DEAD BOYS

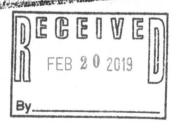

DEAD BOYS

Gabriel Squailia

Talos Press
NEW YORK

Talos Press books may be purchased in bulk at special discounts for sales promotion, corporate gifts, fund-raising, or educational purposes. Special editions can also be created to specifications. For details, contact the Special Sales Department, Talos Press, 307 West 36th Street, 11th Floor, New York, NY 10018 or info@skyhorsepublishing.com.

Talos Press is an imprint of Skyhorse Publishing, Inc.®, a Delaware corporation.

Visit our website at www.talospress.com.

10 9 8 7 6 5 4

Library of Congress Cataloging-in-Publication Data is available on file.

Cover design by Brian Peterson

ISBN: 978-1-940456-24-9
Ebook ISBN: 978-1-940456-29-4

Printed in the United States of America

for Najwa

When the mind renews itself without forming new patterns, habits, without again falling into the groove of imitation, then it remains fresh, young, innocent, and is therefore capable of infinite understanding.

For such a mind there is no death because there is no longer a process of accumulation. It is the process of accumulation that creates habit, imitation, and for the mind that accumulates there is deterioration, death. But a mind that is not accumulating, not gathering, that is dying each day, each minute — for such a mind there is no death. It is in a state of infinite space.

—J. Krishnamurti

I

On Southheap

Holding out both of his leather-palmed hands for balance, the gentleman corpse known as Jacob Campbell thrust a boot into Southheap. Infinitesimal bits of burnt plastic, chipped wood, and styrofoam plinked down the slope. When no landslide followed, he staggered forward with all the grace of a marionette operated by a novice.

"Chin up, now," he said to himself in a tight-throated voice, "just put one foot in front of the other, and you're all but guaranteed not to spend eternity in pieces."

For years, Southheap had hulked in the distance through the window of his Dead City flat, so huge, familiar, and featureless that he gave it no more thought than the sepia skies. Even when he'd planned this journey, it hadn't occurred to him to wonder where all this garbage had come from, much less why a population obsessed with scavenging had tossed it all aside. Now that he'd spent the better part of a week watching it slide and skitter beneath his weight, he knew more than he cared to. With every step, Southheap spilled its grotty secrets between his feet, threatening to break or bury him, or both, if he dwelled too long on what he'd seen.

The surface of this colorless mound had been dumped here one bucket, one barrow-load at a time, that much was obvious. But its core, he'd realized during the past few days, had been deposited by the whims of the river over the course of centuries. Whenever she flooded, Lethe toyed with the structure of Southheap as surely as she reordered the city below, and no dead man knew how or why.

Jacob trod on a trove of moldering newspapers that crumbled into sand and ink at the touch of his sole. He tottered backward, finding his footing a moment before the scree shifted. Trembling, he watched a shelf of garbage tumble down toward the river's edge, exposing a curved talon of iron rebar that would have impaled him had he trusted that step for a moment more.

"I should've sent a damn debtor," he whispered. So far as he knew, no one who could afford this trip made it themselves, for reasons that became clearer every hour. He'd made up his mind, however, that his business here was too important to entrust to a hired hand. Despite the danger, he meant to begin his quest as he hoped to end it: with his own hard-won strength.

As Jacob picked his way toward a remnant of the spiraling path that debtors of old had built to dump their barrows of trash, he heard a clanging from the city below. They were ringing the hour in the crumbling minaret near his flat in the Preservative District. It was four in the morning, though it looked, as ever, like a hazy afternoon. He tallied five days and fourteen hours since he'd left the comfort of home, a length of time that might well have sent him spiraling into despondency had its echoes not been accompanied by his first glimpse of the fortuneteller's dwelling.

Just beyond the edge of the path, an upended water tower was half-buried in a mound of debris, and beyond its rusted curve lay a view of the River Lethe unparalleled in the city proper. Jacob, despite his unmoving lungs, gasped.

Its purplish waters were wide and slow-moving. The motion-less corpses that floated on its surface were surrounded by glittering shoals of refuse and roiling rainbows of oil. There, past the bobbing shape of a claw-footed bathtub, was the stretch of river-bend where he'd thrashed out of the mud and onto his newly lifeless feet nearly a decade ago. With this unexpected glimpse of his point of deathly origin, it all came rushing back: how, after days of toil, he'd propped his numb body up on one palm, then another, only to lose his purchase in the slippery mud and splash face-first into those amniotic waters, where the whole humiliating process began anew.

Dazed by the memory of his quickening, and by that of his death that lay in hiding behind it, Jacob took a single thoughtless step.

One was enough. His arms windmilled, too wildly, too late, and he fell backward, landing with a crash on the lumpen cushion of his overstuffed knapsack. Scrabbling at the surface of Southheap, he screamed for help to no one, then bit off the sound as the ground beneath him gave. The underworld blurred and tumbled, all beige skies and thundering rubbish, and all he could think was how *close* he'd come before the end.

For there could be no question that his quest was over. He could hear the rush becoming a roar behind him as he somersaulted onto his belly. Riding a cresting wave of detritus, he saw a thin wall of scrap metal approaching and jammed his hands down and to the left. With inches to spare, he tumbled away from that serrated edge and thumped into the gray-green curve of a rotting featherbed.

Keening in gratitude, he lifted his head to witness the cascade thundering past. His spine would have snapped in two, and his crumpled halves would have been buried for the rest of time, or at least until the next flood. He fell back onto the mattress and shuddered: if anything could be worse than spending an endless existence buried in a landfill, it would be lying in the mud at the bottom of Lethe, watching his body deliquesce.

The bells seemed to speed up as he lay inert, thanking the starless sky. An hour passed, then twelve, then twenty-four. Finally he sat up, checking his arms, then his legs, then the rest.

Somehow he hadn't broken so much as a toe. It was a miracle. No: a *blessing*.

He tugged the plastic vial from a pocket in his knapsack and pressed it to his shrunken lips. He'd never been so sure of the rightness of his path. Now if only he could stay on it — and stay vertical!

Hampered by the grip of his rotting musculature on his bones, he resumed his ascent, twice as carefully as before, but without any undue worry. In life, such a setback might have distressed him, even sent him into a panic, but in the underworld, the time he'd lost was utterly insignificant. Like any other corpse, Jacob had no need for rest or nourishment, and any occupied hour was a relief so long as his body remained whole, mobile, and suitably preserved.

He spent another seven such hours regaining the ground he'd lost. Giving his full attention to his footsteps, he was surprised at how well-tended the interrupted path became as it led to the seer's door. Someone had packed it down, forcibly and recently. Stepping lightly now, he rubbed his reupholstered palms together, the high-pitched scrunch of their leather soothing his mind.

"Greetings!" he cried, jerking one hand over his head, but as soon as he'd had a good look into the murk of her chamber, he choked on his prepared speech. From the roof to the rust-bitten curve of the floor, the room was packed with filth-encrusted children's toys. Quilts and blankets spewed moldy down onto jacks-in-the-box with broken springs. Board games missing their pieces served as tables for eyeless dolls. In the center of the candy-colored sprawl sat the seer known as Ma Kicks, her body so thoroughly ravaged by time that Jacob felt a professional ache at the sight. From forehead to foot, her skin was full of holes, flashing elbows, cheekbones, and knuckles alike. Her face was a soiled handkerchief askew on her skull, incapable of expression.

"My name is Jacob Campbell," he said, steadying himself enough to bow. "I come with a gift — and an uncommon question."

Ma Kicks still hadn't moved, but at the sound of his voice, something within her did. Startled, he staggered backward, fixing his attention on her belly.

She must have been near her ninth month of pregnancy when she'd died. Since then, her womb had given way, and from its dark cavity two tiny, skeletal feet emerged, dangling over the edge, kicking into the open air.

"What's that?" she whispered, bowing her head. "Oh. All right. If we got to, we got to." Looking up, she seemed to notice Jacob for the first time. "Strange. Strange agent you are. What's your name, now?"

"Jacob," he said, uneasy at repeating such simple information. "Jacob Campbell. May I be so bold as to —"

"Why'd you come?" Her hands drifted with maddening languidness toward her baby's feet.

"As I said, I came to ask —"

"I don't mean what *for*," she said, her voice as slow as molasses. One decimated hand found the child's toes and slowly wiggled over them. "*Coochee-coo*," she murmured, then looked up again. "I mean why *you*. Everybody sends somebody. Nobody comes up here himself. That's the whole point."

"The point of *what*?" said Jacob. Had Ma Kicks been away from the company of corpses so long that she'd gone mad? Or had she always been this way?

"The point of *leaving*." She was playing pat-a-cake now, at the tempo of a dirge. "They send servants, the servants don't want to small talk. And it's quiet that gets us through the years."

Jacob steeled himself and stepped into the doorway. "What I have to ask is too — too personal to entrust to a proxy. Both for me and for you. I'm not here to speak to Ma Kicks."

For the first time, she seemed to give him her full attention, her hands plopping into her lap. Even the baby's restless feet were still.

"I'm here," he went on, "to ask a question of Clarissa."

Her body stiffened. Jacob grabbed the flaking corner of her doorway, suddenly fearful that he'd gone about this all wrong.

"That — that's what they called you, isn't it? In the days when you worked beneath Dead City's streets?"

Her head was shaking, as if palsied. She seemed unable to speak. He could think of nothing to do but press on.

"When you worked in the Tunnels, with that traveler known to every citizen as —"

Then the chamber exploded in a din so abrasive that both of them ducked.

"Remington!" she roared over what sounded like a jackhammer atop the hollow drum of the room. "I told you not to play up there!" Hustling Jacob out of the way, she stomped onto the path that curved up and around the water tower. Stunned by her sudden animation, he followed behind, striding uneasily onto the percussive roof.

There, leaping to and fro with that utter lack of coordination that is the hallmark of a recent immigrant to the Land of the Dead, a teenaged boy as pale as milk was at play. In his hand he held a gutless tennis racket, which he swung with savage ineptitude at the trio of blackbirds flapping and diving at his head, trying for his eyes. The boy's freckled face was seized in an expression of amiable surprise, and his body, clad only in blue jeans, was so perfectly unblemished that Jacob couldn't imagine how he'd died.

"Didn't I tell you to keep off the roof?" scolded Ma Kicks, snatching the racket from his hand and whacking it sidewise into one of the blackbirds. It tumbled down the side of Southheap, squawking in protest. Its partners, impressed by her aim, flapped away, and she aimed the racket at Remington. "Didn't I tell you, now?"

Jacob was still struggling to assimilate the change in her demeanor, to say nothing of her sudden increase in volume.

"But, Ma," said Remington, his voice an earnest alto, "those big birds were picking on a little one! They picked him right apart." Ma Kicks tossed the racket off the roof, and Remington turned to Jacob, as if they were old friends. "This little crow, you should have seen him go. He caught a beetle all on his own, and then those three big guys swooped down and tore his belly open to get it out. Well, he pecked the biggest one of them right in the eye, and then two of them held his wings in their beaks while the other one tore them off, like *kkkkt*!" As he swung his bare arms through the air to illustrate, he lost his footing and slammed onto his back, sending a thunderclap through the roof of the chamber.

Ma Kicks paced close to Jacob, leaning close. "This little fool don't heed a word I say," she said, in a conspirator's whisper. "Crawled straight up here from the river and had his mortis on my doorstep, and now I can't get rid of him."

"That's — quite the predicament," said Jacob under his breath. It occurred to him that Ma Kicks had taken a sort of surrogate, a child who could act where hers could not. He wondered if the bond of motherhood, if nothing else, might stir her from inaction.

"Where did that little crow go, anyway?" Shoving himself onto his bare feet, Remington stumbled around in a circle, and as he turned his back, Jacob saw the jagged wound that had caused his death. The back of his head had been obliterated by a shotgun, and nothing remained but gleaming bone.

"That's why I call him Remington," murmured Ma Kicks. "Dummy crossed over with his brainpan clean as a mixing-bowl. Big toe stuck in a shottie's trigger-guard. Came up the Heap using it as a walking stick. But since he left his brains behind, he don't remember a moment of his life. Boy's halfway between an idiot and an angel, but the idiot half is on my last nerve.

"Aw, Remy, put that bird down!" she cried, staggering off the roof in disgust. "Nasty things got diseases even a corpse could catch."

Remington bounded up to Jacob, thrusting his cradled hands out before him. "See, look at him! He's scrappy. And little. I think he's like a kid crow."

The crow and its wings, stunned by the shock of division, lay perfectly still in the boy's cradled hands. "Let's sit down here," said Jacob, clearing a space in the rubble and depositing his knapsack by its side, sensing a rare opportunity to win the seer's favor. "Put the crow down, if you would, and we'll see if we can stitch him up." With nimble, practiced gestures, he pulled out several plastic canisters, selecting a needle and a spool. "The thread's black, you see, so it will blend right in."

"Will his wings work?"

"No way to know unless we try," said Jacob, teasing the skin loose from the wing-stubs with a dental tool. He glanced at Ma

Kicks, who was watching them sidelong. "I rarely work with post-mortem severance, but since the incident was recent, there's hope."

As Remington stared in mute fascination, Jacob told him to retrieve a film canister full of paper clips from the knapsack and straighten two of them. "We'll fix the wings to the body with those," he explained as Remington fumbled with the cap. "I'll have to jam them into the muscles to keep them in place, but it won't hurt your friend. He's past all that now."

"How do you know how to do this?" said Remington, popping the cap open, spilling paper clips everywhere.

"Not to worry, I'll pick those up in a moment. I know how to do this because this is how I earn my keep. I'm a preservationist: I apply cosmetic, medical, and taxidermic principles to the business of keeping long-dead corpses looking like they were only just living. I don't get many crows for clients, though; I fix people. Although my first client, believe it or not, was a rat named Japheth."

"A talking rat?" said Remington.

"Not that I noticed." Jacob dipped his needle into the skin at the crow's shoulder, then through the wing. "I named him myself. His situation was rather similar to that of your friend: he'd made his way out of the river, and some citizen, in spite or ignorance, had stomped on him. As a result, his front end worked, but his little bottom dragged on the ground, and as he passed by the spot where I'd been sitting since my mortis passed, I found him so pitiful that I determined to fix him using the basic skills of taxidermy, a hobby of mine in livelier times.

"I had a theory I was eager to test, you see. Some of the corpses I'd seen on the streets were like you: they had bodies like living folk, with muscles and organs intact. But some — forgive me, Clarissa — were more like Ma Kicks, little more than skeletons dressed in skin."

"Hell, I know what I look like," muttered Ma Kicks, keeping an eye on Remington while she reached absentmindedly into her womb.

"So what was the theory?" said Remington.

"Since the corpses who were only skin and bone seemed to move just as well as the fleshy ones," said Jacob, testing the flexibility of one reattached wing with his fingers, "I came to believe that bones are the engine driving the motion of the dead."

"Bones are the engine," whispered Remington, as if he might be quizzed on this point.

"To prove this theory, I experimented on little Japheth, who didn't object. With the pocket-knife I'd brought with me from the Lands Above —"

"The what?"

"That's what we call the world of the living, where all corpses come from. In any case: with my pocket-knife, I skinned the little fellow, keeping his pelt on a nearby ledge to cure. Gently, I pulled all the muscles from all his bones, then sat for weeks whittling what's called a body-mold from a piece of driftwood."

"That's gross," said Remington with approval. "What's a body-mold?"

"A carving that replicates the musculature. A fake body, if you will, that fits inside the skin. A tall order, since I wanted to fit his tiny bones inside the wood just as they'd have sat in the muscles. If bones were indeed the engine that drove Japheth's motion, I'd have to leave them in place if I wanted him to be able to move.

"While I carved, Japheth's skeleton waited patiently, holding together all the while, even scuttling around at a surprisingly rapid clip. When I finished, I snapped the body mold into place and sewed up his skin, which by then was as dry as a little rug, enabling him to walk proudly, looking as hearty as a sewer-rat in its prime. After that, I was able to swap him for three years' credit, with which I purchased my first set of tools. And that," said Jacob, snipping the thread on the crow's second wing, "is how I developed the Jacob Campbell Preservative Treatment."

"Preservative Treatment," Remington pronounced, jabbing a finger perilously close to Jacob's cheek. "Is that what's wrong with your face?"

"What's — *wrong*? Whatever do you mean?" Grasping the crow in one hand, Jacob dipped the other into his knapsack, retrieving a cracked compact mirror and rapidly inspecting himself. All was well, he found to his relief: his yellowed teeth still shone through grimacing lips; his milky eyes remained firmly ensconced in their sockets; his kinky hair yet clung to his scalp; and, most importantly, his skin let no bone show through. To achieve this effect at his level of decay, he'd had to patch himself with a dark brown leather that matched his natural hue, then buff the new hide with shoe polish. "My dear boy, this is *intentional*. More, this is the best that any corpse could hope for!"

Remington nodded. "It's freaky."

Jacob stowed his mirror, considering that Ma Kicks' pronounced decomposition was the boy's only basis for comparison. He tried to calm himself. "I can assure you, Remington, that this is a top-notch preservation. Not quite the Campbell Treatment, I admit, as I've made notable progress in the industry since I first worked, with hand-mirror and scalpel, on my own fresh body. But it's still stylish, effective, and envied by all but the wealthiest of my clients. At any rate!" he chirped, handing over the crow. "Your feathered friend should come around in awhile, and we'll see if his wings have recovered."

"Thanks, Jake!" cried Remington, nuzzling its beak with his button nose, an act of intimacy that caused both Jacob and Ma Kicks to turn away in disgust.

Jacob stood, slipping the knapsack over his arms. Ma Kicks crooked a finger at him, starting down the path. As they departed, Remington began humming tunelessly to his pet, stroking its wings against its body as if he hoped to cuddle it back to health.

"I see the little one isn't your only charge," Jacob ventured. "That boy you've adopted is cheerful enough, even if he suffers from a surplus of enthusiasm."

"Please," said Ma Kicks, both hands on her back. "I had enough to deal with before he came. *Another* loudmouth in the cave? No thank you." She hobbled into her chamber and sat heavily on the floor, moaning as if the motion caused her pain. "You got a way with him, Patches. First time he's been quietly occupied since his mortis. Sit." She parted her shawl like a curtain and gently dipped her hands into her belly, resting her baby's feet against their palms as she let out a long, rattling sigh. "Now. Something about the Tunnels, was it? Let's get this over with."

"Gladly," said Jacob, settling in as best he could in those cramped quarters. "I'm tremendously excited to have the opportunity to speak to you about this matter at last. I can't tell you how long the path was that led to your door! But after a diligent search, I found an old acquaintance of yours who let me in on a little secret. Ah, but where are my manners? You should have your tribute."

He pulled a package wrapped in brown paper from the depths of his knapsack and handed it over, bowing his head. Ma Kicks tore it open without ceremony. It was an unblemished picture-book he'd come by at great expense, with an illustration of a girl crawling into a mirror embossed on its cover. She held it briefly in front of her stomach, muttering, "Book," then tossed it into a splintered trunk. The gift elicited a series of kicks from within her womb, which Jacob hoped were demonstrative of excitement, not annoyance.

"In any case," he continued, "I rather doubt anyone else has made this connection. Tell me, Clarissa —"

"Call me Ma." Her body had fallen still again, her voice fallen back to a whisper.

"As you wish. Ma, is it true that you once knew that adventurer known to Dead City as the Living Man?"

No answer came. She didn't budge, but her child began to twitch — unless Jacob's eyes were deceiving him, almost rhythmically.

"Most would call his story a folktale," Jacob said. "But I believe — I *know* better. And my source has told me that you have first-hand experience."

"Ain't a topic I care to discuss," she whispered.

Her silence stung. Jacob felt like a fool for assuming that Ma Kicks would receive him with soft surprise, then joyfully help him when he told her of his intentions.

No matter. She'd hear of his adventures with the Living Man one day. For now, he'd fib a bit. An oblique approach would serve him better than showing his hand. "What bothers me, you know, is how misunderstood he is in the culture of the city. To think that such a remarkable explorer could cheat the laws of life and death, only to end up the object of ridicule — why, it positively pains me." Not a grunt from Ma Kicks. Jacob leaned forward. "Help me tell his story truly. Let's set it to rights. Let us not allow that brave soul to remain a punchline." The baby's kicks seemed to be getting faster. Was that a good sign or a bad one? Jacob, at a loss and possessing no solid information, went out on a limb. "Let us tell the truth at last about — about what *happened* to him."

Her hand drifted toward a pile of blankets. "Who you been talking to?"

"My informant would give no name. He said only that he knew you long ago. Beneath the city."

"Barnabas is a liar. Always was."

"I don't know anyone by that —"

"I got nothing to tell. I'm sorry. It's time for you to go."

"Please," said Jacob, clasping his palms. "I beg of you. Tell me where you saw him last. Is he still in the Tunnels?"

"Don't you drag me down into that muck." With her free hand, she tugged her shawl over her belly, but the baby's skeletal feet kicked it free. "I don't want to remember. I don't want to go down there again. Not even in memory. Now I'm going to ask you one more time. Leave us be."

Ridiculous as it seemed, Jacob had never contemplated the possibility of failure. "I will not," he said. "If it's quiet you so desire, I'll stay for months. I'll tell you stories. I'll — I'll play that recorder. I'll sing! Off-key! I'll do anything it takes, Clarissa, to find my way to —"

The shotgun was leveled at his head before he'd even seen her move. "I told you," she snarled, a quilt sliding from her arm, "to call me *Ma*."

That must have been the weapon that ended Remington's life, Jacob thought. Though he was beyond pain, Jacob had no desire to learn what the obliteration of his head would mean.

"Now I hate to turn away a paying customer. But this is not a topic I will discuss with anyone, for any reason. So you take your picture-book, Patches, and you get your rotten bones out that door before I count to five, or God help me —"

But the shotgun's barrels drifted to the floor. Ma Kicks was staring down at her belly, where the baby's feet were thrashing in a definite, syncopated rhythm, too forceful to ignore.

"Oh, no, baby," she whispered, buckling her arms around her gut. "Don't do that."

Jacob peered at the tantrum. What strength those tiny feet had! They'd have punctured her belly had it not already been broken.

"You just calm down, now," she begged, jouncing. "You just give your poor Momma a break, would you? Just one time, baby, just let me *be*." But the feet flew up to find her ribs, making a drum of her abdomen. "I said that's *enough*, damn it! Hell you want me to do, go back in time?"

For a moment the child fell still. When it resumed, it was kicking harder.

"Aw, Momma's sorry, now," she moaned. "Momma shouldn't have yelled. We'll read the man's fortune. Just you quiet down!"

She glared at Jacob. "Looks like the little one's taken a shine to you, which is more than I can say. Guess you'll get a reading out of this after all. So we can have some *peace* around here." Cursing under her breath, she scooped up a leather cup and rattled its contents over her open womb. "Two shakes for baby. One for me." She dumped it out on the floor between them, and five tiny dice, carved out of bone, clattered oddly across the curved metal, rolling on when they ought, by rights, to have stopped. When they did, Ma Kicks huffed, scooped them up and rolled again.

She and Jacob could only stare. The dice had fallen just the same the second time, with every pip in precisely the same place.

"Oh, come *on* now. Be fair."

But the child inside her started thrashing again, and Ma Kicks turned away from Jacob, falling silent for a long while. "All right, Patches. You want to find the Living Man?" she said at last, her voice cracking. "I'm supposed to tell you where to find him. The bones are clear on that. But I've got two conditions."

Back turned, she wrenched with all her strength. There was a snap, and her whole body shuddered.

"First, you take this," she muttered, "and you keep it close. Hear me? Never let it out of your sight. It'll — it'll keep you on the path."

She held her fist over his open hand. Jacob gaped as she let the object fall: there, plopping into the mottled leather of his palm, was the index finger of her left hand.

Shocked at her sacrifice, horrified by the contact, Jacob whispered, "But why? What — what is it *for*?"

"The dice don't lie. But you ask too many questions, and they'll make you pay. I learned that the hard way. Now, they said it plain, two times in a row. You're taking that with you, and you're gonna take the boy, too."

"The *boy*?" cried Jacob, hearing a crack as he squeezed the finger tighter than he'd meant to. "What, you mean — Remington? Come with me? Impossible! It will be terribly dangerous, and he's a fool, a simpleton, a whirlwind, a —"

"Hey, check it out!" cried Remington, bursting into the room. "The crow's got a new place." Turning his head to one side, he showed Jacob its nest: three squawks sounded from the exit wound, and then the crow poked its head through the jagged bone, clacking its beak in the air, its tail-feathers nestled in his throat.

"That's how it is," Ma Kicks said. "You want to know where to find the Living Man, you take him as your ward. He's too grown to keep himself satisfied on Southheap much longer. And you need someone to rein you in."

Jacob ground his teeth. The last thing he wanted on his journey was a complicating dependent like Remington, but he hadn't spent his fortune following rumors through the Parleyfields only to end his quest before it had begun. "Very well," he said. "I'll bring him along, and do my best to keep him out of trouble."

"Good luck on that front. Kid, it's been real, but you're heading out with Patches now. He's going to take you on some damn-fool trip that'll probably knock that empty head of yours clean off. Sound good?"

"Sounds great!" said Remington. "When do we leave?"

"As soon as she tells us *where*," said Jacob, tucking her twitching finger into the leather pouch where he kept his account-stones, then tying it tightly to his left wrist, where he slipped it under the black cuff of his sleeve. "Where is the Living Man, Ma? Where can I find him?"

The seer was rocking her ruined body like a cradle, singing softly to the child inside. "You got to go deep," she murmured when her song was done, lifting up the brown paper that had wrapped Jacob's gift. "Deep down to the middle of the Tunnels." She'd found a stub of charcoal and was scrawling a map. "Go where there's no light left, Patches. Find a place called the Bottomless Vat. You'll find him nearby. Right here." With two final strokes, she made an X, then pressed her palms against the baby's unquiet feet. "And keep in mind, brother: time's got a way of making folks odd. Making them do things. Things they never thought they could. Everybody's got a way to cope with eternity, what's passed and what's still to come. I don't judge people for how they choose to get by. Not any more.

"Let's hope, for your sake, that the Living Man's done the same."

CHAPTER TWO

City of the Dead

They walked through hours that bled into days, illuminated by the desultory, sepia light that fell through the skies, without variation, forever. Jacob's mind worried ceaselessly at the X on his map — where it was, how he'd find it, whether he had enough time banked to get there — but he was regularly torn from obsession by Remington's steady patter of questions, which only ceased as the pair came around the curve of Southheap, uncovering a panoramic view of Dead City.

As Remington gave way to wonder, gasping and exclaiming, the crow launched itself from his skull. Wheeling lazily between Remington's eyes and the cityscape, the bird drew his gaze over the metropolis, a heap in its own right, built of monstrous fragments of buildings from all nations and eras, extending as far as he could see.

"Look!" he cried as the crow's wings swept over a parking garage ramp spiraling around a sky-blue onion dome; "Look!" as its tail-feathers fluttered over a minaret bursting through the rooftop of a factory; "Jacob, look!" he said, again and again, as the crow flapped over the arches, churches, courtyards, tenements, trailers, shanties, apartments, shacks, bodegas, castles, and mansions that were slumped, mashed, and mangled in a grand confusion around the wide curve of the River Lethe. In the distance, the jagged edge of the mountain range called the Wall of the World cut off the knowable from the unknowable.

Taking it all in, the boy fell into a surprisingly long-lasting reverie. Jacob had been chastising him through the many hours of their descent to take greater care with his motions; now Remington chose his steps with deep attentiveness, and stopped when he needed to consider his next move. Most unexpected was his newfound silence, which persisted until they were near enough to the streets of Rottening Green to hear the barked complaints of its inhabitants and feel the hourly ringing of its bell tower vibrate in their bones.

The path Jacob chose did not end so much as it spewed South-heap into the street. "Let's hurry to my flat," said Jacob as they clambered down. "I hate to deprive you of a proper tour, but I've spent years in preparation for this moment, and I'll need to pack before we depart. So: to the Preservative District we go!"

"To the Preservative District!" cried Remington, careening down several blind alleys before Jacob convinced him to follow.

The word "street," in these neighborhoods, was a euphemism: Jacob and Remington clambered over the mud-packed roofs, walls, and corners of underground buildings, some of which offered views into their inhabitants' conversations through open windows. "There are people down there!" cried Remington, leaning down and calling his greetings into a buried flat where three bone-bags cursed him extensively in an ancient dialect, the burlap sacks that covered their bodies rustling with disgruntlement.

"Wherever a body can fit, you're bound to find two," said Jacob, "and there are plenty of nooks and crannies in this chaos. The city buries itself once or twice each generation, when the floods add new buildings to the pile. The deepest levels are rumored to contain corpses who haven't seen daylight since the days of Tutankhamen."

It was hard to imagine that corpses any older than the ones walking by could still be standing. Although Remington saw, here and there, a body whose bloom was still passing, the streets were overwhelmed by those whose decrepitude was only matched by the ends they employed to cover it up. There were corpses dressed in plastic from head to toe, others sewn into patchwork body-bags, and some who coated themselves in river clay to keep the bones from showing.

Though the Preservative District was architecturally indistinguishable from any other heap of ruins in the area, it was clearly demarcated by the rickety stalls that thronged its streets, stalls whose owners were hawking everything from embalming to plastination.

"What they call embalming is nothing more than a chemical bath that softens you up for tears and abrasions, and as for plastination, it's the biggest scam in the business," Jacob explained to Remington. "Any preservationist worth his salt has a proper flat, but few can afford our services, so they flock to these stalls for stop-gap measures."

They passed a crumpled hot-dog stand whose sign had been daubed with muddy letters reading "HIDE YR BONES." Its proprietor, who glared at Jacob as they passed, was stuffing shreds of newspaper into the ruptured skin of a client whose face was buried in his hands, hidden from the disapproval of passersby.

"As for your own preservation, Remington, while I'd love to offer you the full Campbell Treatment, I'm afraid we'll have to be quick about it. I'll harden your skin and replace your elbows, knees, armpits, and so forth with a supple material, one of the more recent artificial leathers, perhaps. Then I'll pack the necessary materials to replace your innards when they liquefy, so that as we travel —"

"I'm fine the way I am, Jake."

Jacob glanced up and down the street to ensure that no one he knew had overheard. Stopping beside a brick-walled elementary school wounded on one side by a wrecking ball, beside which a pair of headless corpses leaned against each other for support, Jacob whispered, "If you're worried about owing me, Remy, rest assured: there will be ample opportunity for you to assist me on our journey.

You'll never be in debt to me. Think of the treatment as a gift! After all, the ward of Dead City's preeminent preservationist should be suitably natty, don't you agree?"

"Nope," said Remington amiably as the crow hopped from his shoulder into his head. "Thanks and everything, but I don't really get the point."

"The point is that you've already begun to decay. In a few days, your flesh will be irreparably damaged and begin its slow slide off the bone."

"Oh, sure. But bone is the engine, right? I mean, all you're doing is pulling out guts and muscles, then covering the bone up again. So I'm thinking, skip the middleman, you know?"

"Lower your voice, please," Jacob whispered.

"I don't get what's so bad about skeletons, anyway," said Remington, his voice defiantly loud. "I think it'll be fun. You'll be a skeleton, too, Jake, sooner or later! We'll have xylophone ribs. Right, crow?" The crow poked its beak through the back of Remington's throat and squawked, sending the boy into a giggling fit that Jacob's admonitions only intensified.

"Ja-cob Camp-bell!" came a voice from the street, interrupting his lecture. The voice's owner waddled past the headless duo, waving a dog-headed cane overhead in greeting. His three-piece suit was patched together from two dozen fabrics, though his skin was of a piece and hard as a shell; his face, however, had been improperly cured and was several sizes too large for his skull. Though he flattered himself that the matte surface of his skin was too lovely for anyone to notice the error, this preservationist, whose name was John Tanner, was known throughout the District as the Man in the Moon.

"Ja-cob Camp-bell!" he burbled again, pronouncing the name as if it were an off-color joke. Drawing near, he tapped Jacob on the shoulder with the head of his cane. "Old boy, did you polish your hide today? You look rather less like a muddy quilt than usual."

"Ah, is that the mighty head of John Tanner?" said Jacob, gracing his competitor with a condescending bow. "My eyes must be failing me: I thought a low-flying zeppelin was attacking the District."

Tanner hissed, for though he began every conversation with such an insult, Jacob knew he couldn't bear to receive them. "Perhaps it's the sharpness of your tongue that's been sending clients in droves to my side of the street."

"Lord knows it isn't your technique, unless drying one's face on a beach ball has suddenly come into vogue."

"Hahaha! Yes, quite!" Tanner brightened suddenly as a woman passed behind them who looked like she had centuries banked. "All jokes aside, Campbell, I've been searching high and low for you," he said, rocking on his heels and clacking his hardened fingertips together. "I have a proposition that I'm positive you'll find irresistible."

"Spare me your machinations, Tanner; I'm in a hurry."

"Now, hold on, don't be so damnably paranoid! Dear boy, why must you always assume that I'm out to get you?"

"Your frequent threats to hire thugs to disassemble me and throw the bits in separate bogs do not inspire fraternal feeling."

"Bah! Mere joshing. Don't be such a stuffed shirt!"

This stung, for Jacob, in the early months of his death, had been unable to afford the same treatment he offered his wealthiest clients. His own preservation ended at the collar and sleeves of his night-black shirt, beneath which he was as shamefully decomposed as any alley-dwelling bone-bag.

"Let's speak as colleagues rather than rivals for once," Tanner went on. "But tell no one what I'm about to tell you. Do you swear? Do you promise?"

"Tanner, I simply haven't time."

"Oh, shush, it won't take a moment." John Tanner tapped his lips with a finger, causing his hollow face to echo like a drumhead. "Now, I have it on good authority that the Magnate's river-rats have just dredged up two intact barrels of chemicals: one of acetone, one of epoxy resin." When Jacob failed to react, Tanner did a kind of jig on the tips of his toes. "Acetone! Epoxy! The raw materials for plastination, old boy! We need only to pool the time we've saved, and we'll introduce the underworld to the most expensive preservative treatment ever conceived."

"I have no interest in becoming your junior partner," said Jacob.

Tanner leaned in close and growled, causing his face to vibrate. "It's the name you're after, is that it? Very well. I'll hate myself for it later, but I relent: we'll call it Campbell and Tanner, Limited. But you can print the bloody signs all by your —"

Suddenly, Tanner's jaw froze. Looking over Jacob's shoulder, he pointed a shaky finger across the street. "That — that immigrant of yours — why, Jacob, he's fondling the headless!"

And fondling them he was.

Remington, left unattended, had wandered over to the pair of headless corpses who'd recently appeared on the street below Jacob's flat. They were a male and a female, both naked and just beginning to turn. How they got to the Preservative District without drawing anyone's attention was a mystery, but the neighborhood favored a more fanciful question: whether they'd died with heads or stumbled out of the river without them. Because they never spoke and never moved, they'd been quickly adopted as a bit of local flavor, and had been nicknamed Adam and Eve.

Now Remington had hit upon the bizarre idea of helping these unfortunates with a massage they could not feel. Patting them on their shoulders and the stumps between, kneading their muscles with his bare hands, he hummed tunelessly into their nonexistent ears.

As Jacob staggered over, shouting Remington's name, the crow launched itself from its bony nest and flew out of sight, cawing three times as it went.

"Remington! Unhand them at once!" he cried. "This is a breach of every kind of decorum Dead City knows."

"But Jake, they can't see anything. They're frightened. I'm helping them, you'll see."

Jacob shot a look over his shoulder, where John Tanner had overcome his shock and was looking for a confidant. "In that case," said Jacob as evenly as he could, "won't you invite your new friends up to my flat? It's just down the street, and the three of you can get better acquainted there."

"That would be lovely!" said Remington.

Communicating to the headless through taps and nudges, he urged them to their feet. Surprisingly, the corpses stood, and though their motions were stiff, they took the hands that Remington offered and followed after. "They say they'd be delighted," he said.

"He's richer than Trimalchio," whispered Jacob to Tanner as they passed, "and twice as eccentric. He's paying me by the decade to preserve every downtrodden corpse he finds!"

Tanner simply gaped, but as soon as the company had passed him by, Jacob knew he would waddle off to spread the gossip: Campbell was in league with a groper of amputees!

Passing through the first of the many doorways that led to his flat, Jacob paused to ensure that Remington and the headless were following after, then walked on, muttering over the loss of his hard-earned reputation.

Because so few Dead City habitations stood on their own, it was rare that one could reach an apartment through its front door. To access his flat, Jacob and his visitors were obliged to tramp through a number of hallways, parlors, and anterooms before coming to a fire-gutted convenience store, where, respectfully skirting a group of lady corpses shouting in an extinct Eastern European dialect, they came to a wooden staircase rising through the store's roof to Jacob's flat.

Climbing with practiced ease, Jacob contorted himself through his open window, leaving Remington to get his headless followers through on his own, expecting it to take an hour or two and teach the boy a lesson in the process. Instead, he found Remington helping Adam and Eve inside moments later and closing the window after them.

"You have quite a rapport with those two," said Jacob.

"Yeah, they're easy to talk to."

The flat was on the third floor of a skinny, four-story building known as the Leaning Dutchman. Its interior was bare but for a massive metal worktable bolted to the floor, a mirror on the wall, and a wooden rocking-chair in which a well-preserved woman sat perfectly still.

"Good even, Shanthi," said Jacob, pushing gently at the back of her rocking chair. "My thanks for keeping the flat so well in my absence."

Shanthi said nothing, nor did she move the smallest bone in her body.

"Is she your housekeeper?" Remington asked.

"In a manner of speaking," said Jacob. "Shanthi died after a short, futile struggle with an undiagnosed disease, which left her corpse completely unmarked: a perfect death. Thus, while she might not have been a looker by the standards of the Lands Above, she caused a sensation as soon as she stepped onto Lazarus Quay, for comeliness here is nothing more or less than the semblance of life.

"Scores of men and women were propositioning Shanthi, not with sexual advances, of course, since the only stiffness the average corpse can attain ends with his mortis. Still, there are wealthy men who would pay unthinkable quantities of time to keep her, and everyone wanted to deliver her to one.

"Of course, to make a prize like Shanthi last, a man would have to be wealthy indeed, and bring her to the best, that is, to me. Toss her to John Tanner and you'd end up with a scarecrow stuffed with rags, who'd be lumpier than a featherbed in a few years. But dear Shanthi, who knows her apples from her oranges, decided to take matters into her own hands. She'd heard my name in their promises, and she came straight to the Leaning Dutchman.

"When she turned up at my window, she told me that she wanted to look this way forever, and that she was happy to give her body to me for the privilege. I told her the offer was timely and that I'd take her up on it for reasons which had nothing to do with conceptual lust: I needed a squatter.

"These flats, you see, are too mercurial for even the Magnate to rent out. What stands one day might collapse the next, and the floods could move them about at any moment, making the owner-ship of property a losing proposition. Instead, squatter's rights are absolute, and any time there's a flood, every room in the city changes hands.

"When Shanthi came to me, I was hobbled by this custom: when I wanted to leave the flat, I had to pay several weeks to a flat-sitter and hope they were as good as their word. But Shanthi, by staying in the flat at all times, solved my problem indefinitely, at the cost of the finest treatment time can buy.

"We agreed on a direct exchange of five years, cheap for the Campbell Treatment, but I liked her style. Besides, I needed the practice: Shanthi's was the first human body-mold ever created."

"But can she move?" asked Remington.

"She could if she wanted to," said Jacob, unpacking his knapsack on his worktable and taking a full inventory of its contents. "Her joints are perfectly designed, and her five years are up, but here she sits. As to why, I doubt it's strictly a matter of loyalty.

"Think," said Jacob, removing a silver object from his floorboards and sliding it into the leather pouch on his wrist, "of a stone stairway in some populated avenue, weathering the dragging of footsteps for hundreds, even thousands of years. What happens to those stones over time?"

"They wear away," said Remington.

"They wear away!" cried Jacob, striking the table with a metal scraper. "These solid stones wear away. And what becomes of the shoe? What becomes of its sole, made of simple rubber, dragging against street and sidewalk over the course of years?"

"It wears away faster," said Remington.

"Even faster! What, then, becomes of dead flesh and skin, unable to heal, powerless to regenerate cells, more vulnerable to the forces of entropy than rubber, let alone solid stone; the bones grinding away in the sockets, unlubricated by blood and lymph; skin rubbing against skin for unmoisturized decades? What, Remington, becomes of our bodies?"

"They fall apart," said Remington dutifully.

"Yes, Remington, they fall right apart. Even the best-preserved body decays, given time and motion, which is why Shanthi here remains so perfectly still.

"Now! Given what we know about the damage one corpse can do to itself just by moving about from day to day, what can we conclude about two, or, heavens, three corpses, all but fully nude, none of them having taken the slightest of preservative precautions, rubbing against one another in the most violent manner in the middle of the street?"

"They should not!" said Remington, who was enjoying the increasing volume of this discourse.

"They should absolutely, in the name of a reanimated God, not," said Jacob, "nor should any citizen touch any other citizen, for the simple reason that it will do damage, however slight, to the integrity of that citizen's flesh.

"The dead are a vain people, I don't deny it, and contrary to whatever opinions you might have formed about me, I find it sad even in myself. This business of making mannequins of corpses — forgive me, Shanthi — is the baldest of farces. But whatever you may think of our vanity, I beg you to respect it, otherwise your time in this city will be hard indeed, and so, to be perfectly blunt, will mine."

"No touching," said Remington.

"No touching," said Jacob, "and I thank you."

"But what about Adam and Eve?"

"Actually," said Jacob in surprise, "they seem to be getting on all right by themselves."

While Remington and Jacob had been distracted by their conversation, Adam and Eve had begun to move, though very slowly. By now, after many tiny steps and tentative touches, they had identified their positions beside one another and were standing side by side, facing the window like they were gazing at the street with invisible eyes.

As if they'd been waiting for an audience, they lifted their hands to the pane, grasped its base, and pulled the window open. The reconstructed crow, who'd been waiting for such an opportunity, swooped into the room, settling on Eve's shoulder with a cheerful squawk.

"How did they do that?" said Remington.

"They're your friends," said Jacob, "why don't you ask them?"

CHAPTER THREE

The Hanged Man's Laughter

Jacob watched them as he packed his things, vacillating between amazement and crawling unease. Remington had taken his sarcasm at face value and set about finding a way to learn how Adam and Eve could see. He and the headless marched around in a conga line; they played soldiers and tag; they struck poses and made speeches with their hands; but only when he taught them to play blindman's buff did the truth emerge.

"Good lord," Jacob said, "they stop moving as soon as you cover your eyes."

"I know!" said Remington. "That's why I keep winning."

"But, Remington, can't you see what this means? Somehow, though I can't imagine how, it's quite impossible and hurts my head to even contemplate, but somehow they're –"

"Seeing through my eyes! I know, it's pretty neat. Plus, we don't have to touch each other to get around, so you don't have to worry about your reputation any more."

"Yes." Jacob stared at Adam and Eve, who were wiggling their fingers behind one another's stumps. "That's a relief."

It was odd in the extreme, as the headless had been help-less before Remington came along, but there was no time to sort out another of the city's mysteries. Jacob forced his bag shut, snapping its clasps over a fortune in preservative tools. "Remington, fascinating as your menagerie has become, I must beg you to focus for a moment. Ma Kicks has given us a location I've been seeking for years, but it won't do us any good on its own. The Tunnels are a labyrinth, and as I'm not a drinking man, I know nothing of its intricacies.

"We'll need a guide. Unfortunately, those who frequent the Tunnels are drunks and ripoff artists, as likely to lead us into a trap as to bring us to the X on this map. Thus, I've determined to take the lesser of myriad evils: there's a boy, a one-time client, who has worked up a reputation considerably worse than mine. If anyone can help us find this hidden corner of the Tunnels, it's he, for though he's a scoundrel, he's connected to every other scoundrel in the city.

"What's more, in the five years since his treatment, he's caroused and gambled his fortune away. Poor as he is, I'm hoping he'll take us to this pub for a few months' trade. Between you and me, I have only a little more than that left in my account.

"We'll leave immediately," said Jacob, approaching Shanthi's motionless rocking chair. "Shanthi, my dear, this is goodbye. Whether or not I am successful, I won't be coming back. Consider this a bonus for your faithful service." Between his leather-tipped fingers, Jacob extended a single sewing-needle and slipped it into her pocket. "You can trade that in for some walking-around money, should you ever decide to walk around. The flat, of course, is yours. Keep it well!

"Now, Remy, let us make our way to Caesar Augustus' Gambling Den, where I have no doubt we'll find my old friend Leopold striving to win back his fortune, one hour at a time."

It was a short walk, which, considering the speed of the aver-age corpse, meant hours of staggering in the midst of the crowd. This time, it took longer than usual, since Remington, having taken Jacob's speech to heart, froze with his hands in the air every time a corpse came near enough to brush against him, hollering, "No touching!" at the top of his voice. As they finally approached the great, gray walls of Caesar Augustus' Gambling Den, his antics drew fewer stares and titters, since the crowds had grown so large and loud that his shouts were subsumed by the clamor.

The Den's walls had been knocked down, punched through, and trampled so many times that Caesar now utilized a crew of ragged, black-robed workers to circle the perimeter around the clock, making repairs when needed. Remington gaped: the corpses hammering scraps of plywood, corrugated tin, and cardboard onto the rickety wood-and-wire frame had bare skulls for heads, each with a short alphanumeric code chiseled into his brow.

"No faces!" said Remington, giggling. "They're so cute."

"Don't stare at the debtors, Remington, it's rude."

"What do those letters and numbers in their foreheads mean?"

"Something to do with the term of their indenture, I think. I've always kept my distance, to tell you the truth."

Narrowly escaping a collision near the entrance, Jacob led the way through the drooping front gates into a thousand-throated roar that never found reason to end. At tables and around the edges of pits, gamblers and spectators howled, cursed, and celebrated in a thousand tongues, all obsessed with a single subject.

"By no means are you allowed to play," said Jacob as they passed by a high-stakes pit. Remington (and, through his eyes, Adam and Eve) peered down into a small room sunk into the dirt, its ceiling pried off, its doors and windows boarded up to discourage the game's inevitable loser from fleeing into the Tunnels.

Inside were two gamblers, a pit boss, a hefty pair of hand-carved dice, and the charcoal diagram that held the colored betting-stones. Side bets littered the lip of the pit, painted pebbles changing hands rapidly between spectators.

"Can we watch?" said Remington.

"Oh, I suppose so. But just one game." Jacob stood behind the trio, listening closely to the crowd.

Below, a wizened gambler with one dangling arm tossed the bones against the corner with an angular jerk. A glance at her opponent explained why the cheers celebrating her win were so raucous: he was the kind of gambler the Den despised, an immigrant fresher than Remington who had yet to lose the shoes he'd died in.

"Are those painted rocks money?" said Remington.

"More like chips at a poker table. We have no proper coinage in this city."

"So what do you spend?"

"We spend time, whether our own or someone else's. Let's say you wanted to pay me to sew a pair of leather moccasins over your feet. You might offer me a year of your future for the service, and I could either put you to work in the shop or bring you straight to the exchange, where you'd be turned into a debtor."

"One of those skull-head guys."

"Precisely. The Magnate's men would send you to work in the Debtor's Pool, putting your face on their shelves for safe-keeping, and I'd get a full year credited to my account."

"So these guys in the pit are gambling the time they have in the bank?"

"Until it runs out. Then, more often than not, the loser will get excited enough to start gambling fragments of his own eternity. Nine out of ten debtors begin their indenture right here in the Dens."

"But why would anyone gamble his own time?"

"Time is the answer!" cried a woman beside Remington, a creature clad in rags of Lethean purple, whose body, despite its relative freshness, was missing nine fingers, six toes, both ears, both eyes, and a nose.

"I'm sorry, what?" said Remington. "Time is why they gamble time?"

"Ooh, you've got it, ducks; you're nearly a citizen now! Too heavy to bear when it's empty, too light to hold onto when it's full: that's time in the underworld, pumpkin. It might seem strange to you, who ain't used to not sleeping at night, but for them, who bear the hours of their flibbertigibbet existences like boulders on their backs, servitude is a gift!"

"What about you?"

"Why, I've more sense than that!" She leaned her mutilated face close to Remington's and whispered, "You'd be surprised how many men will gamble a year for the chance to win a toe."

Down in the pit, the newcomer called out his surrender. A hundred years was as much as he could stand to lose.

"But what happens now?" said Remington, looking at the celebrations surrounding the pit, where the immigrant had slumped against a wall while the winner picked up the purple century-stone and held it over her head.

"That man is a debtor now, indentured for the hundred years he lost. The Magnate's men will come for the loser and remove his face," said Jacob, threading his way through the crowd. "It peels off like a stocking, if you're curious. For some, it's the best entertainment the city has to offer, but we haven't time to spectate."

"Right! We need to find our tour guide."

Jacob led the company on a long circuit around the room, combing through various games of chance, listening carefully all the while. There was no lack of variety in the Dens: low-stakes games of craps rattled on squares of linoleum next to the tracks laid down for twice-daily crow races, where wingless birds hobbled after a beetle dragged on a string; and, for the wealthy, there were private rooms where eras were swapped over actual decks of cards. Yet none of these sites held the dandy they were looking for.

Just as Jacob had begun to despair, wondering if his former client might be less predictable than expected, he heard the sound he'd been searching for, that unmistakable, unforgettable peal, wildly theatrical and unbound by breath, swooping and oscillating through all the octaves in human range, that was the aural signature of Leopold l'Eclair.

"That's him!" cried Jacob, making a beeline for the origin of that rippling hilarity.

"You mean that lady screaming?" said Remington, the headless at his heels. "Wow, he is a scoundrel."

"No, that's actually him: that's the Hanged Man's laughter. All a part of the persona Leopold drummed up after his treatment. Foppery never went out of style here."

Pushing carefully through the crowd around a craps table, they caught a glimpse of Leopold at play. His face was caked with clay, paint, and powder, and topped with long, blond hair into which locks snipped from the heads of drunken women had been woven. His neck, which had snapped at the moment of his death, was held up by means of a crimson scarf tied to a broomstick jutting from the collar of his shirt. Though he could have bound it tightly, allowing the broomstick to support his spine directly, the scarf was loose enough to let his head dangle, so that he could turn it in a given direction by flinging his shoulders violently, whipping his head around in a most dramatic way. The same sense of drama informed Leopold's dress: his tattered, sky-blue topcoat was the outer layer of a parti-colored proliferation of matted ruffles, moldering frills, and manky scraps of lace that descended to the rusted buckles of his boots. "It's like a bomb went off in a costume shop," muttered Jacob.

Just then, Leopold was rattling the dice in his fist, keeping the table waiting while he held forth. "My history, you say?" he cried, though no one had. "Oh, but everyone here has already heard the Legend of l'Eclair a thousand times over, and surely wouldn't — oh, you insist? Very well, then, but may this telling be my last!

"I was hung a century ago, or maybe three, in France, or was it England? You'll understand when you've been dead as long as I have: the details of a life so long extinguished begin to fade.

"What offense was I hanged for? Pathological caddishness, resulting in an epidemic of bastardy!" He waited for a response, and when none was forthcoming he supplied it himself, laughing long and trillingly. "A chorus of three hundred and one weeping milkmaids stood by the gallows, with mischievous babes at their milk-white breasts.

"Why, no, it's not enchantment that keeps me so well! I'm no warlock, friend: the splendor of my corpus is the result of simple pickling. Yes, I was an opium fiend, and now those twenty grains per diem are my greatest blessing. Which goes to show that living vice paves the way for deathly virtue. If only the vicars could see me now!"

"By the mask of the Magnate, fling the bloody dice, or we'll have your deathly virtue cut off at the root," snarled a bone-bag by his elbow, whose face was wrapped in a plastic sack emblazoned with the name of a supermarket chain in the Lands Above.

"Don't get your wrapper in a bunch!" cried Leopold, tossing his head back and tittering. He made a show of dangling his face over his fist, as if he were about to blow on the dice for luck. "Oh, dear: fresh out of breath!" he cried, dissolving in giggles as he tossed them at last.

When the dice came up in Leopold's favor, he cried, "The wages of sin are mine!" At the ensuing chorus of groans, he threw open his arms and began scooping up his winnings, an action that led to a far larger uproar.

"This blight-born bollock-boil swiped half me betting-stones," roared the bone-bag to the dealer as Jacob shouldered in. "I demand a count! I demand justice! I demand — the Mortar and Pestle."

"A moment, now," said the dealer, creaking to his feet for what looked like the first time in a decade. "A moment, no more, and we'll have the pit boss over to handle it."

"Outrageous!" cried Leopold, his hands in a frenzy of motion as he tucked betting-pebbles into every pocket on his person. "Nefarious! Scandalous! To think that an establishment as renowned as Caesar's would even entertain the word of a man whose skull is ensconced in plastic. I promise you I'll take this indignity to the highest authority, unless —"

"Unless we can come to a more expedient understanding," called Jacob, stepping into the fray with an engraved account-stone held high. "Maybe your friend could be convinced to overlook this unfortunate imbroglio, Leopold?" Dangling the account-stone over their heads was crass, but effective: the bone-bag went silent.

"Campbell!" gasped Leopold, and for once that was all he had to say.

The bone-bag snapped his jaw shut behind the tear in the shopping bag that served as his mouth. He'd zeroed in on the pebble's carvings, which any time-conscious citizen could decode: it was linked to an account that held far more than they were squabbling over. "Possible. Probable, even. We'll let the matter drop. Though I'd caution you to consider who you cozy up to, citizen."

"The account is Campbell Preservation," said Jacob, handing over the pebble and whispering a short alphanumeric code. "And I thank you for your concern, but this isn't my first encounter with Monsieur L'Eclair."

"Indeed," said Leopold, regaining his composure as he staggered into the crowd, "what a surprise to meet you here, of all places! I've been meaning to stop by your flat for ages, old spoon. The preservation you performed has held up impeccably, for which I feel I owe you a great length of gratitude. Well, I'll just deposit these stones, shall I, and then we'll make a date sometime in the near future —"

"I'll pay you six months to forget these trifles and escort us through the Tunnels," said Jacob.

Leopold, who'd been dodging and weaving in an obvious attempt to lose the company, stopped short, head swaying at the end of its scarf. "Sorry — *six* months, did you say?"

"I did," said Jacob. Shuddering as he brushed against Ma Kicks' wriggling finger, he withdrew an intricately-carven pebble from the pouch around his wrist. "Leopold L'Eclair, this is my ward, Remington, and his — compatriots, Adam and Eve."

"Hiya! Your hair's real pretty," said Remington.

"Jacob, that boy has a bird roosting in his head."

"And precious little else." Jacob unfolded the map. "We need only to reach this point, near the Bottomless Vat, here. Once we've arrived, half a year is yours."

"Half a year," whispered Leopold, making some rapid calculations on his fingertips. "And the drinks are on you? Splendid!" Jacob stammered as the map was whisked from his hands. "A generous offer, Campbell, and one you won't regret in any lasting fashion. Bring your little menagerie along, then, and we'll wet our whistles whilst wending our way to your treasure!"

CHAPTER FOUR

The Underground University

S o if we're just going to a bar," Remington asked Jacob, "why do we need to pay this guy to take us? Can't he just tell us where to go?"

"Just *going* to a *bar!*" cried Leopold, his head jerking wildly with laughter. "Oh, Jacob, what an adorable little halfwit you've adopted. Remington, allow me to enlighten you now, as you'll soon be too confused to formulate a coherent question.

"One would be better off giving directions to the Minotaur's residence than to a place as well-hidden as this. It's quite impossible to overestimate the difficulty of travel in the Tunnels, and the primary reason is that they aren't a neighborhood at all: they're Dead City itself, buried and re-buried over the centuries by the caprices of Lethe. Each time our royal river floods, driving the citizens into the hills for safety, she thoroughly reorders the cityscape, tossing its buildings about like a child's blocks while dragging in new ruins from the Lands Above. Old-timers tell of a Great Swelling in which every building on the surface was driven underground by the weight of half-destroyed architecture, and lesser disasters occur constantly, making navigation below the streets a constant source of adventure.

"Thus, there are myriad strategies for exploration. A timid reveler might climb down through a gaping hole in the street, mosey to the nearest watering-hole, drink away weeks or months, and climb up again when he's had enough, or run out of gewgaws to trade for swill. Most guzzlers, however, end up too muzzy-headed to stay in one place, and end up lost in the labyrinth, emerging after an absence of years in some far-off corner of the city! And those are the lucky ones: go alone, and you're liable to be caught in a collapse, or trapped by a riot, or swallowed in a flood. The whims of the city are wondrous; why, I could lead you to the lip of a well at the bottom of which two lovers are arguing in Sumerian, where they've been trapped for thousands of years! Every so often we drop a bottle down to them by way of rope and bucket, and are rewarded with their renditions of ancient Babylonian drinking songs.

"But we won't be touring such wonders on this trip, I'm afraid, due to that cross on Jacob's treasure map, which needs baring, and quickly! Am I right, Master Campbell?"

"You are, Leopold, you are," said Jacob from the rear of the train, gazing up at the mangled buildings of his erstwhile neighborhood as if he didn't know whether to curse them or bid them a maudlin farewell.

Remington, fascinated by Leopold's stories of the Tunnels, kept up a steady stream of questions as they walked. "Why do they call it the Underground University?"

"It's the best place in the underworld to learn new languages. Simply sit down at a table where everything's Greek to you, let the liquor flow, and a few months later, you'll stand up fluent in a language lost to the Lands Above for hundreds of years."

"Where do we go to get down there?"

"I'll tell you all," said Leopold, "but first, I have some difficult news to break. Bring that bird below, Remington, and you'll never fluff its feathers again, for nothing is more unwelcome than a crow in the Tunnels, except for an open flame. Crows go for the eyes when they're cornered, you see."

"Oh," said Remington, knocking at his skull. The crow flapped out and perched on a nearby turret, squawking mournfully at their backs.

"Excellent! Now, regarding entrances and exits, the Tunnels have all sorts: some are no more than ragged holes punched into aboveground buildings, while others are great ramps built for the masses. We could take one of those, but then we'd end up in a bar full of immigrants — no offense, boy, but the ones with brains are often odious. The die-hard debauchees prefer out-of-the-way apertures, such as this shaft you're about to plunge into. Watch your step, boy, or you'll never walk again!"

Remington tottered at the edge of a mineshaft echoing with distant voices, located incongruously at the end of a zig-zagging alley. At Leopold's urging, he climbed out of Dead City's perpetual afternoon into an equally endless night, lowering himself down a rope of knotted bedsheets into pure, obliterating darkness. "You guys, I'm blind!" he shouted as his feet scraped the bottom, but then he raised a hand in front of his face. "Oh, wait," he said as he waved it around, perceiving its dark outline, the downy hairs on the backs of its knuckles, even the fading color in its cuticles, "I spoke too soon. There's no light, but I can see — everything!"

"Indefatigability. Post-mortal immortality. Sight without light. Death does have its benefits, I suppose," said Jacob as he touched down.

"Not to mention freedom from the humiliating pain of a stubbed toe," said Leopold. "Onward, fellows. Follow the sound of flowing booze!"

"Not that you'll be drinking any, Remy," Jacob warned. "You'll need to keep sharp — and stay close."

"Don't you worry, my boy," whispered Leopold to Remington, "we'll loosen his apron-strings even if we have to force the swill down his throat."

Remington laughed as he followed Leopold's head down a tilted hallway overflowing with echoes. As they crouched down, then crawled on their hands and knees, he struggled to identify the cacophony. It was only when he'd tumbled through a tiny doorway and into a startling openness that he succeeded: it was the oceanic babbling of the human voice rebounding through a chamber as wide as a football field. Remington goggled as he stood, for the space between this gargantuan pub's improvised pillars was so crammed with the dead that the taboo against physical contact had been abandoned. Skeletons in rags threw their arms around leathery corpses in top-hats and tails, tin cans and brass goblets clanking before a bar built from a shipwreck. Islands of battered furniture shone with the swill that dribbled from a thousand chins, and everyone Remington could see was either laughing, narrating, sobbing, or involved in some combination of the three. Leopold was greeted with fanfare as soon as the party stepped into the room, and when he emerged from the first round of greetings, he pressed a clay cup of swill into Remington's hand. Remington poured it down his throat before Jacob noticed, and whatever happened from that point on involved so many strangers offering him so many drafts out of so many containers that he soon found himself with a drink in each hand and another clenched between his knees.

"It's bad enough that our guide is inebriated," muttered Jacob, "but you — why, you're but a child! To say nothing of the damage the swill is causing your untreated corpse. At least try to keep it on the inside of your body, Remington!"

The woozy rush reminded Remington of something, from which he surmised that he had, at some point in his short life, been drunk, and that it must have felt more or less like this. "Didn't it feel more or less like this?" he shouted at a girl with a face like a jack-o-lantern in late November. "Drinking did, didn't it? When we were —"

"Don't say it," she yelled. "Nobody cares what you used to be. This is better. Death is better. Swill is the best."

"Swill is the *best*!" hollered Remington, tossing back his plastic cup. When he looked up from the stamp at its bottom the girl was gone, and in her place loomed a pile of broken chairs so tall and precarious that it must have taken hours to stack. Looking down again, he found an overflowing coconut-shell in the place of his plastic cup, then lost himself to laughter.

Time was gone. Time was meaningless. He was standing in the midst of the crowd, swaying, directionless, leaning on the shoulders of Adam and Eve.

Consciousness surged in and out of him. He poured drinks into the open necks of the headless. They danced on a splintered table amidst the howls of strangers. Performing for a woman whose lips had melted away, he stuffed his hand through the back of his throat and shook her hand through his open mouth. She bought him a drink and he tossed it back so hard it splashed through the back of his head. "Thar she blows!" the woman squealed.

A child stood on a bar, his skin covered with extravagant mold like the peel of an ancient banana. He was laughing and filling cups from a gourd made of a human stomach. When all were full he poured the rest down his throat and tossed the gourd to the bartender. How old was the child? If he died forty years ago, and he was eight when he died, did that make him eight or forty-eight? Did the years get crammed into his tiny limbs, or would he be a child forever?

"Pardon me. Excuse me. Hiya! Sorry to interrupt, but do you know where we are?" Remington said to the man beside him.

"The Alley of the Shadow."

"Do you know Leopold?"

"Yes. Have a drink."

"Yes."

"Have a seat."

"Yes."

"Yes," said a bespectacled corpse perched at a well-populated table piled high with moldy encyclopedias, "time is the problem, yes, and we're in this mess because we have nothing *but* time, because the Magnate said from behind his mask, 'Our time is infinite, now what shall we do with it?,' and found a solution for all of us in a system of time-debt, a solution for which he cannot be held accountable, for if he exists as a person and not as a moneyed phantom behind a mask, who is he, and more importantly, where? Oh, there he is, over by the bar; he's taken his mask off at last, hello there Maggie! Let me finish, God's bodkin, it's not as if you have somewhere to be; why patience is in such short supply around here I'll never understand. As I was saying, yes, an economy based around an ephemeral commodity is a danger to whomever uses it, an incomprehensible mess that we can only hope is understood by its architect, for we're unable, and therefore we spend what we have in a constant rush, before the poor sod whose sentence we're spending is freed, we drink it away because we've come to believe that this impossible currency really exists, because we're so complacent that we let eternity be reshaped by its artificial pressure, and why? Because our lives prepared us for just this eventuality, and *that's* why the Magnate wins, because long before our deaths we'd already been trained to let him. All right then, Chuck, the question you've been so patiently interrupting me with, let's hope it's a good one, let it rip."

"Why thank you, Matthias: since you've got this all worked out, tell us, if you were the Magnate, what would the basis of your economy be?"

"Teeth," said Matthias, slapping open an encyclopedia to a discolored diagram of the human mouth. "Yes, boys, that's right, yes, teeth, they're simple, yet difficult to forge, yes, Issa, that's right, and we all came down with a mouthful, so it's fair."

"Her teeth?" said a corpse with flesh the color and consistency of beef jerky. He waved a pair of pliers at the woman who was leaning, stiff as a plank, against the bar. "I've no doubt they have fillings, Grum, but that's not in the rules, now, is it?"

"I say the rules is what you make 'em, Grim!" croaked his eyeless compatriot.

"I say that's anarchy," said Grim, settling down to remove her wedding ring. "Bits that's attached are hers by right. You can have her belt, though."

"Hey," shouted Remington to no one in particular, "they're robbing this lady! She can't move, and they're taking all her things!"

No one paid him any mind. "Settle down there, boyo," said Grum, pulling her belt free and starting on her pantsuit. "We've led her safely from the river to the bar, we've bought her a drink for her troubles and another for when she wakes, and she's gone and had her rigor mortis, all of which makes her belongings legally, ethically, and in all other senses, our property."

"They call it the Dead City Welcome, so they do," said Grim, holding the wedding ring up to one eye. "Lucky you escaped it yourself, lad, or you wouldn't have those lovely dungarees to trade for swill!"

"Get you a good rate for 'em if you're of a mind to trade," said the Grum. "Even a back pocket will get you nice and toasty for a week or more."

"Hair of the three-headed dog, Alfie. Hey, kid, that floozy at the far end, is she on the fresher side of the expiration date, or have I got worms in my eyes? Send her one from me, then. Old habits die hard, am I right? It's a pity men don't. Though you know what they say about hanged men, don't you?"

"Have you seen Leopold?" said Remington to a barmaid the color of a deep bruise. "He has a floppy neck. Or Jacob? He's mostly made of leather. Or Adam and Eve? They don't have heads, and they were here just a minute ago, but everyone's gone now."

The barmaid slid a drink in front of him with a chunk of rotting potato floating at the top. "A minute? You've been nursing that pint for a solid week! You'll make some new friends, hon, just sit still a few more days." On either side sat rows of corpses with swill dribbling from their sides. Remington pushed off the bar, leaving the pint untouched.

Determined to find his friends, he sat down heavily in a puddle to cogitate. Since the only approach he could think of was a random search, he abandoned reason: pulling a bandanna from his pocket, he tied it over his eyes and waited for his drunkenness to subside.

His mind wandered freely, and over the course of the days his drunkenness began to recede, not all at once, but in waves of clarity that were obviously tied to the prodigious growth of the puddle beneath his folded legs. Nearly sober, Remington prayed, not to any saint or deity, but to his missing companions, Adam and Eve. When his mind was finally clear enough that he could speak without slurring, he voiced his prayer aloud.

"Dear friends," he said into his clasped hands, "by the power of your corpses, the underworld begs you: be findable."

His prayer complete, he held his joined hands before him like a dowsing wand and stood, putting his faith in his pointed fingers. Within moments he felt a tug, then followed it to where Adam and Eve lay stacked by a publican atop a pile of lumber and shattered crockery. At precisely the moment the headless duo entered his field of vision, they began to lift themselves off of the pile.

"I found you!" cried Remington, attempting to embrace both his friends at once. "I found you because I felt you. But I can't feel Jake and Leo. We'll have to get to them the old-fashioned way.

"You guys can see through my eyes. Can you hear through my ears?"

Eve raised one fist and made it nod. Adam gave a thumbs-up.

"Good! Let's make a totem pole. I need to be as high as I can get."

Eve climbed piggy-back onto Adam, and Remington scaled both of their bodies. From atop Eve's shoulders, he could see across the pub's vast floor, where so many sodden souls were spread that he couldn't do much but stare for a while. "They're out here somewhere. They wouldn't get so drunk that they'd just leave us. Would they?"

Adam shrugged, causing them all to totter. It wasn't long, though, before Eve clapped her hands, then pointed toward a tiny table across the hall. Remington whooped and hopped onto the floor, leading the gleeful rush toward their companions.

"Ah, there you are!" said Jacob, holding up a plastic replica of a golden goblet. He and Leopold were seated at a scarred air-hockey table with the map spread out before them, kept safe from Jacob's drink by Leopold's deft fingers. "Poldy here was just saying that we should give it a count of thirty before we left you behind, but *I* convinced him to give you a full minute. You had seven seconds left."

"Believe nothing this one says," said Leopold. "When I finally bullied him into admitting that a drink to the mysterious task ahead could only bolster his spirits, he revealed a sense of humor that may soon cause you to long for his tight-assed sobriety. I'd invite you to sit, but we were barely able to liberate these." Jacob was seated on a wastebasket, Leopold on a log, and there were no chairs anywhere in sight. Adam and Eve, dissatisfied with this state of affairs, made a seat of flesh and bone by bending down and grasping one another's wrists, which Remington sat upon with gratitude.

"It's a little unholy, what you three have going," said Leopold, standing unsteadily. "In principle, I approve, but in practice, I'll have another drink."

"So far, Remy," murmured Jacob, chugging his goblet. "We'll go so far!" And then he passed into a reverie so near to dreaming that Remington grew worried. Now that he wasn't drunk any more, he could see how easy it would be for the company to accidentally remain in this very bar, at this very table, for the rest of eternity.

When Leopold returned, he set three sloshing drinks on the table and adjusted his head, which had been hanging on one side of his broomstick. "Well, this place has gone to the vultures!" he said. "Just now I collided with a giant lunk of a corpse who seemed to believe such a mistake could reasonably be answered with fisti-cuffs. 'You'd best proceed posthaste to the Plains of War,' I told him before he had the chance to swing. 'The advantages will be three-fold: first, the dry desert air will preserve your bulk before it turns to blood pudding; second, you'll cease to bother those of us who pre-fer to spend eternity enjoying our immortal good looks; and third, you'll find yourself in company you can comprehend, surrounded by other brutes who find the prospect of pounding one another to mulch for centuries on end appealing.' He thanked me for the insult, if you can believe it. Why, to such a brute, I daresay the Plains would be like Heaven!

"In any case, here are the drinks, which haven't lost a drop. Now, what shall we toast to?"

"We drink," said Jacob, "to the Living Man."

"To the Living Man!" said Leopold. "To Saint Nick and his rot-ting reindeer! To Twice-Dead Lazarus and the lotus-scented carcass of Buddha!"

"To the Living Man," said Jacob, "and the path we'll walk when we find him."

"Cheers!" said Remington, and they drank.

"Hold on a mo," said Leopold, "you weren't serious, were you?"

"Of course I was," said Jacob. "Finding the Living Man is the whole of our purpose in the Tunnels."

"You've hired me to help you find a character from a fairy-tale? Why, Jacob, what a delightful little delusion! A pity for you, since a man can only follow a fantasy to its dissolution, but at least it will make a decent barroom tale of your otherwise flavorless existence."

"Why's Leopold poking fun at you?" said Remington.

"For the same reason a sheep bleats. You must understand that the average citizen treats the tale of the Living Man as an urban legend. I first heard the popular version soon after I'd opened the shop, when a client said to me, 'Freshen me up, Jacob: make me feel like the Living Man for a day.' To put her at ease (since your average corpse is nervous as a virgin when under the knife, and will talk about anything for the sake of distraction), I asked her what this figure of speech referred to.

"'He's just what he sounds like,' she said: 'a man from the Lands Above who found his way down without dying.' His story, as most citizens know it, is a corruption of the Orpheus myth. The Living Man was a newlywed whose bride died on their honeymoon; driven insane by grief, he glimpsed the veil between worlds, which he crossed with the aid of the devil."

"Nonsense!" said Leopold. "He sang a song so heart-rending that the veil between life and death parted right there in their honeymoon suite. He bounded from a heart-shaped bed onto the peak of Bald Mountain."

"In another version he's a scientist who builds a machine to open an inter-dimensional portal," said Jacob. "But regardless of his method, our mourner made the passage and found himself in an inhospitable underworld with no idea how to find his beloved. Lost and despondent, he began to search Dead City, armed only with her name.

"The trials that follow make up the bulk of the story, and only exist to show off the features of our decrepit metropolis in ways that mock the limitations of the living."

"Why, those are the good parts!" said Leopold. "The best is the bit at the end where he's lost in the Tunnels and maddened by thirst. After he runs out of piss, he downs a cup of swill, which sends him around the bend; he ends up mistaking a barmaid whose brains are leaking out of her nose for his sweetheart, and drinks himself to death trying to catch her eye."

"Thus ends this ignoble tale, full of anachronisms and Dead City in-jokes, and thus the greatest explorer the worlds of life and death have ever known becomes a laughing-stock."

"And why not?" said Leopold. "What about this quaint little tragedy makes you think there's any truth in it?"

"Nothing, on the face of it," said Jacob, "and in fact I had put the story out of my mind until I came across a peculiar piece of evidence."

Removing his knapsack, he pulled a plastic vial from one of its pockets. Remington examined it with particular care for the benefit of the headless, then passed it along to Leopold, who rattled its contents and snorted. "This could be anyone's. I myself have ten of them." Inside the vial was the tip of a pinky finger, its flesh and nail blackened around a brilliant white core of bone.

"The day that I came across this artifact," said Jacob, "was in the midst of a curious season that Leopold will no doubt recall: for several months, the River Lethe dwindled to a muddy stream, and its current brought no corpses into the city. Old-timers told us of past droughts and insisted that the river would soon be restored, but the city succumbed to a lassitude that concealed the panic in its heart. Precious little flotsam floated in, and the scavengers sat idly on the quayside, while rumors of the Magnate's bankruptcy quieted the action at Caesar's to a mere rattle. For months I received not a single client, and since this was before Shanthi's tenure, I couldn't leave without risking a squatter.

"I don't expect you to understand what transpired in my flat, left alone with my own thoughts for such a prolonged period. How I coped with that — nothingness." He drank deeply, thumping the cup down hard enough to slosh. "Suffice it to say that was a trying time, and one that led me to think, time and again, 'You must find a *purpose*, Jacob, before you tear yourself apart!' And that was when I heard the voice, caroming off the buildings for hours before it reached my window, rendering sensible the single word it had been chanting: '*Blessings!*'

"Recklessly excited by the sound of a human voice, I rushed to the window and invited the salesman up. Into my flat climbed a mountain mummy, a man patient enough to sit atop Bald Mountain until he'd dried out entirely, his bark-like flesh lending him an ascetic air despite the portable storehouse of charms, trinkets, and amulets strung around his neck with knotted scraps of shoelace. 'Blessings,' he said, time and again, 'blessings,' showing me object after object, observing the mess I'd made of the flat with a keen eye. 'You are need of blessings. I sense — wait — yes. Yes! I sense — loss. Great loss. You have lost — someone. Very close someone.'

"I could only stare at him, astonished by the idiocy of his tactics, but still more astonished that they comforted me. 'I — suppose I have,' I whispered, so near to the end of my rope that I was only vaguely aware that this carnival-psychic's argument applied to every last soul in the underworld.

"'The loss,' he said eagerly, 'invites the soul-maggots. You know soul-maggots? You have the fat ones.'

"'Fat soul-maggots,' I pronounced.

"'This one, he is small, but very powerful spirit.' He held up a discolored rubber frog strung on a length of fishing line. 'Named Bimby the Voracious. He eat them up. Snap! Make your maggots go away. Your crazy go, too. Make you whole.'

"Even in my weakened state, I thought this was a bit much, but I didn't have the strength to dismiss him. Instead I attended to his every guttural word, willingly feeding him those small details about my existence that he needed to perfect his pitch. At last, having exhausted both his repertoire of invented maladies and his stock of worthless tchotchkes, he knelt, digging deep into his tattered cloak. 'Let us be honest, Yacob. You need not many cures, but one. All these maladies can go at once. Curse of the river-ghast. Poof. Bone-blight. Poof. Even soul-maggots. Poof,

poof, poof. All will be gone if spirit is healthy. Awake. Strong. But now? Spirit of Yacob — is *lost*.' He pulled a small object from the folds of his cloak, keeping it covered by his knotty fist. 'One man can find it. Find *you*. And point the way. From now until end of eternity. Make you free.' He opened his palm and held out this vial, swinging it around until the tip of the finger was pointing directly at the husk of my heart. 'Make you stop searching for him you've lost. Find true path instead. The Living Man knows how. This is the last piece of his corpse. Last, and most powerful. Always point the way forward. *Forever*. So tell me, Yacob, how much forever is worth to you?'

"It took hours for the glow of that purchase to fade. When at last I realized how much I'd paid that mountebank, how many months of tediously-accumulated credit I'd spent in that moment of weakness, and how pathetic my gratitude had been, I hurled the vial against the wall, cursing myself for falling for his tricks. But more hours followed those hours, and in the emptiness of their passing I dug the vial out of the mess I'd made of my flat. Lacking anything more sensible to do, I began to dissect the fingertip.

"I thought I'd prove that the mountain-mummy was a huck-ster," said Jacob, withdrawing a piece of charcoal from his knap-sack. "Instead I found definitive proof that the Living Man was real." He quickly sketched a cross-section of the human finger on the back of the map. "Here, inside the fingertip, the distal phalanx is couched in a tiny pillow of fat. I've scooped this fat from hundreds of fingers, and each dollop has borne the unmistakable stamp of the river: like all the body's fatty tissues, it's dyed a murky purple by its long soak. Even after decomposition, that stain remains as a dark rind between skin and bone, but this fingertip bore no such markings. The body this finger was cut from didn't enter this world by way of the River Lethe." With that, Jacob leaned back, lacing his stiff fingers behind his head with the satisfied air of a trial lawyer who'd just delivered an unassailable closing argument.

Leopold swirled the liquid in his cup, humming loud and low before he spoke. "What I understand from all this," he said slowly, "is that by way of a taxidermist's misreading of forensic science you've convinced yourself that a man once magicked himself into the underworld. Now you'd like a bit of company in your starry-eyed obsession, but while the boy may follow you, being a little light in the skull, I remain skeptical, if fascinated by the means you've invented to fill your time.

"I must ask, though, what it is that you hope to prove by finding this Living Man. My guess," he said to Remington, "is blackmail! He hopes to rebuild his fortune by ransoming the pinky back to its erstwhile owner."

"What I want to know is how the Living Man did it," said Remington.

"Precisely, Remington! I'll learn his secrets," said Jacob, "and complete his journey back to the Lands Above. It may well take us through untold dangers, to the very edge of the underworld. But we'll get there, and beyond. If a man can cross the veil in one direction, he can cross it in the other."

"What, go back to *Earth*? What a horrid idea!" said Leopold, snorting. "What could you possibly gain by traveling there? The breathers won't throw a parade for the first corpse who staggers up Main Street, I promise you that."

"You're not being paid for your expert opinion, Leopold," snapped Jacob. "I've hired you as our navigator, nothing more, and once you've done your job, you'll be free to pursue your own aspirations. I'll do you the favor of keeping my judgments about their triviality to myself."

Leopold cackled, then held up a hand, growing suddenly contemplative. "Then again," he said, "despite the patent absurdity of your quest, the paucity of your logic, and the utterly fictive hope you have of returning to the living world, your enthusiasm has plucked a jaunty little tune on my heartstrings. Gentlemen, the decision has been made!"

"What decision?" said Remington.

"Make no mistake," said Leopold, "I am a proud citizen through and through, and aspire toward nothing more than to show Dead City the very girth of my quality, but it has recently occurred to me that a chance to travel might be just what I need to provoke my transformation into permanent greatness. Why, when your little troupe of misfits found me, I was in the midst of raising funds to hire a tour guide of my own! Adventure beyond this city's borders is what I seek, Jacob, and you have just inspired me to raise my fee."

"I beg your pardon?" cried Jacob.

"Six months' credit is a wonderful start," said Leopold, "but if you want me to take you any further, I'll require more: namely, a spot in your caravan! Should you find the man you seek in these Tunnels, take me along for the ride."

"Absolutely not! You must be drunker than I thought. There's no possible circumstance that could cause me to consider bringing you with us. You're hardly what anyone could call reliable, much less trustworthy. No, Leopold, I'm afraid we'll have to stick to our original arrangement."

"Ah, well!" cried Leopold, leaping up from the table with an expansive bow. "In that case, I'm sure you'll have no trouble finding an eager helpmate among this crowd. They all have the best of intentions, I'm sure. Lads!" he shouted to a group of skinless urchins relieving a tattooed corpse of his many piercings. "Six months' credit for anyone who can lose these rubes in the labyrinth!"

"Happy to help," shouted a nearby drunkard, staggering up from his table.

"I'll lose 'em thrice for a year!" said his neighbor.

As more corpses crowded around, Jacob held his head in his hands. "Very well," he murmured. "You may join us."

"Splendid! Then let's drain these dregs, boys, and see what we cross at the cross!"

Remington dumped his swill onto the floor, then followed on, noting how mutable the path became as it progressed. Now it was a subway tunnel, now a sewer pipe, now a dungeon with an unstable floor, and never was it silent, for even when they weren't speaking amongst themselves, the echoing of nearby chambers, slick with swill, brimming with babble, caroused around their silent silhouettes. Remington wondered how many bars there could possibly be, and how many drunks must be lost in them, drifting without direction on currents of swill.

"Not far now!" said Leopold time and again as he consulted the map, until, after untold hours, a single train car hulked over the chaos of a noisome crowd. "Here we are," he whispered, pulling the others close. "Our quarry, the Crowded Car. We're far from any entryway, fellows, so let's take care: the bastards in here have been drunk for so long it beggars belief."

CHAPTER FIVE

The Crowded Car

Dented and scraped but still watertight, the Crowded Car was lodged securely between a low ceiling and crumbling concrete floor. The company entered through its rear door, finding a dining car replete with ancient leather booths, awash in leaked swill and profanity. Presiding over the motley drunkards was an elephantine barman trading a pitcher of swill for a fistful of rags. "His preferred payment is stuffing, the better to keep his belly from collapsing," murmured Leopold as they wended their way toward an open booth toward the front of the car. "That's Barnabas the Barman, stout and surly as ever."

As they passed, a woman missing the skin on the left side of her body banged through the front door, pushing a wheelbarrow overflowing with sodden refuse. "Gotcher gear, Barney," she rasped. "Can I get that drink now?"

Barnabas took a disgusted look at her catch and lumbered to his feet. "What's going on?" said Remington. "Why's she bringing the trash *in*?"

"She's a runner," said Leopold, "an employee sent out to scavenge the river for the basic ingredients of swill. She's botched the job, hence the big man's discontent. Let's take this booth over here."

"You make swill with goddamned vegetables," Barnabas was saying. "Fruits, houseplants, algae, even meat will soak down into a decent batch, but what do you expect me to do with *this*?" He pulled a fistful of purple cotton from the wheelbarrow, slapping it on the bar.

The half-peeled runner looked sidelong at her employer, who'd been shouting into her good ear as if the raw half could hear him any less. "Stuff it in your belly when you think no one's lookin'?"

Barnabas kicked the wheelbarrow onto the floor, one hand on his gut. "You shut your face or I'll smack off the good side. Go on and make another run — and don't even *think* about taking a drink until I get a decent haul!"

"Might get another job first." The runner righted the wheelbarrow and staggered up to the door of the train car, struggling to work it open. "I got options, you know."

"It's a *push*!" yelled Barnabas, snatching up the purple cotton and stuffing it surreptitiously into a hole in his hide.

"Mind yourself," warned Leopold. "The lummox is an inveterate liar, as stuffed with deceit as his belly is with rags."

"Indeed," said Jacob, barely listening as he stepped through the Car's silent scrutiny, sidling up to the bar and laying a small piece of cardboard on its surface. "Barman. A round on me. For everyone."

Barnabas peered down at the circle and approximated a gasp: it was a coaster, printed in faded letters with the name of a popular aboveground liquor.

"A round on the gentleman!" called Barnabas, then stowed the offering and lined up the drinks before his announcement pulled in a crowd from the surrounding Tunnels. Jacob was briefly drowned in shouts of goodwill, then forgotten.

He made his play when the patrons were midway through their drinks. "Now, I've seen moose-heads hanging in bars," Jacob said, "I've seen stuffed stags, bears, and boars. I've seen marlins mounted, and large-mouth bass, and here in the Tunnels I've seen mighty vultures nailed to the walls, but never in all my days, above nor below the ground, have I seen a dead man's head displayed as a trophy. What, may I ask, was this melancholy fellow's offense?"

Barnabas shifted on his stool, regarding Jacob and the subject of their discussion at once. Behind him, bolted to a plank of driftwood, hung the ragged shape of a severed head, white teeth gleaming among blackened gums, eyes squeezed shut against some final, intolerable vision, cracked skin painted long ago in black and white, with a frowning clown's mouth and black tears below the eyes.

"This poor son of a gun didn't do anything wrong," said Barnabas. "This is Pierrot, the Crowded Car's good luck charm! He isn't much of a drinker now, but in his prime he could put a man with no stomach under the table."

"Must be quite the story," said Jacob, hoping to egg him on.

"What's that? You want to hear the tale of the Head on the Wall? Gather 'round, chums, it's time!" A dutiful cheer erupted, and several corpses crowded around, pressing too close for Jacob's comfort. "Now! Before this dive was mine, it was run by a lady so fine you'd think she was breathing if you'd had a few. Old Pierrot was a mooner, and he'd sit right where you're leaning," said Barnabas, waggling a sausage-shaped finger in Jacob's direction, "night after night, just to watch her work. He'd feed her every corny line in the book. He'd overtip her with baubles he'd found in the river. He'd carve her initials into the rotten flesh on his arm. But did she pay him any mind?"

"No!" cried the crowd, which was filling in around him.

"Why, she never even noticed he was there! Pierrot was a kindly soul, but the kid didn't have any game." Barnabas lurched off of his stool, thumping his hands on the bar before Jacob and adopting a stage whisper. "Now you might not think it to see me, but I wasn't always a titan of industry. Why, I used to be a drunk myself!"

"Now he's a whole twenty minutes sober," yelled a woman over Jacob's shoulder. Barnabas gave her a why-I-oughtta, then took a theatrical swig.

"All right, so I'm still a drunk. But a lucky drunk! When the lady of the manor decided to give up the ghost, she tossed me the keys. She must've had a feeling I was never gonna leave! I was as grateful as a vulture after a battle, but that's when Pierrot's troubles started, for she left without telling the poor fella goodbye." The crowd made a mournful noise. "Well, most of these reprobates could give a damn who's serving their swill —"

"So long as they does it quickly!"

"— but Pierrot sure did. The poor fella hounded me for weeks. 'Where'd she go, Barnabas? When's she coming back, Barnabas? Did she leave a message, Barnabas?' So I says, 'Listen, buddy, she just went down the river to get herself a few supplies. But I promise you, she'll be back!' Then I sold the sucker another round. It's my sacred oath to keep 'em in their seats."

"You always was a sacred oaf, Barney."

"Har, har. Now, I had high hopes that Pierrot would let the whole thing drop, but he did not go gentle. No, he paid ahead for a year's supply and went on the worst bender I've ever seen. He was singing serenades! He was crying on the bar! He was hugging folks!"

"Anything but hugging," a man moaned into Jacob's ear.

"Finally he said to me, 'Barnabas, I've drunk all I can and I can't drink no more. I'm going to stay right here until my true love comes back for me. Help me, Barney: pull this head of mine right off my neck and plant it up behind the bar, so that my face is the first thing she sees when she returns.'

"Now, who among us was here to witness what came next?" To Jacob's disbelief, every hand in the crowd shot up. Barnabas guffawed. "That's right, we've all been here forever!"

"Here's to forever more!"

"And it sure seemed like Pierrot would go on forever, too. He was so persistent with his bellyaching and his caterwauling and his carrying-on that I bought myself a nice sharp sword just to shut him up. I laid the poor fella down on the bar, and I said, 'Here we are, old friend! The knife in my paw and your neck on the block. Now, are you sure this is what you really want?'

"'The next words I'll say are *welcome back*,' he cried, and he would not stop his crying until, whammo! I swung the cleaver down and lopped his head clean off!"

"Thought it was a sword?" screeched a woman from the crowd. "Wunnit a sword a moment ago?"

"Everyone's a critic! Pierrot's head tumbled down, mum as a floater's toe, and that, I swear upon my grave, was the last we heard out of him, and the last we ever will. I had my runner carry his carcass up to the river, just as he'd requested, and I hung his *cabeza* right where it stands.

"Poor, poor Pierrot," hollered the barman, lifting his mug in the air. "At least your broken heart is far from your mind!"

Joining in this familiar refrain, the crowd cheered wildly and drank to Pierrot's health, as Jacob had no doubt they'd done dozens of times before.

"A fascinating tale!" said Jacob, setting down his drink as the corpses behind him dispersed. "Do I understand, then, that he's hanging there voluntarily?"

"Well, of course he is," said Barnabas, settling in on his stool. "He don't owe any man a moment, least of all me."

"Then if he wanted to, he could leave the bar for awhile?"

"The head is his own man. But before you go trying what's been tried before, let me make it clear. The head is not a toy. The head is not a dartboard. The head is not a ball for playing games. The head is not for sale, not for any price, so don't bother trying to add him to that broken-corpse collection you came in with. The head stays where he is unless he says he wants to get down. The head does not want to get down.

"But don't take my word for it, let's ask him. What do you say, Pierrot? Want to go walkies?"

The head was silent.

"I guess you're not his type," said the barman, polishing off his drink. "Say, thanks for the coaster. What a find! I remember this one fateful evening, up above, we uncorked two bottles of this stuff and somehow found ourselves —"

"I understand that a lot of oddballs must ask after Pierrot," Jacob interrupted, "but I assure you I mean him no harm.

"My name is John Tanner, preservationist. My associates at the table and I are the vanguard of a research team seeking to achieve a renaissance of our noble art. We envision a future in which corpses like Pierrot will be able to walk again through voluntary partnerships with other disadvantaged dead.

"You say your friend forsook his body willingly, but this is no impediment to his rehabilitation. Men such as Pierrot are, we now understand, victims of post-mortal dementia; in other words, his decapitation was beyond his own control. That's not to say that you were wrong to do it, since you were but the agent of his wishes and acted in good faith.

"Now, Pierrot hasn't spoken in awhile, but it may well be that behind the mask of his muteness he has been suffering, wishing that he could walk again, drink again, speak again, for what can't a decade change? Who among us can say what effect hope might have on his silence?

"My friend, we can offer him that hope. We can offer Pierrot the chance to be the first recipient of a full-scale recombinant preservative treatment, free of charge, and we can begin at once, for the cranially-challenged gentleman at the booth has needs that perfectly coincide with Pierrot's."

Jacob and Barnabas turned to consider the headless form of Adam. "Dear Aloysius!" said Jacob. "He was a close friend and associate of mine before an argument with a brute in a pub not far from here left him bereft of capital. A tragedy, to be sure, yet think of the possibilities if he and Pierrot joined forces! Imagine Pierrot as a free agent, engaged in a mutually beneficial muscular collaboration with Aloysius, able to search for his lady friend of his own accord. You may be dubious, dear barman, but I beg you to let us speak the matter over with him."

"The head can hear all right from where he is," said Barnabas, uneasily pouring himself another drink.

"We'd happily pay for the privilege," said Jacob.

"I won't be bought off, citizen. I've got more time banked than I've got time to spend it in."

"Understandable," said Jacob, leaning close. He lowered his voice until only Barnabas could hear. "I'd hoped to avoid this, but since we both know your tale is as full of noxious garbage as your hide, let's stop dancing around the point. If you don't let me borrow your mascot for a few minutes at our booth, I'll tell everyone in this bar that this 'Pierrot' of yours is, in fact, the Living Man. And I'll tell them the little secret that Ma Kicks told me."

The barman's jaw creaked open, but no sound emerged.

"Take this for your troubles," said Jacob, laying a shining object on the bar. It was a little chipped and completely useless in the underworld, but the barman was eager enough to snatch up the mounted oval of a Guinness tap and cradle it in his hands. "If you can undo the screws you can speak to him awhile," said Barnabas quietly.

"Phillips head?" said Jacob, who had already climbed onto the bar and begun rummaging in his knapsack.

Standing before the remains of the man he'd spent most of his death seeking, laying his hands on the mottled driftwood that housed him, and beginning to work out screws that hadn't budged since the day the man had been mounted, Jacob Campbell was so full of emotion that he was surprised to notice that his heart wasn't beating. The sense of excitement that could, at rare moments, overwhelm the dead was so similar to the effect of adrenaline on the living body that the term "bone-rush" was applied as a psychic defense against confusion, a way of reinforcing the reality of death at the moment one could most easily forget it. A dead man's mouth was already dry, no throb afflicted his throat or temples, no sweat dampened his palms, and his nerves couldn't tingle; nevertheless, when a bone-thrower triumphed or a sentimental corpse found an object that recalled her life, something essential about that person's perception changed, and it was hard to say what had changed it. While it was strange for Jacob, who didn't tremble, and who had no breath to hold, to conceive of himself as impassioned, he could not deny that the sight of the Living Man on his knotted mantle of wood was coloring his existence, nor that the sensation he felt when he held the Living Man's head in his arms blazed just as brightly without its mortal trappings.

"I'll be buggered backwards," said Leopold as Jacob returned, "the shiny ponce has done it. That was quite the sales pitch, Campbell: recombinant preservation, indeed! As if two corpses would suffer being sewn to each other for more than an hour without tearing one another to bits."

"What were you whispering to him right at the end?" said Remington. "What changed his mind?"

"I was bluffing. Desperately." Jacob propped the Living Man's plaque at the end of the table.

"Now what?" said Remington.

The three of them stared at the Living Man's face, pondering the paint that peeled from the wrinkles around his eyes. Even the headless seemed to be closely attending to his features, their hands gripping the edges of the tabletop.

"Maybe he'll feel better if you give him back his finger," said Remington.

"Let's be easy," said Jacob. "By all accounts this man hasn't spoken since before the flood."

The party fell into a silence that had the air of a séance, surrounded but unbroken by the Crowded Car's ruckus.

At last Jacob addressed the head, holding his palms open as if mimicking the rhetorical style of an ancient politician. "O brave explorer, O nameless thanatologist, forder of the five rivers, uniter of life, death, and the space between: the path toward you has been a long one, and I grieve to find you so ill-treated at its end."

"Hear, hear," said Leopold, "that looks awfully uncomfortable. Did they nail him to that plaque from inside his skull?"

"See, the bolts went in through the back of his skull here," said Remington. "They must have put the nuts in through his mouth."

"Ingenious!"

"O Living Man," Jacob went on, "the road you trod is one no other man on Earth or beneath it has yet understood, but it need not remain forever obscured. I ask only that we be allowed to serve you and bring your works into the light of day."

"He means himself and the boy," said Leopold, "begging your pardon."

"It is my greatest hope to walk with you into the sunshine of the living world. If it is a disciple you desire, I will bear that name; if you are weary, I will carry on your legacy. If there is a place in this cosmos where you might find your rest, I will bear you thence. The abominable fate that has befallen you can be transformed, if you only speak the word.

"Tell me, O Living Man, will you let us bear you from this dark chamber? Will you once more tread the path that leads between the worlds? Will you, O ancient traveler, be free?"

They waited.

"Was that a sigh?" said Remington suddenly.

"It was gas escaping from your lily-white corpse," said Leopold, "but we could always convince the barman it was a hallelujah."

"Really, Jacob, is this as far ahead as you've thought? The man has been mum and sober on a barroom wall for eons, watching bodies liquefy for entertainment, and your plan for bringing him around is, 'Pretty please, O moldy one'?"

Jacob laid a hand on his breast pocket. "It was worth a shot," he said, "but there are other ways. Since I'm out of alcoholic baubles and the barman has no interest in time, I'll have to resort to a plan I won't ask you to take part in.

"Leopold, you've done me a great service. Here's the payment I've promised you," he said, working an account-stone out of the pouch on his wrist and whispering the password. "I rather doubt you'll want to follow me past this point, but your path is your own.

"Remington, my odd little fellow, I fear that we must part ways here. Take Adam and Eve to safety; I'll wait as long as I can before making my move.

"When the barman asks for his head, I'll take the Living Man hostage. If pressed, I'll use this." Out of Barnabas' sight, Jacob opened the ties of his leather pouch, trying to ignore the feeling that

Ma Kicks' finger was pointing at him as he worked out the silver lighter and laid it on the table.

"Dear Lord!" hissed Leopold. "You moldering loon, you'll go up like the rest of us! These Tunnels are marinated in alcohol. Dead City will blaze from Heap to Heap!"

"It's a chance I'll take if it means climbing from those ashes with the Living Man."

"Sounds like fun," said Remington. "We're not going to miss this!"

Adam flicked his thumb as if urging Jacob to start the fire sooner rather than later. Eve crossed her arms, signaling her discontent, but before any further discussion could be had, Leopold snatched up the lighter and tossed it down his throat.

"Think of something else," he muttered as it clattered to a stop in his ribcage. "I won't spend eternity as a briquette."

Remington ignored the bickering that ensued, focusing instead on the group of newcomers pushing through the door at the opposite end of the bar. They were debtors, with white skulls grinning over black robes, the first he'd seen since his descent. Banging on the tops of the nearest tables with their fists, the tallest of them barked, "On your feet! Routine inspection."

"Hey," said Remington. "You guys."

"Pipe down, boy. The adults are speaking."

"But there's a —"

The grumbling of the Crowded Car's patrons suddenly ceased as the door at the opposite end creaked open again. The debtors stepped aside for a compact corpse in a well-kept robe who threw his cowl back, revealing a skin-tight leather mask elaborately stitched to resemble a grinning skull.

"It's him!" whispered a nearby drunkard. "It's the blessed Gambler!"

Every other booth in the car had taken to its feet, but Jacob and Leopold were still lost in debate, ignorant of the two terrified lines that had formed beside the booths at the debtors' urging. "This is pretty crazy over here," said Remington as the inspection began. His companions paid him no mind until a wave of indignant voices rose, startling them out of self-involvement.

"Well," hissed Leopold, "you couldn't ask for a better diversion than this! The barman's trying to quell a riot, the Car's in an uproar: abscond with the head, and we'll leave through the back!"

Before Leopold could retreat, however, Jacob gripped his broomstick and forced his head toward the scene at the back of the bar. The debtors were yanking down the trousers of each corpse in line, exposing their tenderest decay to the gaze of the Masker, who ignored their curses and moved through their ranks with a business-like air.

"He's *pantsing* them," Jacob said in Leopold's ear. "Almost as if he's searching for someone with a defining characteristic between his legs, wouldn't you say?"

Leopold's body bucked, a shrill, kettle-like whisper escaping his jaws. "The jig is up! The honeymoon's over! The ship has sailed! Let us away, boys, while there's still a chance to escape." So saying, he tore off toward the car's far door, paying no mind to those he shoved aside.

Jacob, scooping up the Living Man's head, followed after. "So help me god, L'Eclair, if you've brought the wrath of the Magnate upon us —"

"You'll be very, very cross, I know," said Leopold. "Now run, while there's still time!"

"What's happening?" said Remington as he was hustled to his feet by Adam and Eve.

"That was a Masker, one of the Magnate's generals. Leopold neglected to mention that he's on the run from the highest authority in Dead City," said Jacob.

As the group burst through the door by the bar, Barnabas hollered, "Everyone stay where you are, the next round's on the house!"

The swinging door knocked a pair of debtors aside like bowling pins, and the band of outlaws escaped noisily, albeit slowly, down a nearby sewer pipe.

"What kind of idiot runs from the Leather Masker?" said one from the floor, still within earshot.

"One who is desperate," said her partner, a lanky debtor who shifted the weight of an enormous gourd strapped to his shoulder from his back onto his hip. "Alert Monsieur, and I, Jean-Luc, shall ride upon the backs of the guilty!"

"There's a debtor on our trail!" said Remington, watching their pursuer with glee. "Why don't we stop and grab him?"

Hearing this, Jean-Luc stopped abruptly, giving them a more generous lead.

"He's only marking our trail," said Leopold.

As if to demonstrate, Jean-Luc scooped a handful of river clay from his gourd and dropped it on the ground behind him.

"Blast it all, but we haven't the time to dispatch him. Our only hope is to outrun him!"

"How?" said Remington. "We can't even run!"

This could hardly be denied: haste only caused them to stumble against one another or the walls around them, granting them no more speed than their leisurely pursuer.

"How far is the nearest exit?" said Remington.

"Miles away," said Leopold. "Do you think I brought us all this way for the scenery? We're in the bowels of Dead City, boy, with the might of the Magnate rushing after us like an enema. Now for the love of your maggoty mother, move!"

"It occurs to me," said Jacob, "that the debtors aren't chasing us because we've stolen a severed head from a pub but because we've made the mistake of associating with you, Leopold. A more pragmatic man might wonder why we don't just hand you over."

"You've already fled, Jacob. We're accomplices now, and there's no use blubbering over it," said Leopold, then promptly collided with the figure turning the corner into the tunnel before them, tumbling ass-over-elbow into her wheelbarrow full of slops. Even as Leopold was bemoaning the ill effects of such dampness on his finery, Jacob recognized the Crowded Car's lopsided runner, covered in the rotting vegetable matter that had spilled from her conveyance.

"God's wounds," Leopold cried, "the barman sent you to the surface less than an hour ago! Speak, wench: where's the passage?"

"No dice," said the runner, scooping handfuls of pumpkin guts back into her barrow. "That's the fat man's secret."

"I see," said Leopold, knocking her barrow to the ground. "Shall I buy this secret from you or twist your arms out of their sockets?"

"Buying it's easier all around," said the runner. "I like your jacket."

Leopold seemed primed to argue, but at the sound of the Masker and his claque entering the sewer pipe he began to wrestle with his blazer, saying, "Remington, help me off with this!"

The runner, unperturbed by the coat's unnatural stiffness, was so pleased with its color that she led them to the exit herself, humming through the din that rebounded all around them.

Jacob envied her leisurely pace, as his company only got clumsier the more excited they became, and gained no speed by rushing. Jostling one another, they slammed their shoulders against the slick walls, and banged their heads off the slumping ceilings. With every awkward step they were dogged by the steady slapping of the rivermud, the rough orders of the Leather Masker, and the clattering of bones and boot-heels. It was enough to curdle Jacob's marrow, but his dread only trebled when the lopsided runner led them to a moldy plaster wall at the end of an alley, where she stopped short.

"It's a dead end, you dizzy slut!" cried Leopold. "Give me back my jacket!"

"It's a push," said the runner, shoving the wall down with her hands. By means of rusted pulleys hidden above, the wall came down like a drawbridge, revealing a great concrete ring through which a dim sepia light spilled onto the floor.

"My thanks, dear woman," said Jacob, bending as he climbed into the tube. "Would you pull the trap-door shut behind us?"

"No use," said the runner, "the bonehead's already here."

Chancing a look over his shoulder, Jacob saw the debtor standing at the end of the alley, holding a dripping fistful of clay. Launching himself up the tube, Jacob clasped the Living Man close to his chest and whispered, "If you can hear me, little Orpheus, pray."

The concrete tube they ascended was an industrial smokestack rising sideways through the city's substrata. Like bubbles from the neck of a champagne bottle, the company burst from its open end into daylight.

"Trapped like rats!" cried Leopold, for they had emerged at the bottom of Southheap, hemmed in on one side by a sheer wall of corroded metal, on the other by the River Lethe.

"They're climbing up the smokestack!" said Jacob.

Remington tottered out toward the dark water at the end of the rubble, where a bathtub floated swiftly by. "Gee, the current's strong here," he said.

"Would that it were strong enough to carry us to oblivion," said Leopold. "I'd plunge in happily, just to deny them the satisfaction of giving us over to the Mortar and Pestle. They'll grind us down, Jacob!"

"For *what*?" shouted Jacob, clenching his leather-lined fists hard enough to hear them squeak. "What have you done, Leopold?"

"All I wanted was time," murmured Leopold, edging closer to the surface of the river. "Just a little more time, enough to plan my —"

"Hey, wait," said Remington, calling Adam and Eve to his side. The three of them, through Remington's eyes, watched the bloated shape of a naked corpse sailing past on the current. "We're not trapped: we can float!"

"Speak for yourself," said Jacob, looking balefully at the smokestack, which emitted laughter in lieu of smoke. "You're fresh enough that you're still full of gas, but Leo and I deflated years ago. You'd bob like a cork, but the weight of our preservative treatments alone would drag us to the bottom, where we'd lie waterlogged for eternity. If only we had wooden body-molds, like Shanthi!"

"An excellent point," said Leopold, snapping irritably out of his funk. "Had your prices not been so exorbitant, I'd be floating to safety as we speak."

"Really, you can shift the blame to me at a time like this? You're the author of this travesty, L'Eclair!"

But Leopold broke off the argument, pointing at the water's edge. "Jacob, look! Your idiot boy's a savant!"

While they were bickering, Remington's companions had stepped arm-in-arm into the current, where they slowly reclined so that he could hold fast to their ankles. Once afloat, each bent one knee, which Remington linked together, so that their conjoined bodies, buoyant with the bloat of decomposition, formed a small but serviceable human raft. Shrieking like children at a carnival, Jacob and Leopold splashed into the river and clambered aboard.

As Remington kicked off Southheap's edge, the Masker and his retinue spilled from the smokestack, staggering to the end of the rubble as the company spun off on the current. There was no time for Jacob to bid his city goodbye. The last thing he saw was the Masker striding past the edge of the rubble, where he planted both boots in the river, paying no mind to the water that tugged insistently at his robe. His eyeless stare, the cracks in his mask, the single finger unfurling from his gloved fist, the laughter that rose from his skull-faced debtors when he spoke in a voice like gravel in a meat grinder, his words incomprehensible to the company: these were the things that haunted Jacob long after the raft had left the city's mangled skyline behind.

II

CHAPTER SIX

On Lethe

The River Lethe narrowed as it outran city limits, passing swiftly between the rising walls of the Lethean Valley, offering the company's fleshy raft no place to rest. While Jacob and Leopold clung to the headless corpses, bickering fearfully as they picked up speed, Remington lay face-down behind them, his hands clasped around Adam and Eve's ankles. He was immersed in a calm analysis of the river, though the only conclusion he had reached so far was that it was deep and murky. Lethe swirled through his head, stirring hundreds of questions that came and went without any hope of finding answers: its color was a mystery, as were its cargo, purpose, and connection to the world of the living, to say nothing of its rumored droughts and floods, or its points of origin or ending; and yet, to Remington, the greatest mystery was what the river would taste like if the tongue he thrust into it were operational.

Grape jelly? he wondered. Red wine? Ketchup?

Maybe the Living Man will know, thought Remington, setting his mind on waking him. Pulling his head above the water-line, he called out to the others, "Make room!"

"You're doing a fine job as our rudder," snapped Leopold. "Don't spoil it now."

Remington moved his hands from the headless' ankles to their calves, causing the raft to rock.

"Really, Remington, these two aren't structurally sound," said Jacob. "You'll have to stay where you are."

"No fair," said Remington, ignoring the increasing velocity of their spin. "How come you two get to ride the whole time?" As the valley whirled around them, he slapped a hand on Eve's thigh, pulling himself out of the water. "Stay down, boy!" snarled Leopold, aiming a savage kick at his chin. Teeth clashing, Remington flew backwards, snatching Eve's ankle as he plunged beneath the surface. The current caught his body and twisted it like a loosely-held oar, turning the raft's spin into a sudden somersault.

In an instant, the entire company was submerged. The river wrenched Remington free from his fellows, flinging him about in the bubbly murk with astonishing force. Down he plunged, then up he came, buoyed briefly into the air before smacking against the river's surface. As he thrashed upright, he let out a cry: his friends were nowhere to be seen.

That's horrible! he thought. They'll be so sad, stuck in the mud, waving around like little weeds — except for the head.

Just as he began to wonder if the headless had deflated, Eve surfaced, her arms wrapped around Leopold, who would otherwise have sunk like a stone.

Adam popped up a moment later, with Jacob clinging to his legs, howling, "The head, Remy! I've lost hold of the Living Man's head! Dive, boy, dive!"

Remington did his best to oblige, tilting his torso into the river and flailing his arms and legs, but due to his natural buoyancy, his legs were still scissoring in the air when the plaque rose to the river's surface, carrying the Living Man's head on its underside.

"Look, the river washed off his makeup!" said Remington, tossing the head to Jacob before linking his elbows and knees with those of the headless to become the raft's middle plank. He was facing skyward this time, and as the waters of Lethe filled his empty skull, he started to feel a little funny — not intoxicated, but profoundly, almost passionately awake — and began to question the monotony of the hazy sky.

"We ought to chastise him for dunking us, I know," said Jacob to Leopold as they climbed aboard, "but it's nearly impossible to stay angry at the little bugger, wouldn't you say, Leopold?

"Leopold? Are you all right?"

But Leopold didn't answer. He was perched atop Eve's ribs in a fetal crouch, his face buried in his folded arms as if he were about to weep.

"I know how you feel," said Jacob. "I thought we were done for. As soon as the water closed around me, all this leather started to pull me down to the bottom, and it was only by chance that I caught on to this fellow, who, as luck would have it, was headed in the opposite direction. Even then, it was a battle between my ballast and his gas!"

Leopold made no sign that he'd heard, and Jacob noticed that the scarf holding his head erect had slipped from its broomstick and was dangling amidst his dripping hair.

"It's all right now, we're floating freely. Look, there's some riverbank up ahead! Perhaps we'll stop for a moment."

Leopold muttered something into his knees.

"Come again?" said Jacob.

"I said, 'You were right.' It's not a phrase you're likely to hear again, so savor the moment."

Grasping the crimson scarf from behind, Leopold hoisted his head aloft. The last clumps of painted river clay fell away from his cheeks, plopping onto Eve's belly. Denuded of cosmetics, his face was like an acid-eaten cheesecloth.

"You told me not to put all of my eggs into one basket, didn't you? 'Treat yourself to a full-body treatment,' you said, but I treated you like an opportunistic salesman, and now I've paid the price.

Well, go ahead and laugh: laugh through all of that fine, waterproof leather! Don't worry, these withered ears can still hear the echoes, even if I emulate your disembodied friend and squeeze my eyes shut, so as not to catch sight of my reflection on this rancid river's surface."

Slowly, with his head lolling freely on the shattered pivot of his neck, Leopold began to peel off layer after layer of clothing, littering the river behind them with frills and ribbons, until nothing remained but a long-sleeved black undershirt, a pair of purple corduroy trousers, and his boots. Carefully, as if approaching a strange dog, Jacob extended his hand toward Leopold's neck and looped the scarf over the broomstick.

"If you didn't give him a regular treatment, what did you do?" said Remington from below, startling both men, who had grown accustomed to riding a raft that didn't speak.

Jacob looked uncertainly at Leopold.

"Oh, out with it," Leopold said. "We'll leave the legend of l'Eclair back in the city."

"As you wish," said Jacob, rubbing his palms together.

"I first met Leopold in the months before Shanthi's arrival, when I was still tied to my studio and could only rely on word-of-mouth for business. Word was spreading, slowly but surely, as the success of my first full-body casting prompted a savage rivalry between myself and John Tanner, who was, believe it or not, my toughest competition. As my star rose, he lost his hold on the richest corpses in Dead City, notably that notorious pervert known as the Plucker, whose appetites kept me busy renovating the fresh young ladies his minions found on the riverside.

"Weeks earlier, Tanner stood outside my window backed by two rejects from the Plains of War and threatened to bury me in quicklime if I didn't agree to become his partner. So, when I caught sight of his massive head floating up my street like a piebald parade balloon, I shut the window and prepared to ignore whatever vitriol he might utter.

"Ultimately, I found it impossible to ignore his roaring apology, followed by a declamation that he needed, nay, begged for my help in a matter that was quite beyond his skills. The last part intrigued me, and against my better judgment I let my rival inside.

"'Now, Jacob, you know it was only a little ribbing,' he said, 'fraternal in nature, a sort of initiation ceremony or brotherly encouragement, quite similar to tough love. I meant no harm, and I certainly wouldn't know where to find enough lime to eat up more than a few of your toes! We're builders-up, after all, not breakers-down. Let's put the past where it belongs, let us amend, for I really and truly need you today.

"'It's this ghastly boy the whole city is talking about, the kick-stool who won seventeen years on a single throw!'

"Sequestered in my quarters, I'd missed out on the gossip, and Tanner was delighted to fill me in. 'Some sullen, teenaged madman,' he said, 'his neck still warm from the friction of his belt (you can count the notches!), walked into Caesar's yesterday and staked his lifespan on a single throw. Well, wouldn't you know the lucky little dangler won and took his credit-pebbles to the District, where someone was kind enough to refer him to me.

"'I was thrilled to see him, and with seventeen years lining his pockets, why wouldn't I be? I offered him a top-of-the-line Tanner tanning, thinking that I'd suggest some additional enhancements once his skin was off, since, as you know, the indignity has a way of loosening their wallets, but the awful child said no! "There's only one thing I'm interested in preserving," he said, and then he showed me what he meant, and I realized I'd have to turn away business for the first time in a decade.

"'First of all I wouldn't know how to go about it, and if I did I wouldn't want to, but I thought that, given your recent innovations in the preservative arts, you might enjoy the challenge.

"'I beseech you, Jacob, get this nasty man-child off of my divan, where he has insisted on remaining until, to use his phrase, his *situation* is made *permanent*. Isn't that just a darling way of putting it?'

"Putting what, I wanted to know.

"'Well,' said Tanner, 'it turns out that what they say about hanged men is true.'

"'And what do they say about hanged men?' I asked him.

"'Zounds, Jacob, do I have to spell it out? He passed priapic! He ended engorged! His last word was "yes"! The filthy bugger's bell-end is hard as a bone, and he wants to have it fixed that way before it drains! Now are you or are you not the man to handle it?'

"I didn't care to answer that question as it was posed, but I told him to bring Leopold up and I'd see what I could do.

"When he left I began to consider the problem. True, I claimed to offer a full-body preservation, but I'd never considered the rehabilitation of an organ before, least of all that one. Where women were concerned, I dealt with their affairs simply and with decorum; as for men, all my male clients had died flaccid, resigned themselves to the rot of their privates, sewed up their flies, and never looked back.

"Suddenly, I realized that I'd fitted the penis into the same category as the tongue: organs made useless by death, not worth the effort to preserve. Now that such a preservation had been requested, however, I had to consider it carefully, for to my mind it wouldn't do merely to lay the skin over a carved reproduction as I would with an arm or leg, since this would result in nothing more than a glorified dildo. No, it was clear to me that a man willing to go to such lengths to retain his genitals would need them preserved in their entirety, meaning that I would have to salvage every last vein and vesicle by teasing them out of their casing, drying them individually, hardening them by the application of lacquer, and fitting the entire puzzle back together again, with whatever resinous filler might be required, giving the client a direct and visceral sense that nothing had been lost."

"Gross!" said Remington.

"Indeed," said Jacob, "but fascinating, and entirely dependent on the freshness of the corpse in question. Luckily, the boy who stumbled through my window was so fresh his pimples were still pink, having just gone through his mortis on John Tanner's divan. So, without pausing for niceties, I laid him down on the table and pressed Tanner into service as my assistant, since I needed materials and couldn't leave to get them myself.

"The job was intricate, but I had to start immediately, and I credit Leopold's strong stomach with the swiftness of its completion, for even with his manhood vivisected, he never flinched from the task. In fact, he hardly spoke a word: he was shy to the point of muteness, hard as that may be to believe.

"In any case, when his organ's constituent parts had been safely dissected, I took a break to let things drain, and it was then that curiosity got the better of me, and I asked Leopold why it was so important that this feature be preserved.

"He said nothing at first, and when he did speak, he would only say that it would be his secret weapon. At first I was confused by this answer, but I saw what he meant when everything was sewed up. The boy who'd climbed through my window was a sullen thing who looked like he'd been slapped in the face at least once a day for the entirety of his adolescence, but the boy who pulled up his pants and walked to the mirror in my flat was swaggering.

"Now, although my prices were high enough to make such an exhaustive operation worth my time, they weren't so exorbitant that he couldn't afford a full-body treatment, but young Leopold refused.

"'What you've given me is what counts,' he said. 'Pride is all. The rest is smoke and mirrors.'

"When I asked what he meant to do with his pride, he said only that great things lay ahead, and implored me to keep his preservation a secret, even offering to pay for my discretion. Of course, I took no payment for this professional courtesy, and while John Tanner is a notorious gossip, he was either too embarrassed by his incompetence or too mortified by the experience to mention it again, and so far as I can tell, Leopold never mentioned it, either, since in the years that intervened between our first and recent meetings I never heard a murmur about the work I'd done, which begs the question, doesn't it —"

"Say!" said Remington, popping his head up from the middle of the raft. "If everyone kept the secret, how come the Masker knows you have a boner?"

"Curious," said Leopold as he dipped a hand under the river's surface. "The waters of Lethe, according to the ancient Greeks, induce forgetfulness in all who drink them, and yet here we are with our bellies full of river, contemplating old times like a bunch of biddies at bingo night. What happened when, and to whom, and with whom, and to what end? We make such pretty noises reminiscing, and it gives us a sense of power to revel in hindsight, but really, boys, it tells us so little about where we are.

"Oh, I could talk for days about my proud little member, and in the course of our journey it's likely that I will, it being a subject my afterlife has given me little opportunity to indulge, but while the two of you, and, who knows, maybe Adam and Eve to boot, have your minds thoroughly invested in the contents of my trousers, I am more attentive to the fact that we are floating due south up the inner rim of nowhere, without any apparent care for our alleged quest.

"Really, Jacob, how long do you intend to follow the directions of a deaf-mute who has yet to open his eyes?"

Jacob drummed his fingers on the Living Man's driftwood plaque. "Truthfully, gentlemen, I'm stumped. If we stop to consider our options, the Masker will catch up, but if we sail on, we're that much more likely to end up miles from the Living Man's original path."

"For that matter, who's to say that's really the Living Man's bonce you're cradling like a babe in your arms?" said Leopold.

Jacob bristled. "His flesh lacks the river's signature, just like the fingertip. He could not have come to the underworld by way of the river — or, if he did, he was alive at the time."

"And what if he was dead, but crossed over in a waterproof body bag? What if his casket had a trick bottom, and he fell right through the earth onto the Heap? You're a reasonable enough man, Campbell, but when it comes to this second cranium of yours, you insist on ignoring every possibility but the most magical, and to what end?"

"You think I'm a fool," Jacob said quietly, "but you're following me all the same."

"You think worse of me," said Leopold, "but you're letting me follow. Look here, it's possible that your pet noodle really is the last vestige of some world-vaulting hero. It's also possible that he's just an unlucky drunkard who lost a bet with a sadist. But we'll never know the difference if you don't put some energy into waking him!"

"And how would you suggest I do that?"

"You could always set him on fire. Isn't that your standard backup plan?"

Deciding nothing, they drifted upstream. Jacob and Leopold nursed a long, hostile silence, the import of which was lost on Remington. He was so saturated with river-water that when he closed his mouth abruptly a little spume shot out of it.

I am the river, he thought. I'm an eddy, an eel, a piece of driftwood! We're two of a kind, Lethe and me.

But we weren't always. Or were we? I don't think I thought about myself that way when I washed up. I don't really think I thought about much at all. I got up, I saw a big pile of stuff, and I climbed it. I wonder who I was before?

I was born the day I died, that's what Ma used to say. Just like Adam and Eve were born the day they lost their heads.

Is that really how it happened, though? Did they start over again when their heads got cut off?

Are they whole people — or *parts* of people?

If they're parts of people, are they parts of the people they used to be?

Or are they parts of *me*?

Remington's mind, full of the River Lethe and all that its waters contained, began racing, leaping ahead of itself, finishing his thoughts before he'd had a chance to examine them, hurtling him toward an inevitable conclusion whose shape he couldn't see.

The headless can't be parts of me, he thought, or I'd feel it.

Or would I?

I can't feel my hands any more, but they're still parts of me, aren't they?

Of course they are, and I know it because they move when I want them to.

And so do Adam and Eve!

Remington's body jerked, provoking some complaints from above.

I should test it, he thought. I can move my hands without telling them what I want them to do out loud. If there's no separation between Adam, Eve, and me, I should be able to do the same thing with them.

It'll be just like when I quickened.

He remembered that day clearly: the slow slog from darkness into light, the lack of breath in his lungs, his body's surprising numbness, the thought itself: *I'm dead.* Then the struggle. His limbs failing to respond, his will coursing like hot liquid through his bones. His first twitch, his first thrash, his first unsteady step. Then down in the mud, then up again, then again, then again.

He'd had to reach into his bones to learn to walk. This time he'd just reach a little farther, into the bones of his friends.

In his mind's eye he saw Adam and Eve spreading their arms into the river, hands extended like paddles, angling the raft smoothly toward the banks. Then, with an open, flowing patience, he moved the image from his mind toward their fingertips.

There was no result, but a calm seemed to suffuse the water around him. I can't do it yet, he thought, but I'll learn. We'll learn together.

He closed his mouth, and the river bubbled over his lips.

Maybe I'm not reaching far enough, he thought. Maybe it's not enough just to be myself, or to be myself *and* Adam and Eve. I have to think as wide and long as Lethe. If I could do that, moving an arm or a leg would be easy!

Remington softened his gaze and entered something like a day-dream. He saw his mind as a blanket, a flowing, purple quilt made up of millions of tiny patches, a quilt that he draped with ghostly fingers along the length of Lethe, watching it billow from Dead City far into the darkness of the unknown. It wasn't long before he felt the river tugging on its fabric, and then, in satisfaction, he started to hum a little tune to himself.

Above Remington's unsettlingly musical torso, Jacob alternated between two types of anxiety, the first concerning the Masker, whom he had begun to imagine pursuing them on a motorboat, and the second about the Living Man, whom he had good reason to doubt would ever wake up. As his attention swung from one to the next, his worries deepened into terrors, and just as he was approaching a state of frenzy that would certainly have led to an embarrassing outcry, he was distracted by the arrival of an unexpected visitor.

For long minutes a dot in the sky had been approaching, attended by none but the mumbling Leopold, who shook Jacob from his thoughts with such exclamations as, "Is that a vulture?" and, "No, just another bloody crow." As it drew near, however, Jacob noted an irregular wobble in its wingstroke, and by the time it had drawn close enough that all the company could hear it cawing, it was clear that their visitor was none other than Remington's reconstructed crow.

The bird swooped through exclamations of surprise to land on Remington's face and squawk three times.

"This is bizarre, even by your elevated standards," said Leopold. "However did that bedraggled thing know where we were?"

"What if he was captured and trained by the Masker?" hissed Jacob as the crow hopped onto Remington's chest. "What if he flies off and leads them back to us? I know you're fond of the bird, Remy, but I'd feel safer if we took off his wings, at least until we're clear of the river."

"No," said Remington from beneath them. "He came because I called him. I reached out to all the parts of me, and he's one of them."

"Jacob, the boat has gone crazy! I demand another."

"But it's true," said Remington. "There's no difference between me and them!"

"Of course!" said Jacob. "The river has saturated his skull. No wonder he's babbling. Let's shore up here and dry him out."

"All right," said Remington, dipping his head backward into the river and humming tonelessly.

At his unspoken urging, the headless turned their arms and legs like rudders, navigating straight into the shore beside them.

The raft scraped to a halt below a little cave in the valley wall, and the reconstructed crow disembarked, hopping along the stone as Jacob and Leopold staggered away and the headless let go of Remington's limbs. As the water that rolled off their corpses stained the ashen rocks, Leopold cried, "What is this, Remington? By what dark magic have you enchanted these wretched creatures?"

"No magic! Just a blanket. Now let's all gather around and see if we can help the Living Man wake up. If he wants to, I mean. Jake, can I hold him?"

Jacob passed the head into Remington's hands and followed him into the deep, bell-shaped enclosure of the cave. Remington sat at the back of the bell, before a squat, forking tunnel whose branches quickly became too dark to make out. Adam and Eve sat beside him and clasped his wrists, holding out their other hands, waiting for Leopold and Jacob to join the circle.

"You guys coming?" said Remington. The crow flapped onto his shoulder, preening.

With obvious discomfort, Jacob and Leopold sat and clasped the hands of the headless. The five of them formed a circle around the Living Man, whose grimace was aimed at the alcove's ceiling.

"What now?" said Jacob.

"It's hard to describe," said Remington. "I'm sort of making it up as I go along. Clear your mind, I guess, and try to reach out to him, like he's on the bottom of the river and we're all one long arm."

Clearing the cluttered anxieties from his mind was no easy task, but Jacob did his best to honor his ward's wishes. Calm had never come easily to him, so he kept still and did his best imitation of someone relaxing. His gaze wandered to the Living Man's face, where an expression of suffering seemed, if anything, to be more pronounced now than ever. Unsettled, Jacob lifted his gaze to the alcove walls, and had just descended into a level of boredom that bore a passing resemblance to serenity when Remington broke his concentration.

"Oh!" said Remington.

The crow cawed, took flight, and landed inside his skull, and Remington unclasped the headless' hands to lay his own on the Living Man's temples.

Remington made no sound, but his body jerked as if he'd received an electric shock. With a terrible creaking, the Living Man's head wrenched open its mouth and began, in a voice as strong and constant as Lethe, to scream.

CHAPTER SEVEN

The Living Man's Remains

The scream began as the hoarse complaint of a man roused from catatonia by shock treatment, then widened into a roar as its utterer slowly returned to awareness. His throat-shredding bass was soon joined by Jacob's oboe-tones and Remington's earnest alto, additions that managed, in a few minutes, to transform his roar into a howl of disbelieving angst, and then, when it was clear to the screamer that his tormentors had no intention of letting up, into a brief moment of silence that led them to cry out in excitement.

Their joyful noise was short-lived. What followed was an outpouring of speech more ragged and emphatic than the scream, but no more coherent: he was cursing them, that much was clear, but in what language Jacob could not begin to guess. It sounded at first like the religious rush of glossolalia, but proved too discrete and consistent for babble. The sonic torrent was unsettling, but more so was the Living Man's visage: the severed head, gnawed by shadow, raking the walls with its shriveled eyes, its skin fluttering around a jaw loosing an endless stream of syllables, gave Jacob bone-chills. Though it shamed him to do it, he led the company out of the cave to reconsider their strategy.

"We're sunk," said Jacob, sitting heavily on the bank, bowed beneath his soggy knapsack. "We'll never get back to the city without being audible from miles away, and what are the chances we'll find a translator abroad?"

"We don't need a translator," said Leopold, peering upstream. "That's not his mother tongue, nor any other man's. I'll bet you my favorite bone that your Living Man is speaking a language of his own invention. Leave him to me and I'll have him chirping straight before we're caught loitering in the path of our pursuers."

"What are you going to do?" called Remington.

"I'm going to talk some sense into him," said Leopold and strode into the murk at the mouth of the cave.

"Well," said Jacob, staring despondently at Remington's toes, "what harm can it do? Things can't get much worse for him, the poor sod. He suffered through years of consciousness in the Tunnels, according to my informant."

"Who's that?" said Remington, plopping down beside him. "Your informant, I mean."

"A fair question. Nearly everything I learned about the Living Man was told to me by a dried-up drunkard in the Parleyfields, a wide expanse of open land on the bank of the river opposite Dead City. While most of the corpses who occupy that territory do nothing but gossip, retelling the same stories, again and again, to every unoccupied ear they can find, there are some true philosophers out there, too, attempting to work through the problems of existence one extended jaw-session at a time. The Parleyfields are to conversation what the Tunnels are to drink, and this man, a one-time habitué of the bar where Ma Kicks once worked, was attempting to replace one of these vices with the other.

"'I need to keep myself on the straight and narrow. All I desire,' he said when I'd offered him the world, 'is a stool strong enough to sit upon for a decade or two,' and so I spent a small fortune finding him one. When he'd been better situated, he told me as much as he could bear to recall. 'No stories. No memories. I was there, my conscience is as dirty as hers, and that's enough. I'll tell you that he went round the bend, after. I'll tell you that he babbled, and that the woman Clarissa, Ma Kicks they called her after, used him as her crystal ball. But no more. I could stand his voice no more. I could stand his incomprehensible accusations no more. I could bear the weight of our actions no more. It's worse to think of them now than ever it was. Each day drives the memories deeper. My thanks for the stool, but may I never see you again. You're now one more reminder of what we've done.'

"That vague confession wasn't much to go on, but it led me to Ma Kicks, and from there to here. And from here, I've begun to suspect that what happened with the Living Man down in that pub had something to do with the secrets he holds, secrets that will one day enable me to return to the Lands Above. Whatever went wrong down in that bar, it trapped him here. And we'll be the ones to right that wrong. Assuming, that is, that Leopold has talents he hasn't yet revealed." For a time they listened to the voices echoing from the cave, both equally inscrutable. Recognizing that this might be their last moment alone, Jacob leaned close. "Speaking of what our floppy-necked friend may be hiding," he said softly, "I hope it has occurred to you that he can't be trusted."

"Oh, sure! I like Leo, but he only thinks about himself."

"That seems not to bother you, which is admirable, in its way. I would, however, ask you to remember that the Living Man is our responsibility. Mostly mine. But you are becoming — a fuller partner in this enterprise."

"That's true. I *am* the one who woke him up."

"Then let us agree," Jacob whispered, "to help one another keep an eye on Leopold. We don't yet know what he's planning."

Remington stood and saluted, flanked by Adam and Eve, who held their flattened hands up to empty air. "Aye-*aye*, sir! We'll be the best spies you've ever seen, just you wait!"

"Well, and that's that!" cried Leopold, strutting out of the cave. Jacob jumped, then relaxed: Leopold was too fluffed up with pride to have paid the slightest attention to their conversation. "The head hates me more than the Magnate does, but at least the horrid thing is talking sense now. I'll accept your lavish praise any time, gentlemen."

Jacob leapt to his feet, wobbled dangerously, then froze. "Is it true?" he cried, listening intently to the silent cave. "But how?"

"Have you ever wondered how I paid for my drinks during my tenure in the Tunnels? It wasn't with time, I'll tell you that for free: I was employed as a bouncer, ridding the pubs of their most abhorrent customers in exchange for swill. But I never used force, or even threatened it. Rather, I provoked others to attack *me*, a violation of underworld protocol so severe that any barroom would unite in ejecting the offender. In short, I have never met a corpse I couldn't annoy into action, and so my plan for rendering the Living Man sensible was to do what I do best: I insulted him. I couldn't be sure what language he spoke, so I cycled through as many as I could recall.

"I've studied the dozens from some of history's preeminent practitioners of the pejorative, after all, and our bodiless friend was the beneficiary. In Italian, I told him, 'The sperm that found your mother's egg had no tail.' In Arabic: 'My left testicle weighs more than your mortal remains.' In Hindi I compared the head to a kidney-stone; in Swedish to a fishing lure; and in Japanese I called him a disgrace to the category of the sphere. In French, I expressed my doubts that the head had ever possessed functional reproductive equipment, and in Spanish I wondered if he might be useful as a shot-put. Tiny breaks in his babble followed each of these jabs, so I dug deeper, into a store of languages I can barely recall, spewing insults in halting Hebrew, mangled Mandarin, and execrable Urdu, at last provoking a heavy sigh, then silence.

"I had only one arrow left in my quiver, which I'd learned from a crumbling professor of ancient literature at a pub called the Drunken Boat: it was the Persian word for 'homeless,' and as it struck home, the head spoke his first comprehensible word."

"What did he say?" asked Remington as they scrambled for the cave.

"He may be a bit — confused," Leopold admitted. "I believe he was asking for his grandmother."

Jacob was trembling as he stepped into the murk of the cave, where the Living Man's consciousness washed over him like a wave of heat from the door of a burning building. He forced himself to hold his hero's gaze.

"There should be nothing left to tear down," said the head, his voice as tremulous as a dry leaf on the branch. "There's no hide to pierce, no wrist to slap, no heart to break. All that's left of Etienne is a little ball of bone.

"It should be too small a target, but it isn't small enough, is it? Something flinches: not Etienne Rassendren, but not his ghost. A ghost is what remains when there's nothing left, and there's just enough left of me to hurt.

"When the skull is dust, will you mock the dust, and watch the cloud recoil?

"This has been an experiment, hasn't it, to see how much you can subtract from a boy before he's not a boy any more?

"Well, we aren't there yet, are we? Not just yet."

Etienne's eyes rolled over Jacob's face, then over his shoulder to the silhouettes of Leopold, Remington, Adam, and Eve. "Look at you: too excited to be ashamed, too ashamed to be excited. You have a question, don't you? Like all the others. You want me to find something, or tell you something about the future. Go ahead. The sooner you ask, the sooner you can be disappointed and leave me to my mourning."

"All we want are directions," said Remington.

"Remington, hush!" said Jacob.

"No," said Leopold, "the boy's quite right. I've browbeat this leg-less lump of self-pity enough, and stroking his ego won't bring him any solace. Pay him the respect of telling him plainly why you've taken him hostage, Jacob.

"Remington, let's leave these two to get acquainted. You and I are going to prepare a welcome for the Masker and his boys."

"A trap?" said Remington.

"More of a diversion, but if a brilliant plan comes to you, you'll find me receptive, not to mention astonished. Now come along, boy! Bring your pets — we'll need their help."

Gathering his calm, Jacob knelt before the head of Etienne Rassendren. "Remington speaks the truth," he said. "I need directions. I know what you *did*, and I want to know how. I plan to cross into the world of the living."

"Oh," said Etienne, "one of those. Well, let's make this quick. The world between worlds will not return you to life. The translation doesn't work that way."

"Nor would I want it to," said Jacob.

"Oh, no?" said Etienne. "Do you think that your living friends will welcome you as you are? That your mother would embrace you? That anyone you knew would accept this rotting bundle of bones as someone they loved?"

"It makes no difference to me if they do," Jacob snapped. He caught himself before he said more: giving in to his frustration was hardly going to win his case. "I need this. Let's leave it at that."

"Even," said Etienne with a weary sigh, "if I were partial to the chase of wild gooses, there would be no point in chasing this one. Hasn't it occurred to you that if there had been a way back, I would have taken it before I died?

"The way is closed, Jacob. There was a — a kind of key that opened the way, and it's gone now. I lost it. Believe me, I'm sorrier about it than you are, but you can't get there from here any more, not by any means I know."

"I respect your hopelessness," said Jacob carefully, "and, from all I've been told, you've earned it. But I beg you to return the favor: respect my hope. You may not want to return to the world of the living now, but try to remember when you did. That feeling that once spurred you is the very same that drove me to find you, to wake you, to beg you for help. And if it gains me nothing in the end? Well, then you can enjoy a chuckle at my expense. But if I'm right, and we can find a way across, you won't have lost a thing."

"What could I lose that hasn't already been taken?" said Etienne. "Loss isn't the issue, it's absurdity. I've had my fill of pointless questing, Jacob, and if anything in this world could be worse than those reeking Tunnels, it's watching you fail in my footsteps."

"And what if —"

"Give it up!" shouted Etienne. "There's nothing you can give me that can change what's been done, and nothing you can threaten me with that I haven't already suffered. I'm stuck where I am, and the best thing, the *only* thing that you can do for me is to leave me here in this cave."

Jacob had run out of ideas, but for one. He stood, pacing around the head in a slow circle. "Do you really believe, Etienne, that *nothing* I might do could affect you?"

Etienne sighed. "Perhaps I lack imagination."

Crouching, Jacob reached down and wrapped his hands around the wood of the plaque. It felt somehow heavier now that the head was awake. "For example," said Jacob softly as he lifted. "If I were to carry you back — there." He put his lips to Etienne's ear. "To the Crowded Car. If I were to carry you back to that place and nail you right back on the wall where I found you, awake and aware."

The head said nothing, but his teeth squeaked.

"Would you welcome that fate, Etienne? How long would it take you to hide away in your own mind again, I wonder?"

Etienne struggled to wrench his eyelids shut, but they'd been open too long.

"There is a degree," said Jacob, "to which your circumstance affects you, however small. And if there are places you find repulsive, there must be places that displease you less, whether in the under-world or in the Lands Above."

"Perhaps."

The silence went on long enough that Jacob feared he'd pushed Etienne too far. But he held still, and in time he was rewarded.

"They said I should wait," whispered Etienne. "When I crossed, they said to wait there, that the Poet could help me. But they didn't know for how long: it might be days, or it might be years. I've always wondered what would have happened if I'd waited.

"The place is called White City. Until we get there, I'll tell you nothing of my crossing. I won't be disposed of again."

"Understood," said Jacob. "Which way does White City lie?"

"To the south, past the end of Lethe. For now, we follow the river."

Jacob, overcome, held the driftwood plaque to his chest and carried it to the riverbank, eager to share the news. As soon as he stepped out of the cave, however, he was struck speechless. Adam and Eve were up to their chests in the river, pulling to shore a bloated corpse in a frilly turquoise dress, while Remington knelt on the chest of a second corpse, a naked man whose head Leopold was twisting to and fro like an apple stem.

"What are you doing?" said Jacob, his voice tight with revulsion, but there was no need for an answer. The next twist made it clear, snapping the motionless corpse's head clean off his neck.

"There we are!" said Leopold. "The water's loosened them right up."

Remington tottered over to Adam and Eve, who held the second floater upright as he dragged her dress off of her body.

Etienne, trapped on his plaque, was attempting to writhe away with the power of his lower jaw. "Please," he moaned, "not again."

"Leopold," said Jacob, "what harm have these floaters done to anyone?"

Leopold regarded the curly-haired head in his hands. "Probably nothing," he said, "but who knows? This one might have been a serial killer. He could be napping off his sins." He tossed the head into the river, where it sent up a plume of purple water. "Really, Jacob, I don't see why you're so squeamish. They're vegetables whether they're whole or chopped. If they had a strong enough objection to beheading, I'm sure they'd be motivated to quicken like the rest of us!"

"I don't think they mind," said Remington, struggling with the female floater's head. "These ones aren't like us. They can't even see. Their lights are out, Jake! You can tell."

"Twist and pull, boy, twist and pull!" said Leopold.

"Right!" Remington popped the head loose and staggered backward, heaving it high into the air. By the time it struck the water, he'd dragged the newly headless floaters side-by-side on the river-bank, where he and Leopold wrestled their arms and legs together before standing back to survey their work.

Seeing how they'd linked the floaters, Jacob suddenly under-stood their purpose. "Disgusting, but effective. The Masker arrives, spots these decoys, believes them to be our abandoned raft, and sends his men into the caves to find us."

"And by the time they find their way out of that maze," said Leopold, "we'll be well on our way to wherever it is we're going. Now, have the two of you come to an understanding?"

"We have." Jacob laid his hands on the side of the plaque. "We're heading south, to White City."

"A second metropolis! What a delightful development. We might find anything there! Think of the traditions we'll learn, the corpses we'll meet. Think of the shops they might have, the goods they might trade! They might well have a bazaar that puts the markets at Lazarus Quay to shame, wouldn't you say?"

"I don't think I would," said Jacob, his suspicions aroused. "It's not as if corpses *need* anything. Perhaps we'll find a city with no economy at all."

"Perish the thought," said Leopold, horrified. "We're creatures of habit, surely! Destined to spend our time spending time, or some-thing very like it. Aren't we?"

"We'll find out soon enough," said Jacob, unable to fathom what Leopold was after, but sure that questioning him would yield nothing but lies.

Soon they'd rebuilt their three-corpse raft and were safely afloat, watching their decoys recede. "White City," said Leopold. "To think I've never even heard of it! Etienne, while I will only be convinced of your pedigree when the gates to the living world open and I can see the dancing girls on the other side, I am nonetheless pleased to welcome you to our little tribe, particularly at a moment when our fortunes are on the upswing. I think I speak for all of us when I say that any information you would care to impart about the customs or economy of this White City would be greatly appreciated, as not a word of its existence has reached its doubtless dingier counterpart."

"It's better seen than discussed," said Etienne, his voice tight.

Leopold peered at him. "Good Lord, you're offended by that business with the floaters, aren't you? Solidarity among heads: who would have thought it?"

No one knew how to break the silence that had fallen over the little raft, but while the other three were caught up in the awkwardness of the moment, Remington stared up at the valley walls, which were in the midst of such change that he exclaimed, "How beautiful!"

Jacob recoiled from the word, which, after years of disuse, had become repulsive, but in the end he was unable to argue against it, so thoroughly was he overwhelmed by a sensation that brought his mind into union with his field of vision. "Beautiful," he said aloud, for the first time in years.

For miles, the rock on either side of the waters underwent such remarkable changes in color, shape, and texture that it seemed to metamorphose as they watched, as if it had mastered some marmoreal art forgotten by its neighbors. Legitimate volcanic formations were trumped by structures impossible outside of the realm of dream: here a gnarled wheel of purple rock sprouted thirty-foot spokes the color of bone; there a pale hill was cloven in two, revealing what appeared to be organs of stone within; and for miles beyond, the valley walls were low, slate-gray, and etched with playful, chalky abstractions.

When a shining, obsidian sculpture-garden rose, Jacob and Leopold joined Remington in exclaiming at the sights they imagined they saw there, the three of them like children under a sky of fast-moving clouds. Though every phenomenon (from the rippling taffy-colors of a stone aurora to the pitted walls that looked like corrugated tin) appeared to be a natural work of stone and mineral, their collective effect was a declaration that the world of death was more than they'd imagined.

"I'd stopped wondering what the underworld was," said Jacob as they passed a spiral stairway jutting from a sheer wall. "Now I'm not sure I'll be able to stop."

"I once heard a drunkard in the Tunnels," said Leopold softly, "insisting that this world was nothing but the final dream of a dying woman's brain, and that all of us are nothing but the old girl's figments. At the time I thought it was ludicrous."

"A customer once told me he believed we're sharing a dream between our graves, a joint hallucination originating from a single graveyard," said Jacob. "As I put the knife to his face, he murmured, 'Who knows what dreams they're having in the next cemetery?'"

"This world is real enough," said Etienne as four massive, impassive masks glowered down at them from the sides of the river, their ovoid faces as featureless and placid as those of infants in the womb. "Which isn't to say it wasn't dreamed, once."

"What the devil does that mean?" said Leopold, but Etienne would not elaborate.

As they floated farther into the stone garden, they caught occasional glimpses of the geography beyond the valley. The land they were floating into was rising steeply, and the walls around them were dwindling, becoming more tentative and ill-formed until the garden melted into flat earth.

"It's coming," said Etienne. "The Terminus. Run these corpses aground, and quickly!" Without a sound, Remington aimed Adam and Eve onto the banks.

Finally on solid ground, the band of corpses trudged upward for hours, gaining what seemed a pitiful distance for their efforts now that they were accustomed to the speed of river travel. The steep ascent left the river far below, sunk between steep walls, and made every step difficult.

"It's worse than Southheap," said Jacob, glancing down and wishing he hadn't.

"You're crazy, Jake!" said Remington. "At least this mountain is solid. Besides, the view is incredible. Check that out!" he shouted, leaning over the edge. "There's a little floater there, way down in the distance! See him, in the red shirt? Hello, little floater, hello!

"I'm going to race him. Crow, see if you can get a better look!" The bird squawked thrice, but declined the invitation, loath to leave its nest. As for Remington, he toddled as quickly as he could, but between the incline of the hill and the growing force of the river below, he had little hope of keeping up. The floater, visible despite the distance because of his bright red shirt, was tossed above and yanked beneath the surface repeatedly. This sudden, cruel streak of Lethe's currents was the only thing that kept Remington from losing sight of him completely, since each time the floater went under he emerged further upstream, tugged backward by a powerful counter-current.

"What's changed the river so?" said Jacob. "It hardly seems like Lethe. It has whitecaps!"

"It might," said Leopold in a strangled voice, "have something to do with *that*." With a toss of his head he called attention to the Terminus, whose depths came into view as they rounded the gorge's ultimate curve.

The floater leaped and shuttled along the frenzied river, which plunged ahead until the edge of the valley closed it off in a sudden curve. Miles below gaped an abyss twice the width of Lethe, a darkness devouring her rushing waters.

Upstream, the red scrap ceased thrashing and tipped over the edge. There was a flash in the darkness, and then there was nothing.

Staring down into that void, Jacob felt it again: an echo of that long-ago drought bobbed up out of the black. He could see himself falling, fluttering as he plunged into the great nothing.

One step and he'd forever be free from the burdens of existence.

"What is it?" whispered Leopold as another pair of floaters approached. "What's down there?"

"You already know," said Jacob, trying to turn away. "You've always known."

"Maybe it's another world," said Remington doubtfully.

"It's Hell," said Leopold. "All this time we've wasted perching on its mouth, when we ought to be climbing to the highest peak we can find, as far as we can get from this darkness!"

"There is no Hell," said Jacob. "There's only us and that hole in everything, that gash in our dreams, that —"

"Oblivion," said Etienne. "True death. This world is teetering on top of its open mouth, and always has been."

The Terminus took one floater, then the next, without sound, without comment.

"No need to romanticize it," said Etienne. "It's where we're all going. What we're all hiding from. It's not a sight you forget. And when things became too difficult to bear, I thought of it, again and again, not as a nightmare, but as a missed opportunity. I had my chance to jump, and I passed it by.

"You might find yourselves thinking back on this sight with longing, too. If there's any faith in man left burning in your hearts, the Plains will grind it out like the end of a bidi."

"The Plains?" shrieked Leopold, snapping them out of their reverie. "You're leading us to the Plains of War?" He reared back, as if the head of Etienne Rassendren had tried to bite him. "Why, this is madness! The cranium's a charlatan! Those savages will tear us apart like a rack of ribs! Oh, if only one corpse in the history of Hades had been a cartographer, I might have bought a map and avoided this horrid trip. I ought to surrender to the Masker. I'll get a kinder reception from his minions than the Plainsmen!"

"Come now, Etienne, there must be another way," said Jacob.

"None that you can survive," said Etienne. "To the east are sand-storms strong enough to grind you to dust. To the west is the Wall of the World, which only the men of White City can cross. For us, the only way is straight ahead, through the Plains."

"Will we have to fight?" said Remington.

"You can try," said Etienne, "and the one who's best at dodging can carry what's left of the rest."

Kneeling on the sloping ground, Jacob opened his knapsack and drew out his tools. With a hand-drill he bored two holes in the back of the driftwood, then strung the holes with a length of wire. Once the tools were replaced and the knapsack secure on his shoulders, he hung the driftwood plaque around his neck like a giant pendant. The severed head of the Living Man stared straight ahead from his breastbone, leaving Jacob's hands free.

"I think I know what that garden was for," said Remington. "All that crazy stuff we saw, all those sculptures: I think that's supposed to be the last thing you see before the end."

"The finale," said Jacob, "before the night goes dark."

"You speak as if there's a sunrise," said Leopold.

"Maybe there is," said Jacob, more out of stubbornness than hope, turning away from the Terminus and starting up the hill.

Remington, with the crow peering suspiciously from the back of his skull, set off behind him, and Adam and Eve followed once Remington had turned away from the Terminus, as if that pit had spoken as clearly to their limbs as it had to the heads of their companions.

CHAPTER EIGHT

The Plains of War

"How did this war begin, anyway?" asked Remington as they climbed.

"It didn't," said Etienne. "Despite its name, there's no war in the Plains: there are no armies, and only the loosest of rules. But what looks like chaos is unity. All the corpses you will meet and fight and flee from have agreed on their terms of engagement for a single reason. If you're going to survive the long walk to White City, your only hope is to understand that reason — which the passing ages have embedded in the legend of the Last Man Standing.

"Long ago, when Tutankhamen ruled Dead City, two warrior-women lived on the Earth. Each warrior was tall and strong, and each was the champion of her people, bound by honor to defend them in single combat if they were ever threatened.

"The two warriors lived in neighboring villages connected by a path, and on the path lay a sacred site where a banyan tree grew beside a freshwater spring. The tree was sacred to one village, the spring to the other.

"One day each year, the people of the village of the tree held a great festival there, dancing and singing to honor the tree spirits. On another day, the people of the village of the spring held their own festival, dancing and singing to honor the spirits of the spring. Since one village kept their calendar by the sun and the other by the moon, these festivals began on different days but drifted closer and closer together, until one day the people of both villages arrived to worship at the same time.

"Once there, the villages' holy men began to argue, and the argument spread through the people. But before their words turned to violence, the two warriors strode into a clearing across the path and began to fight on their behalf.

"The people were silent as the warriors fought with hand and foot, arm and leg, tooth and nail, but not with their blades, for they had left their weapons at home on this holy day.

"Their blows fell like hard rain and made their bodies wet with sweat and blood. They fought from dusk to dawn, and from dawn to dusk again, while the people of their villages sat apart from each other, waiting, at first in silence, then with growing discontent.

"When the second night came and neither woman had fallen, the people began to argue with the holy men. 'Our warriors are strong,' they said, 'so strong that mere flesh cannot undo them. While we wait, the gods wait, too. Will you have them wait until they are unhappy enough to curse us all?'

"The blacksmiths were especially loud. 'It's true!' they said. 'Our warriors will fight with their bare hands for a month before one remembers she can fall. But this is not a tournament! These wild women are fighting for our village, for its homes and stones, for the harvest we reap, for the metal we dig from the earth! It is right that they should fight with that metal in their hands. Maybe that will remind them they're mortal! Send for their blades, O sages, and save us from certain destruction!'

"'No weapons may be brought to sacred ground,' said the holy men.

"'This earth below our feet is sacred,' said the blacksmiths, 'but not where those warriors are fighting. It's the blades, not the fighters, that will decide this. Send children to fetch the blades from the warriors' homes!' The holy men, hearing a threat in the roar of approval that rose from the crowds, relented.

"The warriors, however, were already wearier than anyone knew.

"When the weapons arrived, the warrior-women were called apart and armed. They staggered back into the clearing and crossed their blades. In the moonlight their silhouettes were as alike as paper dolls. Each summoned the last of her strength, leapt into the air, and with a single stroke sunk her blade into the other's heart.

"Each warrior was dead before she hit the ground."

"Who told you all this?" said Remington.

"I read it in a book," said Etienne. "Now hush.

"As the villages fell into confusion, the warriors descended to the underworld, both washing up at once on the banks of Lethe. They rose from the banks, pulled the blades that killed them from their own hearts, and, though their bodies were sluggish, they fell to fighting at once. The ringing of their blades could be heard all up and down the riverbanks.

"Now, as different as Tutankhamen's necropolis was from your Dead City, one thing was the same: Tut's citizens abhorred violence. In his time, it was said that one's physical corpse and spiritual essence were a single substance, and that losing so much as a finger could damage the soul.

"Tut's lawmen so outnumbered these two that the warriors quickly surrendered. Instead of being brought into the Halls of Welcome, where corpses were educated in the ways of death as their rigor mortis passed, they were carried out of the city as they stiffened, deposited on a great plateau in the midst of the desert.

"'Out here you can cut each other to pieces,' said the lawmen, 'but don't leave this place until your fight is settled.'

"When they began, the warriors' bodies were stiff and plump, graceless and pretty, slow and muscled. As time went on, their bodies dried, their hides cracked, and their flesh fell away. Their blades clashed, they stomped and twirled, generations of their relatives were sent down the river, and the two women's corpses were worn down to the bone.

"They fought so fiercely for so long that their claw-like feet dug out the rock, wearing a great, flat floor into the middle of the plateau, yet because they never crossed the boundaries set by the lawmen, a wall of stone stood around these plains, closing them off from the rest of the underworld.

"In the end, it was the blades that decided the winner. After countless clashes, the blade of the moon notched the blade of the sun beside the hilt. The warrior holding the blade of moon and spring struck again, cleaving the blade of sun and tree in two, and then, without hesitation, she cut her enemy's skeleton into pieces and scattered her bones to the west. She threw the broken blade across the Plains, where it struck the wall left behind by the Plateau and left a great hole behind: the Torn Curtain. As for the fallen warrior's skull, the victrix left it where it lay.

"Standing above it, she raised the blade of moon and spring above her yellowed head, but it was a sunbeam that fell upon her from the heavens. Though she only now remembered it, she was the warrior who hailed from the village of sun and tree. Since each woman had, upon quickening, drawn the blade that killed her out of her own heart, each had fought the battle with her enemy's weapon, and so it was that the blade of the moon cut the moon-woman's body into pieces.

"The victrix was brought back to life, and more. The sunbeam falling from the land above made her flesh immortal and stronger than that of any living warrior. She rose through the earth to the land of the living, where she led her people in the war that had erupted during her long absence. And when she had conquered her enemy's people, she found another war to fight, for though she lived again, she had lost the taste for food, drink, love, and song, caring only for that art that she'd spent a dozen lifetimes perfecting: slaughter.

"As for the warrior who remained below, she could no longer move, let alone fight, and was obliged to remain in the Plains. When the next warriors were driven there by their own violations of Tut's law, she told them her story, and so it has come down through the years.

"Thus, the Plainsmen believe that the next time a warrior stands over the Plains in victory, she'll be granted eternal life and return to the Lands Above in immortal glory."

"Then it's melee," said Jacob. "Every warrior for himself."

"Melee on the grandest of scales."

"What happened to the loser?" said Remington.

"They put her head in a niche high in the rocky Rim that surrounds the Plains. She was the first of many honored spectators."

"And the book you mentioned," said Jacob, "where you found this tale —"

"Is lost," said Etienne. "Look ahead: the Rim is on the horizon."

Only scrutiny revealed the shape of the Rim, for the air was thick with motes of dust. Through their lazy currents, at the top of the long incline, the Rim rose like the stump of a mammoth tree, thick-walled and hollow. Its walls thinned as they rose, then terminated suddenly half a mile from the ground. They were the color of ancient vellum, smooth but for a single, jagged rift wide enough to admit a platoon of corpses — the Torn Curtain.

"Well," said Jacob, "there's the door. I suppose there's nothing left to do but walk inside."

"Has it occurred to you that we're unarmed?" said Leopold. "The thuggees lying in wait on the other side will churn us into pâté!"

"Etienne, are you certain we'll be safe?"

"Safe?" said Etienne. "Of course not. The entire population of the Plains wants to do you bodily harm on principle. Was anyone listening to my story?

"But if it's weapons you want, there's a market within that sells nothing else. They'll take city-goods if you have them to trade."

"A market, eh?" Leopold brightened instantly. "Splendid! Then we'll arm ourselves forthwith."

"Right," said Remington. "And we shouldn't have any problems staying out of trouble. I mean, if Etienne got through when he was soft and squishy, what do we have to be afraid of?"

"The living move faster than any lurching corpse remembers," warned Etienne, but Remington and Leopold had already moved on, and Jacob, despite his trepidation, trudged on behind them.

The company's bravery was quickly extinguished. Visibility worsened as they neared the Rim, the thickening air giving the company the impression that they were walking into a mist. Since even Remington was hesitant to enter a realm he could not see, the little group was slowly coaxed inside by Etienne, who convinced them that a raging battle would make some kind of noise, while this dust-cloud was chillingly silent.

"Plainsmen are anything but stealthy," he said. "If you don't hear them, they aren't there."

Against their better judgment, they passed through the Torn Curtain, beneath the Rim's tall ramparts, past the sheer drop of its cliffs, and onto the unreadable floor of the Plains. Jacob led them toward the first shadow they saw, a boulder in the midst of smaller stones.

Pressed against its backside, they strained to parse the noises that reached them: a shuffling, as of heavy fabric being dragged across a dirty warehouse floor; a squeaking and rattling, as of ancient, lightweight chain mail; and a steady, muted thumping that brought to mind a monstrous, beating heart.

"I might find this comical," whispered Leopold, "if I were on the right side of a rapier."

"Stay still for now," hissed Jacob, "and quiet! The dust will settle soon."

It did, slowly enough that their tension grew into violent anxiety by the time Etienne remarked that the stone closest to them was not, after all, a stone, but a pile of severed limbs whose occasional shifting explained the shuffling they heard. By then they could see well enough to note that the ground all around them was strewn with grasping hands, twitching calves, dissociated joints, and butchered torsos, as if a thresher had recently plowed through a field of men. An arm severed at the shoulder dragged itself by the fingers toward the nearest cairn of human parts, nestling itself with agonizing leisure at the base of the pile. Nearby lay a pair of severed legs still joined by a pubic bone, one of which was pinning a disembodied chest to the ground while the other kicked it, endeavoring to cave in its yawning rib cage.

As the company stared at this grisly tableau, a booming voice startled them into perfect stillness.

"Otho!" said the voice, its gurgling depth only matched by its volume. "Otho, canst thou hear me?"

"If he can't," replied a shrill voice from farther off, "half the blooming Horde can! Let it alone, Oxnard. His Crushingness is gone."

From Oxnard's direction came the squeaking of tiny wheels and the rattling of thin metal. "Curse thy mealy-wormy mouth, Elspeth!" bellowed Oxnard. "Here's the grand man's thigh-bone now, still festooned with his helmet-hard flesh!"

"Still yourself, you great dead puppy!" said Elspeth, drawing close. "By the time you've put together half his puzzle, all the other Plains-pickers will have picked the Plains clean and driven the Armory's prices sky-high to boot. Leave Otho to the fate his judgment earned, and let us trade this bounty for some proper crashers and smashers!"

In a temper, Oxnard shoved his vehicle toward Elspeth and into Leopold's line of sight: it was a dented shopping cart from a long-extinct chain of grocery stores, its bottom piled with the brick-red flesh of the once-mighty Otho.

Elspeth, a slight, purple woman with a leather jerkin and an imploded face, caught the cart in her claws, dropping the handle of her own conveyance, a child's wagon, all but denuded of paint and piled high with weaponry.

Oxnard stumbled into view to reclaim his cart, prompting the company to hasten their creep toward the hidden side of the boulder, away from his massive expanse of skinless flesh, which was crowded with spears, arrows, and broken blades, none of which seemed to bother him in the slightest.

"Otho raised thee from a pup, ungrateful bobbin!" he cried to Elspeth, lifting the cart and shaking the bits of Otho about in dismay. "Thou wert squatting in the Parleyfields, squeening down at that bumble-blighted city, when unchoppable Otho rescued thee from future indebtitude!"

"Unchoppable," said Elspeth, "is a poor phrase."

"He it was that plucked us up and armed us with fearsome hacker-uppers bought dear at the mouth of the Bypass, and led us frightened as sheep-shorn lambs through that darklish path, and made us mashers of men! Hast thou forgotten, ungratitudinous Elspeth, whom it was that taught thee the stroke that severed the bean of Beano McGee?"

"'Twas Otho," said Elspeth grudgingly.

"'Twas our dear dismankled Otho-man," said Oxnard, and folded himself over to moan into his knees.

She stopped for a long moment, poised like a dog that's noticed its quarry. Jacob, noting her sudden attention, left off his creeping, but the rest of the company kept scraping around the edge of the boulder.

Elspeth turned. "Ox," she said, "make me an oath."

"What oath wouldst thou have?"

"If I reunite you with the missing head of our Otho," said Elspeth, "you'll call me sir from that moment on."

"But find him, and I'll call thee goddess!"

"Sir will do."

"Then I oath it, but find him quickly, dear Elspeth!"

"And Ox," she said, "another oath: if I find folk who swear to bring Otho's bits to the stitchery, you'll leave off yowling and follow where I lead."

"But Elspeth, there's nobody here but thee and me and Otho-bits."

"Then you lose nothing by the promise, do you?"

"Truish!" said Oxnard. "I oath it."

"But hark!" cried Elspeth. "Is that the mewling of Otho I hear? It is!"

"It is!" cried Oxnard, spotting the dusty head past her outstretched finger, as silent as the rock it resembled.

"But soft!" said Elspeth, restraining Oxnard's bulk with one withered arm. "Who's that, behind the boulder? Why, a band of fearful recruits, eager to do our bidding or be minced!"

Staggering around the boulder, Elspeth and Oxnard confronted Jacob's little band, holding their weapons at head-level.

While Remington and the headless threw their hands to the sky, Leopold and Jacob exchanged a curious glance, for the sword-shaped implements wielded by their assailants were cut from aluminum siding, their hilts wrapped in electrical tape.

"You overheard our negotiations," said Elspeth.

"We did," said Jacob.

"Then you agree to carry Otho to the stitchery?"

"In exchange for armaments from your wagon," said Leopold, "and the cart to carry them in."

"In exchange for your unsevered spines!" said Elspeth. "Resist, and Oxnard will mash you to Plains-paste."

"Leopold," said Jacob slowly, "don't you wonder what would happen if, on the way to the stitchery, we were attacked by a second band as fearsome as this one?"

"Dear me!" cried Leopold. "Then Otho would be scattered to the winds for sport!"

"And we could hardly defend him with our arms full of his constituent parts."

"I dare say we might lose a chunk or two."

"Poor Otho," said Remington, his hands still in the air.

"O, do as they demark, Elspeth, sir!" said Oxnard. "O, thou must give them mashers and the wheely-gig, for to protect our dear Otho-man!"

"Very well," said Elspeth, irritated at this unexpected deviation. "Leave Otho in the cart, and bring them three bashing-sticks from the chariot, Oxnard."

"But there are five of us," said Remington, at which Elspeth laughed uproariously.

"Oxnard, hark!" she cried, pointing at the headless. "These feeble-minded recruits would have us arm their meat-shields!"

"Oh, ho!" said Oxnard, bringing a pool cue, a ski pole, and a slat from a picket fence, all worse for the wear, and tossing them at Leopold's feet.

"A free lesson in tactics before we depart," said Elspeth, picking up the severed head of Otho and heaving it into the shopping cart. "This is the bit that does the seeing on a corpse. Lose yours, and you'll have a hard time swinging those bashers!"

As Oxnard rolled the cart before them, Elspeth drew up to her full height and shook her imitation sword at Jacob. "Swear on your posts in the Ultimate Army that you will bring Otho safely to the stitchery three miles hence, along the curve of the Rim."

"I swear it," said Jacob.

"So be it. Oxnard, hie! We make for the Armory before the choicest blades are sold!"

"Fare thee well, brave Otho-bits!" said Oxnard. "Mayst thou tower and glower again, and be the last to fall beneath my vorpal blade!" He lumbered off behind his new general, pulling their little wagon behind him.

"If this is the caliber of corpse we have to contend with," said Leopold, "we'll do more than arrive safely at the other end of the Plains: we'll be its conquerors."

"The individual warriors aren't the problem," said Etienne, "it's their numbers. You can outwit a warrior, even a platoon, but what the Plainsmen call the scrimmage defies strategy."

"There's hope, in any case," said Jacob. "Now let's honor our agreement. I confess, I'm curious to inspect this stitchery."

Though Elspeth had claimed the establishment was three miles away, the company trudged ahead with no idea how much ground they'd covered. If distance had lost much of its meaning, the passage of time was so effaced that Jacob found himself missing Dead City's bells. Time and space seemed to be slipping away from him, and he found himself wondering, childishly, if they'd ever arrive.

Despite the gusts of dusty wind that overtook the Rim from time to time, the air slowly cleared, and in time a ragged construction appeared in the distance. Two long, flexible poles had been bent over each other and buried in the ground, forming a large tent enclosed by an unraveling tarpaulin, its sides marked by fat-limbed crosses daubed in flaking mud. A ring of crates surrounded the tent, stuffed with wire and scrap metal, encircled by a defensive perimeter of sharpened poles and barbed wire fencing that was currently being deconstructed by two spectacularly damaged corpses. The pair turned toward the rattle of Otho's cart, a length of barbed wire suspended between them as they considered the newcomers.

He was a lean, naked man with a striking, two-toned corpse. His back, sides, and limbs were a rich mahogany color that indicated a natural Plains preservation, while the entire core of his body was a bombed-out black, as if he'd died by throwing himself onto a live grenade. The destruction stretched from his empty pelvis, through his charred ribs, and into the upper reaches of his face, where his jaws, teeth, and nose had been blown clean off, leaving two piercing brown eyes and a pair of bushy brows below a curly head of hair.

His eyes, once they'd determined the newcomers to be customers, returned to his gloved hands, which swiftly drew a loop of barbed wire from the long line his assistant was feeding him from beneath.

The woman, who stood a full three feet shorter, never took her eyes off the company and could be heard muttering her appraisal of their worth in an unfamiliar dialect, slapping the ground with one of her sturdy work gloves for emphasis. She was so low to the ground that this gesture required no amendment to her posture, for she had been chopped in two just below her breast and rested now on the stump of her torso, leaving her hands free to work.

Once she'd fed the last loop of barbed wire to her employer, she rose onto her palms and padded to the front of the encampment on her hands. Behind her, the two-toned man stowed the wire in an open barrel and withdrew into the tent. As the company approached, the half-woman barked out greetings in a number of languages until she found one that stuck.

"All right, fellas," she said as they drew closer, inspecting them through a ferrety face that was, like the rest of her, riddled with evidence of post-mortem battles. "I'm the RN, and that there's the Medic. Alls we need to know is if you got trade." Her dusty hair was close-cropped to deny grasping hands any purchase, and her flesh clung tightly to what remained of her skeleton. "If you got trade, we can talk about your buddy in the bucket seat. No trade, you got to turn it around. No offense, but we're running a business here."

She plopped herself onto her stump before the shopping cart and stopped it with her hands, climbing onto its wire basket and peering down at unlucky Otho. "Your buddy's a real jigsaw job, too, and I can tell you right off that he's got pieces missing, which costs extra, on account of the replacements."

"You use parts from other corpses?" said Remington.

The RN squinted at him. "How would that work? No offense, kid. But how's somebody else's leg going to know which way you're walking? We use prostheses: metal, wood, plastic, rubber. So, you got trade, right?"

"To be perfectly honest," said Jacob, "we don't even know this man."

"Huh. So what did you bring him in for?"

"We traded the favor for these weapons, such as they are."

The RN slapped the side of the shopping cart. "Okay, so whose is the shopping cart, yours or the jigsaw's?"

"They were a package deal."

"Good enough. You give us the bucket, the doc fixes up your buddy, everybody wins." She loped on her palms toward the front of the tent. "Roll him in!"

While the Medic's tent, on the face of it, had nothing in common with Jacob's flat, its layout, arranged around the professional necessities of the Medic's trade, felt instantly familiar to him. The tools, laid out on barrels and rough wooden shelves, illustrated the ingenious solutions that the Medic had found to those problems of reconstruction particular to the Plains of War, necessitating an approach to preservation unknown in Dead City. As a fellow tradesman, Jacob felt such excitement that he could hardly keep still.

In the midst of the cramped tent was an improvised table made of a barn door and two sawhorses, beside which stood the Medic. His hands, now gloveless, were so perfectly skeletal that it was clear their bones had been intentionally excavated by the Medic himself. With these brilliant appendages, he motioned for the shopping cart to be drawn up beside the table, then withdrew its contents one segment at a time.

Whether mute out of preference or because of his injuries, the Medic made himself understood solely through gestures. The RN occasionally interpreted them for Jacob's benefit, for it was clear that this newcomer had a genuine fascination with their work.

Leopold and Remington inspected the rest of the tent, regarding with curiosity a large metal trunk at the back, whose open lid revealed that its latch only locked from within. "Is this a refuge from the Plainsmen?" said Leopold.

The RN, elevated on a metal step-stool, looked over at the trunk and nodded. "That's our last resort," she said. "The scrimmage usually sticks to the middle of the Plains, but every once in a while it hits the Rim. The fence keeps them from pushing in here by accident, but if they want to loot, they're going to find a way inside. Most of them leave us alone — I mean, you never know when you're going to need us, right? But we have to have somewhere to go. Handy, since I can't fight and move at the same time, and the boss doesn't have the stomach for violence."

The Medic clacked his fingers to draw her attention, then made a knocking motion with his hand, at which the RN climbed off the stool and pulled a rubber mallet from a shelf. She held it in her teeth while she crossed the floor, then tossed it into his hands with a swing of her neck.

He gripped the tool and lifted Otho's head with one hand, striking it sharply in the forehead with the mallet. The blow produced a sound like a coconut hitting concrete, and a startling side effect: every segment of Otho's brick-colored body twitched at once, as if the Medic had struck the table-top instead of his patient's skull. The Medic then passed the mallet back, crossed his arms, and stared down at the table with a chess-master's intensity.

"Why'd he hit him?" said Remington.

"Checking for separation of consciousness," said the RN.

"Separation of consciousness," murmured Jacob as the Medic began fitting the parts of Otho's human jigsaw together with startling speed.

"Sure," said the RN. "You get diced up, you go into shock. It's like quickening all over again. For a while you're completely blacked out, and we can stitch you up no problem. But after that window closes, all the hacked-up parts give up. They can't reconnect, so they stop trying and start moving for themselves. Nothing we can do to put them back together again after that."

"Like those piles of parts outside," said Remington. "They all think they're different people."

"And the mallet?" said Jacob.

"A quickened corpse has one reflex: not in the nerves, but in the senses. You can hamstring a guy on the Plains without him noticing, if you're quick enough, but hit him in the shinbone, and he twitches. The vibration makes him jump, even if he's in hack-shock. So if your left leg is cut off, and it doesn't jump when the rest of you does, then we know it's too far gone. Might as well be a stranger's leg then."

"But all of Otho's pieces jumped, so he's going to be all right," said Remington.

"Well," said the RN.

The Medic jabbed a white finger at the problem areas of Otho's puzzle: though the cart was empty, his left bicep and right shin were missing.

"We've got some work to do."

While the RN dug through crates and barrels to find an appropriate substitute for Otho's lower right leg (whose foot she tossed unceremoniously through the front flap of the tent), the Medic assembled his tools: the home-made, double-barbed hooks that were inserted around the bone, anchoring flesh to flesh; the thick fabric sewn into either side of a severance like a grafted bandage; and an assortment of rock-sharpened, improvised blades and picks.

The RN offered up her prosthesis, a rusty length of pipe jammed into a flat rubber rectangle, and hustled everyone out of the tent while the Medic operated, leaving Jacob and Etienne behind after a sharp nod from her employer.

Jacob, humbled by the gesture, opened his knapsack, withdrew his canister of needles and proffered one to his host. The Medic pinched the needle between the white tips of his thumb and forefinger, his eyes showing wonder.

He touched his own chest, cocking his head to one side.

Jacob bowed his head.

The Medic nodded, emitting a long, hushed rattle of thanks. With a series of precise, eloquent gestures, he invited Jacob to lay out the rest of his tools on the table, assuring him of their safety.

Jacob, who had not until that moment noticed that he had missed his practice, accepted the needle, now threaded with fishing line, and laid down his first stitch.

When Otho at last awoke, it was Etienne's grizzled head he saw first, hanging from Jacob's chest a few inches away. "Don't look down," said Etienne, a warning the warrior promptly ignored.

"Yeargh!" cried Otho as he surveyed the ruin of his once-mighty body, which, though its basic integrity was assured, was still being stitched up by the hands of his two surgeons. "Yeargh!" he shouted at his left arm, which now proceeded directly from shoulder to elbow, resulting in an ineffectual limb that would never again swing a warhammer (though it did prove useful in knocking half of Jacob's tools to the ground, causing the preservationist to curse him in a language he didn't speak); he shouted it again at his right leg, which was nothing more than a length of pipe jammed into the stump below his knee, so snug against the bone that it would never come off without a hacksaw.

"Yeargh!" he said again, and continued thrashing about on the table, causing untold damage to those parts of his person that had not yet been fully reconstructed, provoking the Medic to lean over his face with a stern, bony forefinger extended. The gesture startled Otho into obedience, as it had hundreds of patients before him, for even a corpse as battle-hardened as Otho was vulnerable to that combination of paternal condescension and facial mutilation that passed for the Medic's bedside manner. However, although Otho no longer struggled, he complained as they finished his stitching, utilizing blunt, guttural syllables that were incomprehensible to Jacob but which Etienne finally and definitively responded to in kind.

"What was that?" murmured Jacob.

"Plains-Deadish," replied Etienne. "He was cursing his under-lings for leaving him here with us, and I told him to be grateful to Oxnard that he wasn't left where he lay."

"You learned an entire language when you passed through?"

"It's mostly 'smash' and 'run': you can learn the basics in an hour or two."

The Medic, having inspected all of Otho's reconstructed parts, clacked his fingers together, signifying that the work was done. Otho, once he'd looked at the Medic's eyes for permission, lurched off of the table and onto his feet, stomping irritably on his prosthesis and waving his shortened arm with a bellow of dissatisfaction as he made his way through the front of the tent.

Once outside, his demeanor changed: staring past the loung-ing forms of Jacob's compatriots, he fixed his eyes on the Plains, which were clear now for miles around and sparsely peopled with far-off figures returning to the business of beating each other with sticks. Two such corpses were engaged in a barely visible duel, each far-off blow provoking an agonizing break in the action as both fighters struggled to regain the balance, composure, and grip they needed to continue. Miles beyond them, a dark, earth-hugging cloud marked the outer edge of that ceaselessly churning mass of corpses called the scrimmage, which Otho stood silently watching by Remington's side.

"Hey, you're all fixed up!" said Remington, patting the giant's shoulder. "So — so why are you sad?"

"He's not much of a talker, this guy," said the RN through her teeth. She padded out of the tent on her palms, then rested the stump of her torso on the earth between them, spitting a button into one hand. "I think I understand him, though. He used to be somebody. He used to have a shot at this." She waved at the scrimmage. "So did I, once. Or I thought I did. But it gets harder to head back into the scrimmage every time you leave it, especially once you start leaving parts of yourself behind."

"Yeargh," said Otho in agreement, sitting awkwardly down beside her.

"But look at him," said Remington. "He's huge! He's scary! Why couldn't he still be the winner?"

The RN hobbled over to Otho, squinting into his craggy face, where a flinty compassion had arisen. "Kid don't understand. Still got all the parts he came with."

Otho trembled as he buried his face in his knees.

"But hey," she said, slapping him on the back. "I wasn't trying to get you down. Like the kid says, you're a big guy! And *real* scary. Look, here's a little pick-me-up." She held out the button, large and navy-blue with an anchor etched into its face, and dropped it into his palm. "This'll get you a bashing-stick from the Armory or a mug of swill back in the Tunnels. Choice is yours. Good luck.

"Come on, let's leave him be." She loped back inside, and Remington, with a glance at the broken warrior, followed.

The Medic, who'd been waiting for the RN's assistance, gestured under the table and folded his arms.

"You're kidding," she said. "The lock-box? What for?"

The Medic directed her onto the stool where she could see Jacob's gifts: the needle, a pair of pliers, and a dental pick. She held up her hands, retracting her complaint, and when the Medic scooped up these prizes and tipped the door onto its side, she scooted the sawhorses out of the way and swept a thick layer of dirt off of an object buried below.

"This is our stash," she said as the Medic dug up the handles of a buried trunk and lifted it from the ground. "We don't collect these on purpose, but every once in a while someone like your buddy comes in, gets fixed up, and decides he's had enough. If he leaves behind a parting gift, we have to wait for the merchants to come around before we can unload them, and obviously it's better if nobody else knows we have these in here. So let's keep this quiet, okay?"

The Medic threw open the lid, revealing a modest selection of weaponry, from which the squadron selected their first bashers and crashers.

"Generous as this is," said Leopold, "I rather think we ought to stop by this Armory before we step into the fray. Who knows? We might trade these in for even more fearsome accessories."

"Nonsense," said Jacob, digging through the supplies. "These will do nicely. We're not trying to decimate the population of the Plains, merely cut a path through them."

"But there will be other advantages to an exchange," Leopold went on. "For instance, we might learn the fastest route to White City!"

"White Gate is due south," said Etienne. "Straight as an arrow flies."

"I must insist, my friends, that we think this through —"

"And I must insist," said Jacob, leveling a crowbar at Leopold's face, "that you either show your hand or put the cards away. Convince us with the truth of what you're after, Leopold, or it's full steam ahead."

"I'm sure I don't know what you mean," said Leopold. Irritably, he withdrew his suggestion, pulled a length of chain from the box, and followed on.

Once they'd said their goodbyes, the company stepped past the bowed shoulders of Otho, Jacob using his crowbar as a walking-stick, Remington cheerfully swinging a traffic sign over his head (it read 'SPEED LIMIT 35 MPH' and was sharpened to a point at the end of its post), Leopold slinging his chain around his shoulders, Adam holding a rusty chef's knife, and Eve with a ski-pole in one hand and a trash-can lid in the other. Without a backward glance, the company strode into the Plains of War.

CHAPTER NINE

Recruits!

Recruits!"

"Hey yo, peep the shiny-ass hides on these recruits!"

"Twenty paces remain until your dismemberment."

"Recruits!"

The voices came from the top of a hillock, where three heads were impaled on a tall, pointed pole, each pointing in a different direction, each shouting over the heap of limbs and severed heads that lay below.

"Impaled," said Leopold, "like cubes of lamb on an infernal kebab! Is this some savage punishment?"

"Just the opposite," said Etienne. "They're spectators. Now that they've lost their bodies, watching is all they have left. If somebody thought they deserved punishment, they'd be face-down, left to endlessly examine the dirt before their eyes."

"Recruits!"

"I pray for the arrival of the Horde."

"The Hordesmen gonna cut y'all into teeth and nuggets."

"Recruits, recruits, recruits!"

"Is that a bad word here?" said Remington.

"We're newcomers," said Etienne. "We've earned no respect, and they'll show none until we do."

"We're immigrants all over again," muttered Leopold, annoyed enough to tug the chain from around his shoulders and begin swinging it provocatively as he climbed the hillock. "What do you say, gentlemen," he called to the company, "a spot of target practice before we enter the fray?"

All at once, the severed heads in the pile below the pole erupted with indignation, and though they lacked the means to follow through on their threats, their volume alone was enough to stop Leopold's progress.

"Wow, look who's tough now!" said the top corpse on the pole, whose parchment-like skin held the remnants of the cornrow braids his minions had maintained until his beheading.

"Recruits!" yelled the lumpen head beneath him.

"You lack the conviction to attack us," said the head on the bottom, her face hanging off the bone.

"Lack the balls, too. We got the good seats for a reason, heard? My name's Killer Clay, this here's Gork, and that's Desi the Destroyer. Remember the names — you'll be hearing 'em again!"

"We'd better leave them be," said Jacob, looking around uneasily. "It seems likely that their elevation was a mark of respect."

"Respect!" said Gork.

"Got that right," said Clay. "We're only up here until El Ultimo Hombre chops his last neck-bone."

A cheer went up from the heads on the hillock. "And then," said Desi, "we become generals in the Ultimate Army."

"The Ultimate Army," said Etienne, intrigued. "Does the Last Man Standing bring it with him when he ascends?"

"*Por supuesto*," said Desi. "We shall conquer the living, and he shall rule them."

"A new chapter in the story!" said Etienne from his plaque. "And will your lives be restored as well?"

"Dag," said Clay, "I wouldn't complain."

"Sacrilege!" cried Desi, scowling up the pole. "The Last Man Standing alone shall have life."

"We do get our bodies back, though," said Clay.

"Recruits!" said Gork.

"Enthralling as this anthropological study is," said Leopold, "it's time we hastened from here. The longer we let these bodiless braggarts announce our presence, the slimmer our chances of safely reaching White City."

"White City?" said Desi over the horrified murmurs of the spectators below. "What business have you with those *brujos*?"

"Damn," said Clay, "getting hewn in twain ain't enough for y'all? It's dust or nothing for these recruits!"

"Recruits! *Recruits!*" cried Gork.

"Leopold's right: we should go," said Jacob, but by then it was too late. Gork's repetitive holler, no mere function of his idiocy, had reached a marauding squadron to the south that was now making its way toward the hillock. Their numbers and armaments were obscured by a grand, oaken door turned sideways, carried like an enormous shield by two fighters who were completely hidden but for hands and feet, plodding toward the hillock with funereal persistence.

"Have we anything that resembles a plan?" said Leopold, contemplating the gouges on the face of the door. "It's been some time since my swashbuckling days, and I'm not sure that I recall the proper protocols. Etienne, old bean, you've been through this before: how did you survive?"

"I ran."

"I cannot see," complained Desi.

"Hey yo!" said Clay. "Desiderata's got a bad angle. Can one of y'all turn her to face the action?"

"Help this remnant of wench to view the destruction that you brought upon us?" said Leopold.

"If you're salty about it, let's trade," said Clay. "That half-assed formation is gonna get y'all diced. Do right by Desi and I'll hook it up."

"Go ahead," said Jacob. "We have no better alternative."

After Remington turned Desi toward the approaching squadron, Clay began directing the band into a defensive position. He was startled into silence, for as soon as he'd mentioned that the headless ought to be shoved out front, they walked there.

"Hold up, did those meat-shields hear what I said?"

"Sure," said Remington. "They use my head."

"Say what now?" said Clay.

"They use my head," said Remington. "They see what I see, hear what I hear."

"I'll be damned," said Clay. "Now that's the kind of trick you want to keep in pocket, dig? Make them play dumb until that squad is attacking, 'cause nobody's going to expect them to fight. And keep yourself out the way: if you go down, half your boys go with you."

"You tell them too much for such a tiny favor," said Desi.

"Nah, we're fitting to have a proper fight now," said Clay. "You watch."

While the door was still in the distance, the warriors behind it knelt down, leaving a single, scrawny corpse standing upright, bearing a bulging satchel and whirling a leather sling from which a stone the size of a child's fist flew. The stone popped Remington square in his open mouth and pitched the crow out of his skull with a squawk of alarm.

"First strike!" called Clay, elevating the spectators' chatter to an uproar, to the distraction of those under attack. "Forget the surprise, get that chick working her shield!"

Eve lunged across the hillock, attempting to intercept the stones that were thudding into her companions' bodies. While the squadron advanced, still crouching behind the lowered door, the stone-thrower knocked Jacob off-balance with a stone to the hip, twisted Eve's shield on her wrist, and knocked Adam's knife to the ground: impressive feats of marksmanship with an arm that was no more than bone and gristle.

Leopold, however, remained unmoved. "A decent trick, but I fail to see what tactical advantage can be won by pelting men whose nerves are incapable of — *Zwounds!*" he cried, for the stone-thrower's latest projectile snapped his broomstick in two, at which his broken neck folded, his head struck his chest, and his chain fell to his feet. A moment later another stone, striking his knee, sent him sprawling to the ground, where he remained for much of the battle, struggling to right himself with one hand while holding his head up with the other.

"Man down!" cried Clay, who could barely be heard over the roar of the spectators. He was drowned out completely as the enemy general's war-cry drove her underlings into a frenzy, pounding their weapons against the back of the door and howling.

In moments, the door reached to the base of the hillock, leaning diagonally over four crouching warriors, one of whom popped up with a baseball bat, forcing Jacob to defend himself with his crowbar.

Remington, who had the task of seeing for two headless combatants, found it difficult to determine what he ought to be focusing on, and while his eyes were on Adam's scuffle with one of the door-bearers, the other sprang up and swept Eve's legs from under her with a billy-club — an event he witnessed too late to stop. The spectators went mad as she struck the earth, hooting at Clay that his team was already finished, and the enemy general, agreeing with their estimation, lurched around the side of the hillock, withdrawing an antique short-sword from a cardboard scabbard as she made her way toward Leopold's fallen form.

But Remington had little attention to spare for Leopold. As soon as Eve went down, her assailant began pounding on her with his billy-club, and Adam, hearing the crunch of her ribs, hurled himself neck-first off the hillock and into the oaken door, slamming its bearers to the ground beneath it. As he landed on his backside, his knife slipped out of his hand and skittered to the feet of the rock-thrower, who uttered a long, jubilant ululation as he took possession of his first edged weapon.

"Shut him down!" said Clay, who, expecting no sensible response to this order, was astonished when Remington launched his signpost like a javelin straight through the rock-thrower's stomach, turning his war-cry into a bleat of surprise as he was pinned to the ground.

In moments, three of their five opponents had been knocked off their feet, but Jacob was oblivious to this change in their fortune, being preoccupied with the curious duel he was waging against the batter. They were swinging at each other, but given their general unsteadiness, their weapons were more often used for balance than aggression. As Jacob took advantage of a rare moment of equilibrium to prepare a competent swing, the batter, hearing a sharp whistle from the hillock, loosened his grip, and as Jacob's crowbar connected, the bat flew from his hands.

"Nice one," said Clay. "Now mash him!"

"Mash!" cried Gork, overcome with emotion, but before Jacob could comply, the batter turned and stumbled into the Plains. Adam, finding his feet, staggered after the batter, and Jacob, using his crowbar as a walking-stick, tottered down the hillock after him, more out of a desire to protect his unarmed companion than any sense of wrath.

Jacob was likewise devoid of fury, terror, bravery, or any other state he'd associated with battle, yet an undeniably violent haze had enveloped him, rendering certain alterations to his consciousness: for instance, it obscured the sounds of the hillock (including certain shouted warnings that he would no doubt have found useful) but rendered gloriously the little plumes of dust rising behind the batter's footfalls as he led them into a sandy patch of the Plains.

Jacob had begun to wonder, given their relative speeds, if it was possible to catch the batter before they reached the opposite side of the Rim. As it happened, he only followed for a few more paces before the general shrieked an order.

The batter stomped three times on the ground, and the earth below Adam's feet exploded. A desiccated lieutenant, who'd clearly been buried in the sand like some bellicose jack-in-the-box, sprung up with surprising force, swinging his machete in a wide arc; the blade severed Adam's thigh in one stroke, and the lieutenant landed on his feet, lunging toward Jacob, who was suddenly forced to take the business of war more seriously than he cared to.

Here they are, thought Jacob: the terrible foe, the blade that may undo me, et cetera; but where is the fear? He raised his crowbar, blocked the blow, and braced himself for the next, feeling nothing but a touch of dread. The machete was hacking through the air, rising and falling, and his crowbar was rising and falling to meet it, causing the two of them to shudder without straining, to stagger without toppling. It all felt comfortable, even natural, as if the dust that covered them were a narcotic.

We're drugged, he thought. The Plains are reeling us in. Making us a part of them.

Then the lieutenant plunged his scimitar into Jacob's belly, missing Etienne's chin by an inch. Jacob took the opportunity to bash his crowbar into the lieutenant's head, knocking some inessential bones into disarray.

We could spend days like this, thought Jacob as he regained his balance, but before another moment passed, Remington's crow swooped into the lieutenant's face, digging its beak into his eye, blotting out his vision with its wings.

"Do it," said Etienne, and Jacob yanked the scimitar from his own gut and swept it through the lieutenant's neck, trimming an inch off the crow's tail-feathers in the process.

"My apologies," said Jacob to the crow as the lieutenant's body flopped back into the pit, "and my thanks."

The head had landed face-down, and with the tip of his boot Jacob righted it.

The batter who'd led them here was now far in the distance, waving Adam's severed leg like a trophy as he loped away.

"Oh, Adam, I'm sorry," said Jacob. "There's not much point in chasing him now, I'm afraid."

"It's only a leg," said Etienne.

"Perhaps, but the poor fellow doesn't have much left," said Jacob, hefting Adam over his shoulders and turning toward the hillock, where he was surprised by how much of the general's squadron was on fire.

"Everything turned out all right, then?" called Jacob. Standing at a safe distance from the blaze, he set Adam down and allowed himself to become mesmerized.

The entire hillock was silent, as everyone from the stone-thrower pinned to the ground to the heads on the totem pole stared into the dancing flames, awed by a sight none had witnessed since they walked the Lands Above. Fire, however eerily it recalled life, was no foreigner to the land of death; it was simply unpopular there, for reasons ably demonstrated by the general and her two minions, who writhed, slowly and involuntarily, one above and two below the raging wreck of their formidable oaken door, muttering their dissatisfaction as their flesh turned to ash.

"How?" said Jacob, a question Leopold was happy to answer.

"Really, old boy, I couldn't have done it without you. While you and the headless wonder were traipsing merrily into the trap laid by this bunch of ne'er-do-wells, their slattern-in-chief was standing ominously above me, waggling her blade and calling me terrible names that Clay was too happy to translate. This whole pile seemed to find her amusing, encouraging her to precede injury with insult, leading to that rhetorical flourish that was her undoing: her final gibe was to call me 'gutless,' a state she sought to illustrate literally by slashing open my stomach. Of course, I wasted no time reaching inside and retrieving —"

"My lighter!" said Jacob, catching it in the air.

"While the doxy stood distracted by her own declamations, I sparked its wheel. This desert air had dried her out so thoroughly that the merest lick of flame at the hem of her garments engulfed her in an instant. She dropped her weapon into my lap (no damage there, thankfully), and dear Eve, who'd recently righted herself, used her buckler to knock the floozy onto the door, birthing this bonny blaze."

"And you, Remington," said Jacob, "how did you fare?"

"I watched. Hey, now that Adam's lost his leg, I'd like to try an experiment. I know the guys at the stitchery said it wouldn't work to replace somebody's leg with somebody else's, but I have an idea."

"Very well," said Jacob, "you can all do as you please while I'm repairing Leopold's neck. Let's set up camp near the pole; with any luck, the spectators will be excited enough to tip us off if a threat approaches."

The spectators, in fact, were happy to play lookout, stimulated as they were by the victory of these underdogs, which they attributed to Clay's intervention. As they spun the tale into a legend, putting Plains-Deadish to its best use, Jacob began to saw off a section of the billy-club recently wielded by a door-bearer, retaining a cylinder of lightweight metal. "I'll drill some holes in it and secure it to your spine with wire," he said.

"Carry on," said Leopold.

"From now on, you'll be unable to turn your head without turning your shoulders."

"An improvement over the old method."

Jacob inspected the remains of the broomstick-apparatus, which, it turned out, was lashed between Leopold's shoulders with duct tape: a durable solution, but impossible to remove without flaying his back. Jacob sawed the broomstick down instead and turned his attention to the crimson scarf that hung limply from Leopold's neck, its knots so encrusted with filth that they couldn't be untied.

"I'm afraid this can't be salvaged," said Jacob, withdrawing a pair of scissors.

"Let it fall away, then. Let it all fall away."

As Jacob's fingers peeled away the fabric, he saw that Leopold's neck had, at some point since the preservation of his nether regions, been torn open, resulting in a ragged edge of skin hanging loosely over the exposed innards of his throat.

"Would you like me to try and sew this up for you?" said Jacob, wondering with some distaste who had performed such a sloppy job, and to what end.

"There's no need. We'll all suffer greater indignities before we reach White Gate. It's time we left vanity behind, Jacob: the Plains mean to change us."

Beside the pole, Remington had found a leg about the same length as the one Adam had lost, and sat down with it, clamping its thigh between his knees, staring at its stump.

"This cannot work," said Desi from the pole. "You are attempting the marriage of apple and orange."

"Don't seem like it ought to," said Clay, "but it don't seem like those meat-shields should be able to see, either."

Remington took Adam's knife in his right hand and began paring the flesh from the tip of his left index finger. "Bone is the engine," he said, carving down to the knuckle. He repeated the operation with his opposite hand, then peered at the exposed tips, two white spikes emerging from tubes of rotting muscle.

For a moment he sought the state of mind he had attained in the cave, but as the breeze blew dust through the bowl of his skull, he found it unnecessary: his mind was already perfectly suited to the task at hand. There was no need to reach out for the hands of his fellows, for something steady and infinitesimal already joined them, something that suffused him as he reached his fingertip to the gleaming femur of the severed leg.

No spark occurred when the two bones touched, and if any physical force was at work, it was subtler than Remington could perceive, yet once the connection was made, his mind went rolling down the thigh, swirling around the kneecap, plunging along the shinbone, down five metatarsals, to the tips of five toes.

Slowly, drawing on the leg's will as well as his own, he unbent its knee, then kicked its foot into the air.

"*Brujo,*" whispered Desi.

He touched his other finger to the stump of Adam's thigh, joining the two severed femurs with his skeleton. For a moment he felt uncomfortably crowded, then he simply abdicated. His body slumped over, and Adam took control, lifting and lowering the severed leg through the conduit of Remington's bones.

"You can stitch these guys up now," said Remington over the spectators' murmurs. "Just make sure the bones are touching."

Jacob, who was testing the integrity of Leopold's reinforced neck, looked up to see Adam holding his new appendage flush against his stump, wiggling its toes.

"Well," he said, popping open his canister of needles. "This simplifies matters."

CHAPTER TEN

The Scrimmage

The company couldn't ignore the battle's losers for long. A severed head awakened and started cursing, first at his own body bashing itself against the walls of the sand-pit below him, then at the smoldering ruins of his general, who responded in kind. As the disagreement infected the rest of their squadron, engulfing them in an argument fueled by enough acrimony to last for the rest of time, Etienne began fretting aloud. "We can't stay here," he said from Jacob's chest.

"Well, of course not," said Jacob, victory lending him a certain breeziness. "I'll finish up here in a jiffy, and we'll be on our way!"

"Look at that leg," said Remington as Adam stomped around the hill. "You'd think he was born with it!"

"Perhaps," mused Leopold, "I ought to have you slap a second sword-arm on my back. Or do you think the front would be more useful?"

"Oh, shut your *traps!*" shouted Etienne. "You think this is a game, don't you? But our eternity is in your hands, hands that will be ripped off as soon as you step into the scrimmage if what you showed in that scuffle is all the fight you have!"

The company was too stunned to reply.

"Jacob, stand and face the others," he said. Jacob complied without a word.

"You know, this is my fault," said Etienne, a jagged edge in his voice. "I'm acting like a passenger on this journey when it's my directions that put you on a path you have no chance of surviving without my help. I mean no disrespect, but everyone who saw that fight knows that you'll be pulled apart if you step into the scrimmage as you are, and then *we'll* be the ones arguing in a heap of parts for the rest of time."

"What battle were you watching?" said Leopold. "We emerged from our first encounter victorious! Our adversaries are mangled and charred! By what mad measurement can you consider us failures?"

"The head's right," said Clay. "Y'all can handle the Shallow End, but the scrimmage is a whole other deal. They're hard on squads out there."

"The violence is constant," said Etienne, "and it comes from all directions at once. You'll need more than luck and timing. You'll need a solid defense. You'll need to learn to move and react as a unit, and the only way that will happen is if somebody takes command."

"And I suppose," said Leopold with a snort, "you'd have us believe that someone is *you?*"

"I'm the only one with the necessary experience. Besides, I know my history. Tactics will get us to White Gate. But in order for those tactics to do us any good, you'll need to respond, without questions, without witty asides, to my orders.

"Your training starts now."

They followed, however reluctantly, through an interminable succession of drills and exercises, and while it was unsettling to take orders from someone they'd grown used to regarding as cargo, it was impossible to deny the results. At Clay's suggestion, Etienne recruited the stone-thrower (who was so eager to escape beheading that none doubted his allegiance), adding a crack shot to the roster.

In their standard formation, the five would-be soldiers stood in a ring with their backs to Remington, who held Etienne on his chest and aimed him like a flashlight. At a word from Das Kapital, as Leopold dubbed their bodiless commander, the ring could expand outward and overwhelm an enemy or retract into a defensive huddle. Once enough Plains-Deadish had been drilled into their heads, they could take orders as swiftly as any seasoned scrimmage-rat.

It only became evident how long they'd been training when Etienne declared them as ready as they'd ever be, and Jacob noticed, as if waking from a dream, that his body was coated in grit, that his leather had lost its shine, that his skin was cracking at the joints. He bent one elbow and shuddered: for the first time in years, he could see the unwelcome brightness of his own skeleton.

Etienne thanked the spectators for their advice (for they had offered much, and he'd treated them like elder statesmen), then rotated the ring toward the south, where the scrimmage loomed like a thunderhead, its dark, heavy, mutable front of battle-stirred dust letting glimpses of carnage peek through: the glint of a rusted breastplate, the proud blue of some forgotten army's uniform, the bright gleam of bone. Waves of voice and violence washed over the company, a hideous magnetism drawing them into the dust. They pushed into the fray, knocking warriors into an ever-shifting kaleidoscope of teeth and knuckles, chains and helmets, gloves and cuirasses. The company offered a constant barrage of wild attacks, their rare successes measured in severed extremities, each one resulting in a scuffle over fallen armaments. Not that their formation kept them safe, exactly: as they swayed and staggered on, they were subject to hundreds of bludgeonings, piercings, and changes of course, making Etienne's sense of direction their only compass.

He and Remington, removed from the action by a precious few feet, had the leisure to analyze the madness around them, but to the rest it was a blur, and they made no distinction between lone warriors and the rare squadrons who recoiled from their blind efficiency and ricocheted off in search of easier prey.

Clenched together, the five soldiers labored through yards that felt like miles. The thudding vibrations of battle became commonplace. They'd push, they'd bash, they'd strain, they'd holler and hoot, and then, without warning, the mass would loosen around them, allowing the opportunity to travel unmolested for short periods of time.

In the pauses, there were matters of martial hygiene to attend to. Adam had been disemboweled again, and his guts needed trimming; various sharp weapons were extracted from stomachs and buttocks and thighs; and an arrow that had been wielded as a dagger had to be pulled from the stone-thrower's eye socket, where it was lodged with uncommon tenacity.

The struggle kindled a sense of camaraderie, and each time they pressed forward, exchanging blows with Confederate soldiers, Mongols, and Crusaders (or warriors who'd inherited their equipment), they'd trade their opinions on the efficacy of various techniques. Jacob and Leopold would debate the efficacy of various two-handed attacks, Remington would pester Eve to hold her shield arm higher, and everyone would praise the stone-thrower's sling, which pitched many a weapon to the ground. (The little man spoke little, but always gave a flattered titter after a compliment.)

Ankles and ribs were strewn about, hands scuttled like crabs between their feet, and heads that were giggling, sobbing, and telling tall tales to no one at all littered the ground. The company grew used to these sights, as they'd grown used to the rising and falling tides of the scrimmage. Time itself seemed to fray, lending each moment the hazy, predetermined weight of a living dream. An attacker who'd broken their ranks was held down in the dirt, and a blade sawed back and forth through his spine until it snapped — but who'd done the holding, and who the sawing, none of them could say, nor whether it happened many times or just the once.

In a rare moment of clarity, Jacob glimpsed himself in the blade of the broadsword he'd pulled from the meat of his shoulder, recognizing with a queasy thrill that the leather patches that once had distinguished him as a man of wealth had all been torn out of his face, that he was coated in the yellowy grime of the Plains, and that his nose had been smashed into his skull, leaving his visage as grisly, battered, and anonymous as any he faced in the crowd.

"A Plainsman," he whispered. Turning to survey the damage done to his fellows, he noted with alarm that Eve's shield arm had been severed below the elbow, and wondered how long ago she'd lost it. Beside her, Leopold loosed a long, wordless scream and lashed a barbarian in the face with his chain, time and again, until his opponent was a heap of shards and skin. Remington screamed and cursed, his voice a low and rasping thing. Who have we become? Jacob wondered, as a noise unlike any he'd heard shook him out of contemplation.

The usual soundtrack of the scrimmage was a chorus of voices raised in triumph and defeat, insult and mania, hilarity and hysteria; a raucous blend, to be sure, but nothing so jarring as the roar that now erupted. It was a pure expression of terror, and as it crested, the scrimmage devolved into a stampede, which at Etienne's command the ring faced head-on, digging in their heels and bracing their weapons in an attempt to send it around them.

"What spooked them?" said Remington as his companions, stumbling back against his body, held their ground.

"*Horde!*" shrieked a warrior, shedding his helmet, his basher, even his boots in an attempt to gain speed. The word, once it was recognized, could be heard echoing around the company in every language they knew.

"Why, they look like they're fleeing a volcano!" said Leopold, lashing a crazed warrior aside with his chain.

"Maybe they know something we don't," said Remington. "Should we run?"

"And lose the ground we've gained?" said Leopold. "Fie! Whatever evils may fester in these lands, there are no monsters here. This Horde is made of nothing more terrifying than dead men, and I say we've proved ourselves fierce enough to face them."

"There's no time to talk it over!" said Jacob. "We'll stand and fight. With all these warriors fleeing, we'll have a straight shot to White Gate once we're through. If we win, Remy and I will patch us up in White City, and if we lose, well, there's always the Medic."

"Adam, Eve, you'll sit this one out," said Etienne, "and carry us to the stitchery if we fall."

Holding their weapons to their chests, the headless slumped to the ground, feigning hack-shock as the last of the stampede passed by.

"Remington, it's your turn to fight. Whatever happens, don't let them get hold of your head!"

"Oh, stop worrying, you old hen!" said Leopold. "The stampede is past, and this Horde has yet to materialize. Perhaps they've passed us by entirely."

The exodus of so many warriors had filled the air with such a massive quantity of dust that it felt like nightfall — and dusk was such a distant memory that even its echo shook them. Soon, the shifting and clattering of armed men in the darkness dispelled Leopold's hope, and though the company could discern the vague silhouettes of armed corpses, they had no sense of how many there were.

The Horde stood twenty feet before them. With excruciating slowness, forty of the oldest corpses that Jacob had ever seen became visible, standing in a crescent before the company.

In his days as a preservationist, Jacob had come across any number of citizens who, like Leopold or Caesar Augustus, claimed to be superannuated while clinging to the very flesh that revealed their vintage. He had often remarked that giving in to skeletonization would have allowed these blowhards to claim whatever date of death they liked, but the sight of the Horde dispelled this theory in an instant, for it was clear in the presence of these ancient, fleshless creatures that all bone was not the same. The Hordesmen were skeletons, yet nothing about them was blank: every bone was an artifact inscribed with proof of the passage of time. Lavish coats of desert varnish lent a golden-brown sheen to their skulls, shins, and patellae, filling the hashmarks scored by hundreds of thousands of blows with a sticky, dark resin.

They wore tarnished breastplates, cracked jerkins, and tattered robes; many of their joints were lashed together with bands of metal, leather, and rope. The implements of destruction that were, for now, held loosely in their hands induced in Jacob a perverse desire for the fight to begin, simply to see how corpses so slight could wield weapons so massive. Lengthy spears and swords abounded, as well as hammers and axes that brought gods and heroes to mind. From the talons of a tiny black-robed woman sprouted a scythe worthy of the Grim Reaper, and at the back of the crowd, borne by a seven-foot giant, was the great, two-bladed propeller of some antiquated airplane.

As the air cleared, three Hordesmen bearing spears beat them in unison against the rock floor in an intricate rhythm. One warrior strode forward, speaking eloquently in some outmoded rhetorical style as he tossed a great battle-axe from hand to hand.

"What language is that?" said Jacob in wonder, for the idiom was so ancient it was alien to him, but before an answer was offered, the spear-bearers, hearing the language of their opponent, beat out another rhythm, summoning three warriors fluent in their enemies' tongue.

The little reaper ambled forward, using her scythe as a walking-stick, and from the midst of the Horde two skeletons in chain-mail vaulted forward on a twelve-foot pike, the bands in their joints jangling as they landed on the rock behind her.

"Idle threateners!" cried the reaper, her voice as bright as a bell, while the warriors behind her brandished pike and sword. "You stand accused of banding together, that your combined force might challenge the supremacy of the Horde."

"Feh!" cried the swordsman, and the pike-bearer tapped out a rhythm on the rock, prompting the Horde to chant their Latin motto, which Etienne translated for the benefit of his fellows: 'The Last Man Standing shall a Hordesman be.'

"Listen to these spindly blowhards!" scoffed Leopold. "Decayed as they are, I doubt they can even swing those weapons."

Suddenly, the pike-bearer leapt onto the swordsman's shoulders and dipped his weapon into the ring, skewering the stone-thrower. The little reaper, standing under the midpoint of the pike, propped it up with one hand, and as the pike-bearer dropped from his partner's shoulders to the ground, holding the end of his weapon, the stone-thrower was launched into the air. The pike-bearer yanked his weapon free, the reaper swept her scythe upwards, and the stone-thrower tumbled to the ground with his stones, bisected.

"Then again," said Leopold.

"Huzzah!" cried the pike-bearer, booting a bit of would-be ammunition at Remington's head. "The Horde, supreme: and woe to your team!" He seized the stone-thrower's torso while the swordsman grabbed his legs, and the two warriors launched the two halves in opposite directions, where they were lost in a wasteland of human detritus.

The three Hordesmen advanced, the swordsman reaching his mark first and swinging for Leopold's neck. Leopold wrapped his chain around the blade, yanking with all his might in the hopes of dislodging it from the swordsman's grip. Failing this, he swung his own rusty blade at the swordsman's wrist, snapping the leather band around it, which did not, as he'd hoped, cause the swordsman's hand to fall off. The little reaper, while Leopold's hands were occupied, twirled around and swung her scythe through his middle, and with an indignant yap he fell variously to the ground.

Distracted, Jacob stumbled out of range of the pike-bearer's jabs, steadying himself on his crowbar as he swatted the air with his scimitar. While he searched his mind for a gambit that would bring him close enough to engage, the little reaper danced to his side. Too late, he realized that the pike-bearer had merely been toying with him to allow her to reach him unopposed.

Her crooked blade swept through him, and the snap of his spine resounded like a snare drum struck in his gut. Though years had passed since he'd felt the cold, something like a chill touched him as his legs toppled down beside him, and then his mind ground to a halt, and the world passed through it like river-water.

Remington ambled forward as pike-bearer and swordsman melted into the Horde, leaving the reaper alone to finish him.

"Comprehend me, challenger!" said the reaper. "The Horde suffers no alliances in the Plains: nay, not even a band of four! We have fought for centuries beyond reckoning and have seen tiny threats grown large when some untested urchin rises to command. Such audacity must be answered with swift disassembly, for the role of the Last Man Standing is too important to leave to chance.

"Leave it to the Horde, instead. Once we have cleansed the Plains, we shall elect our King as champions ought: in a civilized tournament, wherein each warrior faces her brothers until all have fallen but one.

"We tell you this that you may spread our message from the ground: the Last Man Standing shall a Hordesman be!"

"Can I hit her now?" said Remington.

"You can certainly try," said Etienne.

As the crow took wing in fright, the reaper met the signpost's swing with a flick of her wrist, puncturing the metal with her scythe. Their weapons thus entangled, she and Remington wrangled them to and fro in the air like long-distance arm-wrestlers until the reaper let go with an irritated sigh. The weapons crashed to the earth, and when Remington bent to extricate his, she pulled a cleaver from the folds of her robe and swung it with a butcher's surety towards the curve of his neck.

In that terrible moment, a quintet of Hordesmen strode forward, eager to scatter the pieces of their defeated opponents; Remington, distracted by a sudden squawk from above, glanced up at the reconstructed crow, who'd been forced to swoop in order to avoid a severed head launched with great, mechanical force from afar; and the head, an airborne blur, howled, *"Vengeance!"*

Before the cleaver struck, the head pounded the reaper's back like a cannonball, the collision making it clear why the Hordesmen's joints were banded together, as all the unsecured bones burst from her frame and skittered across the rocky floor behind her knife. She scurried after them in a panic, fitting the bones into her skeleton before they were lost to her consciousness, and shrieking, "The Collectors! The Collectors approach, from south-southwest!"

A second head struck, pounding a Hordesman full in the chest but failing to scatter his bones.

"Interesting," said Etienne. "That one expected the blow."

"Thy doom drops from above, body-robbers!" cried the head, bouncing past Remington's feet. "Draw near, that I might gnaw thy hated ankles."

Its fellows were falling like hailstones now, and the Horde, enraged, charged to the south-southwest, toward a distant congregation of wheeled catapults whose operators bore severed heads by the bushel. Before the clash between these mighty battalions could be glimpsed, however, the Horde's exit drew a dusty curtain over the southern Plains.

"Well, enough gawking," said Etienne. "Adam, Eve, arise!"

The headless stood, and with Remington's help divided the halves of Leopold and Jacob between them. Remington put Jacob's knapsack (thankfully undamaged) over his shoulders and carried his upper half. Eve hefted Leopold's torso with her good arm, leaving Adam to lift two filthy pairs of legs over his shoulders.

"Should we find the stone-thrower?" said Remington.

"He's lost," said Etienne. "At least his arms were attached when they threw him. Maybe he'll crawl away before the Plainsmen come back."

The northern Plains were eerily calm. "Where are all the fighters?" said Remington.

"At the Armory, most of them. Sometimes you'll find thousands milling around those markets, more or less peaceably. Then they'll all run out and start fighting again, as if someone had struck a bell."

"And the Armory's that away, so we should be able to get these two to the Medic before they wake up."

"I hope so, but it's too early to celebrate. Although — hold on, is that the Rim?"

"Oh, yeah! Look at that. It wasn't too far after all."

"Which means the ground we've covered in all this time is negligible."

"I won't tell Jake if you don't."

As they neared the stitchery, they were startled to see hundreds of warriors standing in an ungainly column before the Medic's tent, all waiting for attention from within.

"Imagine if the Horde could see this," said Remington. "All these squadrons in one place! That reaper girl would go ballistic."

"Remington," said Etienne in a low voice. "I want you to walk right past this line, like you've got a special pass. And while you're at it, find any spools of thread that might remain in Jacob's knapsack."

Just ahead, a chopped-up warrior came noisily to her senses, forcing her squadron to realize that they had no hope of seeing her reassembled. Making hasty apologies, her fellows dropped her, without ceremony, right where they'd been standing. The rest of the queue, in their haste to fill the vacated space, kicked her parts out of the way, half to one side, half to the other. As the poor woman's head distracted the crowd with screaming, Remington took the opportunity to trot down beside the line, and got about halfway without provoking comment.

But before he reached the end, a rattling voice cried out for the destruction of "them varminty line-cutters," to which Etienne responded with a startling, nasal cry: "Supplies! Supplies! Thread-and-needle man, make way for supplies!" While the men in line gaped at the equipment in Remington's hands, which certainly looked more medical than martial, Remington slipped into the stitchery.

Within was a scene of utter chaos: disassembled corpses who'd failed the mallet-test were strewn about the floor, crawling and bemoaning their newfound predicament when they were not attacking one another outright; barrels and cabinets had been overturned in a desperate attempt to find forgotten supplies; and four angry corpses in threadbare Royal Air Force uniforms were thrusting their proffered payment across the table while demanding that Flak-Jacket Josie be sewn up with sinew from the Medic's own arse if he were in fact out of wire.

"There's a bleeding red cross hanging off your tent," squawked an aggrieved flyboy. "Now get on with the red-crossing, or we'll pull the bleeding thing down!"

As fists struck palms with increasing velocity, the RN pretended to search for a spool of thread, using the pantomime as an excuse to fortify a bulwark of empty containers tossed between the operating theater and the front of the tent. Behind her the Medic jiggered open the lid of their strongbox, rapping on its side to let her know the time was ripe to lock themselves inside.

"Supplies!" squawked Etienne as Remington, Adam, and Eve clambered over an overturned filing cabinet. "Here you go, chief: three spools of stitch-grade medical thread, in exchange for the immediate reassembly of these two scrimmage-rats."

Remington slapped the spools on the operating table. "Here you go, chief!"

"Good timing," muttered the RN, and the Medic, who had already climbed inside the strongbox, popped out immediately, motioning for the halves of Leopold and Jacob to be laid out on the operating table posthaste.

"Now look here," shouted a flyboy, "we was here first, and we'll be served first!"

"With what?" answered Etienne. "We don't get paid, they don't get the supplies, and your friend don't get stitched. Now pipe down and move outside the tent, before I cart this crap to the Armory and sell it for twice the price!"

Cursing, the flyboy dragged his squadron outside, where the news that reinforcements had arrived set off an argument that broke the informal ceasefire, distracting attention from the tent for a few precious moments.

The Medic bowed in thanks, and the RN hopped onto her step stool. "You guys are a godsend," she said, tossing the mallet into the Medic's hands and emptying the last handful of double-headed hooks from a jelly jar.

"Problems, boss?" she asked, for the Medic had slapped the table with his open palm in alarm.

For their benefit he repeated himself, striking first Jacob, then Leopold on the noggin: the top halves of the two men jerked, but their bottom halves were still.

"Separation of consciousness," said the RN. "Tough luck, but you know, a body can get by with only an upper half. What do you say we sew some work gloves on their hands, maybe tidy up their torsos, in exchange for two of those spools?"

"No need," said Remington. "Just sew them up like normal, and I'll handle the rest."

"You're the boss," said the RN, and while the Medic weighed his misgivings against three spools of thread, she prepped the table.

They set to work with astonishing speed, rolling back the edges of shirts and trousers, puncturing flesh with needles, and filling the air with a flurry of jerks and tugs. Before the flyboys had time to complain, Leopold and Jacob, still unconscious, were carted outside on a stretcher borne by Remington and Adam. At a safe distance from the tent (which was experiencing an unholy rush now that the flaps had been thrown open again), he laid them belly-up on the ground in the long shadow of the Rim.

"I'd hoped we wouldn't have to test your art this way," said Etienne, "but since it's their only hope of walking south, I wish you the best of luck."

"I've got it under control," said Remington. He hummed to himself as he laid his hands on each man in turn, caressing forehead and shin, chest and thigh, until a jolt ran through him.

"All set," he said, dusting off his hands. "They're fused, both of them."

"How can you be sure?"

"One way to find out," said Remington, picking up a fist-sized rock with which he struck Leopold on the forehead, eliciting a full-body jerk. Before he could repeat the test, however, Jacob moaned, then sat bolt upright, staring around like he'd woken from a nightmare.

"Can it be?" he cried, slapping his legs. "I'm awake! I'm intact! I can stand!"

In his excitement, he strove to demonstrate this last statement, but found it more difficult than he'd anticipated; he staggered and swayed for several long moments before he could steady himself enough to stand still.

"Take it slow," said Etienne, but Jacob was too perplexed to stop. Stepping forward, he felt his feet thudding beneath him as if he were miscalculating the distance to the earth.

"Jeez, Jake, you'd think you'd never used those legs before!" said Remington.

Jacob, seized by a sudden dread, bent down to inspect his trousers, and found, beneath a thick coat of desert grime, that they were made of purple corduroy. "Why have you dressed me in Leopold's pants?" he cried, clawing at the zipper like a man in a nightmare.

As Leopold himself began to come around, the purple trousers fell to the ground. The first thing he saw when he awakened was his own proud member standing at attention below Jacob Campbell's grimace. As soon as he found his footing, Leopold began staggering around like a newborn colt and shrieking, "I'm a monster! That crater-faced quack has Frankensteined me! I'll have his head sewn between his legs! Malpractice! Malfeasance! Abomination!"

"We'll fix this at once," said Jacob, glaring at Remington as he wrestled with his trousers. "Won't we, Remy?"

"Gee, I don't know," said Remington, soothing the crow, who'd been ruffled by the noise. "I fused you guys pretty good. I don't think cutting you up again is such a good idea."

"Really, you haven't suffered any harm," said Etienne, who was trying not to laugh, "and for all we know, there are limits to Remington's gift."

"For all we know," cried Leopold, "there are none at all! If our bits are as interchangeable as this, why the deuce can't we swap them back? Why not chop them up and slap them higgledy-piggledy back together again? It's time we learned precisely what the demonboy can do, before —"

"Hah!" cried Jacob.

"What is it?" said Remington.

"Hush!" said Jacob, pacing in an oval precisely the length and width of his old flat in the Preservative District.

"A hint, perhaps?" said Leopold.

"Shut your damned mouths, I'm thinking," said Jacob, and that was all he would say for almost an hour. When he finally shared his epiphany, however, even Leopold forgot all the fuss.

"There's only one problem," said Etienne when the excitement had worn off. "Your plan calls for everything you have in the knapsack. Without that, what do we have to trade for weapons?"

Jacob opened his mouth and shut it again. "Damn!" he cried. "You're right, of course. We'd need a benefactor to pull this off, and we're in the wrong part of the world to be looking for charity."

"A benefactor, you say?" said Leopold, who was hopping from one of Jacob's former feet to the other, his spirits restored. "Well, my hearties, tell me how this strikes you: I, Leopold l'Eclair, shall fund this endeavor entirely, providing whatever supplies might be necessary for our ascension, in exchange for command of the army, effective as soon as we reach White Gate."

"Fund this endeavor — with what? Your pockets are empty!" said Jacob, pulling them inside-out.

"Jacob," said Leopold with an obvious thrill, "I must confess that I've been holding out on you." He pulled the skin clean off of his head, revealing a lily-white skull with a curious carving in its brow.

"Leo, you were a debtor?" said Remington.

"Oh, no, nothing so desperate as that. But I found it helpful to dress like one to get my hands on these." Plunging his fingers into a hole drilled through his crown, Leopold withdrew a black velvet pouch. Out of it he pulled five functional timepieces, one of which, a burnished, golden pocket watch of ingenious design, was still ticking.

Jacob gaped. "But that's —"

"A fortune," said Leopold. "The Magnate's fortune, in fact!"

CHAPTER ELEVEN

The Last Man Standing

I t took me no more than five days," said Leopold, "to spend every moment of the seventeen years I'd won — a fortune, I'd thought! And what I'd purchased seemed well worth the expenditure. Dressed as a dandy, I was as impossible to ignore as I was to take seriously, and so I could dig up a wealth of information without being suspected of anything more sinister than a predilection for gossip.

"As I adjusted my crimson scarf, I was startled by the ringing of the hour, its discord drawing my attention to the clock-tower beyond the window of my tenement, where a debtor struck his misshapen gong time and again — twenty-*one*, twenty-*two*, twenty-*three*. I was hungry to learn more about the operation of these clock-towers, which I'd heard were run on the reliance of functional time-pieces. Just the thought of those ticking watches made me feel feverish. 'Died with a watch in her pocket,' the gamblers would say of a woman on a lucky streak, who stood to win an account stuffed full of years.

"And yet time was also our prison, converting the grand expanse of eternity into a series of measured cubicles as dreary as any in the life we'd left behind.

"Just as the Magnate robbed me of my time by shackling me to these ruthlessly passing hours, so I swore to take my first step toward usurping his power by stealing a little time back. I knew that watches and clocks were the most potent symbols of the Magnate's power, as surely as I'd known when I rose from the muck of Lethe that I'd come into my inheritance at last. Would the theft of a few watches make any impression upon the Magnate, considering how many more he held in his towers? Doubtful, but think of the symbolic heft! I had to start somewhere, even if I were the proverbial mosquito attacking a pachyderm.

"This city will be my kingdom, I thought from the start: I need only the patience to claim it. I have known since the night I chose to snuff out my own life that death was the best choice I ever made; that true power, power eternal, was finally within my reach; and that the qualities innate to my soul would elevate me, in due time, to godhood.

"In essence, I am the same boy I was in life, but it was the act of passing from world to world that brought about my apotheosis. In that sense, I have much in common with this pocket watch," he said, dangling the object from his fingers, "a bauble before the river transformed it, now a treasure. Setting my sights on stealing at least a few of its fellows from the hundreds in the Magnate's stores, I began my reinvention in the Tunnels, where I spent years in dank barrooms in the service of idle conversation, revising my persona from room to room until I felt more natural in my adopted self than the one I'd strangled.

"Slowly, as I became a polyglot and an expert in Dead City culture, I became certain that I would need to find an informant before I could gain access to the secrets of the Magnate's rule. After months of searching, I found the right corpse for the job in a pub called the Rag-and-Bone Shop, a man whose hands looked fifty years more decrepit than his face.

"'Was I a debtor?' said the man, swabbing the inside of his cup with his finger and rubbing the last drop of swill on his teeth. 'Sonny,

I been a debtor so long I don't remember what you call the thing I was before. In fact, I don't remember a thing that happened before they scrubbed me, not in life, death, nor dreamland.'

"'How odd!' I cried, laughing rather more uproariously than the occasion merited.

"'It's odd, all right,' said the man, cheered by his own apparent wit. 'I might have been born with a skull for a head, for all I can recall!'

"'Oh, indeed!' I cackled, jerking my head like a ball on a string while paying for the man's next round with an account-stone that would keep him drunk for a year. 'Now tell me: how well do you recall your indenture?'

"'Where that's concerned, sonny, it's etched as deep in my memory as the debtor's code in my skull,' said the man, knocking his knuckles on the loose skin of his brow. 'Torture like that no man can forget.'

"To be brief," Leopold went on, slipping the pocket watch into its pouch, "this corpse served for decades as a bell-ringer, a post that combines the mind-numbing boredom that is every debtor's lot with regular installments of shattering noise. His assignment was to stare for fifty-nine minutes at a time at a small collection of watches, noting any deviations from the norm to keep the Magnate's time-keepers aware of any necessary adjustments. When the watches neared the hour, he was to bring one to his bell — a fanciful moniker, as he rang the hour on an uneven slab of scrap metal — which he struck thrice for three a.m., fourteen times for two p.m., and so forth.

"His only solace was that midnight was marked not by twenty-four bells, but twelve; it was also the last bell he rang at the end of every week-long shift, for the developers of the time-keeping system had concluded that no human mind could endure such repetitive clangor for more than seven days before job performance was adversely affected by certain mental eccentricities. Thus, his weekly break was spent in the Debtor's Pool, where he was debriefed, then stultified into mental fitness before being relocated to another bell tower where some other ringer was at the end of his own workweek.

"I was thrilled by the news of this changing of the guards, not to mention that the city was full of such bell-towers, each with a wealth of watches inside! I endeavored to hide my eagerness from this ex-debtor, though it scarcely mattered. He'd loathed this detail so much that the slightest hint of mischief made him a willing informant, and as soon as our interview was over I hastened to the surface, eager to explore the tower he'd described as 'begging for a break-in.'

"Back in the city, I was delighted to discover that my combination lock, aided by the noise pouring into my building from the bell tower across the way, had kept my apartment uninhabited in my absence, and by way of celebration I gathered the bulk of my possessions and took them to Lazarus Quay to trade. Returning with a bundle of black cloth and a clay pot full of river-water, I sat down against the wall and put the shard of mirror to my throat, sawing my neck open from nape to Adam's apple. After peeling off my face, I scrubbed my skull clean of flesh and gristle with the river-water and a wire brush, then checked my handiwork in the mirror before carving a debtor's stamp in my brow with the edge of a chisel. As the alphanumeric code carved into the average debtor's skull was unknown to me, this fanciful carving of a lemniscate was not intended to pass close inspection, but I hoped its presence would satisfy the glance of a ringer greeting me in exhaustion at the end of a shift.

"I tried on my robes then, arranging their cowl to hide my broomstick and scarf, then dressed and undressed repeatedly until I was certain I could do it blind. I replaced my face, which had already begun to feel like a mask, and changed into my frippery; tucking the black bundle beneath my belt, I descended into the Tunnels, where I sought out the bell tower my informant had named.

"If Dead City's buildings truly are brought in by the floods, then this bell tower must have been carried on the crest of a mighty wave and plunged like a lancet into the boil of Rottening Green, for its base was buried deep in the streets of that district, its dungeon sunk below the Tunnels. Luckily, the dungeon's walls were so compromised by the collision that I was able to climb into a crawl-space below the floorboards of a neighboring pub and slip right in.

"Winding my way through murky passages and finding no access to the upper levels besides an unreachable trap-door, I located that architectural quirk that my informant had so helpfully described: a long, narrow cistern running the length of the tower. I attacked it with chisel and mallet, beating on a single stone until the skin chafed off of my palms; and although the regular noise and vibration produced by this method continued long enough to deliver the eccentricities the ringer had described (fancies, figments, and fakeries of the mind that distorted my living youth into the stuff of waking nightmare), I persisted, cursing, moaning, and babbling, until the block of stone crumbled into the dark floodwater below.

"Grateful that I'd punctured the cistern higher than the water-line, I wiggled inside, wedged my limbs into the shaft, and began to inch my way up toward a distant point of sepia light. I felt nothing, saw nothing but bare rock, and had no sense of distance above or below; the figments multiplied in that claustrophobic darkness, subjecting me to a hell that only the unwavering strength of my ambition could propel me through. It was a trial so severe that I would have believed years had passed by the time I reached the hole through which ancient scholars had dropped their buckets.

"When I'd climbed close to this aperture, I waited to hear the ringing of the hour: it was seven p.m. I waited in the shaft like a human cannonball until midnight came and went.

"Since no debtor replacing the ringer on duty had passed on the stairs, which I could see through the bucket-hole, I persisted until the day grew long enough that its bells provided cover for my entry. At last, as noon rang, I hurried through the bucket-hole and chose a chamber off the central stair, where I changed into my costume, keeping still unless the bells were ringing and avoiding the windows.

"I remained in that chamber for three full days.

"At moments before midnight on the fourth, I heard my cue: a shuffling of robes on the stairs below.

"The sound of the ringer's replacement sent the bone-rush through me like a sudden flame, for to escape detection, I would have to dispatch and replace him in the space of twelve bells.

"As the ringer above me dragged his hammer across the floor, I launched myself around the bend, suffused with a savagery familiar to any Plainsman.

"As the first bell rang, I sprang down the steps; at the second, I crashed into the ringer, who was so shocked that he made not a sound; at the third bell, I heaved his body over my shoulder; at the fourth, he was screaming blue murder; at the ringer's fifth strike, the replacement covered my eyes with his scrabbling hands; at the sixth, I crashed headlong into the wall of my chamber, knocking the replacement to the floor; at the seventh bell, I climbed atop my adversary, planting my knees on his chest; at the eighth, I twisted his head off his neck, crying out in glee at that wicked little snap; as the ninth bell rang, I stood and shot his head at the bucket-hole, astonished that he could still scream as he flew; and horror! as the tenth bell rang, his head had struck the bucket-hole's edge, and rolled back between my legs; as the eleventh and penultimate bell tolled, I scooped up his head and shot again, ignoring his slurred curses; and as the twelfth and final bell was struck in the chamber above, the replacement's head plunged howling into the cistern, tumbling to its doom as the bell's last reverberations echoed down the stairs.

"I hurried back to the steps, swallowing my excitement: head down, shoulders slumped, I plodded up the stairs like a man on the brink of a hated chore.

"The ringer above had no sooner finished his twelfth strike than he'd dropped his hammer and begun descending, and he passed me without so much as glancing at my fraudulent debt-stamp.

"Dazed, I reached the top of the bell-tower, saw the rotting card-table where the watches lay, swept them into the pouch I'd purchased at the Quay, hurried down the steps, stowed my clothing beneath my robe, and stuffed the headless body of the ringer down the bucket-hole before descending an inch at a time toward the Tunnels.

"The heist was flawless, unlike the rest of my plan: for I had overestimated the strength of Dead City's black market and was sentenced to squander month after ticking month searching for a fence capable of converting these stolen goods into credit, for I required a vast quantity of time to bankroll my scheme. As fate had it, I could find no buyer brave enough, and so I turned my ambition beyond city limits, down-river and into these very wilds, where at last, with your help, my destiny shall be realized. Rest assured, your part in my timely ascension shall not be forgotten when my foes have been ground to dust beneath the mighty pestle of Leopold l'Eclair!"

The crow squawked irritably at the close of this monologue, which it had now heard twice in its entirety. Leopold kicked a spray of sand in its direction, but the crow only clacked its beak and continued staring.

"Interesting," said the cross-legged merchant sitting before them, inspecting the dagger he'd been sharpening all the while, then laying it on the straw carpet between them with exaggerated care. "This story, with the snatching and the crawling and the derring-do, it's good at a museum, on a laminated placard, or maybe at an antiques shop, to help the hand find the wallet, but it is not, I think, so useful to us at Mahmoud's. My offer stands, Mr. Eclair, right where it stood, unless you let me nail this odd little bird to a board and sell it as a curio. Then I throw in a chess set."

Mahmoud the merchant, naked but for a paisley waistcoat, his oblong head standing at the apex of so tall and precarious a frame that he trembled when he spoke, sat in the midst of a dozen carpets, curtains, and lengths of upholstery laden with unbroken blades and armor, above which a dozen well equipped and faultlessly silent warriors stood: Mahmoud's Guard.

"You are as displeased as your blackbird," said Mahmoud over the crow's indignant cawing, "but consider the fate of the merchant: in order to exchange these watches for something I can use, I have two choices: I can wait here for the city folk, the blade-traders, who are not so easy to impress with tales of adventure as a simple man like myself, and who will drive such hard bargains that I will thank myself for holding to my offer; or, if I feel like having an adventure myself, then I must roll up my carpets, pay my servants with their blades, trade in my stock for city-goods, and make the long hike down the Bazakh Bypass to Dead City, where I will try and pawn these dirty goods without attracting the attention of your, ah, nemesis, as you have tried and failed to do already. Either way, the risk is mine, and your story, which you hope will drive my offer up, only gives me more to worry about; and since worry takes time, and time, more than ever, is money, I really ought to lower my offer to compensate. Therefore you can put your mind at ease, for since I hold to my initial offer, it is the same as if I had given you more, do you understand? Of course you do; we are both reasonable men."

Mahmoud rose seismically to his feet, his hand extended in a gesture that still struck Leopold as obscene: the offer to shake hands.

"Now tell me, my friend," said Mahmoud, "do we have a deal?"

Leopold, reduced to his last resort, closed his fist around his pouch, turned on his heel, and stalked away, as if he were about to sell the watches posthaste to Mahmoud's most hated rival.

"All right, my friend, relent!" cried Mahmoud, waving his hand at the ground. "The sight of your back reminds me that a man must sometimes take a chance to reap a reward, isn't it? And so I present you my final offer, which I hope you find agreeable: I can give three dozen blades per watch, with armor to match. This truly is a deal that only Mahmoud can make, for no other merchant has the stock!"

"We'll need delivery, too," said Leopold, offering his profile. "Our tent is along the Rim, past the Torn Curtain, about a mile before the Medic's: do you know the place, or shall I draw you a map?"

"Delivery?" spat the merchant, investing those four syllables with such disbelief and outrage that he had to steady his head with his hands. "This is not a service we offer at Mahmoud's! A man comes with his army and he takes his goods! He does not ask the merchant to take the risk of transport, and through this war zone, and for nothing!"

"I offer four watches," said Leopold, undeterred. "One as downpayment. The other three you will receive at the camp. Meet me there, and you'll be rich enough to buy several districts, which I, as ruler of Dead City, will let you keep. Who knows? There may even be a place for you in my administration." Leopold dangled the pouch from his fingers, favoring the merchant with his ruined teeth. "So tell me, my friend: do we have a deal?"

"We have a deal," muttered Mahmoud, his rancor dissolving into deep satisfaction as his customer turned his back. "Moron," he said under his breath, "all the swords in Tutankhamen's army are worth less than the gift you've given!"

The crow turned its tail on the merchant and took to the air, following closely behind the bobbling head of Leopold l'Eclair.

As Leopold threaded his way through stalls of imitation swords and makeshift clubs, he squeezed the pouch in his fist. "What audacity, l'Eclair!" he said to himself. "The very audacity that shall carry you like a guardian angel through these Plains, for if any quality is favored by the gods of this land, it is surely brazenness."

He continued in this vein as he walked into the Shallow End, going so far as to recite his first speech before a united Land of the Dead. His mood was further improved when two recruits with sharpened sticks charged him, their river-moist bodies falling in slabs beneath the edge of his sword before their battle cries had been fully articulated.

"Tell those who kick pebbles into your eyes," he said as they sank into torpor, "that the Last Man Standing has arrived!"

He grew less ebullient as he approached the hinged gates of his camp, where the sounds of argument soon spilled over the walls and onto the pitted surface of the earth. Enclosed within a tall fence constructed entirely of scavenged weaponry and patches of plastic and cloth was a wide swath of earth divided by barbed wire into a multitude of little pens keeping hundreds of quarrelsome body parts organized by size and type. The bickering company worked in a clearing between the pens, and their dispute concerned the plans drawn in the dirt before them, which had, as the weeks passed, grown so elaborate that the company couldn't proceed without them. A miniature tent had been built to protect them from breezes, footfalls, and discarded tools — and this had seemed like protection enough until Etienne's head was installed at the top of the framework of flesh that was shrouded in shadow by the camp's high walls. Since then, his spasmodic attempts to control that errant body had crushed the tent, erasing the plans entirely.

"It was faulty wiring that did it," he shouted from above the company. "Look to yourselves before blaming me!"

"Come on, E," shouted Remington from the ground, where he was attempting to join a string of body parts with both hands and both feet, "what happens when the parts get joined to you is *your* problem! We're working overtime down here, so why don't you just kick back and wait for the grownups to tell you what to do?"

"Enough of this verbal spew!" screamed Jacob, tearing the little tent up by its roots. "Let everyone be quiet unless anyone has anything even partially relevant to say, at which point everyone will be amazed at anyone, since there's been nothing but jabber for hours, if not days, of wasted time!"

Then Jacob shouted at Remington, flinging the tiny tent aside; Etienne hollered at Jacob while trying to gain control of his enormous limbs; and Remington hollered at Etienne while Adam and Eve tossed him up one side of the human scaffolding below Etienne's neckline, where Remington strove to fix the connection between two lengths of spine in a grand hoop around the creature's midsection.

"My friends!" cried Leopold, planting his sword in the earth and holding out his hands as if he were carrying a large platter of hors d'oeuvres. "Let us all take a well-deserved break and settle our differences without — dear lord, Remington, are you climbing that beast with my watches? Come down slowly, damn you, and give them here!"

Thus the argument intensified, and might well have led to violence, had Jacob not scrambled over to the ruined plans and begun scribbling over them with a ski pole. Etienne, noticing the diagram, pleaded with Remington to disconnect him from the bony clamp that held him in place above the creature, and with a last wheeze of psychic energy Remington obliged. Etienne, who had been unscrewed from his plaque, and whose few remaining vertebrae had been stripped of flesh for a cleaner connection, was passed down to Adam, and the company crowded around Jacob's sketch.

In the sand, two human forms were depicted beside a harness made of limbs and ribs, parts whose cuneiform was instantly recognizable to all through a system of anatomical notation developed in the planning stages. "Of course," muttered Jacob as he sketched, "of course! If bone is the engine, its mass is the horsepower. Of course!"

"What are you saying, man?" said Leopold. "Enunciate when you jabber."

"Yeah, Jake, en*un*ciate," said Remington.

"A living man doesn't move the way we do," said Jacob, pointing to the first drawing, the shape of a man with arrows descending from his head into his body. "When he moves his hand, the motion starts in his brain, runs through his nerves, then moves his muscles." He tapped the grit below the second drawing, in which a human figure had arrows running through every part of his body, in both directions. "But a corpse goes through a total overhaul. When he's translated from life to death, he learns a new way of moving."

"Ooh! Ooh! That's called quickening!"

"Yes, Remy, it is," said Jacob, "now put your hand down. While quickening, the corpse recognizes that his brain and muscles are now powerless to move his hand, which must now move itself. The will to move is no longer centralized; it has spread throughout every bone in his body." He drew his fingertip across the bellies of the two figures. "Thus, if you cut off a living man's legs, they simply die, but cut a dead man in two, and you get two dead men: one who walks on his hands, and one who can no longer see."

"Usually," said Remington, looking up at Adam and Eve.

"Usually. But bring Remy into the picture and you can get different parts of different dead men to agree to function together." Jacob joined arrows from the separated halves across the diagrams. "Get him to merge parts of different corpses, and you make a combination corpse. His will to move has separate origins that Remington unifies. So far, the mechanics are simple, because the parts still add up to one whole body.

"But this creature is more complicated: its body is made up of parts of hundreds of corpses. We want to unify those parts enough for a single operator to control them, and so we've been trying to plug Etienne in at the top.

"But we've been leaning on the model of a living human, expecting his head to control the body as if its brain were operational. Apologies, Etienne, but we've been overestimating the importance of your skull! Attaching it does allow the creature to see and hear, but for our purposes it's only a specialized bone. This isn't about mental dominance, it's about extending the will to move throughout the creature's framework, and where that's concerned, bone mass matters."

Behind them, the creature shifted its weight, dragging a massive appendage a few feet through the sand, alarming the company enough to halt the lecture for a time. When it settled, Jacob began sketching again, drawing a head with a short arrow extending from its neck and a body with long arrows extending from its digits and joints, each of which he connected to a corresponding point on his proposed harness.

"A skull on its own doesn't have the mass to control our creature. To drive it, we'll need to plug an entire body into the core, so that the impulses from every bone in its body can interface with the creature's. What we need is a puppeteer."

The company fell on the theory at once, dissecting it, debating it, and engaging in a heated analysis of the harness, which Jacob and the headless began assembling on the spot. Remington consented to join it to the framework of the creature, clambering back inside its cavity despite the frazzled state of his nerves, holding on while involuntary motions shook its bulk, but before he was through, Etienne, plugged into the creature and hanging above them all, began to protest.

"The plan makes sense, I'm not denying it. The thought that there wasn't enough of me for the job passed through my mind, though I wasn't thinking in terms of bone mass. But this isn't just about mechanics. There's the character of the operator to consider.

"I promise you, this creature is chaos. It's a jumble of wills that wants to devour the man at its reins. To take control of it, a corpse would need to be so forceful and stubborn that he was almost insane; he'd have to be completely self-obsessed; he'd have to be monomaniacal; he'd —"

"He'd have to be Leopold," said Jacob.

Leopold, of course, had already come to this conclusion.

"And why not?" he cried as he laid his hand on one of the creature's myriad flanks. "The beast will be under my control after we reach the gate, so let us be joined now: the king and his people, sharing the body politic! How soon can we begin?"

"We'll have to expose a lot of bones first," said Jacob, "but we can get started immediately."

Noting his ward's exhaustion, he ordered Remington to go off and play with his friends until he was needed, and so it was that Remy, Adam, Eve, and the reconstructed crow had ample time to relax on the rocky ground outside the gates, staring into the Shallow End, watching a number of minor encounters between bit players in the drama of the Plains before spotting a rickety shape on the horizon. Mahmoud the merchant approached, each segment of his body shimmying independently with the strain of locomotion. On his shoulders were the straps of a backpack that rose above his head, containing all the city-goods for which he'd traded his stock, and behind him, twelve of his Guardsmen steered a pallet creaking with cargo.

The crow flew in a silent circle above the fence, and Remington trotted out to meet Mahmoud, flanked by the headless. "Oh, hiya! You must be the delivery guy."

"Where's Eclair?" said the merchant, bristling.

"You mean Leo?" said Remington. "He's busy inside, but I'm on his team. I saw you coming, and I'm on my break, so."

"Saw me coming?" Mahmoud peered at the fence. "Through what?"

"Through the crow," said Remington, poking at the punctured bed-sheet on top of the pallet. "I see what he sees. He's my buddy."

Mahmoud grunted in skepticism. "Show me. Send him under the pallet and read me what is written on its wood."

The crow squawked irritably at this suggestion, but complied, hopping between the guardsmen's feet and under the wheeled conveyance. "That's funny," said Remington, giggling. "It says 'Restrooms This Way.'"

Mahmoud straightened, his head bobbling. "My young friend," he said, throwing an arm around Remington's shoulders, "your talents are wasted with these schemers. I have decided to relocate my business, moving back into the city I left so long ago, with your friend Eclair's watches as my passport. A man with a vision so limited as he would, of course, never be able to unload such finery, but I was once, let me say, well-placed in the economic structure of the city, and know just which wheels such items would grease. Soon, I will return to the position I held before my little misunderstanding with Caesar, and with a newfound and unstoppable momentum will I rise above it.

"In short, *yanni*, death is long, and we survive its passage only if we are willing to reinvent ourselves. I am going to places, do you understand?"

"Yeah, sure," said Remington, nodding as the bird settled in his skull. "You have to go to places, right?"

"Precisely. So go to places *with* me, boy. Tell Mahmoud what they pay you and your bird buddy, and Mahmoud will quintuple the number."

"Oh, *wow*! Quintuple is my favorite. But they don't pay me anything."

Mahmoud roared with laughter, clapping Remington on the back. "Easy to quintuple, then! Stick by me, boy, and you will be wealthier than you have ever imagined, all in the span of a single pay period."

"Hey, thanks! You're the most generous delivery guy ever. But I'm just going to take the stuff and stick with my friends. Here, let *me* pay *you*." Remington reached into his skull, where the watches had been pasted down with clay beneath a piece of folded paper. Pulling the packet loose, he counted its contents into Mahmoud's hand like giant coins. "One, two, and three," he said, then set off for the fence. "I'll open the gates, and you can wheel that stuff right in."

"There must be something that can sway you," called Mahmoud.

"Not really. See, I have to go to places, too. And they're closer than ever."

Mahmoud brightened upon inspecting the watches. "So be it," he said, stowing them in a pocket. "Here are the weapons, as promised, one gross, no more, no less, feel free to count them. Over here we have the armor, a rarer commodity, but you will find none so fine nor so plentiful in all the Armory." With a flourish, he threw back the bed-sheet.

A terrible screeching erupted as the fence was wrenched out of the earth, propelled by a force so powerful that Mahmoud's Guard froze in terror before its source had even been glimpsed. Once the creature bashed the tattered panels across the Plains, exposing itself to full view, several dropped their weapons and took off running, while the rest fell immediately to their knees, shouting the words "Last Man Standing" in half a dozen languages. As for Mahmoud, his body stopped trembling at once, locked in place by a rapt and unifying attention.

The Last Man Standing towered above the kneeling soldiers, a patchwork monument in rotting flesh. Its twenty legs were bundles of thighs and calves, each twice the length of a human leg, each ending in four feet joined at the heel, divided at the midpoint by a pair of hips like a giant knee from which a single severed hand extended, grasping and clawing, ready to defend. These legs were connected to a wide hoop of spines, giving the creature's undercarriage the appearance of a demented chandelier, above which rose a wall of torsos, a defensive girdle festooned with thrashing arms. This bulwark of flesh tapered upward for six feet, and near the top, sprouting from a smaller hoop, were four limbs like giant cables, each comprising five torsos stitched end to end, terminating in a gargantuan hand whose fingers were made of arms, whose knuckles were elbows, whose fingertips were the knotty hands of warriors.

These appendages tore into the piles of swords atop the pallet, each "finger" arming itself, so that the creature seemed to sprout steel claws. No preference was shown to these larger limbs: the creature armed itself evenly, passing swords from hand to hand and buckling armor to its extremities, exhibiting an eerie awareness of its entire mass.

Above it all, a bony clamp held Etienne in place, while Leopold, filleted to the bone at every joint and digit, rode in his harness on the opposite side, giggling shamelessly. Jacob dashed around the creature's feet, shouting directions, gesticulating, and being summarily ignored by the men at the top.

"Good thinking!" said Remington. "With both those guys up there, it can see in all directions at once. But how did you plug Leopold in without me?"

"I have no idea," said Jacob, staggering backwards. "I thought I'd check to see if he'd fit, but as soon as his bones touched the harness the whole thing lurched to its feet. Then it grabbed Etienne and plugged him in itself. It would appear that it's making its own connections now!"

"Mahmoud, old boy!" roared Leopold, his sunken eyes flashing twenty feet above the ground. Twisting his body in its harness, he swallowed the merchant in shadow. "So pleased you could make it," he said, his every word veined with hysterical glee. "I gather from your luggage that you've decided to take the trip down Bazakh way! Tell my city to expect me, won't you? I should arrive not long after you: all of me!" He shrieked with laughter, and every joint below him shook in sympathy, pressing him to new heights of hilarity.

"But of course, of course I will, my friend!" said Mahmoud, stowing his watches in his waistcoat as quickly as his trembling hand allowed. "But look at how late we've stayed, and with such a long trip ahead of us. Farewell, Mr. Eclair and friends: on behalf of Mahmoud's, may your swords serve you well.

"Boys!" he cried, but the eight warriors who hadn't fled refused to budge. They saluted the creature instead, barking out their allegiance in Plains-Deadish, and Mahmoud, cutting his losses, hobbled away without them, his backpack wiggling furiously as he dwindled.

"Last Man Standing, is that what they're calling it?" said Jacob. "Of course. What else could it be called by someone who's spent his afterlife hearing about a single man destined to conquer the Plains of War?"

"Now," said Leopold, sweeping his eyes over the hundred and forty-four swords shining in his hands, "let us cut a swath through the Plains, and through the minds of its denizens as well! You lot," he shouted down to the company, "try and keep up, eh? I want to see what these legs can do!" Beneath him, the Last Man Standing reared up and swung around in a great circle, pointing Leopold's face toward the south. He let out as mighty a roar as his single throat could manage and pounded forward, circled by the squawking crow. As the rest of the company, joined by Mahmoud's Guard, staggered ahead, Etienne gazed back at them over a seething wall of flesh, his lips pulled back from teeth so tightly clenched they cracked.

Since the Last Man's legs were twice the length of a normal man's, it moved at a clip that terrified the scattered souls in the Shallow End, as well as the company that lagged behind, for whom it was all too easy to imagine Leopold charging into the scrimmage and forgetting them in frenzy. However, as soon as that dark cloud of combat was near, the Last Man thrust its forelegs down and skidded to a stop, giving the company a chance to catch up.

Mahmoud's Guard stomped in lines of six on either side of the company, whom they seemed to revere as the creators of their hero. Thus protected, Remington and Jacob were able to focus their attention on keeping up with their companions, both of whom were loosing an increasingly barbaric series of yawps that seemed to begin and end at exactly the same moment.

"Whoa," said Remington after the loudest of these tandem screams. "Do you think they're all right up there?"

"Let's hope they're just getting into character," Jacob replied, but his unease was growing.

"Ah, Jacob," screamed Leopold as they approached, "you can't imagine what fun this is!" He swiveled his head toward the scrimmage, rubbing his swords together in eagerness. "And that was a mere appetizer. Now, my lovelies, let us feast!"

"Leo, can you see what I see?" said Etienne.

"Very nearly," said Leopold, "but the beast can see it *perfectly*!"

Without further discussion, the Last Man Standing thundered into the dust, followed by the Guardsmen, their blades and voices raised in fealty, and behind them the company, whose backs were pressed together in grim recollection of their last trek through the scrimmage. As he glanced ahead, however, Jacob's fear dissipated into awe as the accuracy of the creature's hundred-and-forty-four swords became apparent. It was sweeping its massive hands through clutches of warriors, carving through masses of bodies with ease. The company had no trouble following through the wide and gore-strewn path that the creature created, hearing everywhere amongst the human rubble the shout, "*Last Man!*"

"We're near White Gate now, Jacob," cried Etienne when he spotted the company in their wake, the giant hands below him shaking parts of men from their bladed fingers. "When we arrive, you must get me down; the lines are blurring in here, Jacob, do you understand?"

But before Jacob could reply, the Last Man Standing burst through the far side of the scrimmage, leading the company into the muted light of day, through which they stared at the bone-pale Southern Rim, where a cleft as slight as a hairline fracture was carved, concealing a long, crooked hallway in its shadow.

"The White Gate!" said Leopold, and the Last Man thundered toward it, the swords around its legs shaking like bangles.

The company, still terrified by the sounds of the scrimmage, clambered after the Last Man, stumbling and dragging one another up again. As they approached the crooked shadow in the Rim, Leopold called, "White City today, Dead City tomorrow, and then all the underworld shall be mine!" As the crow wheeled above, he shifted his vantage to the north, planning to repeat this promise in the direction of Lethe, and so Etienne was turned to see the dark mass of the Horde rushing out of the cleft in the Rim, crashing against the Last Man's flanks.

"It's them!" he cried, and then a pole was launched like a javelin straight through his mouth. As its sharpened end shot through the back of his skull, the three heads skewered on it slammed against his: Clay, Desi, and Gork were now jammed against him like olives on a toothpick, laughing and hollering as if the greatest moment of eternity had arrived.

Etienne screamed, and a great arm swept up and yanked the pole from his mouth, tossing it at Jacob's side.

"You traitorous balls of bone!" shouted Jacob. "You gave up our destination to these savages?"

"Come on, man, how much fun you think we get to *have* out here?" said Clay.

"All is fair in the love of war," said Desiderata.

"Mash!" said Gork.

Remington said nothing, but focused his attention on the crow, who was patiently feeding its vision to the boy. Adam and Eve, watching the action through Remington, stood tensed, waiting for an opening. With a few orders barked from their midst, the Horde surrounded the Last Man Standing, taking care to block the rest of the company from reaching White Gate.

Circling the Last Man's feet, the Hordesmen attacked, first singly, to test the strength and speed of their curious foe, and then, following orders uttered from various points in their ranks, in joint strikes: five warriors at once lashed out and were repelled. The Horde kept up their assault, methodically and precisely, until they'd located the weak points in the field of vision established by Etienne and Leopold's twisting heads, whereupon two warriors broke through the Last Man's defenses, each cleaving a minor arm from its knees.

Leopold roared in irritation and began spinning the Last Man around like a top, knocking two dozen Hordesmen to the earth, where they suffered nothing more than dust in their joints. Nor were the Last Man's precision strikes any more effective, for the Hordesmen either parried with their oversized weapons or took the hits directly, shedding a few inconsequential bones on impact, which they gathered up and fit back into their bodies like puzzle-pieces while their fellows provided cover.

"Leopold," said Etienne over his shoulder, "we won't take them with brute force."

"What in hell did we build a brute for, then?" cried Leopold, trying in vain to stomp a Hordesman beneath a four-soled foot.

"Listen! There are two things I noticed when we met the Horde. First, all their most effective moves are choreographed. Second, the only one of them who fell apart when she was struck was swinging her blade at the time."

"Meaning what?"

"Meaning," said Etienne, parrying five blows at once, "that we have to take their attacks until we've learned their moves, then strike when they're in the middle of a long one. They're skeletons, so every joint that isn't lashed together is held by will alone. If we hit them when that will is focused, they'll fall apart!"

At that moment, the Horde gave Etienne the opportunity to demonstrate, as the pike-bearer and his partner the swordsman initiated the same maneuver that had sent the stone-thrower flying. The pike-bearer leaped atop his partner's shoulders while a third man stood before them, ready to act as the fulcrum — but this time, as the pike lunged to strike the Last Man in the foot, a great arm shot out and sprayed the pike-bearer's bones into the Rim. As his jabbering skull rebounded, Etienne crushed it beneath one foot, provoking the Horde to pummel the Last Man's midriff with a complex and increasingly furious series of maneuvers, causing a slow wave of body parts to fall.

This escalation, while it won the Horde a few limbs from the Last Man's lower regions, exhausted their repertoire of maneuvers in a more expedient and methodical fashion than Etienne had dared to hope for.

"They're repeating themselves," shrieked Leopold. "They're repeating themselves!"

"At last," growled Etienne. "The small one feints. The large one leaps. The two behind spin over and smash. We've seen it all. We know their maneuvers now. We know them. We *know* them!"

"He doesn't sound good," said Remington.

Jacob shivered: Etienne's voice had retaken the ragged timbre of his first coherent moments in the cave. "We know them," he was chanting, "we *know* them."

Leopold joined the refrain. Together, they roared, "We *know* them. We *know* them. We *know* them! The Last Man Standing *knows* them in our *bones*!"

"Our?" said Remington.

"We've made a mistake," said Jacob. "We've got to get them out of there as soon as we can. Their minds are being assimilated by the creature's will!"

In a single rhythm, the two men loosed a grand, unhinged cackle as the body below them set about dismantling their opponents with a synergy that was startling to behold, picking apart every recycled attack with the four gigantic arms it had heretofore held over the fray. Bones sprayed in shards and clusters from the Hordesmen, and the tiny bands of metal that once held their joints together rolled and clattered underfoot.

The Last Man's twin-throated voice was raised in victory, but even as it howled, the little reaper, who had not yet been dismantled, ran toward it from a distance of several yards, tossing herself to the ground at the last moment and skidding between two of its massive legs.

"This is it," shouted Remington, and the crow dove into the great cavity inside the Last Man's body in time to see the little reaper climbing up its innards. Cursing, she locked her legs in place around two torsos and started hacking with two push-daggers at a column of spines. The crow heard the Last Man shriek as four of its legs went limp at once, sending its body listing to one side, and before the remnants of the Horde began to cheer, the reaper launched herself to the next column and set to work.

"Get ready," said Remington, but Adam and Eve were already in motion. As Mahmoud's Guard sprung into motion, distracting the remaining Hordesmen with their bellowing attack, the headless duo tossed themselves under the Last Man's legs, sliding out of Remington's field of vision and into the crow's. Astride the creature's second spinal column, the little reaper glanced down at them in surprise, a mistake from which she would never recover, for in the moment it took her to admit that she was being attacked by two decapitated opponents, they had already overtaken her.

While the reaper struck with both daggers at Adam's arms, Eve brought two balled fists down on her back with such force that her skeleton burst. Adam, though his arms were cut to the bone, tossed reaper-pieces through the holes hacked out of the Last Man's body. Before the reaper's stained little skull succumbed to hack-shock, her conquerors climbed through one of these openings into the Plains, where the Last Man Standing was bashing the last few Hordesmen into rattling bits.

While the bones were being scattered, Jacob strode toward the shadow of White Gate, slipping into a crevice so narrow that he could not fully spread his arms. He walked down that crooked hall alone, trying to ignore the sounds coming from atop the creature, needing urgently to be the first of the company to see White City.

This was his moment. Whatever Leopold and Etienne were suffering could be fixed, but Jacob had waited too long to delay his triumph. He plunged deeper, following the swaying and twisting of the path until it ended abruptly in a massive slab of white stone. Laying his hands on its unyielding face, he grunted in irritation, then shrugged off his knapsack, hoping to find a tool that would aid in his ascent.

Before he'd opened its flap he saw the ropes tumbling down the walls. In moments, they were taut with the white-headed, dark-robed weight of debtors. Jacob held up his hands, his jaw working silently as scores of them swarmed the hallway. A gabbling gang peered down from the Rim, where dozens, hundreds, *thousands* of debt-stamped skulls were amassed high above the Plains, stretching as far as the eye could see, every one of them staring at Jacob.

Staggering back against the Gate, he glimpsed a dark skull among the white ones. It was the compact form of the Leather Masker, rattling a pair of dice in one gloved hand.

Jacob screamed for help, thinking that at any moment the Last Man Standing would grind these soft bodies into paste, for these were no Plainsmen, only unarmed debtors. Then he heard the twinned bellow of Leopold and Etienne, and the thunder of the Last Man's bulk slamming against the mouth of the crevice, which was far too narrow to let that body through.

"It isn't me," he blurted in desperation. "I'm not the one you're looking for. I've stolen nothing from you; it was —"

But the debtors had already pinned Jacob's back against the Gate and yanked his corduroy trousers down. A cheer went up when Leopold's cock sprang up below his belly. Jacob, whose limbs went as limp as they had when he'd been bisected, was trussed up and hauled on the end of a rope to the top of the Rim, where the mass of debtors passed him hand over hand, away from the tall Gate of White City.

III

CHAPTER TWELVE

In the Box

The thousands of debtors who lined the Rim in two tidy rows tossed Jacob's hog-tied body southward like a sack of cargo toward a ship. As their skulls flashed past he wondered whether he'd join them in indenture, or if the Magnate had something even less palatable in mind. Leopold's crimes were surely grievous enough to earn disintegration.

Regardless, they couldn't very well punish Jacob for his partner's transgressions. He'd explain, and they'd see that he was an innocent.

But as he prepared the story in his mind, it occurred to him that he'd known full well where the watches had come from when they'd been traded for his monster's armaments, and the theft hadn't bothered him then.

The guilt was his, after all. Treason halved was still treason.

A strange noise tore him from his thoughts, a polyphonic bark rippling through the ranks of debtors, whipping past him before he could comprehend it. The debtors were speaking almost in unison, passing a message from the Torn Curtain to White Gate in some unfamiliar dialect of Deadish.

He stared over the flat top of the Rim, finding that his peculiar mode of transportation granted him lurching glimpses into the desert beyond the Plains, where a dust storm roiled, wider than his eyes could take in.

The debtors around him remained hidden from the eyes of the Plainsmen as they'd hidden from the company, by keeping away from the Rim's inner edge. They had eyes on the floor of the Plains, though: Jacob was tossed past a debtor lying on his belly, peering down at the floor of the Plains through a telescope, his head camouflaged by a dusty blanket.

They must have dozens of spies up here, he thought as he spotted another. They were keeping watch for the Last Man Standing.

Hope kindled in his heart, for the company could pass easily through the Torn Curtain and overtake his captors long before they reached Dead City.

But the Masker knew as much. Why, then, was he transporting his prisoner so openly?

A second message passed through the debtors, traveling in the opposite direction this time, a single phrase leaping from one throat to the next in the same thoughtless, reflexive way they were heaving his body, moving more quickly by mouth than he could be passed by hand.

It's like a disciplined game of telephone, he thought, and then he was hurled face-first off the edge of the Rim.

He broke his fall on a scaffold outside of the Torn Curtain, made of warped, wine-dark wood connected by ladders of rope, rubber, and chain. Its surfaces, like the desert below, swarmed with debtors.

Four of them surrounded Jacob. He stared through their legs at the sloping desert rock to the north, where hundreds of thousands of skulls snaked past the horizon.

"All this for a handful of watches?" he said as he was rolled onto his back.

"Don't know much about the Masker, do ya?" said one of the four.

"Them's the crown jewels you stole," said another, holding Jacob down with her foot while the others unfolded a bed-sheet. "King's got to chase his jewels."

"Whate'er the price," said the third, tying the corners of the sheet onto bamboo poles driven into the platform.

"Such is the weight of sovereignty," said the last, arranging the sheet like a tent around them.

They huddled together to inspect him, drawing so close that their skulls knocked together. Jacob recoiled in irrational fear as their skulls grinned down over the corrupted flesh of their throats.

"Right-o," said one, jabbing a thumb at his neighbor, "he's closest to your height."

They rolled Jacob over and untied his bonds.

"Time to play dress-up," said the debtor so selected, pulling his robe over his head while the others yanked off Jacob's clothes.

"What will stripping me naked achieve?" cried Jacob, terrified by the prospect of seeing Leopold's legs sutured to his torso. It hadn't been long ago, but he'd all but completely blocked out the memory of their merging.

"You should know, you gave the Masker the idea." Catching Jacob's trousers in the air, the debtor pulled them on, clucking as he wiggled his finger through a hole in the pocket.

"Our co-worker here will be your decoy," said the debtor working Jacob's shirt open. "We brought you this far in case your friends was watching. Now, if they follow, it's the decoy they'll chase, while the Masker takes you the back way."

"But they travel with the beast," said Jacob as the decoy pulled on his shirt. "The Last Man Standing is armed with a hundred shining swords. If you take me, you'll never walk again!"

"That's the plan," said the decoy, tucking in his shirttails. "A debtor disassembled in the line of duty joins the Order of the Ossuary. Thereafter he is carried about on a velvet pillow according to his whim. Every debtor on this detail hopes to be 'hacked up'; your friends will be doing us a service if they catch us."

They lifted Jacob to his feet, pinning his arms behind his back. One of them paused, noticing the little leather pouch tied around his wrist and squeezing it suspiciously. "What's this, then?" he asked, tugging at its strings and peering inside. "Ech. Nothing here but dust and rubble."

Jacob ground his teeth, but kept silent. He'd long forgotten about Ma Kicks' severed finger, which must have been pulverized in its pouch while Jacob fought in the scrimmage. He felt a stab of guilt that he'd allowed it to be destroyed.

Leaving the pouch where it dangled, one of the debtors brought a rusted razor blade to his throat. "Never mind. Let's make this pretty face shine," she cooed, sweeping the razor around his neck, where the skin parted like tissue paper. "Would you look at that? We don't even have to scrub!" Sinking her fingers into his hair, she pulled off the loose sheath of his face and tugged it down gingerly over the decoy's skull.

"How do I look?" said the decoy through Jacob's lips, adjusting the skin until the eye-holes lined up just so.

"You're a vision."

"The spit and image of the Clock-Thief!"

"With one obvious exception."

There was a somber pause while they examined the object of Leopold's pride.

"Are we meant to take it?"

"What if the Masker wants it?"

"Don't be daft. It's a defining characteristic, isn't it?" said the decoy. "That's what he said: 'Make a costume of his defining characteristics.' Off it comes!"

"Then it's on your head if the Masker's displeased."

Jacob couldn't tell which was more disturbing: the sight and sound of Leopold's erection being torn from his body, or the howl of wounded pride that spilled from his own throat at its loss. It isn't mine, he thought frantically, it isn't even mine. But all the fight had left him by the time the cock had been securely stuffed down the decoy's new corduroys. Stunned and silent, Jacob was dressed in cast-off robes, bound by the wrists, and hustled out of the tent. His doppelgänger trudged in the opposite direction, toward the ladders at the front of the scaffold, hanging his head in mock shame as the debtor behind him played warden.

"You look dapper now," she said as she and her partner shoved Jacob back onto the Rim. "Let's hope the Maskers' Council has pity on you and throws your skull in the bogs. It would be a shame if they ground it down, shapely as it is!"

They pushed Jacob through the double line of debtors on the outer edge of the Rim, out of sight of the scrimmage. When White Gate rose high above their heads, they passed him into the custody of the thirteen debtors awaiting his arrival, whose leader, a gangly corpse with pale, clean, and ceaselessly expressive hands, took hold of Jacob's ropes with relish.

"*Il arrive!*" he crowed. "To you we extend our welcome, Monsieur Clock-Thief. Boys, down the plank for our guest!"

As the others laid a board across the chasm, this enthusiastic debtor twisted Jacob's ropes this way and that, hoping to force from him a cry expressive of the misery of bondage. He could not oblige: there was nothing left in his chest.

Jacob's captor drove him across the plank covering the chasm before White Gate, over the site of his capture and onto the western edge of the Rim, where the path became uneven as the foothills of the Wall of the World thrust into the Plains. Ahead, towering flanks of rock closed off the rampart entirely, and although Jacob couldn't fathom how the debtors intended to climb these obstructions, he focused on keeping his footing.

In the midst of the path stood a rickety cage on six bicycle wheels, the remnant of some century-old circus, its rotting frame reinforced with planks and straightened nails. Long chains attached to rubber loops trailed from the front, and a metal trunk was hitched to the rear. A prisoner was already inside, a teenaged girl of whom so little remained that he hesitated even to think of her as a corpse.

Jacob's captor drove him onto a sloping shelf of rock above the box, then shoved him through a trap-door in its roof. He fell bodily to the floor not a foot from the girl.

"Please to meet your new roommate," said the debtor, pacing before the bars. "I would make your introduction, but you I only know as Clock-Thief, and she have no name at all: she must have run away into *le Désert du Sable Mobile* when we arrive here. The sandy storm scrub off her cloth, her skin, even the debt-stamp on her skull, then send her running back into our arms, *comme un poulet plumé!* This traitor, let us call her Mademoiselle Squelette."

Jacob shoved himself as far from her as the cage would allow, overcome by a horror of all that naked bone. For her part, the girl seemed not to have noticed him at all. She sat cross-legged, and her bones, unlike those of the Hordesmen, were so perfectly white that it looked as if she'd just been scrubbed — which she likely had, Jacob supposed, if she'd been lost in the sandstorms of the Moving Desert long enough to lose her flesh.

"She have run from her debt, a crime most full of shame, and for this she will have the biggest punishment available. We shall see her ground down — *oui*, down to the very *dust!*"

Jacob jumped as an inexplicable noise emerged from her empty frame.

The skeleton girl giggled.

"She also is quite mad," said the debtor. "I think it must be the sandy storm still moving about in her head. If she attack you, please be welcome to break her bone.

"Now please to wait here, eh? Go nowhere!" The debtor trotted off, whistling as he went, leaving Jacob alone with the skeleton girl.

Hours passed. Boredom trickled between them like drizzling rain. Jacob could hear the debtors moving and barking, preparing their departure, he supposed, but could see nothing but bare rock and the girl.

For a time, Jacob couldn't look directly at her. Her gleaming bones reminded him that he was on his way to disassembly, that his quest was dissolving, moment by moment, in this acidic silence. And how disgusting it was to see an entire skeleton, up-close and utterly unclothed, lacking the promise of impending preservation, without even the meager accessories of a Hordesman! He lifted his hands to his face to shield himself, however briefly, from the sight of her, but upon feeling his fingertips clack against bone, he realized that his skull was as naked as hers. Ashamed, he was attempting to summon the bravery to greet her when he spotted a sudden lurching on the path and froze in place.

It was the Leather Masker tumbling down the path like some rotting primate — loose, compact limbs flailing under his robe, skull hidden away behind a luchador mask embroidered with a second, stylized skull, nothing of his body visible but grinning teeth and empty eye sockets. In moments he'd rolled up to the cage and pounced onto its bars, slapping gloved hands around them, turning his head sideways to peer within.

"So this is 'im, Jean-Luc? The Clock-Thief 'imself?" He snorted, and Jacob was afraid, not that the Masker would attack him, but that in his tumbling and growling and snuffling he would ferret out the truths that Jacob was hiding. A terrible question occurred to him: what would they do if they learned of Remington's talents? Even if they'd witnessed the monster's construction, they clearly hadn't drawn the right conclusions. Were Remington captured, would he resist, or could he, in his naïveté, be convinced to make something even more monstrous than the Last Man Standing?

With a sudden resolve, Jacob promised himself that they'd never find out. Leopold and Etienne were already suffering for his mistakes; he'd not add Remington to that list.

The Leather Masker pointed a gloved finger at his face. "This is 'im who's cost us all this effort — and what is 'e now that 'e's 'ere? No master criminal, just another turd circlin' the bottom of the bowl." Clanging a fist across the bars, he shouted, "Perk up there, Clock-Thief! We'll require a better show than this, after all we've spent."

"He does not know, Monsieur," said Jean-Luc. "He does not know what time and care you have put into his capture. But I think he should!"

"Jean-Luc thinks you should," said the Leather Masker, tumbling onto the dusty path, where he sprawled extravagantly, digging a hand into his robes. "I guess 'e's got a point," he said, pulling out a pair of dice and rattling them in one hand. "Probably curious 'ow we even knew to look for your knob, innit? Thought you were so careful."

"It was I who discover this detail," said Jean-Luc, strutting around the Masker, who began rolling his dice repeatedly in the dirt. "My master, the Gambler, it was he who put me in charge of searching your clock-tower, for it seem impossible to him that the ringer himself should simply disappear — with no face, and a debt-stamp right in his forehead? *Impossible*! So I inspect every last pebble within, and am finally bother by this hole in the wall you know so well. 'A window to nowhere,' I say, 'and the only escape for our Clock-Thief.' So I volunteer to climb down into the dark, and there I find the hole you have beat out of the stone!"

"Cracked that tower right open, so we did," growled the Masker, still busy with his dice, "and found both 'alves of the ringer you broke in two. That's a treason right there, desecratin' the corpse of one of the Magnate's own debtors! Spoke 'ighly of your bravery, 'e did, but not so 'ighly of your aim."

"You see," said Jean-Luc, "when you pull off his head, you shoot at this window to nowhere, and you miss — and this is when his head roll between your legs, giving him a look up your robe at your *protubérance*! Oh, if only you had wore some trouser, Monsieur, you would be free today."

The Masker scooped up his dice and tumbled to his feet. "Looked all about for the man with a statue for a cock, so we did. Nearly 'ad you in the Tunnels, too. You escaped for the nonce, but snarin' you was a mere matter of persistence.

"Built us a raft 'alf as wide as Lethe. Brung out thousands of debtors from the Pool to tug it upstream, enough to canvass the underworld twice over, should we 'ave needed to. Them 'eadless decoys by the cave were a lovely touch, but we'd an army to conduct our search. And now 'ere we are. And 'ere are you. And now I want to know, Leopold." The Masker leapt at the bars. "Ah, yes, we know your name! John Tanner gave you up, with joy."

"Tanner?" said Jacob, infuriated by the very mention of his competitor's name.

"That's got 'im goin'!" barked the Masker to Jean-Luc. "Aye, John Tanner, whose name you'd given as your own in the Crowded Car, offered up all we needed to know. Except for one damn thing that's been botherin' me all this while. Wormin' in and out of me skull until me sane 'alf's gone 'alfway barmy." He rapped his gloved knuckles against his masked skull. Jacob heard a rattle, and wondered if the man's head were stuffed full of dice. "All I want to know, Clock-Thief, and the only thing that will 'elp me reckon what to *do* with you now, is the answer to one question:

"Why?"

"*Oui, pourquoi?*" Jean-Luc echoed, striding to the Masker's side. "*Pourquoi?*"

Jacob stared at them, trembling. "Why — why what, exactly?"

They exchanged an incredulous glance. "Why'd you take the bloody watches? T'was a damn fool thing to do. And I'm an expert on the subject of damn fool things, as anyone who knows me knows. You might 'ave gambled your lifetime on a throw when you was moments dead — leastways, that's the rumor — but *I* gambled *eternity* to get where I am. Every stinkin' grain of sand in the glass." He rattled the dice in one gloved fist. "And knowin' a thing or two about gambles, I know that every gambler 'as 'is reasons. Secrets 'e whispers to Fortuna, 'oping she'll choose '*im* from the crowd. So tell me, Clock-Thief, one fool to another. Why'd you do it?"

Jacob's mind had seized, offering no answer to this question. "A moment. A moment to gather my thoughts."

The Masker grunted. "S'pose we're 'ardly in an 'urry."

In the overlong pause that followed, one truth emerged: Jacob's continued existence, and that of his companions, depended upon how he answered this question.

His mind raced. He had no way of knowing why Leopold had stolen from the Magnate, beyond an obvious hunger for power. And there was no point in trying to convince these men that he wasn't Leopold, as Leopold's unique genitalia had provided them with all the evidence they'd require.

The truth wouldn't help him now. Anything remotely resembling it would lead them, in time, to Remington.

He was shaking by the time the Leather Masker disengaged from the bars of his cage and plopped down in the dirt, resuming his incessant rolling. Something about the action caught Jacob's eye, some oddly insistent precision. It reminded him of the way Ma Kicks had rolled her own dice, so full of intent, and more: full of *ritual*. Then he heard the Leather Masker muttering a number under his breath before each roll, and saw his body stiffen with triumph when the dice matched his guess.

Jacob had his answer.

"Why does any gambler roll the dice?" he said, taking to his feet in an imitation of Leopold's confident strut. "That's the question, isn't it? Why does any man gamble, and were my reasons any different from those of the braying crowd at Caesar's?" He knelt close to the bars, pushing his skull against them to peer down at his captor. "Which is another way of asking: are yours?"

The Leather Masker scooped up his dice, cocking his head.

"It may occur to us that we can't control the choices we take," Jacob went on, "but that doesn't mean we *believe* it. Instead, we have faith in chaos — faith that the dice we throw will fall at random — or we turn Fortune into our goddess, hoping that our behavior might sway her whims in our favor. But you're too wily for either of those excuses, and so am I."

The Leather Masker shook his head, and resumed his rolling. "Audacious, I'll give you that. Comparin' yourself to me, with your feet a-thumpin' on the gallows floor!"

"I'd already be swinging if you hadn't made the comparison yourself," said Jacob, steadying as he warmed to his role. "It's clear after moments of meeting you that you understand what *really* governs the pips on those dice. What appears to be chance, or the caprice of a goddess, isn't random at all. It's physical. The way those dice fall depends upon a host of minute forces: gravity, air pressure, irregularities in their shape and weight, the way they sit in your fingers, the angle of your hand when you toss them, the force, the spin, the surface of the ground itself. Thus, winning is not an art, but a science so maddeningly precise that no ordinary man could hope to learn it in his lifetime.

"But you're no ordinary man. And you have far more than a lifetime at your disposal. You can throw those dice for the rest of history. You can throw them until you master every variable on that long list, and then, in the end, chaos will have no choice but to serve you.

"Just like a god."

The Leather Masker stopped rolling. He left the dice in the dirt and crept, with uncommon care, to the side of the cage. "And?" he rumbled. "What's any of that 'ave to do with you, Clock-Thief?"

"With — with me? Right. Of course." Jacob had been so excited by his idea that he'd utterly forgotten where it was leading. Having nothing in reserve, he focused on saving his hide. "I ask only for the chance to serve you, at — at the side of chaos. Let me be your acolyte. Let me be your worshiper. Above all, let me continue to *be*." Falling to his knees, he grasped the bars, desperately hoping that theatricality would save him where his wits had failed. "Don't grind me to dust, my liege, I beg of you!"

The Leather Masker stood perfectly still. Jean-Luc was watching, rubbing his hands together slowly.

That's it, thought Jacob, I've bungled it. Imagining his body broken beneath the weight of the Pestle, he was on the verge of dropping the act when the Leather Masker began to chuckle.

"What, the Mortar and Pestle, that's what you're on about? Punitive deconstruction and that? You surprise me, Clock-Thief. After all this time and energy spent, you think we'd just grind you up and toss the remains into an ashtray? You'll not be so lucky, I'm afraid!" Scooping up his dice, he clapped Jean-Luc on the back, sending the lanky debtor sprawling. "We've got somethin' special planned for this one, 'aven't we?"

"Of course, Monsieur!" his lackey cried, scrambling up again.

"Right, then — saddle up!"

Jean-Luc fell to the task with relish, arranging eleven other debtors in two rows beside himself, where they began, in two rows of harnesses, to pull. The Gambler trailed behind the cage, stopping every so often to roll his dice and mutter, and Jacob, exhausted and with no idea whether he'd succeeded or failed, fell to the floor of his cage.

The road flattened as it approached one of the great, vertical flanks of the Wall of the World. Jean-Luc urged the debtors to bring the box as close to the end of the path as they could, then had them remove their harnesses. He and the Masker squatted in conference beside the Wall, consulting a yellowed scrap of paper on which a kind of constellation was drawn. At length, the debtors were arranged in a bizarre configuration before the bare rock, standing on one another's backs and shoulders, forming towers and pyramids with their bodies and stretching their arms to their utmost limits in order to reach those tiny, barely visible indentations that were their goal.

"Very good," said Jean-Luc when all were arranged just so, "and we depress on *trois. Un, deux, trois!*"

A loud click was followed by a bassy rumbling as a slab of mountainside shuddered behind a well-disguised seam, opening a dank tunnel through the rock. As Jean-Luc hollered, his debtors secured their harnesses and lumbered into the dark. Jean-Luc took the lead, inspecting the ground ahead for cracks and pits.

Jacob stared as the Masker led the way, feeling surprisingly little relief. There was no point in wondering what would come when they returned to the city: his existence was now completely beyond his control. He laid back on the floor of the cage, staring up at the roof of the tunnel until it melted into sky.

Days passed, maybe weeks. All the ground the company had covered on the current of the River Lethe passed by again, this time at a snail's pace. His captors left him alone, and his fleshless neighbor never moved.

The silence became oppressive. Hating the sight of the debtors, disturbed by the very presence of the Leather Masker, depressed by the slowly-passing landscape, he began to stare, unabashedly, at the skeleton girl.

He'd thought of her as his mirror, but he couldn't ignore their differences any longer. She'd been sitting perfectly still for miles and miles of bumpy road, while Jacob couldn't keep himself from fidgeting. Every time his mind wandered, he caught his right hand picking at the skin that drooped from his throat, loosened by the knife of the debtors who'd taken his face. Each time he saw a bit of his own flesh pinched between thumb and forefinger, he gasped in disgust, tossed it through the bars, and tried his best to emulate the skeleton girl's stillness.

After unconsciously tearing another hunk from his throat, he slapped his hands on the cage's wooden floor and said, more loudly than he'd meant to, "However do you sit so still for so terribly *long*?"

The skeleton girl didn't budge. For a moment he was afraid he'd offended her. Then boredom drove his fingers back to his neck.

"I'm asking out of genuine curiosity," he said, grasping his right wrist in his left hand and forcing it into his lap. "It's a talent I've never mastered. Stillness, that is. I get uncomfortable, and then I start to move. As if action, any action whatsoever, might save me from the void. You're familiar with the sensation, I assume?" He stared at her placid skull. "Or perhaps not."

Scooting closer, he dropped his voice to a whisper. "It's this feeling of being trapped. Which we are, of course. It's driving me a bit batty. Were there only a sandstorm at hand, I might well follow your example!" He drummed his fingers on the floor, giving her an opportunity to respond. "The last time I felt this way was something of a turning point for me. There was a drought in the city, and — well, I suppose it wasn't as bad as this. But it *seemed* just as awful, being trapped in my apartment for months on end, without a thing to keep me occupied. I *gave* myself something to do, of course: I tidied, until I couldn't tidy any more. Then I started, well, making little figurines from everything I could put my hands on. Little people, you see, people I could pretend to preserve. I built them from scraps of wood and cloth at first. The scraps didn't last long, so I whittled down an entire chair and cut a fine, black jacket into ribbons. When *that* was gone, I improvised. It was filthy, I suppose, but I won't lie to you, I did it. I unbuttoned my shirt and began to pick my chest apart. The flesh there had never been properly preserved, you see, so it had gone soft, then hard again. Perfectly pliable, with a sort of rind on the outside. I made an army of little men out of it, little

Jacobs, and it was diverting enough, I'll admit, until I looked down at the ruin. *Bones* showing. *Ribs* grinning up at me like wide-spaced teeth. I buttoned up and started pacing, promising to leave myself alone, but worrying that if the drought didn't end *immediately* I'd literally tear myself to pieces. The truth is that I would have, had I not heard a voice through the window. *Blessings*! it cried, and that's when things changed for me. When I started on this path toward the Lands Above. Which I suppose I'm not on any longer."

He slumped. One of the cart's wheels was squeaking relentlessly. "It was a similar feeling to this one, at any rate. This queer, fidgety desperation, which I'm reminded, every time I look across this box and see you, that you're not feeling at all! That is, if you're feeling it, you're certainly not fidgeting. And yet they call you a madwoman, and you must be, mustn't you, if you walked into that desert? But perhaps you learned something in there about — I don't know, about perseverance? About surviving eternity with such stoicism?

"Tell me. Your stillness. Your silence. How do you do it?"

She said nothing. She moved nothing.

"Very well. You're well within your rights, aren't you." He shoved himself away, over to what he'd come to think of as his side of the cage. "Keeping shtum. Keeping your bloody secrets. Lord knows I'm keeping mine." Before he knew what he was doing, he'd shoved himself back, hissing, "I'll tell you one of them. I'm innocent. Of the theft of the watches, at least. I'm not even a thief. I'm someone else altogether! I'm Jacob Campbell, not Leopold l'Eclair. How do you like that? Does it amuse you? To know that you'll be sentenced next to someone who's only being punished because of a prank of happenstance? It's unjust. It's a travesty. But what isn't, really?"

That wheel again. It squeaked three times per revolution. Jacob looked down. Another scrap of desiccated flesh lay between his fingers. He flung it, banging his fist on the floor. "I actually imagined myself alive, you know. In my apartment. I was tearing my chest apart with my own hands, yes, but what I'd have *preferred*, what I actually *wanted*, was living flesh in its place. Some instinct I didn't recognize, some psychological quirk conferred by death. Blood and muscle steaming as they gave way beneath my fingers, that's what

I saw. Had I been able to find my living self, to stand before that reckless little idiot, what satisfaction I'd take in killing him again!" He covered his teeth with his hands. "What a thing to say, I know. And yet, I'm somehow sure that every last corpse in the Land of the Dead can sympathize. That this is part of why we never speak of life. We hate it, don't we? We hate the living, at least. And I wonder, I really do, if that feeling of vengeance, of violent, annihilating hatred toward my own body, toward any creature with the audacity to breathe while I am forced to be endlessly dead, is somehow related to the urge that drove you to walk into that sandstorm." He took his torn skin in his hand with purpose, for once. "This flesh, which I've wasted so much of my afterlife preserving, would finally fall away. I'd be free of it at last. I'd be at peace, wouldn't I? Like you."

"You want to?" said the skeleton girl.

Jacob, startled, flung himself away from her. The debtors stopped, glaring at him. "Sorry!" he cried.

She tilted her head. "Seriously. Would you like to check it out? Being at peace, I mean."

Jacob laughed. "Yes," he said. "Yes, I really would." He let go of his ruptured neck. "Let's just ask them if we can get off at the next rest stop, shall we?"

"We don't need anyone's permission!" She had a voice like a flute, lilting and easy. "After all, neither of us is who they think we are." With startling speed, she stood. "I know some people who might be able to help you get all those knots untied. They couldn't help me, but they might be just right for you."

"Kn — knots?"

Their captors had stopped again, more agitated this time, hollering and waving their hands. "Get 'er down!" roared the Leather Masker.

"Knots, man! Knots in your story. It's like you're following a string through this giant labyrinth, and where it leads is somewhere amazing. You just got a little tangled up on the way."

"Be seated!" Jean-Luc approached the box, banging on its bars with his fist. "You must be seated!" he cried. "Enough of this senseless resistance! *Garçons*, procure the disciplinary measure."

"I'm happy to discuss these knots at length," said Jacob, holding tight to his knees. "Just be seated, I beg you!"

"Whatever for?" said the skeleton girl. "They call me Bone-maiden, by the way. What we're going to do now, Jacob, is take you to White City. And if Shailesh is angrier when I return than he was when I left, well, I'll just have to put him over my knee."

"Did you say White City?" said Jacob.

"Well, sure. Did you really think I was a debtor?"

Their captors were pulling long poles lashed to serrated blades from the trunk at the rear of the cage. As they jammed them through the bars, Jacob crawled towards the middle of the cage, rolling his body into a ball to escape those toothsome edges. "Oh, do sit down," he cried, "before we're in bits!"

"Stop squealing, Jacob, just tell me you're in."

"If you know of some way to instantly whisk us out of this cage and over the miles to White City, then yes, I'm in!"

"Perfect," said the Bonemaiden, lifting herself onto one toe and whirling around so quickly that her tiny frame became a white blur. A tremendous crack assailed Jacob's ears, and the Bonemaiden stopped, the bones of her fingers and forearms whipping back into place as a great many things clattered to the ground. The bars of the cage and the bladed ends of the poles had all been severed neatly in the middle, and the roof of the box crashed to one side, to the great surprise of the debtors.

"Grab 'em, damn you!" shouted the Leather Masker.

"Let's skedaddle," said the Bonemaiden, sweeping Jacob over her shoulder and leaping over the bisected bars of the box. The debt-ors charged at her, and with a series of motions so fluid that Jacob's body hardly jiggled, she knocked them all to the ground.

As Jean-Luc and the Masker struggled to climb over the heap of debtors, the little skeleton with the corpse on her shoulder dashed out of sight.

CHAPTER THIRTEEN

Bonemaiden

The process of quickening, from the first stirrings of awareness to the final coordination of will necessary to walk, generally took between one and three days, during which an immigrant worked ceaselessly, desperately, toward motion. Watching one's finger twitch in the mud for eight solid hours before it could be moved had a way of permanently lowering one's expectations, and by the time a corpse was up and staggering, he had abandoned all living notions of physical agency and accepted the speed of death as a sluggish, unalterable constant.

The Bonemaiden was a revelation. Even the Hordesmen, unencumbered by flesh and faster by far than Jacob and his cohort, had been slower than a living human in good repair, but the Bonemaiden, even freighted with a passenger, made those warriors look like listing zombies.

Where others lurched, she danced; where others lumbered, she flew; and as she bounded over the heads of the pedestrians they passed, they hardly had time to notice.

Nor was speed the greatest of her qualities; her feather-light frame moved so gracefully and with such elasticity that it was easy to overlook how little she relied on conventional notions of human anatomy. She could expand and contract as she wished, allowing space to blossom between her joints to lengthen a stride into a vault. Her legs could swing freely around her hips to avoid obstacles, then join into a single, flexible bundle of bones that robbed her landings of their ability to jolt. In fact, Jacob, though he was slung over her shoulder, experienced so little turbulence as she ran that it cost him some effort to shake off his wonder in favor of a sense of indignation he felt was well-deserved, and by the time he'd cried out in tones strident enough to earn her attention, the city was far behind them.

"Mercy!" he cried. "Murder! Mutiny! Slow down; stop altogether! Bonemaiden, you must put me down!"

Without slowing a whit, the Bonemaiden flipped him into the air and caught him neatly in her open arms. "Now, Jacob, you agreed to this," she said. "We're going to get you to White City, remember? Anyway, we already ran away, so it's kind of late to back out."

"But we're heading in the wrong direction! You're galloping upstream, away from the Plains. I still have friends there. Friends who are in a good bit of trouble because of me." Briefly, he filled her in on the company's adventures, which seemed not to surprise her. "I can't just abandon them now, not after what I've put them through."

"I'm not asking you to." The Bonemaiden patted his back, as if his mood might have been caused by trapped gas. "*Habibi*, there's a line of debtors running all the way from Dead City to the Plains of War, okay? Now, if we go that way, too, we're going to have to fight them all, and I don't have the patience. Even if they give up halfway, they'll still be lurking behind rocks and reporting on every little thing we do, and I, for one, could use a break from being watched."

"But this is the wrong direction!"

"See, I have a theory that the underworld is round, like the Earth. If I'm right, we can just go around!"

Jacob spluttered, and the Bonemaiden burst out laughing. "Oh, Jacob, you are a goose! Haven't you heard of the Bazakh Bypass? It's the way all the warriors and merchants go. The northern entrance is up ahead, by the mouth of Lethe." Thrusting her legs out before her, she skidded to a halt, sending a sibilant curtain of dirt into the river. "Here, you can even walk the rest of the way, since you love your creaky legs so much. We've got enough of a lead on those debtors for now."

Jacob, climbing out of her arms and onto the ground, began walking forward, though he was painfully aware of how slowly she had to go to keep from outpacing him.

"You're a funny guy," she said as they strode up the riverside, cleaving ever closer to the Wall of the World. "Great big plans, but what a lot of fuss you make along the way! I'm not trying to be antagonistic," she added before he could protest, "just making an observation in the spirit of openness, because I think we should be better friends, and I'm very open with my friends. Also in that spirit, you ought to know my proper name, which is Siham."

"Siham," said Jacob. "Thank you. That will, I believe, help me to think of you more as a person."

Siham stopped short, drumming her fingers on her hips. "Do tell. How do you think of me now?"

"I've never — well, look, you're not exactly — Siham, you pirouetted, and the whole damn cage fell apart! My companions on this journey have exhibited all manners of strange behavior, from eccentric to downright freakish, but nothing I've seen or done could have prepared me for that. I'm at a loss to explain it. Did you cut through those bars with nothing at all? With what, with the power of your mind? Or is it as the Plainsmen suggested? They call your people witches, you must know that, and while I don't want to believe in what sounds like utter nonsense — well, I'm at a loss for a likely explanation," he said again, kicking a rock into the water.

"Oh, that," said Siham, wiggling her fingers. "You are a goose, aren't you? I didn't cut the bars with nothing, of course, and I don't see how using my bones in that way is any more magically freakish than you walking and talking with yours. Anyhow, it's pretty obvious if you stop and think about it: I did it with dust."

"With dust."

"Dust!" She scooped up a little dirt and tossed it into the air before them. "Well, not that kind of dust," she admitted as it fell. "My *own* dust. I keep it on my person at all times. Between the bones. Behind my ribs. In my skull." She flicked her wrist, and her fingertips darted into the air a foot ahead of her, hanging there for a moment before snapping back into place. "See?"

"No, I don't see —"

"Seeing is easier with your mouth shut."

She brought one white hand inches from his face, an intimacy that cowed him more than the scolding. Closing her fist, she left only her index finger extended, then slowly separated its joints, balancing them in midair as if on a thread.

On a thread! thought Jacob, suddenly noticing indeed the dust between the bones, which was very like a thread, after all: a thread made up of infinitesimal particles, barely visible, impossibly still.

"But this dust," whispered Jacob, as if he were afraid that speaking aloud might blow it away, "how do you control it?"

"I don't," said Siham quietly, with a smile in her voice. "I am it." Slowly, her joints began to undulate in the air, though her hand was perfectly still.

"Not magic, then. Mysticism."

"Not that either. My dust is made up of tiny pieces of my bone. My dust is me! Otherwise, how could I have power over it?"

"Mystifying as it is, Remington seems to have no problem exerting power over parts of other people."

"Hey, good point. I can't wait to meet this kid!"

Jacob couldn't tear his eyes off of the thread, which Siham was expanding and contracting for his benefit. "Pardon my befuddlement, but why don't those tiny grains blow away?"

"Jacob, you are aware that you have no flesh on your head, aren't you?"

"It had not escaped my attention."

"And your neck, except for a bit of stuff at the bottom, it's gone too."

"I suppose it is."

"But while I was carrying you upside-down over my shoulder, your head didn't fall off, did it?"

Jacob felt uneasy. "It seems it did not."

"'You citizen,'" she said, strutting about in imitation of Jean-Luc, "'you think ze flesh is what hold you together, *non*? But ze flesh, it is only hold you back!'

"Our bones, Jacob, are solid incarnations of will. You already know that much from your days as a preservative agent."

"Preservationi—"

"Point is, our bones are our beings. They hold together unless they're physically separated. And once the flesh is out of their way, we see what we are and what we can do so much more clearly.

"The way I hold onto my dust is the same way you hold onto your head: I just have more focus, because of my training. Shailesh taught me how to focus with such precision that I can manipulate a grain of dust as easily as you can manipulate your fingers.

"So, like I said, I don't have to think about this thread: I am it."

"But the strength of that dust —"

"It's immense!" She drew her spine up straight and chopped the air with her hand. "'A warrior makes every bone a bullet, Siham! A warrior makes those bones that are not bullets into shields, Siham! A warrior makes the dust between those bones that are not bullets and are not shields into the cutting edge, Siham!'"

She dropped the impression and drew her arm back. "Now behold as I demonstrate the cutting edge of the bone sculptors." Siham flicked her wrist, extending her hand a foot away from her forearm on a thread of dust. In an instant, the thread trebled in size, growing dense and fuzzy around the edges and humming like a tuning fork.

"The dust —"

"Vibrates," she said. She picked up a stone from the path, tossed it in the air, and swung her hand up past it. When the stone collided with the wire of dust between the bones it buzzed, then fell to the ground in two.

"Thus endeth the lesson," said Siham, her hand snapping back into place. "Let's get going, huh?"

Jacob caught up to her, his mind whirling. "Are all of the Bone-men like you?"

"Goodness no. I'm a snowflake."

They continued along the side of Lethe, drawing near enough to its source that the hulking shape of Bald Mountain could be seen through the mist, the cave from which the river sprung a dark shadow at its base. Staring into the darkness that had brought him here, Jacob wondered why he'd never made the pilgrimage before.

He was startled by the sound of three scavengers hauling a box full of dripping goods down the path before them, their bloated faces split with the success of their haul. As soon as they saw Jacob and Siham they fell silent, studying the river's surface intently as they passed by. Jacob was confused by this sudden change in demeanor until he glanced at the river, on whose rippling surface he saw a debtor reflected.

"No wonder they were spooked!" he muttered. "I look like an agent of the Magnate, and you, forgive me, are a fearful sight to any citizen." He pulled the robe over his head and tossed it into the river, cursing at the rippling image of gore-streaked bones peek-ing through decimated flesh. He was naked now but for the leather pouch the debtors had left hanging at his wrist. "Not that this is much of an improvement."

"Me, I like the look of bone," said Siham, who arranged her pha-langes into a chain that ran from wrist to wrist, then began skipping it like a jump-rope. "Fashionable and utilitarian! Come on, Jacob, the Bypass is just ahead." The northern entrance to the Bazakh Bypass proved no more adorned than its counterpart in the Plains: it was a gaping pit in the ground, surrounded by stalls where the Dead City scavengers were haggling with desert-dried Armory merchants. "It's a long road," said Siham, ignoring a vendor of imitation swords who was praising her delicate structure and the refined sensibilities it undoubtedly implied. "You sure you wouldn't rather be carried? I'm super fast."

"This sensation," said Jacob with a sigh, "must be the last vestige of my pride falling away. Very well: you may carry me."

"An excellent decision, sirrah."

She hefted him up, piggy-back this time, and he strived mightily to ignore the stares of the corpses around them. Without warning, she burst into motion, lashing into the darkness of the Bypass, where a long, flat stretch gave her room to pick up speed. She leaped over fissures in the rock and careened around corpses traveling in both directions while Jacob tightened his grip on her ribs.

By Siham's reckoning, they were nearly half-way through the Bypass when an overwhelming uptick in traffic slowed her pace, forcing her to seek openings in the crowd.

"Too bad I can't run on the ceiling," she muttered. "Remind me to work on that when we get to White City."

The tunnel, which at its narrowest could hold ten men abreast, was packed from wall to wall with excited corpses carrying nothing more than the weapons in their hands, which they had no apparent desire to use against one another. In fact, these disenfranchised Plainsmen had nothing more urgent to do than compare notes on what had recently become the talk of the Plains: the emergence of that Ur-monster known as the Last Man Standing.

"I tellest thee, Elspeth, we shouldest have stoodest against that mangle-beast!" moaned a passing slab of cured muscle that Jacob recognized as Oxnard. "'Twas our destiny to do't, and now we are devoid."

"Halt your jabbering jaw and follow where I lead, Ox!" said Elspeth. "No warrior free from the taint of sorcery could stand against that mountain of meat. When they forge corpses of steel instead of bone, we'll return and fight beside them, but for the nonce, we'll not wave bashers in the face of fate!"

"O loathy Lethe!" moaned Oxnard as Siham darted around his bulk. "I oathed nevermore to plash upon her shores. You'll make an oathbreaker of me, sir!"

"You oath too much to be otherwise," said Elspeth. "Now hie!"

"I know those two," whispered Jacob. "They're Plainsmen through and through. If they're leaving, that means —"

"That monster you built is a real game-changer, Jacob!" said Siham, loudly enough to turn the head of every nearby warrior.

"Oh, do let's advertise," said Jacob, whose position made it impossible for him to cringe. Luckily, Siham was able to travel faster than rumor, and the story that the Last Man Standing had been summoned by skeletal witches caused them no immediate harm.

They emerged into an Armory flooded with Plainsmen, where Jacob demanded to be set upon his feet, the better to consider the changes wreaked upon the Plains in his absence. They had arrived at that precise moment when the exodus from the scrimmage had reached critical mass. The Shallow End was buried a mile deep in corpses too astonished by their change in fortunes to fight, and even those merchants whose security forces were strong enough to avoid wholesale looting were packing up their wares and disappearing into the dubious safety of the Bypass. Jacob overheard a squadron, creaking under the weight of Crusader-era armor, discussing the benefits of exiting the Plains through the Torn Curtain and finding a new home by the riverside.

"What a mess we made," said Jacob with a touch of pride. "But how will we find the company?"

"If they're still with the Last Man Standing, it shouldn't be hard," said Siham. "Some of these rumors must be for real. Let's hit the crowds and see if we can't scare up a primary source."

Wandering southward, they encountered many strange features of a melee domesticated by defeat, not least of which was a warrior Jacob had last seen collecting ears on a skewer excusing himself after stepping on the lady's toe-bones. Not all the Plainsmen were leaving; from time to time they came across warriors recruiting members for their militias. On the far side of one such group, whose leader proclaimed his plan to defeat the Last Man Standing "the way the Horde would have done it," Siham spotted the kind of gathering she'd been searching for and pulled Jacob behind her into a ring of corpses listening raptly to a severed head propped up on a cairn of stones.

"Aye, and a fearsome foe it were!" cried the raconteur, her falsetto emerging from a puckered face that was battle-scarred long before death. "Its arms was as long as narwhals, and ten-foot blades chewed the air about its knees. I knew on setting eyes upon it that I had but one hope: to land a harpoon near enough its peak that I might climb aboard and divest it of its hoary head."

Jacob shoved through the crowd. "Hello there! Madam! Are you quite sure it had only the one head?"

"Pipe down there in front!"

"Let the nubbin finish her tale!"

"Aye," said the raconteur, "the beastie were one-headed. Many-arméd, many-leggéd, but with a single bonce, and a grimacing, babbling bonce it were, with gnashing teeth and a spine like a horrible puppy-tail."

"And the beast had no entourage? No headless companions, or a boy with a crow in his head?"

Before the raconteur could answer these queries, a rippling wave of shrieks began at the far side of the crowd. "See it with thine own sockets!" she screamed. "Thar be the beastie!"

The coming thunder of the Last Man's legs drove the crowd into a frenzy, and it was only luck that kept Jacob from being trampled. Seeing the raconteur's head booted from its post, he scooped it up and dodged frantically through the mob, searching for a glimpse of Siham.

A shower of severed limbs and heads pelted the ground around him, and he stared up at the beast's massive, many-bladed hand rising above him. In moments, nothing but dust stood between them, giving Jacob an unobstructed view of his creation.

There was no sign of Leopold, nor of the harness that had secured him to the topmost ring of spines. The Last Man Standing now had but a single pair of eyes rolling within Etienne's skull. From his mouth issued a river of babble, an endless procession of meaningless syllables that stopped Jacob where he stood.

"Oh, my friend," he said, dropping to his knees before the monster, "what have I done to you?"

The beast stopped thrashing and fixed its eyes on him.

"Pardon me, but oughtn't you *run*?" piped the raconteur.

"No," said Jacob, "I'll run no more. I dragged this man from his rest and forced him into this torture. The least I can do is stand before him without cringing — or fall to pieces, as he decides. Etienne, can you see me?" He put a hand out and stepped forward.

Etienne's voice erupted in a gabbling howl, and one great arm swooped through the air, its five blades fixed on Jacob's torso. Jacob bowed his head, girding himself for the sickening snap of his bones — but heard instead a ringing clash, followed by a frustrated stream of speech from above. Jacob looked up in surprise and saw a bulwark of bones branching out like a clump of antlers, bound tightly in place by sturdy threads of dust. Clattering back into shape, Siham said, "Be a doll and keep out of the way now, 'kay?"

Jacob staggered behind a boulder with the raconteur as Siham ducked the beast's hand, only to find two others swinging down from its far side. She had time enough to roll beneath the first, but the second was inescapable; thrusting her tibiae up before her, she bore the force of its blades without suffering a scratch. "We call that 'marrow-grip,'" she said. "Neat trick, huh?"

Before the hand had time to withdraw, she ensnared it with dust, wrapping the dislocated bones of her legs around its blades and riding them into the air. When the beast tried to shake her off, she let go, soaring above it and landing squarely behind Etienne's head.

The beast was in a quandary: desperate to unseat its foe but fearful of beheading itself, it could do nothing but try to knock her loose. Locking her leg into its ring of spines and glancing down into its thrashing innards, she cried to Jacob, "Remington isn't here!"

"I should think not, but Etienne damn well is! Set him loose, Siham."

Siham looked dubiously at the babbling head. "I don't think I can."

"Just pull! The clamp's not half as strong as you."

"No, I mean I've taken a vow not to harm anyone, and this thing you've built seems to be someone. Isn't it?" At this, the beast stilled, as if this very question had been on its mind. Even Etienne's babble quieted to a plaintive moan.

"Ye fight like Bluebeard on a bender," said the raconteur, "yet ye've vowed to hurt none? What be the point?"

"My skills are defensive," said Siham. "I have vowed never to divide that which died whole. It's a whole big thing they make you say before they'll teach you anything."

"Well, there you have it!" said Jacob. "The Last Man Standing didn't die whole."

"Hmp. Well, look, how's this for a compromise," she said, slapping her hand onto Etienne's brow, to the beast's evident unease. "We'll swap out the heads. Matey, would you like to be on the winning team?" she asked the raconteur. "No pressure, there's a field full of potential donors."

"A lookout for the beastie?" The raconteur considered briefly. "Aye, that'll pass the time." Jacob hurled the raconteur to Siham, who followed his directions in releasing the clamp.

Once the heads were exchanged, the first wave of warriors representing the Horde's less terrifying incarnation fell upon the beast, employing various ineffectual tactics with great enthusiasm. During the wholesale rending of flesh that followed, Siham, carrying Jacob and Etienne, dashed toward the center of the Plains, where the recent slaughter had removed all but fallen warriors, and the endless stream of verbiage rushing from Etienne's mouth could be studied in greater detail.

"He's totally out of it," said Siham.

"It's his first level of psychic defense. Next comes catatonia."

"Maybe he'll come around?"

"I doubt it," said Jacob. "He's demonstrated a remarkable resistance in the past, and what he's suffered as a part of that creature might be as traumatic to him as his death. He's used to being bodiless but autonomous. To be reduced to a mere appendage, particularly by a creature as fractious and violent as —"

Suddenly, as if he'd been tuned to another channel, Etienne started talking sense, if manically.

"Nothing could be bad as that," he spat, "not Last Man crashing down upon us Leopold torn out of us they fled toward the gate and we were lost inside the beast inside the Plains inside the death inside the void inside —"

"Did that mean anything to you?" said Siham, for Etienne had taken up again in his unintelligible language as abruptly as he'd left off.

"Mutiny," said Jacob. "The beast threw off its reins. I think we'd better try White Gate."

"Forward motion!" said Siham, kneeling down and offering her back. "Gee up."

"If it's all the same to you, I'd rather walk. This pony-ride business is a trifle degrading."

"I'm a racehorse, I'll have you know," said Siham, tossing Etienne's head into Jacob's arms. "Thoroughbred!"

On the way, Jacob studied Etienne's speech. Certain phrases were becoming familiar, patterns were beginning to show, and there was an appearance of syntax that suggested a legitimate language; but even phrases offered to Etienne in his own idiom did nothing to interrupt his steady jabbering. It *did* grow more subdued as they approached White Gate, becoming an insistent, slithery whisper as they fell beneath the shadow of the Rim, as if Etienne, through the haze of madness, had sense enough to fear returning to this place.

"I'm sorry, Etienne," Jacob whispered. "All I ask is the chance to make things better for you. May this not be a step in the wrong direction."

Though Jacob was confident that Siham could defend them from any number of debtors, returning to the site of his abduction frightened him, too. With each step he took down that pale hall he flinched at the motion of some imaginary rope. He stared up at the edge of the Rim and gained nothing by it. Were there debtors watching, they were quiet and well-disguised.

"Even if they're up there, it doesn't matter to us," said Siham, but as they edged around a corner, she stopped, holding up a hand as Jacob caught sight of a body sprawled on the floor.

For a time he could only stare at that pathetic jumble of limbs, so limp and various in direction that it took on the appearance of a man-sized puppet discarded after a grand performance. Then he saw the familiar shapes of his own boots, at the ends of his own legs, and noted the dusty blond hair at the top of it all. "Leopold," he said. Etienne yelped and was silent for a time.

As Jacob knelt at his side, Leopold, who had yet to look at them, lifted his head from the floor of the hall. "Ah," he said softly, "so you've led them to me. I can't blame you for your betrayal. There was never room on this journey for both our quests, was there? One was destined to be sacrificed for the other. It's as it should be. This folly must end, Jacob. Let it end at last." Without so much as a glance at Siham, he dropped his face into the dirt again.

"I haven't—"

"I thought it would end with death," he said to the earth below. "The boy thought so, anyway, the boy Tanner brought through your window, the boy who tried to fashion a man out of lace and bluster. But that boy never left the man's bones: he's still here, still as broken as he was at birth, making the same noises, the same messes, only now through time eternal. That cycle of degradation is what I saw so well when I fit the belt around my neck. I see now how ludicrous it was to believe I could escape, but a good joke never really ends, does it? Just keeps on punching."

"Leopold —"

"Let me speak." He dragged himself partway up, though he had yet to face his audience. "I always knew, you see, that I'd been born into the wrong world. The words that I spoke, the books that I'd stolen them from, confused every relative whose blood and features forced them to acknowledge me as one of their own. I stood out among them like broken crockery, whether in speech or in silence. My father tried to drive the me from me with the strength of his hands, my mother with her screeching voice. But there was no cure for what I was, and the only palliative came in dreaming — the only arena in my existence where I could be king. It wasn't power itself that I desired, but the freedom from the bottoms of their boots that power could lend me. What I wanted was reversal.

"It will come as little surprise to you that I found my salvation in the most dramatic of places: I found the theatre, and for a short while I was free.

"I was only a boy, I can see that now, and like any boy I had faith that I'd soon conquer the world. Those above me were destined to bend to my will, to surrender at my slightest advance. And that fuming arrogance is what I brought to my audition for Hamlet, Death's Ambassador.

"'To think that he perfected the role of a lifetime,' they'd say, weeping as they stood and ovated, 'to think that his genius has reached its full flower at such a young age!'

"Lord, how trite my story sounds, removed from the hormonal torrents of teenaged angst. How inconsequential were my problems then, and yet how momentous they'd seemed! But you know already how this story ends. When I learned that the directors had cast a professional in the role, when I learned that I was not to be so much as a nameless Lord in that production, I climbed out of my window and walked the five long, moonlit miles to their theatre, where I broke off their doorknob with a stone from the driveway and stalked to the dressing-room. On the mirror I scrawled NOT TO BE in lipstick, which I thought was terribly clever until I'd already kicked out the chair and felt the belt bite my neck. Swinging from the pipes, I'd have done anything to wipe away those words — but not the act, not even then.

"I have never doubted the wisdom of my death until now. I was convinced, since I learned of his existence, that usurping the Magnate would make sense of my short life. I also believed that I'd succeed in unseating him, though I was never quite clear about how. But now I see that it has all been folly. Even the monster built to serve my desires would rather hack me out and drop me like a fewmet upon the floor of the Plains than use me for its eyes. This world, like the last one, hates me, along with all the people in it — and only the thought that I could triumph here, that I could keep the joy of supremacy forever in my grip, was keeping me on my feet. Now that it's gone, what's left for me to hold? In my palm there's nothing but a single pocket watch. Besides that paltry sum, all I possess are questions, and they're heavier than I, sitting on my chest and thumping their sooty fists in my face. I can take no more. So give me over to the Magnate, Jacob. Let him cure me. Let me go."

Holding Etienne against his chest, Jacob looked up at the top of White Gate. "I'm afraid I haven't brought him. Nor have I brought any answers for you, Leopold, only questions every bit as heavy as your own. How much must we suffer, how long must we strive, before our quests become tragic comedies? I can offer only a morsel of cold comfort: that I, at least, have forgotten the trick of hating you. I understand you, I think."

He shifted uncomfortably. "I should also mention that I've lost your penis." There was a sigh from below, but no hysterics. "At any rate, I've made a new friend, and despite my best attempts to prepare her for your theatrics, I found I have, yet again, woefully underestimated your potential. Leopold, this is Siham."

"Hiya! Sorry about your miserable existence. Listen, I have a question for you, too, but it's not all that heavy. Where, good sirrah, is the rest of your company now?"

Leopold peered for a while at the Bonemaiden. "Well. They're naturally buoyant, those three, as certain idiots are. I believe they are currently attempting to climb White Gate by hand."

Jacob stood, offering his hand. "Leopold, I have nothing to offer you but more path. Would you care to walk it, or would you rather be carried? I'm afraid that leaving you to your own devices is out of the question, considering the condition you were in when we found you."

"No matter where I go," croaked Leopold, "the Mortar and Pestle will find me. What's the point of moving when my eradication is inevitable?"

"Ah, I forgot to mention that bit. The Masker decided not to grind you into dust after all. You'll be sentenced to the Debtor's Pool, I believe. It'll be dreadfully boring, but at least you'll be intact."

Leopold propped himself up on his elbows. "Truly?"

"If I wanted to kick you while you were down, Leopold, I'd have done it quite literally by now."

"No Mortar and Pestle," he murmured. "Then they mean to make an example of me. Keep me close. Close enough to punish. Close enough to watch." He executed half a push-up, then collapsed. "But no! Absurdity has finally broken my back, Jacob, after decades of constant effort. Leave me where I lay, and trouble yourself no more with my sordid tale."

Jacob sat down, determined. "For God's sake, Leopold, you're many things, but you're no nihilist. Think of all the things you might still accomplish, even if it is on the other side of indenture. However dim your immediate prospects, there's always a chance to beat your naysayers at their own game. Given eternity, who among us might not reverse his fortunes? Why, I was in a very similar situation once, during that drought I once alluded to —"

Leopold dragged himself onto his feet. "Well, if it's come down to a choice between your memoirs and centuries of indenture, let us press on. White City awaits."

"I do hope I don't regret that encouragement," murmured Jacob to Siham as they followed. "One can never tell with Leopold."

At the end of the hall, they came upon the remarkable sight of Remington, Adam, and Eve striving to mount White Gate. Remington, after discovering minute chinks in the stone, had cleaned all the flesh that remained on his hands and feet with a scalpel taken from Jacob's knapsack, and Adam and Eve had followed suit. With their newly denuded digits, they'd set about teaching themselves to climb the sheer face of White Gate one body-length at a time. Remington had begun, holding fast to the stone a few feet off the ground, then Eve had climbed his body like a human ladder, standing on his shoulders and seeking purchase above him, then Adam had climbed her, and so forth, until the lot of them tumbled in a pile at the bottom, eager to try again. After days of practice, they had managed to climb halfway to the top of the Gate, where the reconstructed crow hopped impatiently, squawking encouragement.

"My word," said Siham, "these three are persistent, aren't they?"

"Whose word?" said Remington, high above. "I can't see who that is. Can you guys see who that is?"

"It's only Jacob," shouted Leopold, "and his skinny friend Siham."

"Remy, can you get down from there without breaking yourself in half?"

"You know, I don't think so," said Remington, trying to see over Eve's shoulders, tottering dangerously.

"Stay where you are!" said Jacob. "I'm sure there's some sane way to open the gate, hopefully without dislodging you three — isn't there, Siham?"

"Nope," said Siham, "he's got the right idea." She crouched beneath White Gate, well to the side of Remington, then burst up like a coiled spring, stretching her bones as far as their dust would allow and catching hold of the stone with her fingertips. From there, she swung her body end-over-end, catching hold of the chinks in the rock now with her toes, now with her fingers, until she reached the climbers.

"Siham, the Bonemaiden," she said as she flattened against the rock. "Pleasure to meet you. Grab some rib."

"Yes, ma'am!" said Remington, taking hold of her ribcage. Eve hung from his foot, Adam from Eve's, and as Siham began to climb, the three of them ascended in a chain along with her.

Remington whooped with laughter as Siham pulled them up onto the beveled top of White Gate, high above the Rim, where she left them to their wonder. The trio sat enraptured, watching the crow swoop as near as it dared to the pale constructions and the spindly citizens below.

It was over an hour before Siham could be persuaded to bring the others up to join them. "I'm sure you'll catch up, Jacob," she said, "but these three are natural Seekers like I've never seen. They deserve a first look at their city on their own."

CHAPTER FOURTEEN

City of Bone

D ear God," said Leopold, "those are buildings."
"Built buildings," said Jacob. "Constructed. Designed!"
"Built *by* corpses *for* corpses," said Remington.

"Yeah, that whole thing about dwelling in ruins always confused me," said Siham. "Why not just pull apart the bricks and make something new? Is that some kind of zombie aesthetic or just laziness?"

Jacob and Leopold were too engrossed with White City to reply. White Gate, atop which the company was perched, was one of four massive, marble slabs rising out of a circular outer wall. Only White Gate lacked an actual entrance — an understandable design choice, considering their neighbors in the Plains. An avenue began below Remington's dangling feet and ran to the city center, where a grand, open-roofed edifice stood, a hybrid of mausoleum and amphitheater whose classical features were accentuated by the homely facade of every other construction in sight.

"Most of the buildings are made of giant jigsaw-chunks carved by the bone-sculptors," said Siham. "You just slap them together to make whatever kind of construction you might need. See?" In the city below, a clutch of skeletons pushed a three-walled room along a grooved street, sliding its open edge to rest in the archway of a larger building. "Nothing looks the same here for very long, although that's mostly because no one can agree on anything for more than an hour at a time."

Remington sent the crow to swoop over the open rooftops, where it spied bone-fighters leaping and whirling in a grand arena, mazes of sheer marble walls with skeletons scaling them in a variety of physically improbable ways, vast laboratories and tiny cubicles, and a group of sculptors, masons, and architects using whirring ropes of dust to carve stone in a titanic workshop near the foothills.

"The elders encourage diversity, once you jump through enough of their hoops," said Siham, "but woe to the hoop-averse."

"How many of you are there?" said Jacob.

"The official number of Seekers is five thousand," said Siham, "though half that number haven't been seen for centuries. I've never seen more than five hundred at once. I'd say we've got three and change down there now."

"Where are the rest?" said Remington.

"Seeking. Marrow-grip, a deep meditative state, is achieved, and then a body goes out into the world until she finds her way home. Now and then a seeking is a mission, an investigation, or some kind of a quest, the more hare-brained the better, but sometimes you just pick a direction and go. That's what I did when I, uh, decided to leave. I walked into the Moving Desert, and when those debtors put me in their cage, I figured I'd see what the Debtor's Pool was all about. It's not a subject we've dedicated much thought to."

"This place sounds disgustingly civilized," said Leopold. "Utopian, even! I mistrust utopias on general principle."

"Yeah, me too," said Siham. "This isn't that, though. Seekers can only tolerate each other for so long before we start to drive each other nuts. All the best seekings begin right after a disagreement. Like Shailesh says: 'We are drawn to the City in order to leave it, Siham!'

"Which reminds me. Jacob, I'll try to keep you out of it, but there's probably going to be a giant-sized argument when we climb down there. I left sort of — abruptly."

Jacob did his best to pay attention, but he was distracted by the whispering babble of Etienne, whose distress was no less profound for its diminished volume.

The street below White Gate had been attracting Seekers since Remington and the headless first ascended. It was now filled with dozens of warrior-skeletons of unimaginable strength and power, none of whom looked particularly pleased to see them.

With one hand, Siham gripped the top of the Gate, then let out her skeleton beneath her, her bones aligning like links in a chain separated by lengths of dust. Remington and the headless were the first to climb down, and once Jacob and Leopold had been convinced to follow, Jacob gripping Etienne's babbling head in one arm and cinching down awkwardly with his legs, the skeletons in the street lent a grudging hand, climbing up the chinks in the wall and hefting the newcomers down one at a time.

Jacob was grasped around the waist by a sand-colored skeleton who scampered down the vertical surface of the wall as quickly as he could, eager to distance himself from the newcomer's rotting flesh. "Another of Bonemaiden's disasters," he muttered as he backed away.

"Bonetown!" cried Remington as he touched down. The woman who'd carried him tried to rejoin the crowd, but he clapped his arms around her spine and hugged her close. "Gee, it's good to be home!"

"Is it good?" she said as she disengaged. "A concept difficult to define. Is it home? More slippery still. Be less hasty in your conclusions, visitor. Study slow knowing. That's the Seekers' Way."

"Ignore her advice," whispered a second skeleton. "Know like a mote that dances on the wind! Define with the impulsive strength of a frog's tongue! Do whatever comes to mind — *that's* the Seekers' Way."

"I've already had my fill of this place," said Leopold, holding up a hand. "Would you be so kind as to fling me back over the wall now?"

Jacob stared at the crowd, which had swelled to at least two hundred. A few of them shone like Siham, but the rest were covered, to various degrees, in a resinous stain that reminded Jacob of the Horde.

"What does the patina signify?" he whispered to Siham under cover of Etienne's whispers.

"The brighter the bone, the more recent the scouring. Some only do it once, some as often as they can. It's a thing. Since the Liminal Ode came out it's been real sectarian around here."

"Beg pardon?"

"The Liminal Ode. The Poet's latest."

Suddenly, a delicate skeleton with bones the color of eggshell skidded into the street at the back of the crowd, cried "Maiden!" in an alarmingly piercing voice, leaped over the Seekers, collapsed into a pile of tumbling bones, and reassembled at Siham's feet. "Oh, dust-hearted Maiden," she cried, shaking her fists so hard her bones jangled, "you left me!"

"Not you in particular, Yasmin," said Siham. "Anyway, look: I came back!"

"That's not the point," said Yasmin, jouncing to her feet the better to turn her back. "You left without even a goodbye!"

"Well, I'd hate for a sentimental moment to spoil my air of desert stoicism."

"Oh, Maiden, dwell on it no more. I forgive you!" cried Yasmin, falling to her knees and wrapping her arms around Siham's legs. "Your new technique was wonderful! I hate you for it, just a little."

Leaping backward, she shook her hands at the ground, launching her fingertips at the stone, but they halted a few inches above her knees, and she retracted them with a stomp of her delicate feet. "I'll never make it out of this place."

"Next time I'll take you with me," said Siham.

"That assumes you'll ever make it out again," said Yasmin. "Mistress Ai has been demanding your expulsion ever since you expelled yourself, though she's lately turned to talk of jailing you. We've been arguing the legality of your punishment ever since. Oh, Maiden, here she comes!"

The crowd began to disperse, swiftly and with obvious regret, as a skeleton the hue of iced tea glided into the street. Stretching a finger toward Siham, she tipped her head at the city's center and began drifting backward, her body rigid above motionless feet.

"Witches!" hissed Leopold. "Utopia is lousy with witches!"

"Siham, is that woman *floating*?" said Jacob.

"Nah. No witchcraft there, just the underworld's single greatest reserve of stubbornness. Ai is the leader of the eternalists."

"Eternals!" said Yasmin. "You demean us with your 'ists' and 'isms.'"

"They're the ones with the yellowy bones. Yasmin here's a junior member."

"We hold that eternity is within the grasp of the individual," said Yasmin, "and refrain from the reckless expenditure of bone mass."

"They don't like repeat trips into the Moving Desert," said Siham. "One scouring either turns you into a skeleton or baby powder, so they need that first one to get into the club, but they claim that too much time in the storm will fry your brain. Anyway: Ai, rather than degrading her bones even the slightest bit by taking actual steps, coats itty-bitty pebbles with her dust and lets them do the moving for her."

"A roller-corpse," said Remington, bumping hips with Adam and Eve.

"They say the motion Mistress has conserved will one day be expended in a single blow of unrivaled power. She strikes fear into the heart of all Seekers," said Yasmin.

"Except me," said Siham.

"All Seekers who are sane," said Yasmin. "But come! We'd better make haste to the Plaza of the Ancients before Mistress Ai gets any angrier, assuming that's possible. Oh, Maiden, what a mess you've made for yourself to clean up!"

The Plaza of the Ancients towered over White City, the interlocking blocks of its walls as snug as puzzle pieces, their outlines describing the shapes of corpses and skeletons, organs and weapons, mountains and rivers, all so expertly carved that no mortar was needed. The company entered through an archway, staring up at a delicate marble honeycomb that covered the walls in filigreed chambers, each one holding a fragment of a weathered skeleton: skulls, bones, and ribcages sat as motionless as museum pieces, though they buzzed with sentience. Each chamber was a sculpture in itself, combining the styles of hieroglyphics and heraldry to relate some intricate, if obscure, chronicle.

In the Plaza's center stood a sculpture of a willow, its branches so delicate that Jacob expected them to sway in the breeze traversing the Plaza's archways; its leaves, thin to the point of translucence, obliged, gently tinkling on thin silver chains. Mistress Ai stood below the tree, and the company followed Yasmin to its circular base, where they seated themselves like students before a lecture, Jacob painfully aware of how much noise Etienne was making. As Remington settled, the crow launched itself from his head in the direction of a bird-faced gargoyle on the Plaza's open roof, announcing itself as it flew.

"A bird," said Mistress Ai, "spilling black feathers on white streets.

"A pack of corpses, shedding skin and tissue, fascia and muscle, dirt and excrescence.

"A severed head, lost in madness, filling the air with tortured noise.

"The shame that trails like a poorly harnessed thread of dust from an unauthorized departure and swift return."

She drifted to the edge of the platform, looking down on the company. "The Bonemaiden brings many gifts to our City."

Siham sighed. "I have a name, Ai."

"The Seekers' Meeting has granted the Bonemaiden no name, and little wonder: when Master Shailesh indulged you, you repaid him with violent betrayal. Were it left to me, you would have been hunted and buried beneath a cairn of marble slabs. Now, as it was then, your fate is for him to decide."

The pebbles beneath Mistress Ai's feet trickled to the floor. Gently, she drew her foot forward, stepping onto the tiny stones and gliding past the company. "Master Shailesh will deal with you presently," she said, rolling toward an open archway. "Yasmin, consider well the company you keep."

"Now there's a skeleton I can understand," said Leopold. "I can always make time for mystic crypticism, provided that it's concealing an insult."

For a long while, the only sounds in the Plaza were the tinkling of marble leaves and the ceaseless monologue emerging from Etienne's mouth. Then Siham began pacing below the watchful sockets of the disembodied warriors, her feet clacking angrily on the floor.

"Why do they call you the Bonemaiden if your name is Siham?" said Remington.

"Because there are no dogs for them to kick."

"That's unfair!" said Yasmin. "Even Ai was called Bonemaiden until she passed her first review. Every apprentice must foreswear her name until she's recognized by the Seekers' Meeting."

"But I'm too willful to name," said Siham, "or too strange, or too contrary. I'm always *too* something, that's the consensus, although it's rarely the same thing twice."

"What did you do, anyway?" asked Remington.

"Oh!" cried Yasmin. "What Maiden did was terrible! And a little amazing. After she failed her review for the tenth time — is that right, Maiden? Ten times?"

"Who's counting?"

"Well, after her most recent failure, she built an enclosed room and remained there for months. What noises she made! Some Seekers said she was carving up her own bones, so she could emerge in a cloud of dust and slice us all to pieces!"

"We have more than a few drama queens in our fair City."

"When she emerged, she challenged Master Shailesh, her own teacher, to a duel."

"Shailesh is a hothead," said Siham. "It took about a goad and a half to get him to agree that I could go seeking if I could best him in battle."

"Even before this duel, Maiden's skills as a bone-fighter were legendary. Master Hamish says she's as fast a learner as Inpu the Faithless! A frightening proclamation, I'm sure you'll agree. But however advanced she may be, no apprentice may go seeking without passing three reviews and an ordeal, which usually takes twenty more years of training than the Maiden received — so you can understand how scandalous this was!

"Master Shailesh cleared the training grounds, and White City stood around its edges to watch. For those who haven't met Master Shailesh, I'll tell you, he's a terrifying man!"

"If you find large puppies terrifying."

"He's so dedicated a fighter that he ground his own left kneecap into powder in order to wield the longest dust-thread ever seen."

"He also lost half its mass when a strong wind interrupted the grinding."

"When, at the start of that terrible duel, he let out his cutting-arm to its full length, everyone knew that he was serious. Swinging it over his head, he cried, 'I will teach you this lesson if it costs me my vows!'"

"He says that to rocks when he stubs his toe."

"Master Shailesh bounded at her like a white lion, but before he had drawn near enough to strike, Maiden drew her arms behind her back and flung them forward, propelling her fingertips like ten arrows toward his backbone! A huge quantity of dust was required to shoot those arrows, but more impressive still was the force behind them: each struck one of Master's vertebrae hard enough to send it bursting from his back, so that his dust-whip was sucked through his spine! And the moment his whip was gone, Maiden entangled him with her ten threads and drew so close that many feared she'd gone the way of Inpu and was about to behead her own Master. But she only whispered something to him. Oh, Maiden, tell us what it was!"

"I said, 'Our teacher had no teacher,'" said Siham.

"Hum. Well, I suppose you had to say something. And then she was gone! Without an instant's thought, the Maiden left White City! Since then, the debate over her fate has been fierce. She's insubordinate — on that everyone can agree. But to develop a brand-spanking-new technique, after so little training! That's where it got complicated, as no one could agree on how to handle such reckless power."

"I'm neither fish nor fowl," said Siham. "Too strong to call Bone-maiden, too unruly to name. But no one named the Poet Laureate of the Underworld, did they? He'd never pass the Meeting's end-less batteries of tests, but without him, all this would be nothing but desert."

"Nothing?" roared a voice from the eastern archway. "It is you who will be nothing, Siham! As the apple that falls far from the tree is devoured by that tree's very roots, so shall I grind my student into a shameful powder!"

The skeleton who spoke these words, his ribs as thick as tusks, backflipped all the way from the archway to the central platform, then launched himself into the air to land several feet from Siham, his fists extended on dust-threads so wide they hummed in baritone.

"Your former master, now your enemy, shall forsake his vows to teach you this lesson — but it is a lesson your fragments shall never forget!"

Siham sighed and shook out her arms, letting out a finger from each hand on a thread of dust the length of a bullwhip. "Shailesh, you're a masochist," she said as the twin wires began to hum.

"I am a realist," said Shailesh, "and you, Siham, are a figment of my imagination!"

They sprang into the air, only to be thrown to the floor by the grinding clash of their dust-blades; both landed on their feet, skid-ding backward only to leap, clash, and rebound again; and so began a spectacle that continued long enough to stultify.

"This is pointless. Why doesn't she just knock his spine out?" said Leopold after a time to Yasmin, the only member of the audi-ence who was making enough noise to satisfy Master Shailesh's sense of drama.

"Oh, she can't use that technique here," Yasmin said between outbursts. "What if she hit one of the ancients?"

Remington strolled toward the bones in the honeycomb, peering up curiously at their broken forms. He stopped beneath a well-formed skull of obvious antiquity, gazing deep into its eye-sockets and waving a fleshless hand in greeting. "Hi there," he said. "How's your day?"

"For Gielgud the Great there have been but three days," the skull replied. "The first was a blink of my eyes in the Lands Above. The second was cut short in the Battle of the Plains when my own apprentice struck me down. Only the third day has been long enough to be worthy of note, though its only interesting element is the promise of oblivion that lies at its end; unless, perish the thought, the eternalists are right, and bone lasts forever."

"You guys are veterans? Neat!" Remington looked up at the various bones arrayed in the honeycomb around Gielgud. "Do the rest of them feel the same way as you? Bummed out, I mean."

"We are unlike this new breed of philosophers and artisans, mystics and scientists. We who people the walls were the first wave of Seekers, the warrior-clan who studied beside the Poet Laureate of the Underworld. Every one of our number was a Plainsman before he scoured. Without the poetry of bone-fighting, eternity for us is a long, gray, joyless journey."

"So, pretty bummed. All right, let's cheer you fellas up." Remington pulled Gielgud from his compartment and solicited his aid in retrieving the bones of those warriors he felt the greatest affinity for. Gielgud, luckily, had a better grasp of anatomy than Remington, and advised him as to the proper placement of various bones, assuming the boy to be a madman, but far from upset by the distraction.

Jacob, meanwhile, was pacing around the edges of Siham's fight with her master, growing increasingly agitated. Their clashes were monotonous enough to bring Etienne's eternally combative warrior-women to mind, and Jacob was beginning to suspect that he wouldn't be able to solve his own problems until Siham had solved hers, for it was clear that the company's Gordian knot could only be cleaved by a sword of buzzing dust.

Striding directly between the bodies of the fighting Seekers, both of which were skidding backward from a clash of predictably stunning force, he stomped his foot, albeit with more peevishness than power, then shouted, "Would the two of you please resume acting like the skeletons of adult humans?"

"Siham," said Shailesh, pausing in his assault, "if this shrill personage is the only fruit of your unauthorized seeking, I demand that you concede this argument immediately."

"I'll admit, Jacob's a little high-strung. But he's a Seeker if any of us are, Shailesh. He just needs someone to help him through his existential crisis. I brought him here for guidance, but I'm starting to wonder if you have any to offer. It's not like you had much for me."

Roaring out his wroth, Shailesh leapt into the air, slamming his whirring bones against Siham's a good half-dozen times before thudding back to the ground, where Jacob had withdrawn, shaking his head.

"Is *this* what Seekers are all about?" said Leopold at his side. "Terribly sorry, Campbell. If all you wanted was to witness passionate squabbling over eternally moot points, you could easily have stayed behind in Dead City. At least in the Tunnels they serve refreshments with the show!"

"Leopold's right," said Jacob, "which ought to concern you both deeply. With all this *power* you have — power that's desperately needed elsewhere — is this really the path you've chosen?" Siham and Shailesh paced around him, crouching low and gathering their dust into compressed balls that sounded like nests of hornets simultaneously struck by slingshots.

It was in the midst of the resulting clamor that Remington raised his hands from Gielgud's skull and intoned the words, "Easy-peasy lemon-squeezy." The newly assembled Seeker, of whom Gielgud was now a part, leaped to his feet, suppressing a triumphant bellow that would have caused the ancients to tremble in their cubby-holes. Raising a finger to silence Remington's excitement, the warrior launched himself up the wall, scaling the honeycomb as nimbly as a lizard and pulling himself onto the sill of a great window, from whence he flung himself between Shailesh and Siham, letting out a swashbuckling yodel as he struck both combatants square in the brow. Their heads flew so far from their spines that their dust-threads were forcibly retracted as they slid across the floor.

"Gielgud the Great!" cried Shailesh, too punch-drunk to right himself. "No: head of Gielgud. Ribs of Rahel. Scapulae of Abernathy, right leg of Lamia, left arm of Luther — but how can this be? It is an amalgamated ancient!"

"It's the boy," said Siham, lifting herself into a woozy crouch. "He's got some out-there mojo I knew the Meeting would go nuts over. I would have introduced you, but you were too busy erupting with machismo."

"The boy?" Shailesh took to his feet and whirled around, pointing an accusatory finger at various members of the company. "I see many boys! Which one is responsible for this audacious and impossible act?"

"He is," said Gielgud, pointing to Remington.

An orgy of explanation followed, in which Siham's prior indiscretions were, at least for the moment, set aside. A smattering of elders were summoned, and many Seekers of more recent vintage arrived and could not be driven out. Within a few hours there were so many skeletons in the Plaza that its former stillness was replaced by rambunctious clamor.

"What we must all set our minds upon," shouted an elder with an oblong head, "is the question of how Remington's gifts can exist. No one doubts that your power is legitimate, my boy, but it has never before been seen. It flies in the face of all that we hold dear!"

"Oh, sure," said Remington. "While you're talking, though, can I put the rest of the veterans together? There might be an extra bone here and there, but Gielgud can help me figure out where to put them."

"Caution, Boneman," said Mistress Ai. "Until we understand the nature of your gift, it shall not be used at all."

"To the winds with your caution!" said Shailesh. "He's no apprentice, Ai — if any Seeker is deserving of a name, it is he, who has developed this preposterous technique without scouring!"

"I grant you that he is more than an apprentice," said Ai, "but his privileges must be restricted. The boy still wears his flesh."

"And imagine the power he'll have when he's out of it," said Siham, stepping into the elders' circle to the shocked whispers of the crowd. "Nobody's made such strides on his own, not since the first wave of Seekers, all of whom developed their techniques without the benefit of this Meeting's approval. Why should we have to pass your arbitrary tests when the ancients never did?"

Jacob looked up sharply, wondering if he ought to involve himself further in this argument, but before he could make up his mind, his attention was drawn to Etienne's voice, which had gradually quieted to a whisper. Could catatonia be far behind?

"Let us focus on the matter at hand," said an elder. "How can this young Boneman have dominion over bones that are not his own? I issue a challenge to the group: let silence reign until truth emerges."

Yasmin leaned over. "How exciting!" she whispered. "A challenge is serious indeed. We might be among the elders for weeks of contemplation!"

"What I wouldn't trade for the power to nap," said Leopold.

In moments, the entire Plaza settled, all of its standing Seekers dropping with a clattering rearrangement of bones into half-lotuses. Awkwardly, the company joined them, each one wrangling his legs into some semblance of a meditative posture, then falling silent. The crow wheeled down to land on the sculpted branches of the willow, causing a tinkle of stone leaves as it looked around the Arena. Remington, peeking out at the Meeting through the crow's eyes, found himself able to dial the thoughts of the Seekers like distant radio stations. At rare moments, he could feel all of them stumbling into silence at once, and in that calm he could feel another, larger silence just beyond White City's boundaries.

That's where he wanted to be — past the walls, where the quiet was *moving*. He was about ready to stand up and start walking toward it when he noticed Jacob rocking beside him, his distress steadily deepening.

In Jacob's lap, the skull of Etienne Rassendren had stopped whispering, having fallen so far into suffering that he was now unreachable. Etienne's quiet, so unlike all the other silence in the Plaza, rose like a wall between the Meeting and the truth it sought.

But before either Jacob or Remington could decide what to do, Siham stood. "The source of Remington's power has been in front of us all along," she said. "It isn't his at all: it belongs to the underworld. It belongs to us all. But Remington, for some reason, isn't getting in its way.

"That's a truth that belongs to every Seeker in this city. The Poet explained it to us long ago. We tried to return his gift, but nothing could be simpler than his words:

> *All roads below the Earth lead us to dust.*
> *In dust, a single seeking brings us home.*

The response was immediate and explosive. Over the ensuing debate, Leopold shouted, "What could possibly be so controversial about a couple lines of doggerel?"

"Isn't it obvious?" said Yasmin. "One can't help but have some kind of feeling about the Poet's recent work."

"One *can* if one hasn't a clue who he is," said Leopold.

"Why, you've never heard of the Poet Laureate of the Underworld?" she cried, drawing horrified glances from the Seekers around them. "But he's the first Seeker! The first corpse to pass through the Moving Desert, the first to be reborn through scouring." She raised her hands in twin mudras, saying serenely: "By maintaining his focus on the marrow of his inmost being, he survived the sandstorms intact and climbed up White Peak to compose the first of his great poems, a work that took him a century to complete.

"Just as he left, two Plains warriors, disconsolate after losing their arms to Inpu the Faithless, wandered up to White Mountain. When they saw the Poet's bony little figure, they knew they'd found their guru. They sat at the base of the mountain waiting for him to descend, speaking not a word for a hundred long years.

"When the Poet finally returned, he recited the poem he'd been composing on the mountain. (History does not tell us whether they understood it, but I doubt it.) When he was done, he brought them into the Moving Desert, where they experienced the rapture of scouring and gained insights into one another's wills in a way that only those who scour together can. The Poet then understood so much about being a warrior that he climbed right back up the mountain to write his first great battle-poem, the Book of Bone, while Hamish and Althea stayed below and developed the art of bone-fighting.

"Anyway, the point here is that his early works are beloved by all Seekers, but things have changed in the past century or so. His last two poems have been confusing, to put it mildly, and Ai says they're actually blasphemous!

"The first, the one the Bonemaiden was quoting from, was the Infinitesima, which he composed about fifty years ago. It's all about dust. I mean, literally about nothing but dust, hours and hours of verses about it, and not about cutting or threading or anything interesting, but about dust in sunbeams and dust settling on surfaces and dust blowing around in houses with the windows left open. Some Seekers say it's about what will happen to our bones eventually, and that's why it became so controversial, because some of us believe that so long as we practice marrow-grip we never have to break down.

"When the poet returned to the mountain, Mistress Ai spoke out against the Infinitesima. She said that maybe spending so much time out in the Moving Desert was to blame for the Poet losing his touch, maybe even his mind, and she got together a group of elders who developed the creed of the eternals.

"While this was going on, the Poet was composing on the mountain for an awfully long time. In fact, he only returned a few months ago to present the Liminal Ode, which made even his defenders think he'd gone senile. Cosmic dust, giant creatures in the worlds between worlds, all kinds of strange things. Even Master Shailesh calls it a delusional fantasy."

"But the point the Poet was making," Siham was arguing, trying to maintain calm despite the increasing volume of the argument, "is that all of this is temporary! Eternity is an illusion. Every last one of us is going to become dust sooner or later, and when we are, we'll be unified. We all know this is true; we've felt it in the sandstorm. Remington can accelerate that union on his own, one piece at a time — but somehow we don't believe it even when we see it with our own sockets. And why not? Because we're trapped in our old habits. Ways of thinking, acting, arguing. We're defeating ourselves, over and over again, trapping ourselves in —"

Just then, she caught sight of Jacob curled around the skull of his companion and dropped to her knees. "Please help," Jacob croaked. "He's gone out like a light. I've made his suffering worse. Please, Bonemaiden, help us!"

As the Meeting dissolved in confusion, Shailesh's booming voice rose above the rest. "Wait," he said. "An awareness thrusts like a mountaintop from the molehill of my mind!" Bounding through the field of seated Seekers, he landed before Jacob, peered down at the head in his lap, then gasped, falling back on thick-fingered hands. "People of White City, hear me," he cried. "This visitor has been here before! He is the one who walked bleeding out of the desert; he is the living boy we brought to health and begged to wait for the Poet's wisdom; he is the boy who refused us, the boy I carried over White Gate into the Plains; and he has returned, incontestably dead and irreparably broken; oh, fate! All due to our weakness! All because we saw a human who was breathing and alive and, despite our years of training, felt a flame of jealousy that would burn him down to blood and ash."

"What is he on about now?" said Leopold in a fit of annoyance. "I haven't understood a thing since we sat down in this wretched square."

"Oh, we're about to go into the sandstorm," said Remington, patting his shoulder.

"He's *right*," said Shailesh and Siham at once.

"We need to go scouring," said Siham.

"Posthaste!" said Shailesh. "May it bring this suffering soul to clarity!"

"Let those who so love the loss of their minds chase that dragon," said Ai as she withdrew. "May the rest of us take this time for quiet reflection on the truth that Master Shailesh has uncovered. All who met this boy in the bloom of his life can recall the urge we felt to destroy it. None were moved to help him, least of all myself. Let each of us examine this breach of our vows, and return to the Meeting when our emotion has settled."

The company, bolstered by Shailesh, Siham, and Yasmin, strode through the hubbub that followed. "*Scouring*?" Leopold shouted at their heels. "Is that what you call it when the sandstorm rips every remnant of flesh from your bones?"

"You've got it," said Siham as they approached Sandy Gate. "You up for the ride?"

"I am not," said Leopold, stopping abruptly. "But we've known that for some time, haven't we? I'm not like the rest of you, and I never will be. Whatever the future holds for me, it isn't in that desert."

The company paused, the Seekers looking to Jacob and Remington as if to ask whether this were worth the delay. Remington knocked at his skull, and the crow flapped out.

"If it means anything to you," said Jacob, "know that I bear you no grudge. Your contributions, whatever inspired them, got us here — and I believe, despite all this unrest, that this is precisely where we need to be."

The sand between them whispered, grains bounding onto the white stone between Leopold's feet, where the crow pecked idly.

"I'll be Leopold's guide while you're gone," said Yasmin. "We'll take good care of your pet bird. This is all very exciting, but not worth displeasing Mistress Ai, I'm afraid. Oh, Maiden, do come back soon!" she cried at their backs. "This place is so boring without you."

"Enough speech!" said Shailesh. "The maelstrom insistently invites us. Who are we to refuse its susurration?"

CHAPTER FIFTEEN

Song of the Sands

Past Sandy Gate, the air grew as opaque as tracing paper. A roiling mass that blotted out both earth and sky hung in the distance, dwarfing the dust-cloud of the scrimmage so definitively that Jacob was amazed such a paltry thing had ever daunted him. The Moving Desert hissed loudly enough that he had to shout to be heard, even as he shielded his eyes from its intermittent, blue-white flashes of light.

Jacob clutched Etienne's head to his chest and leaned into the rising wind, lest he be left behind. Behind the walls of White City, crossing this crackling threshold had seemed like a reasonable plan, but now that the storm was close enough to rattle his joints, doubt was creeping into his mind. He saw, with an unruly burst of emotion, how unprepared he was to bid farewell to his flesh. It was rotten, ripped, and in terrible repair, but it was all he'd ever known, and he'd clung to it for so long — beyond his own death, after his unwitting swap with Leopold, deep into the wilds of his afterlife.

"Well," he called, hoping to cover his anxiety with good cheer. "So this is scouring! And what precisely is it that we'll find inside that cloud?"

"It's a sandstorm, Jacob," said Siham. "Chances are good there's gonna be a lot of sand."

"Sand and dust," boomed Shailesh. "Wind and electricity! Leaping and shifting, threatening to bury all that does not rise above it."

"So it's rise or be buried?" said Jacob. "That's the idea, isn't it? See, it's the particulars that interest me. If you don't mind, I'd like to be a little better educated before we go any farther. Mightn't we be putting ourselves in harm's way? Has there ever been a case in which a Seeker *didn't* make it out of the sandstorm?"

"Jacob, relax," said Siham as a jittering eddy passed through her frame. "Center on the marrow of your bones. Imagine there's a magnetic force holding you together, pulling in from the core. There's a power in there strong enough to keep your body intact — even from sword-strikes! So whenever you feel like you're in danger, focus on your marrow. And remember that the dust you're made of is just the same as the dust that's flying all around. You'll do fine."

Shailesh threw an arm around him. "Twin wills, in the bones and in the sands! Together they will uplift you. It should not be a source of worry."

"Of course not. No worry whatsoever." The storm was now so close that the air between them blurred. "Will it happen quickly?"

"Decidedly not," shouted Shailesh.

"It takes a good long while," said Siham, "but it might feel like minutes."

"Alternatively," said Shailesh, "you may feel as if you've been lost for years!"

"Metaphorically lost, you mean."

"He means lost," said Siham, taking Jacob by the shoulders and steering him behind Remington, who had, by some unspoken agreement, been chosen as the conductor of their train of Seekers. "Actually lost. 'Where-am-I?' lost."

"Embrace the literality of your lostness," said Shailesh, lining up behind the headless, "for it is the very heart of the scouring!"

"Right," said Jacob. "So let's compromise, and attempt a trial run. An hour's jaunt, at lower risk, before we come back and regroup, and maybe *then* we'll be ready to share some concrete details regarding best practices."

"Just follow me, Jake!" said Remington, tugging him over the brink of blindness. Slapping Jacob's trembling hand on his own shoulder, he resolved to make sure it remained there, no matter how bewildering things became.

The storm had no borders. It was impossible to say when they'd entered it. It took Remington over one agitated grain at a time, and then it was everywhere, inside and out. Sand rattled into his nostrils, bouncing through his brainpan, then spilling down his back. Sand trickled down his throat until a gut's worth of storm split his carcass open, the weight flowing through him like swill through a drunkard. Sand slid under his skin, making him feel like he was sloshing through a downpour in loose, soaked clothes as he walked. It ground between his sockets and his eyeballs, which registered nothing but granular static. It swarmed in his ears, making them roar from within as it ripped them apart.

He felt Jacob's hand rattling on his shoulder. He felt Jacob's fear rippling through his bones. He could hear Jacob asking, again and again, What will hold us together? What will keep us from being buried? He remembered Siham's answer: the marrow of your bones.

Remington turned inward, settling inside his own skeleton. In every segment of his body, he felt the dust holding fast to the core. He pushed that rippling calm backward, passing it through to Jacob, meeting the Seekers behind them in their struggle to persevere.

Six Seekers strode into the storm, bearing a seventh. Their sense of time was scrambled, as was their sense of self, for every mote of dust contained a tiny story waiting to be told. Fragments of the corpses who'd passed through this desert before collided with the corpses of Remington, of Adam, of Eve, of Jacob, of Leopold, of Etienne, of Shailesh, of Siham, of the Living Man. Some stories rang out louder than others; some were faint murmurs in the distance. But all of them were swirling at once, and Remington could feel them all, as if he was and had always been a part of each and every one.

He was more than himself now. He had been for some time. He'd peeked into everyone and everything he'd encountered, even the River Lethe, which was enormous, after all. But being inside this cloud, feeling all of the people inside it, was his first taste of being as large as the cosmos.

Six Seekers carried a seventh, surrounded by a vastness ringing with voices and tales.

Remington centered on the dust of the Seekers walking in the sandstorm, gently sweeping aside the voices of those who'd scoured before them. The six Seekers' stories were jumbled, overlapping, but all present, concurrent.

Nor were the visions they shared confined to the underworld. Bits and pieces of their *lives* were splitting open, revealing themselves not only to Remington but to each member of the company. Suspended in the swirling winds before them were images of their deaths.

The flash of a bomb blowing a teenaged girl to bits.

A windshield raining glass into the open mouth of a kinky-haired youth.

A husky lad swelling like a balloon as he howled at the crushed body of a bee.

The bucking belly of a young woman strangled by the father of her child.

A man and a woman bent double, their severed heads thumping to the ground, reflected in the lens of a camera.

The freckled face of a boy with milk-white skin, the barrel of a shotgun sliding between his teeth.

Remington stopped, and the company stopped behind him.

There was still one among them whose stories they hadn't seen. Etienne had found a way to keep himself apart, even in the face of such immense power.

Remington reached back to touch Jacob's hand and felt bone scraping bone.

They were already skeletons, then. They were Seekers, and this was their seeking.

Remington led his friends to a rock that rose above the sands and helped them find their seats. Through the haze he reached out and took Etienne's skull, hearing its tuneless humming echoed by the storm. Remington hummed along with it, harmonizing. Feeling his fellows around him, he reached into Etienne's mind.

You can open up, he told him. You're safe here with us.

The skull's jaw creaked open, and the sand blew clean through it.

Rattling, crackling, the sand scoured the skull, prying loose an infinitesimal piece of bone.

Six Seekers bearing an seventh split open that mote of dust, releasing its contents into the swirling winds.

Etienne laid a hand on the cover of the Book.

It was leather-bound and dusty.

He found it in his family's house.

His family was dead, except for his Amma, who was dying.

Etienne Rassendren was raised by the dead, or at least by the books they'd written in many languages and left in the house by the mountains. He had his grandfather's gift for tongues and had taught himself all the languages on the shelf, but he couldn't make sense of the language in the Book.

"It loops like Tamil," he said.

His Amma glanced at the pages and wrinkled her lips. "An elephant's tail hangs like a trunk," she said, "but don't try to feed it. I don't know if that's a language, or a code, or a game. It came from a box of old things my mother left to me — which is probably still around here somewhere. It's yours if you can find it."

"I should copy this out. The pages are crumbling."

"Then do! It's yours now. All of it is. No one in the family ever knew what to make of it. Maybe you'll be the one to solve the puzzle."

After she died, he remembered her words and found the velvet-lined box buried in a tall stack of keepsakes. Inside the box was a crown made of bones.

The bones were small, arranged in clusters and branches that formed a flexible loop. They had come from hands and feet (*human* hands and *human* feet, he thought, and wondered why he felt no chill), except for a cluster of vertebrae that seemed to be the front of the crown. There were too many bones to have come from a single body. All of them were ancient, some yellowed, some browned.

Stranger still was the crown's construction. He could spy no wires, screws, or threads between its flexible parts, yet it held together even when he pulled it with all his might.

At last, he stopped analyzing and accepted its invitation. Etienne put the crown on his head.

"Prince of the dead," he murmured, walking to his room to look at himself in the mirror on the dresser. The pages he'd copied lay on its wooden surface. His eye caught on an error he'd made in transcription, and he realized that he could read the Book.

His fluency came and went with the crown, which he could wear for roughly an hour before he risked a crippling headache. Slowly, sixty minutes at a time, he compiled a second book, a glossary of the language of the Old Ones, as the many voices in the Book called it. Soon he could read, write, and speak without the crown, which he kept in its box on the bookshelf. As he studied, he learned the stories the Book's authors had told of the Land of the Dead, where his forebears had once traveled as a rite of passage. Some entries were nothing but lists of births and deaths, while others taught Etienne about Tutankhamen's Second Rule, the Plains of War, and the Walkers, giants "with strides three times the width of Earth," who had journeyed through the world between worlds in the time before time. Wherever the Walkers slept, a new cosmos arose, "each with the seed of a world of little dreamers embedded within."

"Ours is a twofold cosmos," said the Book. "Two dreamings birthed it, on two consecutive nights, each as long as an age of men.

"The first dreaming birthed the Earth and the endlessness around it.

"When the Walkers awoke from that dreaming, they decamped.

"When they decamped, they left one of their number behind.

"He whom they left behind had fallen ill.

"The second dreaming was his alone.

"The second dreaming was his last.

"The dying Walker dreamed alone, his fever gnawing through the world that was. The power of his dying dream birthed a little world, a world without an endlessness around it, a world like a growth on the side of the first.

"In other worlds, when little dreamers die, they pass into the world between worlds, the substance of their will diffused, to be drawn into life again.

"Ours is a twofold cosmos. Our little dreamers are tugged through their deaths into the waters of the dying Walker's dream, dragging fragments of their dreams behind them."

Beside such riddling tales were the rudimentary foundations of what might be called a travel guide to worlds beyond the reach of the living: lists of suggested supplies, etiquette for greeting centuries-dead ancestors, travel restrictions, geographical descriptions, and cultural ephemera. Etienne searched the pages for a detailed account of a crossing but found only the vaguest of references. He learned that those who crossed were required to be "at the age of living-in-death," a term for late adolescence, and that one was a "wearer" while the rest were "carriers." But beyond these terms, which must have referred to wearing the crown and carrying the supplies necessary for the trip, the catalyst that would reveal the veil between worlds remained a mystery.

He'd been sleeping poorly since he'd first put on the crown of bone, and his obsession was only deepening. Had something sealed the door between the worlds? Had the ceremony been forgotten? Was the cosmos breaking down, preparing to end? As questions piled up, he grew convinced that his translation of the book was at fault, and after another sleepless night, he wondered if wearing the crown while he read might offer clearer insight.

That evening, as a thunderstorm rolled over the mountains, Etienne lowered himself into his Amma's armchair, vowing to study until the sun came up, headaches be damned. When the power went out, as it so often did in that part of the world, he read by the light of a pocket-sized, battery-operated torch, and in its glow, with the crown heavy on his temples and the rain drumming on the ceiling, he fell asleep.

Later, in the leisure of his starvation, he would reflect that in the language of the Old Ones, one was said to "wear" his dreams, "the many masks of sleep." Thus "wearer" had a double meaning: in order to part the veil between worlds, he wore the crown and dreamed. Likewise, the "carriers" carried not only their supplies, but their little dreamer, too, keeping him safe during his slumber.

Etienne had no such luxury. When he awoke with the Book in his arms and the torch in his fist, the veil was already closing behind him, granting him only a glimpse of the world between worlds before his eyes were forced shut by the sands of the Moving Desert.

His body thudded on the sands, and the cloud was everywhere, grating against his skin, shaking and rebounding in his eyes and ears. He found his feet and began to run, falling down, dragging himself up, choking and coughing, barely noticing when the crown tumbled from his head; he was suffocating, and would have died then had he not collided with Shailesh, who was just embarking upon his third scouring.

Six Seekers bearing a seventh shifted their weight, reassembling above the rising sands. The storm, too, shifted, settling a crackling mantle of dust around the broad shoulders of Shailesh. He reached out and accepted the sand-heavy skull of Etienne, cradling it in his hands. He lay his thumbs on its brow, between the empty sockets of its eyes, and all the company saw his memories projected against the shifting screen of the sands.

Shailesh was deep in the marrow-grip when the living boy fell into his arms, and his first thought was that the eternals must be right: repeated scouring caused madness, after all. Then the sight of the boy's blood smeared on his bones sobered him, and with haste Shailesh bore him out of the cloud, into the safety of White City.

The boy was thin, his body soft and far more fragile than a corpse's. His skin was very dark, darker than Shailesh's had been, with a reddish glow that seemed to boast of the blood within. His eyelashes and sighs alarmed the Seekers who crowded around his place of rest, to whom he was at once an angelic and a shameful object; while none denied his beauty, Shailesh, like the others, struggled with his hatred for the boy. He even fantasized about killing him, and Shailesh had never been able to stomach bloodshed.

"It's what a woman seeing God would feel," said Mistress Ai. "In the presence of the original, we experience a violent awareness that we are but imitations. Each breath he takes recalls us to our last. We'd do anything to avoid that memory. We'd even kill, were it not for our vows."

They nursed him all the same, though out of wary obligation, not tenderness. His skin was raw and wanted washing, and he badly needed sleep, which they watched with quiet mistrust. When he awoke, he complained of hunger and thirst; they could only satisfy the latter, and though he said the river-water tasted sour, "like rotting vegetables," it seemed to revive him.

He had not meant to come without supplies, he said. He needed the crown to return to the living world, he said, but no one who ventured into the storm could find it. He spoke hopefully of his ancestors, but none of the Seekers had heard of his Old Ones.

"You should speak with the Poet," said Shailesh, "the eldest among us. If any will know of your ancestors, it is he."

"Where is he?" said Etienne.

"On White Peak, composing."

"When will he return?"

"No one knows."

"Well, I can't afford to wait," said Etienne. "I've got to find the Old Ones before I starve. They'll know how to get me back."

Shailesh accepted the tome but protested the boy's decision, describing all the ways that a Seeker could travel that were barred to one so breakable. "Your only possible path is through the Plains of War, and I shudder in my soul to think of you there!"

"I know what the Plains are," said Etienne. "I'll take my chances."

"Very well: but I can take you no farther than the far side of White Gate. Our people have vowed never to set foot in those lands again."

"That will be fine," said the boy, his cracked lips splitting in a grin. "I've read about those warriors, and I'm willing to bet that I'm faster than any of them." Then down they climbed, and off the boy walked, setting like a blood-red sun in the crooked hall that led to the Plains. Shailesh launched himself to the top of White Gate, fretting that he'd sacrificed a greater vow to a lesser one. It was a doubt no amount of scouring could clean from his bones.

Six Seekers bearing a seventh withstood the storm, feeling the head's suffering like a prolonged electric shock.

Jacob felt Etienne's story rippling through his body — no, he thought, through his skeleton. He couldn't see himself, not in the midst of this granular onslaught, but the longer he remained in the storm, the more the mass of sand and dust spoke to him. He saw, he felt, in flashes that seemed to belong to the desert. His worn clothes had disintegrated, his boots had been tugged off, and his flesh had been all but stripped away, reduced to a few patches dangling from tangled threads of fishing-wire. As he tore them free, he discovered one last holdout: the pouch was still tied around his wrist, hanging on by a stubborn, gristly strip of leather.

Wondering at its tenacity, Jacob shivered in his bones as he yanked it free, clasping its rumpled oval in one claw-like hand. He'd promised to keep it close, never to let it out of his sight. Now that it had lasted so unaccountably long, should he try to protect it from the ravages of the storm?

It would be impossible, unless he left the desert immediately. But an inexplicable tingle rippling through the sands gave him the distinct impression that this had been Ma Kicks' intention all along.

With two fingertips, he pried the pouch open. White dust and shards of bone rose jittering into the air. The pulverized finger of Ma Kicks swirled into the cloud, pouring through the Seekers' open skulls.

She stood on the riverside with one hand on her belly and one on the handle of a slop-bucket. Lazarus Quay was chock-full of marks, but this boy was so fresh Clarissa caught him trying to breathe when he thought no one was looking. He was hiding something else, too — in the hip pocket of his dusty tunic was some kind of rectangular doodad. It must have been valuable, considering how often his hand drifted there.

But he couldn't guard it forever. Sooner or later, he'd have his rigor mortis. She'd just have to be there when it happened, then turn his treasure into time in her account.

She'd never cared much for the Dead City Welcome — it was a nasty way to bring anyone into this world — but she had her child's future to consider. The baby wouldn't stay in her womb forever. She knew that much from the way it was wiggling these days. Her firstborn would want an afterlife of its own, and what did she have to offer but bad luck, mounting debt, and a dead-end job in the skankiest bar in the Tunnels?

Nothing, unless she took advantage of this immigrant boy's arrival. She'd be a fool to pass him over, and if she did some other enterprising corpse would snap him up just the same. Why should somebody else, somebody with purely selfish motives, benefit from his naivety? The boy would learn the same lesson one way or another.

She glanced at the surface of the river, where she'd already scavenged two buckets of past-due produce. Her reflection was still looking all right. There was no mistaking her for a living girl, not with those marks on her throat. And they weren't the worst of it, not any more. When Clarissa's life had slammed shut she didn't look a day over seventeen, but by now her skin had slumped enough to make her look a little matronly, plastic barrettes or no.

It would have to do. She hiked up her buckets and swung her hips past the spot where her mark was sprawled. As soon as he turned those big, shiny eyes on her, she stumbled, and a bucket full of rotting bounty slopped onto the street between them. She let out her best woe-is-me wail, bending down low.

The boy wasn't looking her way, though. His eyes were fixed on the pile of slops, rifling through half-rotten apples, slimy leaves of cabbage, and heels of bread soaked in Lethean muck. It was only then that she noticed how skinny he was, like he'd starved to death in some shit-heel corner of the Lands Above.

He must still think he was hungry. She hoped she didn't have to watch him try and eat — he'd probably bite off his tongue, which was still so moist with river-water that she stopped looking at his face.

How'd he get so *dusty*? she wondered. It was like his insides were the only part that had gotten wet.

"May I help you with that?" he said, voice wavering.

"You sure you wouldn't mind?" she said, shoving her revulsion aside. "Packed these buckets too heavy for a girl in my condition. Tell you what, though: you give me a hand, and I'll stand you a drink when we get down below."

He scooped the slops back in, making weird little grunting noises.

Damn, but the baby was kicking hard today. Wouldn't be long now.

With the time she made off this rube, she'd fill up a whole nursery with toys.

When he'd gotten a handle on the bucket, Clarissa led the boy through the streets, steering him down a wide, dirt-paved ramp teeming with corpses. Then, when the darkness closed around them, the boy pulled the flashlight out of his pocket and clicked it on, pointing its beam at the floor.

She turned, looking hungrily at it. How the thing was still work-ing after being dunked in the river she'd never understand — was it wrapped in plastic when he'd died? — but she wasn't about to ask any questions. With that thing in hand, she wouldn't just buy out her debt, she'd buy her own bar.

"Honey, your eyes work just fine down here," she said, hoping he'd save the charge in those precious batteries.

"It — it comforts me," he mumbled.

Dead boy scared of the damn dark, she thought, shaking her head. Lethe sure did deliver the goods.

"Hush now," she whispered to her belly, where the baby was going plumb crazy. "What got into you?"

As they passed through raucous bars and crumbling hallways, Clarissa kept her back to the boy, trusting the wobbling beam of his flashlight to assure her he was keeping up. He lagged behind when-ever she went around a corner, and it wasn't long before she heard the awful sounds of his jaws smacking around a mouthful of slops, his gullet working overtime trying to force that half-rotten food down. How he managed to swallow with his throat gone cold she couldn't imagine, but immigrants did the strangest things before the mortis came.

The baby was stomping her guts into disarray, sending an unwelcome vibration through her bones. Her whole body shook as she walked through the darkness.

Was she really going to rob this poor boy?

Course she was. She'd hustle first and kick herself later. That's how things were down here. That's how they'd been up there.

One drink. She just had to get him through one drink, and it would all be worth it.

The bar was even busier than when she'd left it. "Late again," croaked her boss as she took the bucket from the boy's hands and carried it with the other behind the bar. "And customers lined up, waiting." He peered into the buckets. "Is this it?"

Clarissa watched the boy shining his beam wildly around the faces of the drunkards, who goggled back at him, amazed at his gadget. She motioned him over, away from any of the lowlives eager to claim him for their own. "The boy's got something more valuable than the slops he spilled. Give it a minute, I'll pry it loose."

Her boss grunted. "You're better at bullshiting than running for swill."

"Do you mind? I owe Slim here a drink."

The barman sucked his teeth and turned his back, looking side-long at the flashlight. Whatever happened, he'd still turn a profit.

"You've had a long day," Clarissa said, shoving a mug in front of the boy. "Let Ma take the edge off."

The boy tucked his nose in and took a sip. Clarissa watched him drink. The whole room was watching as his light flickered, wondering if the batteries would win the race with his mortis.

It would still be a good haul, even without the batteries, Clarissa told herself, though her spirits had sunk.

"Shall we have it again then?" came a voice from over the boy's shoulder.

"Ad infinitum!" cried another.

"And a-one, and a-two, and a —"

Three corpses were standing on a rickety table, assailing Clarissa's ears with an underworld drinking song. Though tuneless, their rendition had rhythm on its side, and within moments the entire bar was churning to the beat. Clarissa, annoyed by their antics, absently refilled the boy's mug and was surprised to find him with his head on the bar, giggling helplessly.

"You all right there, honey?" she said, surprised at the uncommon looseness his body displayed when he lifted his head. "Looks like that drink hit you pretty hard."

"You have no idea," he said, pulling the mug from her hands more quickly than she'd have thought possible, "how that drink hit me." He shone his light under his face. "I'm aglow with inspiration!" he cried, then tipped the mug into his mouth.

The effects of this second drink on his body were like nothing she'd seen in the Tunnels, and she wondered if she'd judged him wrong. Could a boy as fresh as this already have gone through his mortis? He seemed to be speeding up when he ought to be slowing down.

The flashlight was glowing yellow now. She could kiss those batteries goodbye, but at this rate she wasn't even sure she'd get a crack at his tunic.

He stumbled into the crowd, where after a while she spotted him teaching the singers a new song. The place was soon stomping and howling along, and she was too busy pouring drinks to keep an eye on him. "Win some, lose some," she muttered, and then the boy hopped right up on a tabletop, howling at the top of his lungs:

> *Ten sacks of meat did hit the street*
> *And there they fell to fighting*
> *And what they spilled was red and sweet*
> *And had the dogs delighting.*
> *Tra-la! Tra-lay! We'll all be dead 'ere day!*
> *What God with life invested*
> *Will all too soon be infested*
> *So scrape it to the bone*
> *'Fore the maggots call it home*
> *We've lived too long together*
> *Let's thank Christ we die alone!*

The drunkards were in ecstasy. Half-full mugs of swill soared through the air, bodies lurched in a grotesque parody of dance, puddles were stomped into fountains, and above it all the boy waved his hands in the air like a conductor, weeping with laughter.

Clarissa stared at his face. He must have splashed swill in his eyes, but it looked for all the world like tears.

> *The dogs did drink, the dogs did eat,*
> *The dogs did swiftly die*
> *The whole damned planet perished in*
> *The winking of an eye.*
> *Tra-la! Tra-lay! We've all been dead all day!*
> *Now all our little lives will fall*
> *Into death's wretched protocol*
> *So drink for all you're worth*
> *For the charnel-house of Earth*
> *But prepares us for the truth*
> *That death is just another birth!*

The boy was down in the crowd now, and his lyrics rang out in a muddle, trampled under the stomping of feet, the beating of mugs, the slamming of chairs on tables. The crowd pitched and heaved; every now and then a reveler tumbled to the floor, shouting the song from below, oblivious to the blows his sodden body absorbed.

"They'll tear the place apart," said Clarissa.

"We'll have to weather the storm," said her boss, opening up a drawer beneath the bar. A small arsenal was stashed inside. "Take your pick, but I'd recommend a knife."

Suddenly the beam of the torch shot out of the crowd, bouncing across the floor. Clarissa ducked under the bar and picked it up, clicking it off before the batteries were gone altogether; then the crowd went still all at once, and the only sound was a single voice, rising and falling in pain and fear. It was the boy, crying out from the center of the mob, where he'd fallen hard from a tabletop, the insistent, unnatural rhythm of his breath sending a chill through her bones.

Breath?

The baby bucked so hard it ripped her belly open. A tiny foot split the skin, straining against the fabric of her dress. Too shocked to process the rupture, she shoved her hand against the sole hard enough to force it inside, then elbowed through the drunkards, jockeying for a glimpse.

Breath.

The boy sat rocking on the floor, his chest rapidly rising and falling, his hand clamped to his forehead, where blood poured out of him, thinned by moonshine, a sticky, bright, impossible rivulet mingling with the swill on the floor.

"Bl — bluh —"

"*Can't* be."

"What else?"

She could have stepped in. They always listened when she yelled. But this boy had heat in his veins while her baby was dead and cold. Where was the justice in that? Why should anybody be allowed to breathe when her sweet child never had, never could?

Clarissa didn't speak, didn't move. She just stared.

"Is it?"

"It is!"

"Blood?"

"Can't be!"

Disbelieving, one among them started to peel back his skin, slowly, just to see what would happen. Then, hearing the shout at what he'd seen, what he'd *felt*, the others crowded closer. One by one, they lowered their hands. Rough, sharp-tipped fingers dug into the boy's sides, making fists around his flesh, pulling harder. Every gobbet came as a surprise.

The drunkards were hollering now, but the boy was louder. The screams spilling out of him were like nothing she'd heard, not since her sister had given birth.

"Blood!"

"He's — still living!"

"A living man!"

"Alive?"

He went quiet, soon enough, but the crowd didn't.

They were giggling like children digging into a broken piñata.

The seer turned away; she didn't want to see.

All hundred and one of his killers were singing.

His blood was bright on their faces.

They were singing the song he'd taught them. *Tra-la! Tra-lay!*

But he wasn't singing along, not any more. He wasn't alive any more, either — couldn't be, with so much of him spread around the room. He was shouting, though, trying to drown them out, saying anything that came to mind: multiplication tables, names of relatives, nursery rhymes. But the crowd turned the words back on him, mocking him, shouting him down, and pretty soon he'd switched to a language like nothing she'd ever heard, and his crazy talk kept going on until there was nothing left but his head.

No one would touch it. No one but Clarissa, who pulled it out of its puddle and set it on the empty bar.

The baby thumped, slower now.

"You knew all along," she whispered to her belly. "Knew what he was. How'd you know that, baby? You can't even see."

"There's an idea," said her boss from over her shoulder. He pointed at the head. "A crystal ball. One that talks." He slammed a drink down in front of her. "I think it's time we put your natural talent for bullshit to use. Apparently a hustle as simple as the Dead City Welcome is beyond your capabilities, but *this* is something you might just have a knack for."

She stared at him, then down at the murdered boy's head. It was still yammering on, its eyes landing on the ceiling, the walls, anything but a human face.

"You want me to —"

"Put a cloth on a table. Put the head on the cloth. Put your hands on the head. And pretend that only the head can see the future, and that only *you* can understand the head. We'll make a fortune. Fifty-fifty."

It worked. Better than her boss had ever imagined it would. His cut made him rich, but it wasn't long before she'd bought out her debt, then filled up an account of her own. Inevitably, the two of them had a falling-out, but by then she had enough to buy her own bar.

She didn't know much about running an establishment, but she learned. Learned how to brew swill, how to bully runners, how to squeeze every last year of credit out of a drunkard's account. Nor was that the extent of her education.

Slowly, one guess at a time, she learned to comprehend her baby's kicks and thumps. Discovered that the child had an honest-to-God talent for clairvoyance, one that kept the months flowing into her account. But along with it came a passion for justice that Clarissa was wholly unprepared to handle, and a temper to match.

For it was obvious that the baby was furious, tired of having played the silent partner, of taking part in unsavory business, of swindling good folks along with the bad. She'd learned how disappointed the child could be in her, in what she'd said, in what she'd done, in what she was doing still. Learned that the baby blamed her for making it complicit in any number of nasty endeavors.

Most of all what had happened to that boy.

The severed head learned, too.

Learned to quiet down. To disappear into his dreams.

She envied him that, though it cost her a fortune. What filled her felt like it would never empty, and when Clarissa closed her eyes she had visions of the child disowning its own mother, a passenger fleeing a sinking ship.

It happened suddenly: she knew she couldn't stand another minute underground, drowning in shame, so she picked Barnabas out of the crowd and handed him the keys to the bar. Then Clarissa turned her back on the Crowded Car and stumbled away, lacking the strength to take one last look at the boy's head, let alone apologize. She'd climbed up Southheap and set up shop as far from the Tunnels as she could get, but regret followed like a beaten dog on a long chain, just far enough away that she could forget it was there sometimes, only to hear it scratching for food again.

She'd give anything to be quit of it, or so she told herself.

The child told her a finger was as good a start as any.

Six Seekers held the skull of the seventh high.

The company interlaced their skeletal arms, lifting Etienne into the shifting sands, feeding him memories of their own.

Etienne turned from his howling, only for a moment.

In that moment he saw Jacob laughing so hard he snorted, his head against another boy's chest.

He saw Siham dancing, the bangles on her wrists chiming in time with music that poured from speakers as tall as trees.

He saw Shailesh climbing a branch and peering at a nest full of baby birds.

He saw Remington jumping naked into a creek.

He saw Adam and Eve sitting side-by-side, pointing through an airplane window.

He saw himself, in his chair with his Book.

A moment was enough. He spoke his greeting through the storm.

"That was — heavy," he said.

"A weight you've carried long enough," said Jacob. "Let the dust bear it now."

Lowering Etienne's skull, he followed the others through the storm. There was no need to form a chain and hold on; by now, they were attuned to the glimpses of life and death that rose and rebounded from one another's bones. The visions began to fade as they left the rock buried behind them, trekking toward the blurry boundary of the storm. From blindness, they passed into static, and from static into the dim, dawning light that shone between the grains.

Jacob stared down at his fleshless feet, watching sand and dust shift between metatarsals. He held up the hand that wasn't holding Etienne and willed his dust to gather between the bones. While he'd centered on his marrow, he'd felt the motes being scraped from his skeleton by the storm, and kept as many as he could clinging to the bone. Now here they were, forming a tiny trickle of dust, allowing him to dangle one distal phalange an inch from its neighbor.

He still had much to learn, he thought, returning the digit to its proper place and wiggling his fingers before his eyes.

Through their white bars, he was the first to spot the Plainsmen.

Five warriors trod the sands, pitching rocks at the sandstorm.

"Look," Jacob said, startled by the sound of his voice. The storm was but a whisper now. "Are they lost, do you think?"

"They're coming from the direction of White City," said Siham.

By then, the Plainsmen had seen them. With a unified hoot of excitement, they staggered ahead, brandishing clubs and swords.

Even that far-off threat sent a rush through Jacob's frame. Before he'd decided to react, he was tearing ahead, his talon-like feet pitching sand in the air behind him. The company fell in, their bodies blurring as they skidded in a ring around the warriors.

"All right!" rasped a Plainswoman in a leather girdle. "A little practice before we get down to business."

Jacob saw the axe beginning its swing and leapt deftly aside. As the axe-wielder sank his blade in the sands, Jacob struck and was surprised to see his opponent launched into the air by the touch of his hand.

"What business?" said Remington, sidestepping another slow blow. "Are you trying to get back to the scrimmage?"

From the ground, the axe-wielder shook his head. "Ain't no scrimmage to speak of," he gurgled. "Whole thing's cleared out, from Rim to Rim." Laboriously, he righted himself, then trotted toward his axe, seemingly oblivious to Jacob's strength and speed.

"Now our little squadron will be the first to return," said the Plainswoman, jabbing her sword in the general direction of Adam's ribs. "All we have to do is fight each other until three of our four are fallen, and the remaining fighter will, by definition, be —"

"The Last Man Standing!" they all roared at once, hollering and whooping as they made ineffectual passes at the ring of Seekers.

"Let us leave these simpletons and discuss," said Shailesh, drawing the company away. The Plainsmen were happy enough to stagger on, clashing their weapons together as they went. "Something has happened in the Plains," he said. "Something momentous and unexpected."

"And those four weren't at all afraid of us," said Siham. "Isn't that weird? Don't the Plainsmen think we're all witchy?"

Jacob, peering toward the distant walls of White City, had an awful premonition. "Remington," he murmured, "can you see through the crow's eyes from this distance?"

"Hm? Oh, sure. There he is, flying above the walls." Remington spread out his bony arms and started running in circles, crying, "Whee!"

"Focus, Remy," said Jacob. "What can you see down below?"

"Oh, that. Everybody looks like little ants! The Seekers are the white ants, and the other guys — wow, there's a lot of them. They're kind of everywhere." Remington dropped his arms and looked up at the company. "I think the city's under siege."

"Scaffolds," said Jacob, pointing. "The walls of the city aren't white any more. They're covered with scaffolds."

It was a great while before anyone spoke, and it hardly mattered who it was.

"How long were we gone?"

CHAPTER SIXTEEN

The Mask of the Magnate

The crow fluttered to a landing on the corner of an open-roofed laboratory in the midst of occupied White City. The chamber's walls had been half-heartedly defaced by its occupants, ten of whom lounged about trying to summon the civic pride to do more damage as the other two theatrically decried their situation.

"It's dehumanizing, that's what it is!" cried Elspeth, pacing before a large plastic barrel, waving the blunt-tipped sword she'd been issued by the Magnate's bean-counters.

"O fickle-fettled Fortuna! We're nought but dehumans to thee," said Oxnard, pounding his fist against the barrel's lid, causing the river-water within to slop over one side.

"They made it sound so glamorous, with their tales of ransacking and kidnapping. And did you hear how we were to bring low the beast?"

The ten other warriors added their grumbles to the performance, urging Elspeth on.

"And what did that amount to? Spectating at a safe distance while all ten metal-men cut the Last Man Standing into hanks and hunks, shrugging off its blows as if they tickled their chrome-plated skulls. Well, the Magnate told us one thing truly: we're stronger now that we've joined his army, ain't we? So long as we stand behind the ten of them, we are!"

"A plagueful of poxen on the Manganate!"

"They said they'd make me an officer, didn't they, Ox? But none of us, not even myself, is anything more than a metal-man's lackey. What maneuver has any Plainsman performed here but for leaping into the raining blows of some jumped-up pile of bones? We're agents of distraction, all in the name of giving one of them gilded lilies an opening. And now, as if our lackeyism weren't crystal-clear, we've been blessed with a new assignment: guarding a blooming bucket while the metal-men bash Boners through eternity!"

"Teckmology hath dunked us to the depths of woe," moaned Oxnard, thumping the barrel's lid again and paying no mind when it thumped back.

"And why were the metal-men chosen? Were they the best among us, Ox?"

"Elspeth, sir, they wasn't!"

"Nay, Ox! They were merely — the least."

The Plainsmen, having warmed to the topic, were excited enough to resume hacking at the walls.

"'Twas cheaper to weld blades and hammers to broken men than to plate a warrior entire, so those that fell beneath our swords in the scrimmage were made into our generals. They're the ones were hacked apart, yet we're their spectators now!"

"Indignable it are!" said Oxnard. "We art the lowliest of lowlies now: lowlier than face-lacking debtors; lowlier than hacked-up metal-men; and fathom-depths of lowliness lowlier than them Boners, who art speedier and strengthier than I know not what! All them what's greater than we art lesser in form: yet do you think, sir, that if we wert whittled down to bonishness ourselves we'd rocket through the ranks? Nay, we wouldst not even then!"

Elspeth dropped her sword on the floor. "Oxnard, that's it!" she cried. "You great, moronic genius, you!"

"Eureka!" cried Oxnard, dropping his sword in agreement. "But, sir, what have I geniused?"

Elspeth pulled her armor loose and peeled off the grimy garments beneath, revealing a body more husk than flesh. "Those Boners are quicker than our metal-men, aren't they, Ox?"

"By a muchness, sir," said Oxnard.

The warriors around them stared in confusion as Elspeth gripped the dehydrated remnant of her calf and tore it from the bone. "Their movements are so rapid that they're all but invisible to the naked eye, aren't they? Fast enough to fake, Ox. Fast enough to fake."

She'd stripped her lower half down to bone caked with ages-old grime but was having trouble reaching the rest. "Help me whittle, lummox!"

Oxnard, too confused to protest, began yanking off his commander's flesh by the fistful, and hiccuped in delight when it was done. "Why, Elspeth, sir, you're rebirthed! My own noble commandress, the first Plainsman to abstain the mightiful strength of the Boners." He thudded to his knees, stricken by a sudden fear of her tiny frame, which in its filth could pass for that of an elder Seeker. "But be thou merciful, sir. Chop me not with thy dust-beams, nay, not even for demonstrational purposes!"

"Oh, stop your mewling, Oxnard, I don't have any damn dust-beams. However!" Elspeth whirled about, imitating the martial style of the Seekers, and brought her open palm to a halt at Oxnard's sternum.

"Thou really dothn't have dust-beams, sir. I felt that not whatever."

"No," said Elspeth slowly, "but when I make such a gesture at you, you'll fly backward as if it were the mightiest blow that ever a Boner landed. Thus, when they see me tossing the dozen of you about like grotty little rag dolls, they'll think I'm one of them, and I'll stroll into their impenetrable Plaza forthwith!"

The sense of this plan impressed the Plainsmen, who, in a roaring rush, abandoned their post to practice in the open. The crow fluttered down to peck at the lid of the barrel, broadcasting nothing to Remington now but an empty room.

"I guess that's it," said Remington, running through the desert in the midst of the company, pitching sand behind his skeletal feet. "There's nothing in the lab now but that barrel of water, but I swear, guys, something inside it thumped! Maybe it's an ultimate weapon. It could be a super-warrior built from pieces of the Last Man Standing!"

"Or a platinum-plated vulture," said Jacob, "with lasers for eyes."

"Ooh, what if it is?"

"It could be anything or nothing at all. But with the city taken over, we haven't the time —"

"Remington's right," said Etienne. "If the Magnate thought it was worth protecting, it's worth investigating."

"We'll go there first," said Siham, "with Remy's crow as our lookout."

"What a terrible scene!" cried Shailesh as they spied Sandy Gate. "And what a shame that we've missed so much of the struggle!"

"This can't all really be about a handful of pocket watches, can it?" wondered Siham.

The crow swooped over White City's reconfigured streets, sweeping over bands of vandals, shipments of munitions, and the chaos at the city's center before zeroing in on a maze of empty streets. The company, who'd followed Remington's wordless signals and the crow's overhead surveillance from the unguarded Sandy Gate, dashed through abandoned rooms and disused hallways until the sudden appearance of a group of debtors forced them into the marble room, no larger than a closet, where Siham had perfected her Ten Arrows technique.

As they crammed themselves inside, their ribs becoming fundamentally entangled, Jacob whispered, "Does fighting our way through appeal to anyone else?"

"The Magnate's forces outnumber us a thousand to one," said Siham. "How would we dig ourselves out?"

"Cutting them into manageable pieces has always worked for us," said Etienne.

"Impossible!" said Shailesh. "Every Seeker has taken a vow not to divide that which died whole."

"At the cost of your body?" said Jacob. "At the cost of your city?"

"At the cost of the underworld itself!" said Shailesh. "We are not gods, to decide which men may walk and which must sit on the shelves like weights for paper!"

"Don't be ridiculous, Shailesh," said Siham. "Doing nothing means letting White City fall. Doing nothing *is* doing something."

Shailesh sighed. "You are no longer my student, Siham. But I would still ask you to respect that these debates have occupied the Meeting for centuries."

"So has the question of how to keep the minutes. Look, Shailesh, it's not complicated. The rule against dividing corpses is all about potential. Anybody could end up being a fool, or a sage, or a hero, or a villain, so long as she's around long enough. And Seekers are all about giving people the chance to make good. Right?"

Shailesh ceded the point. "Just as the Plains warriors joined the Poet, then turned to peace, so may any man transform in the fullness of time."

"Then it follows that we have a duty to protect our own first, before our enemies. Your own city, your own people, your own self — those are the things you have control over. Those are the things you actually have a shot at changing for the better."

"So we should cut our way through these weaklings to preserve ourselves?" said Shailesh. "But they are harmless! They lack the means to damage us!"

"Just because they haven't yet doesn't mean they never will," said Siham. "If they've gone from zero to metal-men in the time it took us to scour, how much further will they go if we just stand around and parry their blows for another five years?"

"Aha!" said Shailesh. "So, because they have the potential to destroy us, we should destroy their potential to do it. I see your logic and vehemently dispute it!"

"Hasn't scouring taught you anything? We don't destroy or create — we transform. All we do is change. But Etienne is no less himself because he's lost his body. And Althea and Hamish would never have founded the art of bone-fighting — the art you've dedicated your afterlife to studying! — if they hadn't been hacked to pieces."

"But a man's substance is his will!" said Shailesh. "If we were meant to divide, we would also have been given the power to —"

"To join?" said Remington.

A long silence fell over the marble chamber.

"We're dust," said Siham. "I'm dust, you're dust, everybody is dust. That's the gift he uses: it's just dust talking to dust.

"A man's bones aren't his will, not his alone. Bones are will, period. The *him* in them is on loan, but the will itself belongs to the cloud. It's in the cloud that we can see the truth: our bones are just dust in the shape of a person, but sooner or later, by water, by wind, or by time alone, all of us, all of them, all things below the Earth will just be — dust!

"So tell me, Shailesh, who is it that you think you're destroying?"

Above the chamber, the crow squawked twice, signaling that the coast was clear, and the company extracted their tangled bones. Shailesh argued no more, but he carried their debate as he followed on, muttering arguments and counter-arguments as he went.

The company made for the laboratory, where a sizable stone on the barrel's lid was its only guardian. Adam and Eve rolled it onto the ground, tipped the lid to one side, plunged their arms into the water, and pulled a loose-jointed skeleton free.

The prisoner loosed a rubbery moan as his bones touched the ground, his basic unsteadiness betraying the effects of river-water on the mind of a quickened corpse. His skeleton was dripping with a gelatinous substance, which, as he dragged it from his skull and slopped it on the floor, the company recognized as flesh broken down by Lethean waters.

"What, fleshless?" said the prisoner. "Melted down, melted into weakness, as payment for the strength my molten metal brought his men? Is this the ruin that my nemesis so often, so fervently wished upon me? Is this the end of the man I was, and if so, what possible kind of man can it be the beginning of? You there!" he cried, leveraging a goopy finger at Jacob. "You're a Boneman, aren't you? Tell me what I ought to do in this accursed crucible of an afterlife, since this is what my efforts have earned me!"

"I'm sure I don't know," said Jacob, deeply irritated without knowing why.

"Ha! That's what the Bonemen are, you see," he pronounced to the air before him, "a tribe of warrior-sages committed to the mystical art of not knowing. Isn't that right, eh? Isn't it?" The skeleton staggered forward, shoving Jacob's shoulder with one slimy hand.

"I beg your pardon!" said Jacob, stepping aside. "I was a citizen, and renowned as the finest preservationist ever to wield thread and needle."

"Ha! Double and treble ha! The Boneman mocks me now," he told his invisible confidante. "You know very well that you were no such man, for I was he! The grandest and greatest, the mightiest and most magnificent preservationist ever to wield — well, thread and needle, as you put it. Yet who will seek my services now, now that I am undone? My beautiful face, my flawless body, all have fallen apart in these turbid waters; and though it be no fault of his own, no one trusts a bald hairdresser, do they, Boneman? Oh, what will become of the once-immortal John Tanner?"

"Hey, it's the Man in the Moon!" cried Remington. "Only — out of the Moon now."

"A friend of yours?" said Siham.

"My nemesis, apparently," said Jacob.

"Nemesis!" cried Tanner, backing against the wall with his skeletal arms in the air. "Does the sly-skulled Boneman invoke the dastardly Campbell, who even now is doubled over with laughter at the fate he plotted for me?

"And how could I have foreseen it? Campbell gave every appearance of giving up his claim to the preservative kingdom; he left without warning and without a trace, after he was joined by a suicide, two headless hobos, the Hanged Man, and goodness knows what other Lethean freaks. Where did they go, and toward what end? These were no concerns of mine, no: not Tanner's worries, for he was too busy falling into the trap that Campbell had laid.

"What hunger I had for the business he abandoned! I fell upon it like a starving man at a feast, gorging myself on his clientele; and when the Maskers found me, telling me that my name had been dragged into some sordid head-theft in the Tunnels below, I found a way to turn that, too, to my advantage. I knew it was Campbell's doing, of course, but I still imagined I could best him.

"I told them all I knew, and all that I could do for them: I told the Maskers I'd make them immortal, invulnerable, though I hardly knew how — in truth, my best efforts had only nipped at the heels of Jacob Campbell's treatments. Thus, when the Magnate summoned me to his Council to tell me of his plans to build an army of invulnerable warriors, I fell into a panic. I said yes, of course, and promptly broke into Campbell's quarters, to see what clues he might have left in his wake.

"And there was his book of secrets, written on the pages of the body: Jacob Campbell's perfect specimen, sitting motionless in a rocking chair, waiting to be revealed, piece by piece!"

"Shanthi!" cried Jacob.

"Was her name Shanthi?" Tanner asked himself. "She gave no name; she said nothing at all as I peeled her, layer by layer, away from herself, learning what Campbell had known all along: that we're all Bonemen beneath the flesh. Oh, how I'd wondered at his methods, how I'd marveled at his technique, thinking he'd somehow made their muscles solid, when it was only carven wood clasping bare bone!

"The innovation came in a flash: I'd pick the Magnate's warriors clean and cover their bones in metal. I told the great man of my plan, and he gave me twelve hacked-up refugees from the Plains and a workshop near Southheap, where I could melt down metals and dip bones. But it took so long to do it that the bones forgot their bodies by the time the metal had cooled, and I ended up with nothing but shining parts! I tried bending the metal around the bones next and had some luck with that; the first warrior who worked was an amalgam, if you will, partly welded, with his extremities dipped in metal, his missing leg rebuilt from mechanical parts, and his useless arm replaced with a hammer.

"Yet even this success was too slow for the Magnate. By the time I'd made him ten such warriors, he was demanding a hundred, and within three days! So flush was his city with Plainsmen fleeing some mythical beast, eager to fight for any reason at all, that he declared himself ready to attack White City then and there.

"Campbell's trap had closed around me! Instead of making metal-men, I faked them, pulling off their flesh and painting them silver, or covering them in foil. I told them desperate lies, saying that their treatments had infused them with supernatural powers. Most of all, I made these impostors swear to follow the ten metal-men at their vanguard, for under this leadership, their putative powers would bloom: and the soldiers, being soldiers, ate it up with a spoon!

"Then my ten true metal-men passed the test of the Plains, laying low the bugbear that prowled there, and the Magnate, believing his metallic squadron to be one hundred strong and invulnerable, marched them toward White City, dragging me behind with a host of Plainsmen, all of whom I was meant to plate as soon as we arrived. Too soon, the scaffolds were built, and the Magnate sent the metal-men down to attack White City, to seal my fate!

"When the true metal-men attacked the Seekers, the Seekers felt their strength and struck back in kind. So long as they struck the metal-men, all was well, but when one of the impostors wandered into the line of fire, he was shattered into silvery shards.

"The Seekers reacted strangely to this victory — with grief, with shock, with confusion — and thus the Magnate learned that his enemies would defend, but never destroy. Thus he adopted my deception as his strategy, hiring some blasted-out sawbones and his legless assistant to make dozens more metal-men and hundreds more impostors, so that the Bonemen would hold back their strength for fear of what their blows might do.

"It was luck I'd brought him, and a foolproof plan, but did he reward me? Ha, and quadruple ha! Instead he punished me for the very stroke that bought his victory, ordering his debtors to dunk me in this barrel of river-water to deliquesce!

"And what will become of John Tanner now? Alas, the best I can hope is to eke out a beggar's existence in some disued corner of the

Tunnels, for what self-respecting citizen would do business with me now?"

"None I've met," said Jacob, patting Tanner on the shoulder blade. "Best of luck, old boy."

Turning to Siham, he shook his head. "For a moment there, at the start of that nauseating monologue, I thought I might find a way to sympathize with Tanner's predicament. I'm afraid the cloud hasn't made me any kinder, though — I still find him as loathsome as ever. But what a terrible series of developments he's revealed! Can we really overcome these metal-men?"

"We can," said Etienne, "if we're as ruthless as we were in the Plains."

"Like it or not, that's the path ahead of us," said Siham. "Come on, kids: we need to get to these so-called warriors before they do any more damage."

The company left Tanner blubbering in the laboratory and set out for the Plaza, using Remington's crow as a lookout, dodging even small bands of debtors for fear that any contact would bring hundreds of Plainsmen crashing down upon them. At last Remington led them through a narrow hallway toward the terrible noise at the center of White City.

They emerged into an ocean of corpses whose waves broke on the walls of the Plaza of the Ancients. Around that edifice every able-bodied Seeker in the city had joined in a defensive ring, fighting with terrible focus, though at reduced strength. The combat was concentrated around the archways and windows of the Plaza, from which the Seekers flung their opponents as far as they could, only to meet them again moments later; and while the Seekers were occupied thus, the shining figures of the metal-men and their painted impostors attacked, pressing their advantage ruthlessly with bludgeon and blade.

The Magnate's forces cheered through it all, taking such satisfaction in every blow they landed that they seemed not to care how seldom they did any harm. The Seekers, meanwhile, labored without joy, losing a little more heart with every broken bit of sculpture that was hurled at them.

"Steady and staunch! Keep 'em running, lads! Beat the blaggards to bits!" barked a hooded figure Jacob recognized as the Leather Masker. "First citizen to seize a skull from the Plaza'll be dunked in swill and gold-plated!"

As a roar ripped through the ranks, Siham drew humming threads from her fingertips. "They're trying to take the ancients hostage," she said.

"At this rate it's only a matter of time," said Etienne.

"We'll join the ancients together," said Jacob, rubbing his finger-bones together. "Remington, you'll make a Last Seeker Standing, then draw the army away from the Plaza. Lure them into the Moving Desert, and the job is done — they'll all be powdered at once!"

Shailesh and Siham glanced at each other. "Hm. Yeah, that's a bit much even for me," she said, and then they were plowing through the mob, the apprentices fighting as well as they could behind the whirling bones of Siham and Shailesh.

Any doubts that Jacob had about his ability to keep up were dispelled as soon as he grabbed his first Plainsman. The scouring had taught him nothing of the advanced techniques of bone-fighting, but he was now ten times quicker than he'd been in the Plains, and with the strength of unfettered bone. Tossing the warrior through the air, he whirled on the point of his toe toward the next, who was swinging his sword at Remington; as Jacob's open hand knocked the swordsman to the street, Adam snatched the sword from the air and hacked three Plainsmen to pieces.

The warriors before them recoiled, howling the news through their ranks: the Bonemen at the Plaza's northeast corner were playing for keeps! The mob around the company scattered, loath to verify this rumor for themselves, and Jacob soon saw the whirling shapes of Gielgud, Ai, and Yasmin in the archway ahead, fending off a platoon of Plainsmen with a telltale shine at its center.

Gielgud and Yasmin fought as a single unit. While Yasmin blocked the archway, absorbing great violence through the discipline of marrow-grip, Gielgud leaped and lashed out all around her, tossing as many warriors into the crowd as he could lay hands on. Orbiting the pair was the crazed figure of Mistress Ai, whom

Jacob only recognized after her whirlwind dispatched ten men at once and she came to rest in her usual, motionless stance. When another wave descended on the archway, she broke apart into dozens of twirling, whistling, frenzied pieces, each so far from the next that it seemed impossible that they all belonged to a single Seeker.

As Gielgud and Ai deflected this second wave, Yasmin saw the company approaching; squealing her greetings, she stepped aside to let them into the Plaza.

Before they had the chance, ten metallic skeletons tumbled into the gap, lashing out in a shining blur of such speed and fury that there was no hope of telling the metal-men from the impostors.

While the Seekers fought them back with focus and desperate caution, Eve, falling on the attackers with a bearded axe, cleaved an impostor's painted arm from its shoulder.

"Hold off!" cried Shailesh, but before he could scold any further, he was struck in the spine by the head of a massive hammer and thrown by its weight against the Plaza's outer wall. Mistress Ai, screaming at the company to keep out of her way, knocked the hammer-wielding metal-man toward Gielgud, who pitched his heavy body into the air, and while Gielgud swung his long arms to meet his next opponent, the metal-man landed with a crash at Jacob's feet.

Jacob, unarmed, outmatched, and twenty feet from his fellows, backed away as the metal-man pushed himself onto his feet with the sledgehammer welded to his arm. Jacob feinted to the left and ran to the right, hoping his newfound agility would get him to the safety of the archway, but a fallen Plainsman grabbed hold of his ankle, and he slammed to the street between the metal-man's feet.

The creature's jaw squeaked open, revealing a row of tarnished teeth, and as its mechanical foot crashed down on his chest, snapping several ribs at once, it cried, "*Yeargh!*" and let loose a profane burst of Plains-Deadish. Jacob, as the hammer's massive head reached the apex of its arc, recognized the broken body of Otho, whom he'd stitched together beside the Medic. Jacob wished, briefly, that he'd kept his needle and thread to himself, and then a deafening crack rang through the air.

As the hammer swung, ten white bullets hung in the air around it. Then Siham's fingertips, at the ends of their dust-threads, whipped around Otho's shining frame, squealing against metal as they gnawed through its joints. Before the hammer struck Jacob's skull, Otho's weight was lifted off of his ribs, and the metal-man fell, in glinting, clanging pieces, onto the marble floor.

Jacob stood up in the midst of shining rubble and jagged bone and saw every warrior around him, Plainsman and Seeker alike, staring in shock as Siham's ten little fingertips snapped back into place.

"I know not whether it be for good or ill," said the skull of an ancient beneath the watchful eye of the crow, "but a new era has dawned."

In the hush outside the Plaza, eleven Plainsmen burst from an alley, chasing a brown-boned skeleton over Otho's silent bones. As the skeleton threw a hand into the air, her pursuers fell screaming to the ground, and she staggered backward through the archway of the Plaza of the Ancients.

"Oops," said Remington, startled by the crow's incessant squawking, "that's no Seeker — that's Elspeth!"

The moment she was inside, Elspeth snagged the closest skull from its cubbyhole, lobbed it through the archway into Oxnard's outstretched hands, and exploded in triumphant giggles. As Oxnard melted into the crowd, she howled, "Operation Trojan Corpse is complete!"

"That was Althea," stammered Yasmin, wrapping her skeleton around Elspeth's. "They've taken the honored Althea's skull!"

"A hostage!"

"A Boner's head, at last!"

"Three cheers for Dead City!"

"Four cheers for the Plains of War!"

The chaos around the Plaza grew yet more frenzied. Those fighting instincts that had been blunted by sheer repetition were sharpened, and bone clashed against metal and flesh with deafening force, yet no Seeker was willing to follow Siham in breaking the taboo, and all the clashing that followed represented nothing but a furious extension of their stalemate.

The company was pushed apart by the thousands of bodies that slammed against the Plaza walls, hoping to end the battle there and then, and Jacob, barely able to keep up with the tide, had resigned himself to losing something more vital than a handful of rib-tips when a voice brought both armies to a halt.

"Parley!" came the cry from the top of a tower of blocks recently erected between the Plaza of the Ancients and Sandy Gate. "Parley!" The face of the man who uttered the cry was obscured by the bullhorn he held at his mouth, but the skull held aloft in his other hand was clearly visible: it was Althea, first of the bone-fighters. "Cease-fire and parley, or it's Mortar and Pestle for Granny!"

The order to fall back came rippling through the ranks, and as the Magnate's army obeyed, the Seekers, holding tight to their formation, glared up at the figure on the wall. His bullhorn fell, revealing the gleaming of an iron mask.

"It can't be," whispered Jacob.

"Can't be what?" said Remington. "Can't be who?"

"Dead City legend holds that the Magnate wears a mask of metal," said Jacob. "And there's no question it's Leopold he's looking for."

"Yikes, I kind of forgot about that guy. Yasmin, you seen Leopold lately?" asked Siham over her shoulder.

"Oh, my, not for a while. But he was holed up in the Plaza of Ancients, and they were having quite the struggle keeping him from surrendering."

"From *what*?" roared Jacob. "Do you mean to tell me I was nearly pounded into eggshell because you lot won't let Leopold bloody l'Eclair call off a war?"

"Yasmin, that's bonkers," said Siham. "You've got to admit, it would be a lot less —"

"I don't have to admit *squat*, Bonemaiden!" Yasmin shouted, turning the word into a startling epithet. "Not to a bunch of apprentices too full of their own whoop-de-do to pass some tests that aren't even that hard! *I* took a *vow*, and that vow was to protect people from being ground up into little pieces, and that's the *only* thing that nasty man with the metal face has talked about since he's arrived. *Give him over* this, and *Mortar and Pestle* that, and lots of anachronistic, gender-based insults that I don't care for at all. Anyway. I am sorry to have lost my temper, but I believe the two of you to be out of line. Leopold is this way," she said, sashaying into the Plaza.

"Yeesh," said Siham, but for once she followed along.

Within the Plaza of the Ancients, they found Leopold struggling in more literal a sense than they'd imagined: he was lashed to a chair made of the bones of two apprentice Seekers, both of whom appeared ready to switch sides. "At last!" shouted Leopold as he spied the company. "Talk some sense into these war-mongering peaceniks, would you? Release me from their dusty grasp so I may indeed parley with the madman turning this city to rubble. Jacob. Siham. Remington. Adam. Eve. Cranium. *Do* something!"

"Boneman, Bonemaiden: release this corpse!" said Shailesh. "It is time we acknowledged the lostness of our cause."

The human chair retracted its bonds, and Leopold stood, shaking with frustration. "I thought you'd never return," he said. "When you left, I'd imagined escaping White City would be as easy as slipping out the back door while these underfed lunatics were singing Kumbaya. Instead, they've held me hostage while waging an ineffectual war in my name, all because they heard a few grunts discussing the street value of my knuckle-bones! Enough of this madness: I'm off to face the music, just to have something to *do*."

"Let me walk with you," said Jacob, and in moments Leopold was lurching through the ranks of the Magnate's minions, enduring their jeers without so much as a sideways glance. The company strode beside him, tailed by Yasmin, Shailesh, Gielgud the Great, and Mistress Ai, who had grudgingly agreed to let Siham come along when it was pointed out that she alone could pose a credible threat to the citizens.

"I never would have known it was you," said Leopold, gesturing to Jacob's skeleton. "Adam and Eve are rather more distinct, and Remy's missing the back of his head, but you're indistinguishable from any other newly scrubbed Seeker, at least to my eyes. In a way, it will be a relief to be imprisoned among debtors, who at least have numbers carved in their heads for identification! For months, I've been asking Yasmin questions and receiving answers in a baritone."

"Months?" said Jacob. "We can't have been gone that long."

"Don't be a twit," said Leopold. "Did you imagine all this happened overnight? You've been adrift in the telephasic gallimaufry of the polyphonic dust-cloud, or some such hullabaloo; I'd hardly expect you to be able to account for the time. It's been somewhere between a long while and an age, let's leave it at that, and I've felt every moment acutely."

"So you're really going to surrender?" said Remington.

"With gratitude! You wouldn't think anything could be more stultifying than the hair-splitting these buckets of chicken-bones get up to on an average day, but their wartime posturing actually made me long for another Meeting. Better a cool millennium in the Debtor's Pool than another day of this irritation! May the Magnate do his worst, so long as I'm not disassembled — I've found the cure for ambition, and its name is 'consensus.'"

"I'm still struggling to understand why the Magnate went to all this expense," said Etienne. "He has towers full of watches, doesn't he? Surely a handful must retail for less than a full-scale invasion."

"Yorick here raises a good point — and besides, I don't have a one of them left! The war does send a message to would-be challengers, I suppose, but it seems a bit much for that alone. And since enslaving a race of super-powered skeleton-men is bound to be more trouble than it's worth, I'm out of reasonable explanations. But you may as well ask the man yourself. It's not as if you'll get a better opportunity for Q and A."

As the company drew near to the marble tower, they were met by a squadron of metal-men, this batch decidedly more streamlined than Tanner's. Within the walls was a vision of Dead City squalor brought to foreign climes: the courtyard was buried in shattered blocks, fractured sculptures, and the remnants of any signs of culture that had fallen into the path of the Magnate's men.

Leopold stopped, holding a rotting hand to Jacob's ribcage. "A moment before we go in, old spoon. This is — well, the end of the line for us, that's clear enough." He touched the metal rod that held up his head, seeming to search for the words. "Promise me you won't tarry here when I'm gone, Jacob. I haven't a notion where this quest of yours will end, but it's not in this madhouse. The dust will never settle in White City," he whispered, then strode ahead. Jacob could only follow behind, wondering at the queer discomfiture those words caused him.

At the rear wall of the courtyard, crouched on a hillock of rubble, the Leather Masker incessantly rolled his dice. Near the rear of the room, the Magnate perched on a pile that aspired to the height of Southheap, peering down at the company with obvious amusement. From within the darkness of his cowl his iron mask gleamed, its surface covered in dents, scratches, and grooves. His legs were covered with jointed armor in similar disrepair, and his mail-covered hands held two skulls. The first, Althea's, he held by the eye-socket, twirling it around one crooked finger; the second, carved from marble and wrested from atop an ancient statue, he held before his face, regarding its empty sockets with his own.

"Forgive us," he said. "We've been smiling at each other, we three, while we waited. I like the carving best. One almost expects it to speak." He tossed it upside-down in his hand, working its articulated jaw and grunting out a greeting in City-Deadish. "Such craftsmanship. When all is said and done, I hope your sculptors will make a marble mask for my collection. They've had enough practice — half the sculptures we smashed were of skeletons. But that's the trouble with artists. With all the imaginative power at your disposal, all you can think to make are self-portraits."

The Magnate pitched the marble skull down the front of the heap to smash on the floor amidst an avalanche of debris. Siham, though she saw Althea's skull still dangling from his fingers, could not keep her dust-threads from humming, and the metal-men, hearing the threat, rolled between her and the Magnate, their bladed arms at the ready.

The Magnate chuckled, tossing Althea's skull from hand to hand. The Gambler joined him on the heap, squatting like a gargoyle on its side. "Eager little china doll, ain't she?"

"Indeed," said the Magnate. "My dear, if you ever defect, do it in my direction. Though I seek to avoid armed conflicts as a rule, I must admit that this one, though unscheduled, has worked up my appetite. Think of how much value I've reassigned, and in so little time! Take these sculptures, for instance: what are they worth now that they're so rare? And I've hardly begun on your most valuable possessions, namely these dusty ancients whose bits you revere at the cost of your own well-being."

"Cease this inflammatory rhetoric!" said Shailesh, letting out his wrists.

"Ah, good, they're makin' demands," muttered the Gambler, tossing his dice in the rubble, then scooping them up and trying again. "That always goes well."

"Regarding demands," said the Magnate, strolling partway down the heap, "I find that they are most effective when stated as ultimatums; e.g.: 'Cease this inflammatory rhetoric, or we will strenuously defend ourselves, taking great care not to cause you any bodily harm.' Then again, that does lack a certain urgency, doesn't it?"

"I don't share their qualms," said Siham, striding to the base of the heap. "I'd love to get behind that mask of yours and do some carving of my own."

"I'll bet you would," said the Magnate, tossing Althea's skull over his head and catching it by the jaw, "but if you were willing to sacrifice your elder to cut through us, you'd already be cutting.

"So let's drop the aggression! There's no need to be so tense. This is a negotiation, after all: the sweet dessert at the end of our martial meal. You may resent my successes, but you must recognize that this conflict concerns nothing more than your ill-advised alliance with the Clock-Thief."

"There is no such alliance," said Leopold, striding to the base of the heap.

"Just a mo'," shouted the Gambler. "Who're you, then? No Boneman, that's plain."

"I'm the one you call the Clock-Thief," Leopold said with a low bow. "The other — the one you captured in the Plains — was but a decoy."

Magnate and Masker exchanged a pregnant glance. "I'm afraid that's hardly enough proof to stop a siege," said the former. "After all we've been through —"

"After all you've been through," said Leopold, "you ought to wonder what kind of man would turn himself in without guilt. Did my decoy offer himself freely? Did he leap to sacrifice himself in my place?"

The Gambler scratched under his mask. "Bawled like a babby, more like."

Jacob nearly defended himself, then stopped. He was an anonymous skeleton to these people; no need to let them know who he was.

"My ringer was convincing," said Leopold, "only because he held the single attribute you were looking for. There would have been no point in protesting, considering your surety. And he succeeded in buying me the time I sought, though it did me little good in the end. But ask yourselves, gentlemen: is there any amount of credit that would buy the sort of sacrifice I'm offering you now? Only the genuine article would put his neck on the chopping-block."

This time, his captors didn't argue. "It's me you've sought all this while," Leopold continued, "and I can assure you that the Seekers knew not what they guarded. Their contribution to this conflict amounts to nothing more than misguided chivalry run amok. By their logic, a criminal ought to find his own punishment in the wide-open space of eternity, like water finding its own level, or some such folderol — and they will defend to the point of their own ruin his right to do it.

"They are pig-headed, I grant you, and their ceaseless dithering amounts to verbal water-torture, but they were ignorant of my theft when your armies arrived. Our relationship was nothing more than peripatetic happenstance: we stumbled into each other, and both parties are worse for the wear. Your argument is not with the Seekers, Magnate, but with Leopold l'Eclair. Trade me for the skull and punish me as you see fit."

"A Seeker abducted you — or your impostor, I s'pose — from my custody!" shouted the Gambler, spraying chunks of marble before him as he tumbled to the base of the heap. "May even 'ave been this one, for all I can tell. She was right there, in the cell we'd prepared for *you*, laddybuck, which I call one coincidence too many."

"But a coincidence it was," said Leopold. "My only goal in stealing your watches was to bank myself enough time to challenge your power, by any means I could devise; and because this was a fool's errand, I shared nothing of it with those who crossed my path, not until they were too deeply entangled in my plans to extricate themselves. The men and women who surround me aren't conspirators, they're patsies. All the plans, all the crimes, were my own, and my neck alone should bear the brunt of justice."

"You 'aven't neck enough to bear our brand of justice, sunny Jim," growled the Gambler. "You 'aven't just watches to answer for, but all we've done to recover 'em. 'Ave you the least notion of 'ow many man-hours your chandelier-swingin' 'as cost? Can you even begin to reckon such gallopin' quantities of time?"

The Magnate's fingers clacked to a rest on the brown surface of Althea's skull. All eyes were on Leopold, and Leopold, as if their weight had driven him down, fell to his knees.

"I cannot," he said, "but I trust we can agree to round up." His hands, which held so little flesh now that they were like gloves over the bones of his fingers, sought out the ragged skin around his neck and peeled his face from his skull. He bowed his forehead, showing the Magnate the lemniscate he'd carved as part of his ringer's disguise: a figure-eight turned on its side, a twice-looping ribbon engraved in bone.

"I can offer you nothing more than my future," he said. "In exchange for the freedom of all whose company I've exploited, I offer eternity. Every hour of my existence is yours."

The Magnate paced slowly down the face of the heap. While the Gambler looked on like an actor whose last line had been spoken, he tossed Althea's skull to Shailesh and pulled Leopold's face from his trembling hands. "So be it," said the Magnate. "Our men will depart White City within the hour."

"And what of the damage you've done?" said Ai.

"Don't be coy," said the Magnate. "I've spent months spying on your men. Filling great expanses of time with activities of debatable utility is all you people do."

As the crow launched itself into the air, the metal-men closed around Leopold, withdrawing him so brusquely from the courtyard that he was shocked when, after they'd climbed over the scaffolds that joined White City's walls to the Rim, they deposited him gently into a litter filled with cushions liberated from river-stained couches and bowed as they left him unguarded.

"This is unexpected," murmured Leopold, starting as the crow landed on the litter's embroidered roof. Moments later, the Magnate climbed in, reclining so close to Leopold that a thrill of discomfort ran through him. "Now, that was elegant!" said the Magnate, and then the Gambler tumbled in after him. "Ta," he grunted. A team of debtors lifted up the litter and began, slowly and evenly, to stalk through the human debris of the Plains.

"I do appreciate a classy abdication," said the Magnate, "especially after all we've been through lately. This one was the last of us to give up in style, and that was three hundred and sixty years ago now."

"Say it ain't so!" growled the Gambler. "Feels like a fortnight." Then he found the zipper at the back of his leather mask and slapped it onto the floor between their feet.

Leopold stared. The skull before him bore the same marking as his own: the sideways symbol of infinity.

"It's just delightful to welcome someone to the team who instinctively understands the protocol," said the Magnate, attempting to work his own mask free. "To have carved your own forehead with the loop-de-loop in advance! (We'll have that touched up when we return, by the way: your lemniscate is a trifle lopsided.) Well, it's just like I said before we invaded, 'This Clock-Thief will bring us back to our roots, gentlemen! He has what we began with, and what we most need restored: panache.'"

Leopold drew himself into a sitting position, cramming himself against the cushions on the far side of the litter, holding up a hand as if to brace himself against their revelations. "To welcome someone to the —"

"To the team, yes! Why, do you mean to tell me that was in earnest? Oh, wonderful! Say, would you give me a hand here?" The Magnate leaned over to the Gambler, who helped him undo the straps at the back of his mask. "I beg you, don't be offended; it's just so — so refreshing to speak like this, on the level, with someone so — well, so fresh! Imagine that, the confession of guilt, the falling to your knees, the voluntary defacement: and all of it genuine! And here we thought the entire act was being submitted as a part of your resumé. Why, I'll be asking to swap masks with you in no time; I don't mind spoiling that secret.

"But you don't seem excited. Don't tell me you've never wanted to play the Magnate? I thought that's what all this song and dance was for. Here, try it on!" As the Gambler finally pried it free, the Magnate removed his metal mask and handed it to Leopold, who was so startled he immediately dropped it to the floor, where it landed directly atop the leather one.

"Uh-oh," said both of his captors in unison.

"Uh-oh?" said Leopold.

"Well, look at us!"

"Can you tell the difference?"

"I can't!"

"Mix up our masks and we're all in a muddle."

"Is he confused? I think he's confused."

"He won't be when he's been around as long as we have!"

The stillness that Leopold's body achieved when they scooped up their masks lasted only a moment, replaced by a horrified trembling when he saw that they'd swapped them.

"This is 'ow it works, y'see," growled the Gambler, who had only recently been the Magnate.

"The only men we can possibly trust are long-time debtors," proclaimed the Magnate, who'd just been speaking in the Gambler's brogue. "All our highest-ranking staffers have given up as much time as we'll let them. Only the men at the top are worthy of taking on the Infinite Debt: like you, Clock-Thief!"

"And 'ere," said the Gambler, pulling a briefcase from beneath his seat, "is the new identify you've earned. We recommend you startin' with what you've shown us already."

"Time will take care of the rest," said the Magnate as the Gambler snapped open its clasps. "When enough years have passed, you'll simply forget the difference between yourself and your mask. This effacement is inevitable, after a decade or two."

The Gambler turned the briefcase around to Leopold, who stared down at his new face: a plastic skull, stamped with carnival colors for the Day of the Dead.

"Don't be put out 'cause it ain't classical," said the Gambler.

"Quite right," said the Magnate. "Plastic is ubiquitous, exciting, and all but immortal. The Gambler's always having to replace his leather, but your mask will last forever, if we're careful with it. Go ahead: try it on!"

Leopold regarded the mask with uncertainty, twanging its rubber band. "I must say that neither of your skulls looks quite as old as I'd expect."

"Don't they?" growled the Gambler, digging in his pockets. "I s'pose they wouldn't. We must 'ave been other Maskers before we swapped. These things 'appen, once you've been dead longer than you lived. I say, mate, 'ave you got me dice?"

"I must have!" said the Magnate, reaching into his own pockets to withdraw them. "These masks, you see, they're solutions to a problem that time causes. Or else they're answers to a question that time asked. Anyway, the story starts and ends with time, though what doesn't?"

"It's like this," said the Gambler. "The Magnate rules for eternal time, yet eternal time robs 'im of 'is will to reign. Sad old story, but the best we've got."

"You'll see it yourself," said the Magnate. "The years that pass blunt your memories first, then your feelings, then your very will; we call it 'flattening,' because it leaves a man feeling like a paper doll. At first, one can lean into his mask, drawing strength from his role, if you will, but after a decade or two of that, well, the mask itself begins to seem like the problem. Curious longings beset you: now that infinite power's been won, you find yourself longing to cast it off! Isn't that a twist?

"Hence the masks. These days, when I grow so tired of the years upon years of rule that I can no longer face the tolling of the bells, I can simply trade masks with the Gambler and be brusque and reckless instead. We began the practice centuries ago, except that, as you say, my actual bones aren't old enough for that to have been me, are they?"

"Then that's why you've gone to all this trouble?" said Leopold. "To add me to your collection, as some sort of antidote for senility?"

The Gambler guffawed. "Ain't that a way of puttin' it, Mags? No, Clock-Thief, I don't think we're senile. But the best way to revitalize a flaggin' rulership is to let it swaller up a mouthful of resistance."

The Magnate nodded eagerly. "The new ideas that surge forth from a corpse as fresh as you can be folded into our reign, and they always make it stronger; it was that way with the Gambler, whose brutality restored our hold on Dead City when it had gone a little limp. We simply harnessed his challenge and made it a part of our strength! As his moniker suggests, he had a weakness for the Dens, and so we hired an actor to bet against him, then ran him so far into debt that he proposed, all on his own, a bet of eternal time. He lost, of course, since we'd loaded the dice, and then he was ours: the Gambler joined the Council."

"But after a century or two even my tune changed," said the Gambler sadly. "I've yet to meet a will the years can't flatten."

"And so I traded masks with him, or rather the man who was wearing the Magnate's mask did, and it turned out that a man only playing at being the Gambler was even *better* at being the Gambler than the Gambler had been!"

"Wasn't long before all of us swapped 'em around so much that we forgot who was who, but after a time even that weren't enough. That's when we looked at 'iring from outside the group."

"And here you are," said the Magnate with admiration. "And so you see, all this pursuit has been by way of evaluation. The tower bit was good enough to get our attention; the escape downriver was downright inspired; but it was using the Seekers against us that made us discuss your inclusion in the group. And the use of your friend as a decoy! Well, that sealed it, and just in the nick of time. Overall, it was your flamboyance that swayed us, for at this juncture we need more than another man in the shadows: the Council, like the city it serves, needs *spectacle*."

"A figurehead," said Leopold.

"A mask to stand before the Maskers!" cried the Gambler. "To deal directly with the citizens of Dead City. Throw 'em parties and such. Swill and circuses."

"It's the role of an afterlife," said the Magnate, leaning forward. "But don't forget, should you ever tire of it, you have but to ask, and one of us will gladly trade."

"Think of me," said the Gambler, patting Leopold's knee. "I'm sure you'll agree, Clock-Thief, that I'm uniquely suited to bein' you."

Leopold stared down at the mask, then out at the walls of White City, receding into the empty Plains. "How far away it seems already," he muttered. "What a long, long way from the company we've come, in such a short time. And why shouldn't we travel farther from them still? Why, isn't this the fate I was aiming for all along?

"This may be redundant, chaps, considering that you own me for time eternal, but I accept."

"Lovely," said the Magnate, lying back on his cushions. "Just lovely. But don't think of it as us owning you, Clock-Thief. In our organization, everyone is owned by everyone else."

Leopold and the crow stared at one another in a long, wordless farewell. At last, using its black, beady eyes as a pair of convex mirrors, he fit the plastic mask over his skull, taking a careful moment to arrange its open mouth over his bare teeth: a man without lips doing his utmost to smile.

CHAPTER SEVENTEEN
Infinitesima

J acob held his hand flat before his empty sockets for the umpteenth time that afternoon. Through the spaces between the gleaming bones he saw the scarred surfaces of the laboratory he'd appropriated, then cleaned of rubble, some days or months before. As he summoned the dust to the joints of his hand, it occurred to him that this new workspace bore a certain resemblance to the tilted flat he'd once kept in the building called the Leaning Dutchman, in the neighborhood known as the Preservative District.

What a long way he'd come, only to find himself rebuilding the very place he'd started from. There was comfort in the familiar, after all he'd been through. If he weren't careful, if he didn't get the help he needed, this might well be his journey's end.

But the dust will never settle here, he thought to himself.

His phalanges separated, seeming to float in the air as he focused his vision on the broad marble tabletop where he'd been learning to carve marble with his buzzing threads of dust. Slowly, he waved his hand, watching the digits undulate as he bid a silent farewell to this facsimile of his past.

"Again!" cried Siham, slamming the thin marble door behind her and startling him so thoroughly that his hand snapped back into shape. "Jacob, it happened *again*. Another idea that cuts the time they take on reconstruction in half; another demand that I be brought before the Meeting for testing. I can't even walk down the street here without someone challenging my right to exist." She flounced against a wall, her skeleton twisting in midair, reassembling as it landed. "Everything's an argument," she murmured from the floor, her legs already locked into a full lotus. "It's like the holidays at my mother's house, except everyone's a martial arts genius." She slid her hands over her sockets. "We could be learning so much from each other. But it's never going to stop, is it?"

Now was as good a time as any. Jacob slid down to join her, though he maintained his standard bodily structure. His training was going passably well, but it was clear his talent lay in dust-carving, not bone-fighting. "It does seem as if the Seekers have a certain double standard where the most powerful members of their community are concerned."

She dropped her hands. "How do you mean?"

"You're the one who made the argument. 'My teacher had no teacher,' wasn't it?" He pointed up through the laboratory's open ceiling at the spire of White Mountain, a gnarled finger in the sepia sky. "A Seeker with no more credentials than you or me sits on that mountaintop for a century at a time, free to compose and commit to memory his epic poetry without interference. Then he descends into White City to sit under a willow and recite, knowing full well that whatever he's written will throw the society that's formed around his legend into absolute chaos."

"As usual, the Poet Laureate of the Underworld is in a class of his own," said Siham. "Nice work if you can get it."

"Tell me," said Jacob carefully, "why do you think it is that he encounters no resistance? Is it simply because he was here first?"

"I don't think that's a fair assessment," said Siham. "It's not like they were fawning over him the last time he came down. His latest poems were controversial, and he stuck around for a good bit of the controversy. He takes his knocks, he just kind of has this knack for deflecting. I think it's the pentameter. No one's got a snappy comeback for a heroic couplet."

"I'd imagine that practice helps, too. He's been at this for a while, hasn't he?"

"Sure. And I'd be willing to bet there were as many arguments in the old days as there are now. People tend to smooth those things out of the official story after a while." Siham began pacing around his worktable, hefting a carving of a crumpled automobile and tossing it between her hands. "It's like the Seekers need change, but they still can't stop themselves from resisting it. Anything that alters the fabric of their culture provokes this collective hissy-fit, but they end up changing all the same. It's really unpleasant for everyone involved, but I keep feeling like it's something they have to go through, you know? Like growing pains." Jacob cringed as she slammed the carving down. "So maybe it's *me* who needs to step up to the plate. Right?"

"Are you suggesting —"

"I'm done suggesting," she said. "I'm anointing myself. Hey presto — I'm a full-fledged Seeker, and I get to do what I need to, with or without the Meeting's permission! There you go. That was my graduation ceremony."

"Congratulations."

"Thanks. Now I'll head out on my own, just like the Poet did. Making the path ahead my poem. Blazing a trail for the Seekers to come. I'll show these ninnies what a real seeking looks like!"

"Splendid," said Jacob, leaping up to join her. "When do we leave?"

"We?" Siham stopped pacing. "Whoa there, killer. It's been fun and everything, but this is a one-woman show. I mean, it's not the Poet and his sidekick up there. No offense."

"None taken," he said, without much conviction. "My mistake. It's just that what you described sounds so much like my plan to reach the Lands Above that for a moment I thought it might be a natural fit. A wearer needs a carrier, after all."

"Well." Siham hopped onto his table and sat for a while, dangling her legs. "As far as vision goes, I can see where you're coming from. That's a humdinger of a quest you've got there, and it would take me as far *out* as I need to go. But it's also, and don't get bent out of shape here, completely impossible, at least for the foreseeable future. I mean, you've got no Crown of Bone, and no way of dreaming. And I can't hang around here any longer. This place is getting to me."

"Of course. You need to dash through the nearest gate and find your path as you walk it."

"Exactly."

"Just like you did last time."

"Exac — hey."

"And I suppose it wouldn't interest you to know that Remington is, at this very moment, retrieving the Crown of Bone from the cloud."

Siham unfolded her arms. "Okay, a little. I am marginally interested."

"Or that he believes he's found a way to teach me to dream."

She slid off the table and started pacing again, more slowly this time. "I guess it wouldn't hurt to hang out for a *little* longer. Just to see what happens when the kid returns."

"Oh, I'm back!" came a voice from above.

They stood, expecting to see Remington's skeleton clambering over the wall, but found, unaccountably, nothing.

"Remy?" called Jacob, disconcerted. The voice was unmistakably the boy's, but he couldn't isolate its source. "Where — where *are* you?"

"Whoopsie-daisy. I forgot to be solid. Sorry, it's been a weird week."

Thick, patient tendrils of dust corkscrewed down from the top of the wall, pooling in two distinct spots on the floor, then filtering up, slowly and transparently, into the rough shape of a human skeleton. "Turns out you can really speed up the whole scouring thing if you set your mind to it! It was taking too long to find all the bits of the Crown by wandering around in my skeleton body, so I set the dust to work grinding down my bones. *Yak-ak-ak-ak-ak-ak*! Once you get going, it doesn't take much time at all." A small, hovering cloud was filling in his outlines now, chugging down until his form was opaque. "Then my dust reached out into all the rest of the dust in the cloud, and we asked the Crown if it would come back and help you get to the Lands Above." His transparent hand reached up and knocked on the back of his own skull, and as it fell away he looked, at a glance, like the Remington Jacob was accustomed to. A glance into his eye sockets, however, revealed tiny, swirling sandstorms crackling with energy. "Good news! The Crown said yes."

"Where is it?" said Siham.

"Oh, the other me must have it. Hold on, I'm coming!"

They could only gape as Remington's ghostly double opened the door, twirling a thin oval on one finger. The two Remingtons waved, saying, "Hiya!" in unison, then stepped into each other, merging without a sound. The skeleton that coalesced where they'd collided looked as solid as any other Seeker.

The others followed: Adam, bearing Etienne's skull, and Eve, upon whose shoulder the reconstructed crow preened its brilliant feathers. Jacob lifted a hand to its wing and was shocked at its solidity, for the bird had been rebuilt, from beak to tail, out of powdered bone.

"Here's your Crown, Jake," said Remington, tossing it high in the air to land on Jacob's wrist. Whisper-thin, it was composed of intricate braids that held together no matter how hard he tugged.

"A Crown of Dust," Jacob murmured. "But there's still one problem to tackle. The wearer has to dream, and I can't very well nod off. Unless you've decided to come along, Etienne?"

"I have no desire to return to Earth as a severed head," rumbled Etienne from under Adam's arm. "Nor is there anything left for me to return to. But if I could learn to dream in death, you could, too, I suppose. My catatonia was not altogether pleasant, but it was a subconscious state full of strange visions. I believe it would suffice for the purposes of the ritual."

Jacob peered at him, concerned. Etienne's voice sounded every bit as gravelly and morose as it had when he'd first awakened.

"Should be pretty easy," said Remington, lifting Etienne with one hand and laying the other on Jacob's skull. "We'll just sync you guys right up."

"Etienne," said Jacob, "are you quite sure —"

But it had already begun. The storms in Remington's skull were spinning fast enough to whine, and Jacob's frame jolted as if struck by lightning.

He saw himself through Etienne's eyes, stripped of flesh, grinning and bare.

Is this who I am now?

Is this who I always was?

He felt a powerful urge to launch himself back into his own body. But he remembered what was at stake, and then the rest came rushing in.

Jacob saw through his own eyes and Etienne's at once. Their skulls stared at one another, sensations mingling, memories and abilities arcing through Remington's dusty frame. The knack of deathly dreaming was surging into Jacob's marrow, but with it came a surge of memory that seemed somehow hotter, more urgent than anything he'd seen in the cloud.

The stump of his neck rested on a tablecloth. The seer's hands were gripping his hair. He couldn't shut his eyelids tight enough to block out the sight of the customer before him.

He'd never forget her red hair hanging limp in her withered face as she'd flung gobbets of his flesh through the fetid air. He'd never forget any of his murderers. How could he, when so many of them had returned to ask his advice? This one had lost her lover between life and death, and she wanted Etienne to find him.

But a curious thing was happening: the hotter the embers of his anger burned, the quieter he grew, until he could feel the answer rising, blotting out the world.

He'd disappear inside himself, where none of them could ever find him. He'd go silent. He'd go to sleep.

As Remington released him, Jacob fell to his knees. "We haven't helped you at all, have we? I had hoped that scouring would set you free."

"Free?" whispered Etienne through his teeth. "Oh, I'm free. Free to sit on a shelf with the ancients while the rest of you gallivant through the worlds. Free to be carried around like a damaged antique, dispensing advice from the shadows. Free to watch this wretched world destroy hundreds upon thousands of afterlives. Free to disintegrate slowly, like every other corpse damned to consciousness. I am as free, Jacob, as I can possibly be. But the burden of my freedom isn't yours to bear, and never was."

Jacob grasped his own ribcage. "Then what Clarissa said, what she showed you in the storm, brought you no peace."

"You really think it should have?" said Remington. "I mean, Ma could have helped him. When she found him. When those drunks attacked him. With that baby's powers, she could have helped a lot of people." He shrugged. "She wasn't really big on looking out for anyone but her baby."

"It makes no difference. This isn't about forgiving her. I never blamed her. The truth is," Etienne muttered, "Clarissa and I are built of the same stuff. Sequestered in self-pity, begging to be excused from the constant judgment on how we choose to spend our time. Both of us only want the impossible.

"She imagines her baby playing happily in the nursery she's built, forever innocent of the city below. But you could punt me all the way back to Southheap to accept her apology with all the lavish sentiment I could summon, and she'd still be no closer to achieving it."

"What is it that you want, then?" Jacob said.

"I want to find my family. To tell them my story, and to hear theirs. Not because I believe I'll be any happier when it's done. Because this is how the Book of the Rassendren clan says I might leave my boyhood behind, and I've realized that, despite all the time that's passed in the underworld, I'm still the child I was when I arrived.

"But look at me. What was once my calling is now nothing more than a dream, the faint flickering of a candle in the depths of my mind. I'll watch it gutter out, and you can leave me to it with your conscience clear."

"Let's just slow those horses down a minute," said Siham. "If what you really want is to keep looking for your family, there are ways to get that done. There's a whole Plaza full of partial warriors who'd love to hit the road again."

Etienne ground his teeth. "After what I suffered in the Plains, the thought of joining my will to a collection of fragmentary strangers with a history of violence sounds like a recurring nightmare."

"You've already made up your mind," said Jacob, beginning to grasp the fiery determination he'd seen in Etienne's skull. "As soon as we depart, you're planning on tunneling back into yourself. You're going to end up just like —"

"A floater," said Etienne. "That's all I can be. On the river or on a shelf, it makes no difference so far as I can see. I can't have peace, but I will have quiet."

"Yikes," said Remington, and the laboratory fell into a brooding silence.

In the end, it wasn't broken by speech, but by motion.

First Eve, then Adam clattered down to the laboratory floor. Eve reached out for Etienne's skull, lowering it onto her severed spine, where a line of her dust snaked up and locked him in place. She stood, twirled, hooked an eye-socket in one finger, then tossed him to Adam, who caught him lightly and set him atop his own frame.

"Oh, good idea, you two!" said Remington. "E, you could bounce back and forth between them. You can trust these guys as much as anyone. I don't even think you'd have to merge. I could just let them see through your eyes the way they see through mine." Adam and Eve pumped their fists.

"That's very generous of you both," said Etienne, startled, "but I have no idea where we'd even begin. The Seekers say there are five chambers in the Land of the Dead, and my family could be in any of them, or none. It could take centuries. No, I won't ask that of anyone. It's better for all of us if we never have to face that failure."

Eve waved a hand to dismiss him, then flung herself full on the ground, stretching her bones into a kind of skeletal rope, at the end of which one hand rose, giving a thumbs-up.

"The longer the path, the better," Jacob translated. "I couldn't agree more. Good lord, Eve, how much dust do you have?"

"More than me," said Siham. "Girl's got moves."

"I'm just gonna give you the option," said Remington, extending three tendrils of dust from the center of his skull. "You guys can figure this out on your own." Each tendril brushed against one of their skulls, and a sudden crackle of static electricity intimated that the job was done.

Etienne looked down at the body that now served as his vehicle, flexing the fingers on Adam's hand. He let out another heavy sigh, but his movements — a jouncing on the tips of the toes, a sudden sweep of the arm, a long look from side to side at the tops of the walls in the laboratory — betrayed his fascination. "I should have known you wouldn't make this easy on me. We'll debate this amongst ourselves. No one will mind if we take our time hashing it out, I suppose."

"Not in these parts," said Siham. "But where does that leave you, Remy? Are you coming with us?"

Jacob felt a thrill rush through his bones. *Us.* He said nothing, convinced that speaking would startle her into changing her mind.

"Who, me?" said Remington softly. "Oh, I'm going up the mountain. I could use a break, you know? And I want to be the first one to hear the Poet's new poem. I think we'd have a lot to talk about, cloud-wise.

"There's a lot of adventure still ahead. A lot for me to explore. But I need a nice quiet spot to do it, and a couple of hundred years."

Jacob lifted the Crown to his head. "I wonder if I'll even recognize you when we meet again," he was saying. The Crown didn't settle so much as it clicked into place. "I wonder if we ever will."

"I'm pretty sure we're all going to the same place in the long run, Jake," said Remington, his skeleton beginning to dissipate. "But I don't really know what that means. I guess we'll all find out together."

"Farewell, my friend." As Jacob stared at the swirling bones of his ward, he began to drift into a state that blurred the edges of all the figures around him.

"Bye, Jake!"

"Are you ready, Siham?" slurred Jacob, his joints beginning to loosen.

"Died ready." She caught him as his body slumped, scooping him up in her arms as the threshold rose around them, causing their substance to waver like a curtain in a breeze. She took a single step forward and the veil cinched up behind her, sending a wave of dust roiling back into the laboratory. It swirled around Etienne's skull, rebounding from solid bone, but passed right through Remington, meeting no resistance.

Adam and Eve stood staring at the empty room through Etienne's sockets for a long while, then turned to Remington and bowed. Remington watched them go, then waited for the white-feathered crow to flap slowly down, landing in its old nest to preen.

The change was gradual, imperceptible. The crow was sitting in Remington's skull, and then its ivory talons were settling on the floor. It squawked three times, then launched itself into the air, swooping high over White City in a widening spiral, searching for Remington, finding only wisps. The cloud that had been a boy was sweeping through the nooks and crannies of White City, crackling through its mutable buildings, whispering through its halls. The Seekers whose skulls it filtered through were startled by ineffable sureties, strange visions, snatches of poetry and song. "All roads lead to dust," they murmured, suddenly seeing the truth in the Poet's syllables as they followed dusty tendrils through the maze-like streets, toward the open archway of Poet's Gate, where a bird with brilliant wings flapped and cawed goodbye. As the cloud's last wisps wafted beyond the city's borders, the bird turned and dove, its mass rippling out into a broad teardrop as it plunged, merging with the cloud that drifted, broad as a cathedral, toward the foothills of White Mountain.

It wasn't long before the boy took his own shape again, with the crow's white head peering through the back of his skull. Maybe it was just a habit, but there was something Remington liked about the feeling of his feet on the path.